The Arms of the Creator

TAYLOR FUNK

Paper back ISBN-13: 978-1-963272-70-3
Hardcover ISBN-13: 978-1-963272-71-0
Dyslexic Friendly ISBN-13: 978-1-963272-72-7

ShelteringTree.Earth, LLC Publishing
PO Box 973, Eagle Lake, FL 33839

Did you enjoy this book?

We love to hear from our readers.

Please visit the author and illustrator at
ShelteringTreeMedia.com

DEDICATION

To the lost and the stumbling.

May these words find you

wherever you may be.

CONTENTS

FOREWORD
MEET THE NARRATORS!

Auran

Auran is the Praetor over the region. While his position gives him immense control over many things, it can't help him when it comes to things within his home, namely his sick servant boy. Every day he drifts further and further away from hope, the world becoming dull around him as the life of his boy drains away.

Niemos

Niemos is a Pharisee dedicated to the ways of his people. He's spent years studying the rules of his ancestors and longs to see the common people show the same commitment to them as him and his fellow Pharisees. Whenever he struggles for understanding, he leans on his longtime friend Carian, trusting that he'll have the answers as he always has.

Tirnan

Tirnan is a merchant who sells jewelry just like all the men in his family have. All his life he's been surrounded by splendor, but none of it has prevented him from feeling empty, especially when he sees joy on the faces of everybody around him. He longs for something he can't buy; he longs for connection, and a purpose greater than the one that's been passed down.

Cato

Cato works long days in another man's field for practically nothing. He's never had a good lot in life, and when a grain shortage hits, things only get worse for him and his family. With limited options, he questions who he is and who he's willing to become for the good of his family.

Martha

Martha is the oldest of her siblings and has been taking care of them since her parents died many years ago. She is driven by duty and holds herself to high standards. Though she hasn't been educated in the way that her brother and his friends were, she tends to pick up on things quickly, something she's found to be both a gift and a curse.

Mary

Mary is the youngest of her siblings. She enjoys going for long walks in search of the most beautiful flowers to display in a pot on the table, just as her mother always had. She tends to believe that there is beauty to be found in everything, even the things she doesn't understand.

Lazarus

Lazarus is the middle child, though as the only boy, he sees it as his job to look after his sisters. As a teenager, he was taken under the wing of his best friend's father and taught carpentry alongside him. While he has a good reputation in his craft, he can be a bit accident prone at times, and his sisters never let him forget that.

ACKNOWLEDGEMENT

First and foremost, I would like to give all the credit to God. None of this would be possible if He hadn't made me just the way I am and walked alongside me on every hill and through every valley. During the writing of this book in particular, it felt like we were writing it together, and I could not be more honored to have had that experience.

I would also like to thank everyone who listened to me ramble about random scenes and the various directions that I wanted to take each character both throughout the planning and the writing process. Specifically, Karla Bockrath, Zoë Masters, Mason Conklin, Nicholas Deary, and Mathew Owusu Jr., who have all listened to me go on and on about not only this book, but many of the others before as well.

Next, I would like to thank Evelyn Rainey from Sheltering Tree Earth Publishing for taking a chance on this book. This wouldn't have been possible without all the work she did with me to make this book into the best book it could be.

It would be impossible to talk about my writing without bringing up my amazing cousin, Elizabeth Dippo. It's been such a gift to be able to share this craft with her as we've both grown up. Her encouragement and shared understanding over what it means to call yourself a writer has been crucial to my writing journey.

I wouldn't be where I am today in writing or in life without the love and support of my family. They never questioned me back in high school when I told them that I was writing a novel, and they've been by my side for every writing goal I've set since then.

They've made me who I am today, and I'm very grateful.

And finally, dear reader, I want to thank you. Writing has never been about acclaim for me, it's always been about sharing the stories in my head with other people. While the events in this particular book have already been told a time or two, it was still written with love for you.

PROLOGUE

The world was carefully crafted. Formed and shaped by a creator, the Creator, to be a haven for His creation. His love for them, something incomprehensible, led Him to make each and every little detail perfect. His creation, His children, would lack nothing.

In the beginning, He dwelt with them in this perfect world, made more perfect by His presence. The Creator in community with His creation. What more could they ask for? They not only had everything thought up in the mind of a matchless Being, but they had Him right there with them. It can't really get any better than that.

Here's the thing about creation: they're seldom ever satisfied. In the case of the first humans, the clay had notes for the potter. They felt they were missing something. They felt that their Creator had left something out. They believed that He had left them incomplete.

One day they went searching for what they lacked. They assumed it would be found in the one thing they were told they couldn't do. A command given to them for their own good. A command they saw as a limitation.

There was one tree they were told not to eat from. One tree. The garden was plentiful, yet this tree seemed to have more allure to them than anything else there. The fruit from this tree had to be what they were missing. Surely eating this fruit would make them whole. They could finally fix what was wrong with them.

They picked the fruit. They took a bite. They disobeyed the Lord. The Being who gave them life. The Being who took His time with each and every fiber that made them up. The Being who'd done them no wrong because wrong is not in His nature.

In that action they brought wrong into His perfect world. He could no longer dwell among them. It hurt Him more than they would ever understand. The Father was torn from His children. All He had ever desired was community with them, but that was no longer possible. They had separated themselves from Him. They had chosen their own desires over Him. The Creator went back to Heaven, and His creation was alone in a world that began to sour without His presence in it.

The more time that went on, the worse it became. The Lord was heartbroken. He started thinking of ways He could return it to the way it was, not for the sake of the world, but for the sake of being with His creation again. For though He could start over, though He could just leave them behind, He ached to be with them again. Because though they were broken, they were still His.

Wrong cannot just be erased; it must be made right. His creation couldn't make things right. No, it would take someone without any wrong in them to fix things in this world. It would take someone who could dwell in the tainted world. It would take someone both like the Creator and His creation. It would take His Son.

Only a Man without wrong could justify creation once again. A Man so full of light that He would be able to take on all of the darkness brought in by creation's first wrong and every single wrong after that. When this Man enters the world, He will bridge the gap between the Creator and His creation. They will be able to dwell among each other once more in a new paradise as the Creator has always desired. He is waiting, His arms open to all who choose Him.

1 AURAN

I've always had to rise early for my role as the Praetor of this city. Others are rarely up at this hour when the sun is just beginning to illuminate the sky. The world, normally so busy, so chaotic, is still. The bright, golden rays shine on the stone walls around me, and nothing interrupts them. Birds chirp all around me, their songs clear and complete. These hours used to bring me peace, calm, quiet; not anymore.

Lately the silence has been too much. The golden rays unable to distract me from problems that lie within my home. Peace and calm were fleeting before, and now, they're completely gone. These hours that used to be the perfect start to my day now remind me of what's been missing as of late. The laughing. The running around. Even the trouble I once longed to eradicate. It's gone now that he's stuck in that bed, sick with an illness that has proved to be untreatable.

Maxian isn't my own flesh and blood, but he may as well be. My wife, Domitia, and I have been unable to have our own children. That bothered us once upon a time, but it seemed to matter less and less as Maxian grew. The son of two of our servants, he was always around. When he was young, his father died, and we brought him and his mother in to live with us. The three of us have raised him together since then.

He's thirteen now. Old enough for me to start teaching him all the things I was taught about being a soldier at that age. He's always looked up to me for what I do. Not due to the prestige of my current rank; he finds the role I play in Roman and Jewish relations fascinating. I've never seen things that way until he told me that.

It's a delicate system. When the Romans took over Jewish regions, we allowed them to continue to practice their current belief system. It includes tons of rules, rituals, and leadership positions that we respect as long as they follow our rules and revere our leaders. Any misstep on either side has the potential to cause serious conflict between people groups. A big part of my job as a Praetor is making sure that doesn't happen. To do that I have to be in the know about what's going on with the Jews. Throughout the years, I've worked to understand their rules and rituals, and though I generally don't find the actions of their leaders agreeable, I do my best to find out and remedy their grievances.

Maxian has always loved hearing the bits and pieces I've learned about Jewish culture. With a spirit like that he'd do well in my position, maybe even better than me. Care for and interest in other cultures isn't necessarily popular among Roman leadership, but when it is shown peace between us and the people groups we rule over becomes more attainable. Those who genuinely care about peace rather than their own ambition are the type of leaders that are best for the people, though it's much harder to get to this point with peace as a cornerstone of your actions rather than selfish desire. I firmly believe that Maxian is the type of person who would be able to do it, but he will have to survive this illness if he's ever going to make it to that point, and the odds don't seem very good right now.

We've tried multiple doctors from many different regions, but none of them can even identify the cause of the sickness, let alone treat it. What started as drowsiness turned into him doing practically nothing during the day, then that turned into him never leaving his bed. The speed at which he's worsened has increased, and we have no explanation. I've never felt more helpless than I do right now. All the power I possess, all the prestige that comes with it; none of it can fix Maxian. It can't fix my boy.

My heart aches as I get out of bed and begin to prepare for my day. These quiet hours of the early morning leave too much space to think. I try to shift my focus from my thoughts to my routine. I cover myself in armor but can't escape the idea that the man underneath it is weak. I used to feel strength just from the sight of the symbol on the front, but now that notion feels ridiculous. It doesn't matter what I do once I step out into the city. It doesn't matter how I keep the peace. I can't bring it home with me.

Escaping my thoughts seems to be hopeless. I sigh, then begin to head out of the house, but I stop at the opening to Maxian's room. I can't tell if he's sleeping or not. He barely moves at all no matter the time of day. Taking a deep breath, I walk into the room, then drop to my knees next to his bed and ruffle his hair. That used to make him smile. These days it's met with no reaction. His eyes don't even open. His blank expression in combination with his pale skin makes it seem as if he's already slipped away from us. The slight rise and fall of his chest the only indication of life.

"How's he doing?" Domitia poses, stepping into the room. I turn around just in time to see her yawn. Now that she's here, I try to bring all my attention to her to try and fill the empty hollow in my chest.

"Did I wake you?" I ask, rising to my feet. She sighs as she comes up next to me to examine Maxian.

"You know I don't sleep much these days. How's he doing?" she repeats, uninterested in any form of small talk. We don't talk amongst ourselves much lately, let alone about our own sleep patterns. All conversation not about Maxian feels like it's just a distraction, and I can't handle the topic of him for very long. I learned pretty early into all of this that I'm not as strong as I always thought I was.

"He's the same," I answer her, already itching to find a way to move on from this. Domitia leans down and puts her hand on

Maxian's shoulder and begins to study the rise and fall of his chest. He shifts a little in response, but not much. Again, his eyes don't even open to see who's in the room with him. My heart burns as I wait for more from him that I know won't come. "I'm going to work," I speak up, unable to take it any longer. I start to walk out of the room, but she speaks up, stopping me.

"I know it's hard, but you should consider staying home with him. Sometimes he manages a few words during the day. It's not much, but it's more than we'll have when he's gone," she tells me. When he's gone. How can she say those words so easily? It pains me just to think them. I turn toward her and find quiet intensity in her expression. She wants to talk about this. She wants to, but I can't.

"He appreciates what I do. He wants me out there," I shut her idea down. My eyes drift from her to the bed, but I can't seem to make them land on him. I can't bear to see all the ways he's fading before our very eyes any longer. Domitia takes a step towards me and puts her hand on my armored shoulder.

"You can't run from this, Auran. The boy is going to die. The sooner you accept that, the better," she declares, and her words feel like a punch to the gut. The idea of death doesn't bother me. I've been around it for as long as I can remember. I've lost friends on the battlefield back when we were at war. It hurt, but I had my family to return to. No matter what happened, I knew I'd always have them. Now that doesn't seem to be true anymore. Things are changing.

That's what I'm truly afraid of. Change. How different my life will be without him in it. How he won't be there to greet me when I come home. How much I'll miss him more and more with each passing day. The way I miss him now is almost unbearable and he's still here. I can't even fathom how I'm supposed to contain all of that emotion once he's… *I can't even let the word cross my mind right now.*

"I'm needed out there," I restate, turning around and walking out of the house before she can say anything else to me. Domitia's always been straightforward. It's one of the reasons I fell in love with her. Being in the position I'm in people aren't always honest with me. They're too afraid of what I'll do if I don't like what they've said. She was never like that. From the moment I first met her, she's refused to tell me what I want to hear.

I really wish she would just stop with that right now. She's told me repeatedly that ignoring the reality of the situation isn't healthy. She's told me that I have to face it head on like I would an attack on the battlefield. I've heard her tell me those things over and over, but I cannot live them out. I'm not strong enough. I don't want to hear about the grim truth of what's going on in our lives right now. I want her to tell me that everything's going to be alright. I want her to be gentle with me. I want her to fill me with hope at a time where I feel like I've been hollowed out to the point where a slight gust of wind could knock me over. But that's not Domitia, and it will never be. Hope will continue to evade me. I will remain this husk of a man until-I honestly don't know if I'll ever feel solid again.

I walk through the city trying to shake this empty feeling. My job requires that I be someone greater than what I've been reduced to inside. I must be a symbol of Rome's power not just to the Jewish, but to my own men. They must see me as a man of great fortitude. A man capable of leading them. A man not defined by personal struggle, but by the prestige of his empire and his place in it. By the time I reach the building, I don't feel any closer to being that man.

"Dominus," Deslan acknowledges me, standing at attention as I walk in.

"Anything happen last night?" I ask him, trying harder to dissociate from thoughts of home and slip into who he expects me to be.

"A man on the temple stairs tripped a Pharisee who was walking out," Deslan reports. I think I know the man he's talking about. Even if it hadn't been dark out, I'd still think it was an accident; that man is blind. He was probably just reaching out because he heard noise so he could beg for help.

"How did the Pharisee react?" I follow up.

"He scoffed, then he continued on his way," Deslan answers. Figures. I take no issue with the Jewish faith, but I can't stand their leaders. They preach about following all the rules to a T, and last I checked, taking care of your neighbor was one of those rules. They've never seemed to have that one down. What Deslan witnessed is a prime example. They'd rather scoff at those in need than do something to help them. One time I saw them force a lame man away from the temple because they claimed he was in the way. I haven't seen them do that with the blind man who's been sitting there lately, but it's undoubtedly going to happen soon.

"Anything else happen?" I check.

"No, Dominus," Deslan replies.

"Good. Go home. I'll see you tomorrow," I instruct.

"Thank you, Dominus," Deslan responds, then he heads out. I continue my journey into the building and take a seat at my table where a stack of written issues is already sitting, detailing all the problems the people have reported, from broken fixtures throughout the city to squabbles with their neighbors.

There was a time when I hated things like this. I wanted to be out on the streets interacting with people as much as possible instead of simply reading about their grievances like this and tending to them from behind my desk. Nowadays I find going through the stack of issues a more suitable task. Reading about others' problems tends to distract me from my own. It's the closest to solace I can manage to reach.

2 NIEMOS

"Hear, O Israel: The Lord is our God, the Lord is One. Blessed is the name of the Lord our God; His kingdom is forever and ever. And as for you, you shall love the Lord your God with all your heart, with all your soul, and with all your might. And these words which I command you shall be upon your heart; teach them faithfully to your children, speak of them in your home and on your way, when you lie down and when you rise up. Bind them as a sign upon your hand; let them be a symbol before your eyes. Inscribe them on the doorposts of your house and on your gates," I recite the prayer our people have said for generations.[1]

I've always been insistent upon each and every one of my days beginning with this prayer. When I was young, boys my age would try to get out of it. They found the prayer repetitive, dull even. They thought that their time was better spent running around like animals. They were too naive to recognize its importance.

The life of God is infinite. In His time, He's seen many young boys running around without a care in the world. They don't stand out to Him. A young boy dedicated to reciting prayer and keeping His commands does stand out. It is the boy who asks his teachers questions and pays close attention to the answers who warrants rewards, not the boy who remains silent so he can leave quicker. It is the boy who tells others that someone is trying to play a trick on them who warrants praise, not the boy playing the trick. It

[1] The Shema prayer

is the boy who is mocked and pushed around for reminding others of the behavior we are to emulate who warrants the attention of the Lord, not the boy doing the mocking and the pushing.

I've spent my whole life minding the rules. When I fall short, I make the necessary atonement. On my last day He will recognize all that I've done, and He will bring me into His Kingdom. The life I live, the life of a Pharisee, it may not be attractive to most, but in the end it will be worth it.

I finish adorning myself with the garments worn by Pharisees for generations, then leave my home and begin making my way toward the temple. Merchants are starting to set up for the day, the smells from their perfumes and soaps filling the air. It's nice, but it's frivolous. Money should not be spent on things as trivial as these, yet people line the streets to purchase them. These things may cause them momentary happiness, but they will not lead to eternal rewards. Their money should go towards something that serves the Lord, not something that serves them.

These people like to try their best when it comes to the commands laid out before us, but their attempts are inadequate. They make their lives about enjoying themselves in this world rather than securing their spot in Heaven. Following all of the rules seems too much for them. Who am I kidding? Remembering all of the rules is too much for them. At the end of the day, they're just too short-sighted. They need us to remind them what the end goal is. They need us to remind them to do better. It is the only chance they stand at earning the Lord's approval.

Take the man just up ahead of me for example. He's not wearing the prayer tassels that our people have been commanded to wear each morning. This is one of the easiest commands, yet somehow one of the ones that's broken most frequently. A daily sign of devotion that many of them can't bother with. People think it's a little thing. The little things will add up in the end when it's time to face the Lord.

"Where are your prayer tassels?" I ask as I approach the man.

He turns toward me, annoyance on his face.

"It's not exactly easy for me to get them on," he answers, waving his arm. His wrist seems to be locked in the downward position with each of his fingers following a similar trajectory, and the skin in that area has a greyish tint. I wasn't exactly expecting that, but it's not like it's enough to excuse him from the rules. If he were truly devoted, he would have found a solution.

"You could've asked for help. The rules still apply to you despite your misfortune," I tell him, and he shakes his head. This is what I mean about these people. They can't see how their every action in this world impacts their chances of being welcomed into Heaven.

If it was easy to get into Heaven, then it would be overcrowded. It'd probably wind up soured the same way that this world did. That's why God can only let the best of us in. We aren't entitled to Heaven. We need to earn it. These people that ignore the 'little things' miss that. They seem to believe that if they just mostly get things right, that that will be enough.

"Tell me, have you ever dealt with *misfortune*?" he asks me, cold eyes locked on mine. I began this conversation to help him, but now he wants to turn it into a personal attack. I don't owe him an answer.

"This is not about me. I suggest you find help with your prayer tassels so you don't have to spend any more of the day without them," I state, then I start to walk away, but he calls to me.

"Pharisee," he says. I glace back, but keep my silence. He shakes his head again and a small chuckle escapes him. "You want to lecture me about not wearing my prayer tassels, but not once did you offer to help me put them on," he brings up, pulling the prayer tassels out of his pouch with his good hand and holding them up. *Does he not have other people who can do this for him? I need to get to the temple.*

His eyebrows raise as he waits for a response from me. People around us have begun to look on, and I see the same challenge in their eyes that sits in this man's own expression. I shake my head as I walk back toward him. This was never meant to be a spectacle. Some people nearby applaud mockingly as I put the prayer tassels on quickly, then turn back around and start heading toward the temple again.

"Did everybody see that? This heroic Pharisee saved me from my disobedience! What ever would we do without them alerting us of our every misstep?" the man bellows. He jokes as if the rules set out for us are unimportant. That couldn't be further from the truth. We acknowledge the commands in our morning prayer, vowing to involve them in all areas of our lives.

Does he really believe that saying that prayer then disobeying it will be fruitful? Now that I think about it, he probably doesn't say his morning prayers at all. He's just like all the boys from when I was a kid. He lets other things distract him. Excuse after excuse leaves his lips. The Lord will not hear them on his final day.

"You seem frustrated," Carian observes as I walk into the temple. We've been going to temple together since we were kids. He's the only other person who ever took our religion seriously, and we eventually both became Pharisees together. He probably understands me more than anybody in this world. That's how I know he's going to know exactly where I'm coming from.

"I saw a man not wearing his prayer tassels on my way here, and when I stopped to tell him he should put them on, he gave me attitude. He laughed in the face of the rules," I share, my breathing starting to pick up as I relive the frustration of the interaction.

"You care too much for the people, my friend. Their disobedience is between them and the Lord," he responds, patting me on the back.

"I know. I just feel I should help them, but I always wind up wasting my breath," I say, shaking my head.

"And you'll continue to if you keep bothering yourself trying to make any change among those who simply do not care. We're here every day for the ones who want our help. The others, well, they don't have much of a chance at seeing Heaven at all," he retorts.

"That's grim," I reply.

"It's the truth, and you know it," he declares. He's right. Even if they correct themselves in the way I tell them to, they're still going to fall short in so many other ways when I'm not around. I need to learn to leave their fate to them like Carian and most of the others do.

"How has your morning been?" I pose, wanting to bring my attention to other things.

"Uneventful, though last night I was tripped coming out of the temple," he details.

"What did you do?" I ask, concerned. Though it's not uncommon for the people to throw verbal insults at us, they don't usually resort to violence.

"I continued on my way. His actions are between him and God," he answers. I don't know that I would've had it in me to respond that calmly. I guess that's one of the biggest differences between us; he lets others' actions be their own.

"I'm glad you walked away unharmed," I say.

"You know it takes much more than a fall to bring me down," he reminds me, a small smile on his face. When we were kids and the other boys used to make fun of us and push us around for our dedication to our religion, he always took the brunt of it for me.

He has always cared for me like that. He's the one part of this world that I've grown attached to. Luckily, his adherence to the rules will put him in Heaven with me when our time comes. I look forward to the day we're both basking in paradise as a reward for everything we've done. That's when everything we've put up with, everything we've sacrificed will be worth it. The way we were mocked won't matter anymore when the Lord tells us that He is pleased with the way we prayed to Him every day. The frivolous pastimes we've ignored won't be on our mind when we have more than we could have ever imagined in Heaven. The scorn of the people of this world will be a distant memory when we've finally earned the love of God.

3 TIRNAN

"Saved you a spot," Edrik tells me as I reach the city's center with my cart.

"I appreciate you," I say, unfolding the cart to convert it into my booth. Edrik whistles, still impressed by the cart's capabilities even though he's seen me do this for years. "These things aren't that hard to get. Lazarus will make one for you if you really want one," I divulge, and he shakes his head.

"Do you know how much Lazarus charges for things these days? The soap business is not as profitable as the jewelry business. I can't afford to put that much money into something like that," he responds. He carries himself like someone who grew up with money. Sometimes I forget that he was the first in his family to make something of himself.

We both started as merchants around the same time, but while he was starting from the ground up, I was just the next man in my family to sell jewelry to the people. I've done the best I can to help him. Taught him business skills that are learned from those who've spent their whole lives in this trade. Spotted him some money during the lows of the soap market. I've even run his stand for him when he had to tend to things at home.

"I can go in with you on it. Pay for half of it," I offer, and he sighs.

"Tirnan, I appreciate all that you've done for me, but eventually I'm going to need to stand on my own. Your charity can't be the only thing keeping my business alive," he replies. That's the thing about self-made men; they don't like accepting help. In the past he's only done so out of necessity.

"It's not charity. You always save me a good spot so I can sleep in. It's the least I could do for you," I bring up. He laughs a little, his smile not quite meeting his eyes. *I can already feel the no coming.* He shakes his head, his gaze slowly moving from my table to his own.

"I really do appreciate the offer, but my current table is fine. While it lacks style and ease of set up, it gets the job done," he says, patting the table in front of him. That it does. It's not much unlike him: simple, but effective.

That's one of the biggest reasons I enjoy his friendship. He keeps me grounded. I don't want to be like my father or his father before him who thought they were better than everyone else. Sure, they had more money than everyone else, but they lacked true fulfillment. Edrik has that. His business is fun for him. His wife and kids help him gather supplies and make the soaps, then he comes here during the day to sell them.

I dream of fulfillment like that. I started in this business because it was expected of me. I go home to an empty house full of expensive things that mean nothing. I want to have people outside of this market like Edrik does. I want to feel like I'm doing this all for some sort of reason other than to appease my parents by keeping the family legacy going. I want things that money can't buy, and therefore it seems I'll never have them.

Often, I've wondered what my life would be like if I had been the one making decisions for myself when I was younger. I mean, to this day I still don't make very many decisions for myself. The cart that Edrik loves so much was my father's idea. My wardrobe was handpicked by my mother to draw in the wealthy. The stuff that I produce is decided by a combination of the two of them because they know what sells.

What would it be like for me to chart out my own path? Pick out my own clothes? Sell whatever I want to sell, or not sell anything if that's what I decided I wanted to do? Find some sort of purpose outside of what's been laid out for me? Is that something that I'm willing or capable of doing? And if I did, would it be considered wasting the fortune I was blessed enough to have been born into?

"You have that look in your eye again," Edrik observes, waving to a customer walking away from his booth with a small linen parcel containing his purchase. Edrik told me last week that his daughter has recently started helping his wife prepare the linen wrapping. I had a feeling because they aren't as consistent as they used to, but the customers don't seem to mind that. Most of them know that Edrik's whole family is involved with his business, and they seem to like that. I can't help but envy the way that they do everything together. Things must be a lot less lonely that way. "Tirnan? You're doing it again," he informs me.

"Doing what?" I pose, leaving my thoughts behind and forcing myself to be present.

"Doing this," he states, trying to imitate whatever fleeting emotion he viewed in my expression. He moves his eyebrows, eyes, and mouth around a few times until he thinks he has it. I don't know what he thinks I was doing before, but I've never seen anyone make that face, so I doubt that was it. If anything, his features are saying 'I ate something I shouldn't have.'

"Doing that, huh?" I ask with a small chuckle, and he sighs.

"Ok, so not that exactly, but something similar to it that I can't replicate," he responds.

"Ok," I say, nodding, then I turn my attention to my booth. I start fiddling with things, changing their position, propping them up, but he recognizes my movements for what they are: a deflection.

"What is it that's on your mind, Tirnan?" he prompts me, done beating around the bush. Is this something that I can even talk to him about? He's worked so hard to get his business going, and here I am complaining that I'm not satisfied with my life after everything's been handed to me. He's not the type to judge, but there's no way that he would enjoy hearing that. It makes me sound worse than my father and his father before him; they may have flaunted their wealth, but at least they acted lucky to have it. "Tirnan?" Edrik grabs my attention.

"I'm lucky to have what I have," I blurt out. He raises his eyebrows, clearly unsure of what I'm trying to say. There are people walking near our booths, but his eyes don't leave mine as he waits for more of an explanation. alright*, I guess I have to keep verbalizing this.* "I am. I don't think that I'm not," I insist before I really get into things.

"Ok?" he replies, still confused.

"I'm lucky to have what I have, but I want more. Not material possessions. I want more from life. I want that," I let out, pointing to a family admiring a garment booth on the other side of the market. The little girl excitedly pulls on her father's arm, tugging him toward a booth with wooden toys. The father sighs, whispers something to his wife, then lets his daughter lead him away. "And I want that," I go on, pointing to a group of fishermen laughing amongst themselves as they walk down the street. They're sweaty and an awful smell seems to be shrouding them, but that doesn't bother any of them. Why would it? They have each other. They're happy.

I don't know if I can say the same thing about myself. Yes, I have Edrik to talk to when I'm here, but outside of that I have nobody to truly connect with. Nobody to truly belong to. Success tastes sour when there's no one to share it with. No one to tug on my hand. No one to laugh with. At the end of the day, it's just me in my big, shiny, empty house.

"I'm here for you," he reminds me.

"And I love that, but I have nobody to go home to," I get to the heart of the matter.

"You're always welcome to come to my house for dinner if

you need to be around people," he offers.

"That's not the same," I state the obvious. I appreciate his kindness, but it really isn't what I need. It will only remind me of what I don't have. I get enough of those reminders every day when people come to my booth to buy jewelry for those close to them. They leave here with huge smiles, then go home and make their loved ones smile with the gift they picked out just for them. I get that I have a hand in that, but that's not enough. I need it for myself. I need someone whose face I can put a smile on. I need someone to put a smile on my own face. I don't do it often enough now.

"I know," he sighs. His eyes move around the market as he thinks hard about my conundrum. Being a self-made man, he has a tendency to try and fix things every time a problem arises. I wish he would just let this one be. It's mine to deal with, he shouldn't be wasting his time on it. "Aila has a sister…" he begins, referring to his wife's sister.

"I've met her," I cut him off. He tried to set us up two years ago, but she was only interested in all the nice things in my house. That was almost enough for me, but my mother told me I deserved better. That was kind of ironic to me considering her relationship with my father started exactly like that.

"Right, sorry," he apologizes, his eyes falling to his table sheepishly. He begins to busy himself by straightening things out in front of him. He felt bad enough when this all happened, I don't need all of that coming back up right now.

"It's not your fault," I repeat what I told him back then. He nods, his gaze still locked on the table in front of him, though he's stopped pointlessly moving things. He sighs, then turns back toward me.

"You've done so much for me. I just wish I could help you," he says earnestly. *Me too.*

"How much for this?" a man asks, holding up a necklace. He has the same sparkle in his eye that I've seen many men have as they picture how beautiful whoever they're shopping for is going to look with their new accessory. For once, I'd like to have it, or a version of it, enter my own expression.

4 CATO

I let out a deep breath as I dump the last load of wheat into the barn for the day. The pile is small, though it's not for lack of work. The fields are the emptiest I've ever seen them. I brush myself off, then head to the front of the barn where Jaese is doling out our payment for the day. I'm the last person to reach him, and he dumps the remaining coins from his little pouch into my hand. It's practically nothing.

"This is less than normal," I state as I jingle the coins around in my hand. I'm not confrontational by any means, but the amount that I normally get is barely enough for my family to live off of as it is. Sometimes Kassia and I tradeoff who gets to eat that night to ensure that the kids get enough. The coins in my hand right now are only enough to feed one of the kids. That's not an option.

"You brought in less than normal," he responds simply. His eyes tell me to be grateful for what I was handed and walk away, but I can't. I can't tell my kids to decide amongst themselves who gets food tonight.

"There was less to bring in," I point out. Surely he won't hold me responsible for the less than stellar harvest this season has proved to be. He shrugs his shoulders, letting me know that he's absolutely holding me responsible. How is that fair? These are his fields; if they produce less, it should be on him. "I worked the same number of hours that I usually do. Doesn't that mean something?" I pose, a desperate tone to my voice. It's humiliating facing him like this after all the years I've worked for him, but it would be even more humiliating to fail my family.

"I don't pay you by the hour," he reminds me, his tone curt as irritation seeps in. He glances past me, trying to give me the cue that he has elsewhere to be. Are you kidding me? *He's* irritated with *me*? He lives in splendor! He has no idea what it's like to face his family and tell them that we just can't afford to do this or that! He can manage on less than is normally brought in. I can't. I can't, and I know he knows that, and I'm disgusted he has the gall to stand there and act like it's not a big deal.

"Listen, I have a family to feed, and this isn't enough to do that. I'd let myself starve like I've done before, but I can't let my kids go hungry. You're a father too. You have to see where I'm coming from!" I beg, desperation flooding my voice by the end. I don't like to seem desperate, but right now it's an unfortunate fact of my situation. My family's wellbeing currently depends on how much grace this man is willing to show me.

"You were paid for what you brought in. Take up any more of my time and you won't be given that luxury tomorrow. Understood?" he says, impatiently tapping his foot.

"Understood," I respond. He has no heart, and there's nothing I can say to change that. Maybe the merchants at the market will take pity on me and give me more than what these coins are worth.

Each step I take away from the field, my anger grows. His family will probably sit down to a feast tonight while mine tries to figure out a fair way to split apart a single hunk of bread. The worst part is that it's not even him I'm most angry with; it's myself. Because I have no skills, I had to find a job that barely pays. My family will never know comfort. What kind of man does that make me?

Kassia used to think there was something endearing about

me doing manual labor. She said it's made me an honest man. I'm starting to question if being an honest man is really that important. I think I'd rather be a man with a family that doesn't go hungry. A man who doesn't need to hope for the kindness of others to get by. A man who feels like he has any semblance of control over his life.

By the time I reach the market, my anger has morphed into despair. There have been times in my life where I thought I'd hit rock bottom. When I was a kid and my mom vanished one night, leaving my dad's anger pointed solely at me. When I ran away and struggled to find work. When Kassia's parents shunned us after they found out she was pregnant and we had nowhere left to turn. Each time I always managed to find a way out, but there doesn't seem to be one this time.

The pressure is higher than it's ever been now that I have Kassia and two tiny humans relying on me, yet I can't seem to get it together. I truly don't know what I'm supposed to do. I'm just acutely aware that something needs to be done or everything is going to fall apart in the worst way possible.

"What can I get for you?" the woman behind the booth asks me as I approach.

"However much you can give me for this," I answer, dumping my coins onto the table in front of me. She stares down at the measly collection of coins that I spent all day working for, then looks back up at me, the smile that had been on her face diminished. I hold my breath as I wait for her to show me the same apathy that Jaese did. She turns around, reaches for something in a basket under her table, then turns back toward me bearing what's probably the smallest loaf of bread I've ever seen.

"This is the best I can do," she tells me, setting it down on the table between us. Her gaze is stuck on the measly portion of loaf, her eyes not daring to find mine. I watch her hands shift around at her side, discomfort flowing through her. I can feel that she wants me to leave, but she won't say it. She can't acknowledge the man she's sending home with this sad chunk of bread. It'd annoy me if it had anything to do with her, but it doesn't: I'm pathetic. I'm the one who got paid nothing for an entire day of physically draining work. I'm the one who can't get myself out of this horrible situation. I'm the one who got myself into this situation in the first place.

She has no business giving me more than what she's already offered up, but I need to ask. I need to try everything I can to bring home more or I won't be able to stand before my wife. There have been too many days in recent memory where that has happened.

"Are you sure this is all you can offer? Is there nothing stale you can add?" I check. She sighs and finally meets my gaze.

"What I'm giving you is stale. I'm sorry, but there's a grain shortage, and I can't afford to take any more of a loss than I already am giving you that," she states, true pity in her eyes. Based on her clothing and the state of her booth, I'd say she really is being as kind to me as she can manage.

"Thank you," I say, picking up the bread, then heading out. It's not much, but it'll feed both kids and there may even be a little bit left for Kassia depending on how we split it. It's not the best-case scenario, but it's certainly not the worst case either.

I make my way back through the market and begin heading home. My stomach grumbles and my mouth waters as I think about the bread in my possession, but I refuse to take even the littlest piece. I don't know when my next meal will be, but it can't be at the expense of my children.

My eyes wander about the sights around me, trying to focus on anything but the bread. Women greet their husbands as they arrive home after a long day's work. Children run around shabby little houses, laughing as they go. Roman guards silently watch over it all. Some aspects of it seem like chaos, yet everything seems to fit together nicely. The noise spliced with silence. The giddiness allowing room for sensibility. The hectic nature of it all offset by the watchful eyes of the guard. It's spontaneous, yet there's a pattern.

It's beautiful, yet it also deeply saddens me. I don't know where I fit into all of it. It feels as if no matter how much I'm a part of it, I'm somehow on the outside looking in. I exist to them, but not with them. Things have to be this way. If I were to be a part of them, then I'd throw off the balance. The somber reality of my little loaf of bread would be too much for the children's laughter to offset. To truly be a part of it would be to ruin it.

All that's out there for me-all that's ever been out there for me is struggle. There's the occasional light-hearted moment, but they never last. It's as if God Himself doesn't find me fit for joy. For some reason, He's given up on me. I'm destined to always be the guy carrying the tiniest scraps of food known to man home, hoping that his family will still love him at the end of the day when their hunger remains.

I take a deep breath as I come to a stop at my front door. I shift the bread around in my hands, trying to find a position that somehow makes it look bigger. My heart drops more with each new angle, and I know I need to stop. There's nothing I can do to hide the fact that I let them all down. After another deep breath, I open the door and head inside.

"Daddy!" Viridi calls, jumping up from where she had been sprawled out by the hearth playing with her toy that's past worn. I force a smile to my face as she runs toward me, swallowing the feeling of failure that comes with not being able to provide for her. Hale totters after her, and when they reach me, they throw their arms around my legs.

"Hey sweetheart. Hey buddy," I greet them, ruffling their hair. Though Hale is three years younger, he's nearly as tall as his sister. He gets it from my side of the family, though I'm not taller than average myself. I guess it skipped a generation.

Kassia moves toward us, eyeing the small loaf of bread in my hand. 'Is there more,' she mouths. I shake my head and she sighs. Somehow, seeing the anguish on her face manages to hurt worse than I thought it would.

5 MARTHA

"Where's Mary?" Laz asks as he comes in from his workshop. He grabs the rag on the counter and wipes his brow with it as if that's what it was there for. It wasn't. He doesn't pay enough attention to know these things though.

"She's out picking flowers," I answer. Our mom always liked to have fresh flowers in the middle of the table to 'liven things up.' Mary's been insistent about carrying on that tradition in her absence. It started when she was a kid and would drag our neighbor Jesus with her to various fields because I told her she was too young to go alone. I still don't love the idea of her going alone now, but she's a grown woman at this point so I need to let her have some independence. She finds so much joy in spending hours finding the most perfect flowers that mom would've loved, then carefully arranging them in the same jar that's been sitting on that table long before even I was born. I need to let her do this no matter how nervous it may make me when she comes home later than I may like.

"It'll be dark soon," he states, a protective tone slipping into his voice. He does *not* feel the same way about Mary's independence as I do.

"She knows to come home before then," I respond. He throws the rag back onto the counter right next to the food I'm preparing, and stares out the window pensively. After shifting a few times, he sighs, then turns back toward the door.

"I'm going to go get her," he declares, then he's out the door before I can refute him. He's so overbearing. Mary's only two years younger than him. At some point, he got it in his head that it's his job to watch over us, and he started acting like this. I don't know what gave him that idea considering the fact that I've been the one tending to both of their needs since mom and dad died years ago.

That sounded a little bitter. I'm not bitter. Laz and Mary weren't even teenagers yet when we were all orphaned. I was older. They needed me to take care of them, so I did. I had no problem with it then, and I have no problem with it now. What I do have a problem with is Laz thinking that he needs to take care of the two of us now that he's an adult. I never asked him to do that, and I certainly don't need him to. He should be more focused on living his own life than he is on policing ours.

He refuses to hear any of that though. He's the man of the house so it's his job to protect us. It doesn't matter that I'm the one who dealt with all of the trouble he caused as a teenager, or that I'm the one who was there every time he needed a shoulder to cry on, or even that I'm the one who spread word of his carpentry skills and got him all his most loyal customers. *I* need *him*. Isn't that obvious?

I swear, putting up with him is one of the most difficult things I do each day, if not the most difficult thing. By now I'm a pro at all the cooking and the cleaning that fills my days, but convincing myself not to assault my brother is something that never seems to get easier, and I usually pick things up quickly.

"I really was going to come back soon," Mary insists as she and Laz come through the door. He shakes his head in disbelief. Cue exasperated parent comment.

"Sure you were. You girls are going to be the death of me," Laz remarks. *Are you serious?*

"Us? You have at least one accident a year. You've practically turned Mary into your own personal doctor," I argue. As good as Laz is at carpentry, he's never as careful as he should be when he's in his workshop. Whether it's hammering his finger or cutting his hand, he frequently runs into the house bleeding or bruised.

"I don't mind it," Mary responds. She's too sweet for her own good.

"Mary," I comment, raising my eyebrows at her. She gazes back and forth between Laz and I, indecision keeping her from siding with either of us. *Seriously*? I wait until her eyes meet mine again, then I direct her attention to the inside of Laz's arm where a particularly bad scar sits. She shivers at the memory of the incident, then focuses on Laz, a somewhat stern expression on her face.

"I mean, that's right, Laz; you'll be the death of yourself," she quickly amends, crossing her arms and standing up straighter to try and seem taller. It's a valiant effort, but Laz is about a head taller than both of us no matter how we stand.

"I've been a lot safer lately. It's been a long time since something's happened," he defends. While that's true, it doesn't cancel out the dozens of scars all over his body from over the years.

"Safer isn't the same as safe. You should spend more time worrying about yourself than you do worrying about us," I say, and Mary nods her head, her arms still crossed.

"I could be saying the same thing to you, Martha," he replies, his tone serious. He really wants me to think about his words. Lazarus the wise has spoken. We should be grateful to have been in the room to hear it.

I nearly roll my eyes as I think about just how much delusion he lives in. He thinks he's this big, tough, smart guy that we should be looking up to. The idea of that is preposterous. Nearly everything he does he's learned from me. I say nearly because he does a lot of stupid things that I've never done or endorsed.

"Martha, come see what I found," Mary speaks up, finding an empty spot on the counter and plopping her flowers down to draw my attention away from staring down Laz. If I was as emotionally immature as Laz, then I'd continue staring him down. However, I'm competent enough to know that Mary's starting to get upset and that letting her tell me all about her flowers will bring her spirits up.

"These are beautiful. Where'd you find them?" I pose. A huge smile comes to her face as she thinks back to her recent adventures.

"On the edge of the river. The most beautiful things grow there," she answers.

"Mary, there's no soldiers over there. It's very dangerous," Laz cuts in and Mary's smile falls. *Why is it that he still can't seem to realize how much these trips to get flowers mean to Mary?* It's not just a way to continue one of mom's traditions. It's something to do with her days. I'm pretty sure that's the real reason mom did it in the first place. There's not very much for a woman to do in our society, especially an unmarried woman. Mary would go mad without her flower runs.

"Let's go put these in the jar," I tell Mary, ignoring Laz. She gathers the flowers up and we head over to the table. I pull out the old ones that were starting to wilt, and she begins slowly adding the new ones one at a time. I bring the old flowers over to the waste bin, then head over to Laz. "She needs this, Lazarus," I seethe, and he flinches at my use of his full name.

I only resort to it when I've really had it with him. Lately it's left my mouth almost as often as when he was a teenager, which is saying something. When Laz wasn't starting trouble himself, he was instigating it. I swear, the only reason he made it to adulthood was his best friend, Jesus.

Jesus wasn't like any of Lazarus' other friends. He was kind. He was respectful, even of me despite my age. The only time he ever got into trouble was when he was trying to get Laz out of trouble. He seemed incapable of creating messes himself.

I don't know what we all would've done without him and his family. His father took Laz under his wing and taught him carpentry alongside Jesus and his brothers. His sisters always welcomed Mary. His mother helped me figure out what I was doing as a makeshift parent. Then there's the matter of Jesus himself. He always offered me a helping hand whenever I needed it. Every time I was close to my limit, there was Jesus to walk me away from it.

I haven't seen much of him in recent years. I've asked Laz what he's been up to, but as per usual Laz doesn't know anything. I could ask his mother, but I haven't talked to her much since her husband died. I'm not very good with the subject of death.

With our parents, I had to force myself to be over it so I could be there for Laz and Mary. If the topic came up with Jesus' mother, I wouldn't know what to say, so I haven't really spoken to her about this. I feel bad, especially after how much she was there for me after our parents, but I don't know-I just don't want to say the wrong thing and make things worse for her.

"How does it look?" Mary asks, pulling me out of my thoughts. Laz and I head to the table to admire Mary's work.

"It's beautiful as always," Laz tells her, putting his hand on her shoulder, and she beams with pride.

"I love the color combination. They are all so lovely together," I add.

"Thank you," she responds, leaning over and hugging me. It makes me happy to see her so full of joy like this. I know it's the same for Laz, he just doesn't know how to be responsible for somebody else. Things would be a lot easier if he just admitted that. I don't even know how to help him get there, and it's painfully clear he won't get there himself.

Mary lets go of me and starts getting into the details of the moment she found each flower. Passion laces her voice, but I can tell Laz isn't listening. He taps his foot and his eyes keep shifting to the sitting room. Moments like these make me feel bad for the woman he eventually finds. I love my brother, but he has no regard for anybody else's interests. Mary never notices, but I still get annoyed on her behalf. I think my relationship with the Lord is the only reason I'm able to muster the patience to deal with Laz. The patience God extends to me is probably greater than the patience I'm called to extend to Laz. Probably.

"Martha, when will dinner be ready?" Laz asks when Mary pauses for a second. I'm not trying to discount the grace that the Lord has shown me, but I think Laz actually does require more patience than the Lord extends to me.

6 CATO

Kassia is putting the kids to bed by herself. I couldn't do it tonight, not with the gnawing in my stomach that keeps causing low grumbles to emanate from me. Viridi would ask about it and I'd have to lie, or worse: tell her the truth. That kid is too much like me; she would feel bad that she ate and I didn't. My body already feels weak from the day's work without nourishment after. Hearing my daughter blame herself for my failure would make me cry on the spot.

When Kassia returns to our bedroom, she doesn't say a word. She takes a seat on her side of the bed and stares forward, lost in her thoughts. I want to say something, but I don't know what. 'Sorry' doesn't feel like enough. 'It won't happen again' isn't true because the grain shortage will keep my earnings low. Not addressing the whole situation would be disingenuous. I just don't want to make this all worse by saying something stupid. My stomach growls as I continue to wrack my brain searching for words, and Kassia releases the breath that she had been holding since dinner.

"You've never brought home that little," Kassia lets out, starting the conversation herself.

"There's a grain shortage," I say, not able to think of a better response. I don't want to bring things back to my own failure. *I'm not ready for that.*

"So, this isn't a temporary thing?" she questions, her eyes begging to be understanding this wrong. I wish she was. More than that, I wish that there was something I could do about this. That I could tell her not to worry, then go out there and make this all better. Sitting here in this moment I feel so incredibly helpless, but I can't let her know that. I can't let her sink in the reality of all of this like I have. My stomach growls again, and Kassia shakes her head, her eyes starting to water.

"Kass…" I try, reaching my hand over to her.

"Cato, don't. You do realize how bad this is, right?" she poses, ducking away from my hand.

"I'll find a way to do better," I tell her, and a forced laugh escapes her.

"How are you supposed to do better like this? The longer you go without food, the worse you'll do at work, and the less money you'll bring home. You have grasped that, right?" she questions, her glare piercing through to my soul. I hadn't even thought about what would happen to my own body with continuous days of starvation. This is somehow all even worse than I thought. "Cato, we have to pay taxes soon, and we don't have nearly enough money to do that. We were supposed to be setting aside a little bit every day, but clearly that's not happening. How do you suppose we handle this?" she goes on.

I don't know how to handle this. I tried everything I could've done today. I abandoned my pride in front of my boss. I abandoned my pride in front of the woman at the market. It wasn't enough. One didn't care and the other wasn't in much of a better place. There's not much else that I can do at this point, but I'll never admit that to Kassia. I need her to think that I'm better than this. I need her to think that she didn't make a mistake when she married me. I need her opinion of me to be high, because it's all that I really have left now.

"I'll handle it," I assure her.

"How, Cato? I need to know your plan here because I can't

imagine that there's anything you can do right now," she remarks, her words a punch to the gut. I avert my eyes from her, fixating on a spot in front of me. *She has no faith in me.* She shouldn't, but somehow I thought that she could. That she'd look back on everything I've ever done to get us out of tricky situations in the past and trust that I can do it again.

My stomach growls again and I squeeze my eyes closed, willing it to stop. If I can convince myself that I'm not hungry, then there's nothing wrong, right? The kids ate. Kassia got a little bit. We may not have the money for our taxes, but that doesn't have to matter at this moment if everything else is alright. I'm fine. We're fine. Things are going to work themselves out. My stomach growls again, shutting that idea down before I even get the chance to find solace in it.

"I'll go to my parents to see if there's anything they're willing to do," Kassia speaks up.

"Absolutely not. They made it perfectly clear that we were to never come back to them when we told them about Viridi," I bring up. I tried to own up to my part in everything back then. I tried to apologize. I tried to be a man. Kassia's father made sure I was under no such illusion. He struck me repeatedly, making me the little boy just trying to survive an angry father all over again. Kassia doesn't even know how bad it truly was because I hid as much of it as I could from her, but she knows enough to know that going back there isn't an option. The fact that she would even suggest that is more disheartening than the little loaf of bread I brought home earlier.

"Then I'll try to find some sort of work. Viridi is old enough to take care of herself and her brother during the day," she states, though she sounds like she doesn't believe the statement herself. Viridi may be able to look after herself during the day, but she wouldn't be able to take care of her brother. Hale is constantly getting himself into trouble, most of the time without even meaning to. Without proper supervision he could seriously injure himself.

"That's not an option. You need to be at home with the kids,"

I voice the concern in both of our heads.

"I'll come up with something I can do from inside of the house. Maybe I can learn how to make something and make a deal with a merchant to have them sell it for me," she thinks aloud.

"I don't want you going near merchants; many of them don't have good intentions," I say.

"I can take care of myself, Cato," she insists, her voice fierce, but even.

"You shouldn't have to!" I let out, and she jumps, startled by my sudden increase in volume. I didn't mean to scare her. I just-this isn't how things were supposed to be. "I promised you that I would take care of you. I promised you that, and if I can't keep that promise, then-then I don't know," I spill. I was going to say, 'what good am I?' but I don't think I can bring myself to be that vulnerable right now, even with her.

She takes a deep breath, then scooches closer to me and puts her head on my chest. I hold her close as she rhythmically rubs my arm, working to calm the negative surge of emotions she knows lays within me. My breathing starts to even out, but I can't completely eradicate the tears that are beginning to form in my eyes. One slides down my cheek and falls right next to her head.

"You're doing your best, Cato. I see that," she declares, lifting her head and meeting my gaze. Her soft eyes carry a strength I wish I could possess right now.

"Daddy, is everything alright?" a small voice murmurs from the doorway. My head snaps in that direction, and I spot Viridi cradling her little doll. I must've woken her up when I yelled.

"Viridi, you should be in bed," Kassia says as she quickly slides out of bed and begins to head toward her, trying to block Viridi's view of me as she goes. Viridi cranes her neck, looking past her mother and directly into my eyes. Despite her general air of sleepiness, her gaze digs into me, working to unearth an answer to her question. She may be young, but she's not stupid. She knows something's wrong, and she needs me to tell her that I've got everything under control.

"Everything is going to be just fine," I promise her. Kassia turns back toward me, her eyebrows raised. "I'm going to make sure of it," I add. Despite all the hopelessness I had been drowning in just before Viridi walked in, I somehow believe what I'm saying. My daughter needs me. I won't leave her like I've been left in the past. I'm going to get myself together and I'm going to make sure my family is taken care of, no matter what that entails.

Kassia leads a now satisfied Viridi out of the room, and the weight of what I just promised starts to really settle in now that I'm alone. I have to find a way to bring home more money. There's no other option. Merchants giving me more food than what I can pay for isn't going to pay our taxes. No, it has to be the money that multiplies. If it doesn't, then I'd not only be guilty of letting my family down, but also of giving my daughter false hope. I can't do that. False hope nearly ended me when I was a kid and thought my mother was coming back for me after she escaped my father.

Kassia returns, getting back into bed and glancing over at me. Uncertainty fills her features. I don't blame her. She just watched me breakdown then assure our daughter everything was alright immediately after. She probably can't decide whether I lied or if I'm starting to lose my mind. I certainly didn't lie, and I don't think I'm losing my mind, but I'm not fully sure at this point.

"Do you have a plan?" she can't help but ask.

"Yes," I answer confidently as a potential path to take begins to form in my mind. My eyes find the wall in front of me as the details of it all begin to make themselves clearer. It's not exactly smart, and it may actually be proof that I am losing my mind, but I think I can make it work.

"Ok," she responds calmly, then she lays down closes her eyes, her faith in me restored. I won't take that for granted. I'm going to get our family out of this.

7 TIRNAN

The thing about not having a family to go home to is that I can stay at the market as late as I want to. People were still buying stuff off of me long after all the other merchants packed up and went home, so I stayed. Normally I try to make a point of going home before dark, but time slipped away from me. When I finally decide to shut things down the sun has completed its descent beyond the horizon.

It's not ideal, but it certainly isn't the first time I've done this. When I was first getting started, I used to love walking home in the dark. The streets are virtually empty except for the occasional Roman guard. The silence stretches into peace in an uninterrupted form I've never experienced during the day when the hustle and bustle of people carrying out their daily routines occurs. Though I've aged, that peace still envelops me as I gaze up at the stars above me. Their twinkle feels like it was manufactured just for me as I stroll past the fields toward my home.

It's moments like these that being alone doesn't feel so suffocating. There are no expectations on my shoulders as I stare up above. I could just stop right here and nobody would be affected by it. My decisions and their consequences are mine and mine alone. There's a freedom to that. Under these stars I'm not anyone's problem. Under these stars I'm not anyone's caretaker. Under these stars I'm not anyone's disappointment. I'm just me. My own keeper.

I hear a stick break behind me, and I whip my head around, expecting a Roman guard, but finding no one. Goosebumps pepper my skin as I fixate on the darkness before me, willing my eyes to adjust faster. I might not see the cause of the noise now, but there's no way they just disappeared.

Maybe I should just run away. Whoever made the noise clearly hid once I turned around, and a Roman guard wouldn't do that. Anyone else out this late has to be bad news. I've heard stories of thieves in the night, though I've never come across them myself. I don't want to stop that streak tonight.

I face forward again, tightly grip the handles of my cart, and start to shove it forward, moving as fast as my legs will go. Jewelry bounces around within the cart, falling away from the neat positions I had it all set in. I'm too panicked to care about that at this moment. I just want to be home away from any potential danger obscured by the fields beside me.

"Sounds expensive," a gruff voice lets out from somewhere in front of me. *There's somebody in front of me!? Where am I supposed to go!?* My eyes dart around me as I scan every possible escape route that I have, but none of them seem very fruitful. Maybe if I just continue to run forward, I can knock whoever it is over with my cart and be on my merry way.

I quickly let out a shaky breath, then I start my mad dash forward again, but my leg catches on something before I get very far. The cart goes flying as I release it to try and use my hands to brace my fall. I experience a brief moment of weightlessness before my hand collides with the ground, then gives out resulting in my face crashing onto the road below. Pain rockets through my wrist and my nose, and what little I can see in the darkness blurs.

Rough hands flip me over and a large man with cold eyes stares down at me. I try to convince myself that this is all a nightmare, but if it was, the pain wouldn't be this vivid; I'm living every merchant's worst-case scenario right now. A deep, maniacal laugh slowly gets closer to me until there's another man standing before me. He's smaller than the one standing over me but manages to be just as threatening. Fear crackles through me, and this seems to make him laugh harder.

"Just t-take my cart. I wo-won't put up a fight," I get out through shaky breaths. The smaller man puts his hand on the larger man's shoulder as he continues to laugh.

"You look like you've been at this for a long time, so I'm sure you've heard the stories. You have to know that that's not how this works," the smaller man tells me once his laughing finally dies down. I have heard the stories, but never from the person who had the encounter. Those who come across thieves rarely survive to tell the tale, especially those who come across them at night.

Even in the darkness it's easy to see that I'm wearing valuable clothing. These men are going to beat me, strip me down, and leave me on the side of the road to die. And there really isn't anything I can do to stop them. I thought I was experiencing hopelessness earlier. I thought that my big, empty house was the worst of my problems. It turns out it gets worse. So, so much worse.

The larger man leans down and I know it's the beginning of the end. I close my eyes, surrendering before it's even over. Endless jabs find my body, each sending a new, nauseating wave of pain through me. It's hard to even tell when it all stops. The only indication is that I can feel the cool breeze against my now bare skin.

I open my eyes and find I've been reduced to my undergarments. Blood surrounds me. *My blood.* The men are nowhere to be seen and neither is my cart. I'm alone once again. My eyes drift up to the stars above me as I take heavy, labored breaths. Their twinkle feels deceitful now. It reminds me of all the finer things awaiting me in a house I'll never get to go back to now.

Laying here stripped of everything I had, I'm starting to realize just how much I've taken for granted. Edrik was the brother I never had, but I never told him that. My parents did everything they did to help me succeed, but I never thanked them for it. From the time I was little I've been able to make beautiful things, but I've never appreciated that. Maybe I deserve this. Maybe I…

I hear a noise on the other side of the road and quickly turn my head in that direction, my blurred vision getting worse with the motion. Though I can't see well at the moment, I'd recognize those traditional black garments anywhere. I've never been a huge fan of the Pharisees, but I'm not exactly in a position to be picky.

"Help me…" I let out as loud as I can muster. It comes out hoarse and barely distinguishable, but he should've been able to hear me. The Pharisee turns toward me, and hope fills me. It quickly dissipates as he gapes at me, a look that I can only describe as disgust evident in his features. He faces forward again and quickens his pace. *I thought Pharisees preach helping those in need! Where is that now!?* "Please!" I use all of my strength to muster my last plea, but he doesn't even flinch, though I'm sure he heard me. That was my last chance. I truly am going to die here now.

Time passes strangely as life drains out of you. It feels like the attack was just a moment ago, but it also feels like I've been lying here for a lifetime. Opposites are companions it seems. I've never been in more pain, yet I feel nothing. The sky is starting to lighten, yet I'm plunging further into darkness. I was a good man, yet…

I hear footsteps again, but I'm convinced that turning in their direction will be a waste of the limited energy I have left. What am I saving it for? I'm not exactly sure at this point, I just know that calling for help doesn't feel worth it anymore. If a Pharisee didn't stop after spending all day lecturing people on the importance of being a good neighbor, then nobody's really going to stop, are they? This is the reason people rarely survive these encounters. Other people don't care. No matter how much they pretend to.

"What happened?" someone questions, suddenly next to me. Am I hallucinating? The moonlight is glinting off of something silver on his chest. It's large, covering his whole torso. *It's armor, isn't it? He's a Roman guard.* Would a Roman guard really consider me worth his time? His hand finds my neck, searching for my pulse. I guess he does consider me worth his time.

"Thieves," I manage to get out. He removes his hand now that he knows I'm alive.

"I'm going to get you help," he assures me. He leans down and gathers me in his arms, his armor cool against my bare skin. I don't know if there's much that he can do for me at this point, but I'm not going to vocalize that. I want to have the same hope for my survival that he has. I want to believe that there's still a chance for me. That the end isn't as near as it seems.

The guard returns to his feet and begins to run down the road in the direction of the market. A place I'm so familiar with feels foreign at this moment. Through my spotty vision, I can see little spots of bright colors speckling the sides of the path. They must be flowers. *There's no way I would've missed those, right?* I can hear the rhythmic waves of the sea as we pass through the market. *Surely that's not always been the case?* The guard carrying me smells of the soaps from Edrik's booth. *Has this soldier been a patron at our booths?*

"Deslan!" the guard carrying me calls as he comes to a stop. I think we're somewhere near the temple, though my sense of direction isn't as good as it normally is right now. I can vaguely make out the moonlight gleaming off what must be another guard's armor beyond us.

"Ren? What happened?" Deslan asks as he nears us. His armor rattles as he runs. The sound reminds me there's a sword at his side. I've been taught to fear those weapons and the men who carry them. They are not of our people. They do not have our interests at heart.

"This man was attacked by thieves. I know you functioned as a medic when we were at war. Can you help him?" Ren poses. Silence follows as Deslan looks me over, assessing whether or not he can do anything. My guess lies in the territory of not. *Deslan must know that, right? He's not going to leave his post to help a lost cause, is he? I'm not even of his people.*

"I'll do everything I can," Deslan answers, shaking my view of who these people are. This man owes me nothing, yet he is risking his superior's wrath by abandoning his station to help me. He doesn't even know that I'm rich, and something tells me that wouldn't matter to him. He's aiding me because I'm in trouble and he can do something about it. It seems tonight is revealing just how different things are from how I thought they were.

"Thank you," Ren replies. Ren is thanking him? I'm the one who will owe him my life if he's successful here.

"Th-thanks…" I manage to get out. Deslan smiles and gently puts his hand on my shoulder. His touch feels lighter by the second, and blackness begins to replace what little I could make out of him through my blurred vision.

"Save your strength," Deslan tells me. His voice sounds far away. Or maybe it's me that's far away. My eyelids flutter shut. I want to see right now, but I can't seem to make them reopen. We're moving. I can feel Ren's arms shifting and faintly hear their armor clinking. I lose consciousness before I process where we're going.

8 CATO

My daily earnings are not enough to feed my family and pay our taxes. That's a fact. The only way for us to make it through this grain shortage is for me to find another way to acquire either food or money. People are more guarded when it comes to money, so getting my hands on food should be easier.

I don't like the option I've been left with, but it's the only one I have right now besides starving myself and, eventually, my family. I need to do things I don't like for the sake of my family. It doesn't matter if the thought of getting caught makes me anxious. It doesn't matter that my palms already began sweating this morning when I thought about what I'd be doing. It doesn't matter that I'll be considered a criminal the moment I'm in possession of something that doesn't belong to me. I need to steal.

I know this sounds reckless, and in all honesty, it is, but it's necessary. I tried being an honest man. I tried playing by the rules that were set out. I tried appealing to the humanity of others. I tried, and I failed. I will not fail my family again.

Last night, the emotion conveyed in Viridi's expression reminded me much of my own desperate feelings when I was a child. I would look to my mom, begging her to make things better. Overall, she did, but only for herself. I was left in what was once our shared nightmare.

The entire time I've been a dad I've been insistent on not repeating the actions of either of my parents. I wouldn't be cruel like my father, and I wouldn't put my own needs above the needs of my children like my mom had. I was so keen on these two things that I didn't even think about how I could let my family down in other ways. The thought of them being privy to reality that our survival is not guaranteed, haunts me. The burden of that information should be mine and mine alone. They need to think that we're getting along just fine. That's why I need to steal.

I'm still trying to get used to that term. Steal. It sounds so succinct, yet it carries so much. Our people may not agree on the importance of following all the nitpicky little rules that have been set out for us, but do not steal is one that pretty much everyone can get behind. It's also one of the rules that sits both in our law and Roman law. Basically, what I'm planning on doing will make me everybody's enemy if I'm ever found out.

But I won't be found out. I can't be. My family needs me to show up at home with money to go towards our taxes and food to feed us all. That's what they need, so that's what's going to happen. Plain and simple.

I've spent the whole day thinking about how I want to go about this while I've been working in the field. There are periods where the market gets busy and maybe even borders on hectic. *If I just wait for one of those periods, then nobody's going to notice me taking a few things and walking away with them.*

The times I've seen the market at its busiest have been when I was one of the first people to collect my pay and leave. That means that my best chance at being successful with this will be to hang by the barn toward the end of the day and make sure that I reach Jaese first. He'll probably be suspicious at my eagerness to leave after all my complaining yesterday, but I'm banking on the fact that he doesn't care about me to keep him from asking questions.

The second I see Jaese appear at the far end of the barn, I run in with everything in my arms, drop it, then make my way to him.

He eyes me curiously. *Please don't tell me that the flaw in my plan will be concern from Jaese. I wouldn't be able to handle that after his cruel lack of concern yesterday.*

"Your family alright?" Jaese speaks up, sticking his hand into his pouch but keeping his eyes on me. *Do I push my luck here? Maybe I won't even have to steal.*

"Not really," I answer. He shakes his head with a frown on his face, then drops a few coins into my waiting hands. It's no more than yesterday. Yeah, that seems like him. I grip the coins tight, then break into a run toward the market. People stare at me as I go. Maybe I shouldn't be running so I don't draw attention.

Slowly, I return to a normal pace and all the eyes fall away from me. Good. *It's not like there's anything to see here. I'm just your average upstanding citizen. No plans of breaking a well-known law at all.* I feel vulnerable even thinking about what I'm about to do. *What if someone can look at me and know exactly what's on my mind?* I know it's impossible, but the thought still terrifies me.

It takes me longer than I'd like to reach the market, but by the time I make it, it's still fairly busy with the rush of people coming from work. I scan the booths, searching for one that has food and a bit of commotion going on around it. There's a couple that seem like good prospects. I opt for one with a rowdy group of fishermen in front of it. They're being loud and have a very distinct odor coming from them, so they'll be distracting multiple of the merchant's senses.

"Are you serious? Andrew and I caught more fish today than you've caught all week," one of the fishermen lets out, staring down two of the others.

"Simon, they did catch a lot of fish today," the fisherman next to him says quietly. Simon slowly turns to him and stares him down. "But we definitely caught more," he adds, louder this time to try to portray a confidence he clearly doesn't possess. Simon sighs and the fishermen across from him laugh. Wait, is this interaction near its end? I need them to keep going.

"What my brother is trying to say, but is too kind to even attempt to, is that you two fools have once again failed to beat us," Simon declares, having more than enough confidence for both him and his brother.

"Simon!" his brother whisper-shouts, scolding his behavior.

"*You're* calling *us* fools?" one of the other fishermen questions. This seems like a good time for me to get to stealing. I quietly move to the other side of them where there's some bread and fruit in baskets. I don't want to take too much and draw a lot of attention to myself, but I want to make sure that I get enough for my whole family. These loaves are big, so I think one would suffice. A handful of figs seems fair to go alongside that. I start to reach toward the baskets when I hear a voice behind me.

"Hey!" a woman shouts, and I freeze. *Was it a woman running the booth?* I thought it was a man, but I was more focused on the fishermen, so I could be wrong. My heart is pounding as I fear what might happen next. "I ask you two to do one thing, and you can't even do that without causing a stir," the woman goes on. Oh. This isn't directed at me. Why would it be? I haven't even done anything yet.

"Mom, I swear, we didn't start this," one of the fishermen responds. Something tells me that was the wrong response, though that could just be the damaged part of me talking.

"John, I do *not* want to hear excuses. Apologize to your friends, then get me what I need," the woman demands.

"Mom, they're not our friends…" another fisherman tries.

"James, don't even. I raised you boys better than this," the woman cuts him off. My eyes aren't even on them, but I'm sucked in, so I know this is the best time for me to act; everybody else is undoubtedly staring at them. I grab a loaf of bread and a handful of figs, then just casually start walking away. Nobody sees, or at least nobody says anything.

It isn't long before I'm out of the market and making my way home. I can't get over how easy that was. I spent all day terrified for that moment, and for what? It was as simple as finding the right timing. I'm coming home with even more food than I did yesterday, and I didn't have to spend a single coin. I'm starting to question why I spent so long playing by the rules.

The rules didn't stop my father from doing what he did to me. The rules didn't support me when I was all on my own. The rules didn't keep me safe from Kassia's father. The rules didn't feed my family. I did.

As I walk through the streets that just yesterday I felt shunned from, I feel like I'm on top of the world. The children's laughter brings a smile to my face. Of course it does. I know my own house will be just as joyous when I get to it. Because today I'm not a failure. Today I made my family proud.

9 NIEMOS

My eyes drift out the window of the temple as I finish reading the scroll in front of me. There's a horde of people out there and they seem to be crowding around something, but I have no idea what. Carian seems too enthralled with the scroll in front of him to notice. That's probably a good thing. I should be more like that. Distractions should not be able to get in the way of my devotion. I pick up another scroll and try to start reading it, but I can't help myself from watching the growing crowd.

"What's going on out there?" I pose, finally drawing Carian's attention to the commotion. He looks up from the scroll in front of him and out the window where more people are joining the mass. They're practically the only thing in view now. I still can't see what it is they're gathering around, though I can faintly hear a man's voice.

"I don't know," Carian responds, craning his neck to see if he can get a better angle. Usually, when crowds form the people are angry, or they're watching some kind of altercation go down. Their expressions right now don't seem to tell either of those tales. They seem curious. Some even look delighted. Whatever's going on out there seems like something we should be involved in given that we're religious leaders and it's happening outside the temple. "Let's go out there," Carian declares, having come to the same conclusion.

He sets down his scroll and gets to his feet, not even waiting to see if I'm coming with him. I quickly put my own scroll down, then hop to my feet and jog to catch up with him. His swift movements make it so I just reach him before he makes it outside. I see his head move back and forth, scanning the crowd, so I begin to do the same. The sheer volume of people is even more overwhelming than I had imagined when I first saw them. They press against each other, silent despite their vast numbers. The contradiction of it all makes my head spin.

It takes me a few seconds to get over my shock and locate the thing everybody's crowded around: a man. He doesn't look very remarkable, yet all eyes are on him, thrilled to hear each and every word that he spews.

"What's going on?" Carian questions a woman near us.

"That man just healed the blind man!" she exclaims, pointing to the man who's drawn everybody's attention. *Men are not capable of healing other men. Surely, she's mistaken.*

"Are you sure the man was actually blind?" I press, and she rolls her eyes.

"He's only been on these very steps for years seeking help, so yeah, I'm sure he was actually blind. I wouldn't expect you lot to know that though. You never paid him any attention," she remarks.

"Excuse me?" I respond incredulously. There have always been people who disrespect us but never that blatantly right outside the temple. This is where they come to seek our guidance, not spew accusations. *Has one man's supposed actions really made them forget that?*

"I told you what happened. Can you stop bothering me now? I'm trying to listen to what he has to say," she states, then she turns back toward the disrupter. My gaze shifts to Carian; I find him fuming. He begins to push through the people, and I don't know what to do, so I follow him. Some give us dirty looks, but most are too enthralled with catching the man's every words to even notice that we've pressed past them. Soon we reach the front and the man's eyes shift to us.

"Some will have you believe that you must be perfect to enter the Kingdom of Heaven, but I'm here to tell you that that's not the case. Man cannot achieve perfection no matter how hard they try. That's why God has sent One greater than man to atone for their imperfection," the man declares, staring at Carian and I throughout the entire statement. It sends shivers down my spine, but it seems to have a very different effect on Carian.

"You must stop at once!" Carian lets out, jutting his finger in the man's face with fury. There are calls to let him continue from the crowd, but the man himself doesn't seem to be having much of a reaction to Carian at all. His amber eyes look us up and down, a curiosity in them that bothers me. *Who is he to study us?* He has the same shoulder length dark hair and beige clothes as half the men in this city. He's nobody. We're Pharisees.

"I'm under no obligation to listen to you," the man says simply. *No obligation? Where is this boldness coming from?*

"I am a Pharisee and we are within the temple courts, so I have authority over you!" Carian shouts, enraged by the man's calmness. The crowd goes silent as they wait to see what happens next. I too find myself anxiously awaiting what the man will say next. He couldn't possibly deny Carian his authority as a Pharisee.

"There is only One who has authority over me," the man states, a slight grin on his face. *He finds this all funny? Does he have no respect for our way of life?*

"Who!?" Carian demands.

"My Father," he answers, that grin still there. It's a smile that would be nice were it not for the situation in which it occurred. Instead, the curve of his lips feels pointed, as if he's trying to use it to hook the crowd. And it's working. They're enthralled.

"Who is your father!?" Carian interrogates, clearly annoyed with the fact that this man is leaving out information with each response. Carian's annoyance only seems to further amuse the man. There's a gleam in his eye that I can only liken to joy. This man is finding joy in his disrespect and the crowd is loving it. They lean in around us, itching to hear what's said next.

"I think you know," the man responds. *What's that supposed to mean?* I expect Carian to question him again, but he seems frozen in place. "The time is coming where creation will be reunited with their Creator. You must only believe," the man adds, then he turns and starts to walk through the crowd. I try to follow him, but he doesn't appear to be in the mass of people. *How did he do that?*

People chatter amongst themselves as they disperse. Before long, Carian and I are the only ones left. He still hasn't said anything. It almost scares me; he's always had an answer to everything I haven't understood, and I certainly didn't understand much of what just happened. I need him to explain it all away for me.

"Carian, what do we do?" I ask him. He looks up at me. It's his first movement since the man last spoke. His face is a jumble of various emotions I can't seem to identify, though confusion doesn't seem to be among them. He shakes his head, takes a deep breath, then looks right at me.

"We need to go to the Sanhedrin and tell them that a man is out here performing false signs and claiming to be the Son of God," Carian declares.

"That's who he was referring to?" I gasp, unable to hide my shock. Usually I try not to seem this clueless around Carian, but I can't contain my reaction to this news. Our people have been waiting for the Son of God for countless years. I never imagined we'd even come close to His arrival in my lifetime.

"He supposedly performed a miracle, then he said that I don't have authority over him. Who else would he be talking about?" Carian challenges, irritated. I've never seen him this thrown off. Not when we were kids getting pushed around. Not when his parents questioned his choice to become a Pharisee. Not even when Izal got the temple leadership position that Carian was more qualified for due to all his intense preparation. This man has managed to get under Carian's skin in a way that no one ever has. I'm not quite sure what to make of it yet.

"If this man was claiming to be the Son of God, how do we know he's not?" I pose. He didn't seem like much, but I never really had a picture of the Son of God in my head. Well, I did when I was much younger. I thought He'd be tall. Well-built. Flames would surround Him. His strength would be evident well before He ever uttered a word. That wasn't a completely realistic expectation, but I can't get over how average the man I saw earlier was. He was nothing special, yet the crowd couldn't have been more captivated. *Could that mean He is who He says He is?*

"How do we know he's not? Would the Son of God disrespect a Pharisee? Outside the temple no less? Would the Son of God be trying to convince the people that their actions don't matter? Telling them that someone, presumably him, would pull them into the Kingdom of Heaven with him? Think Niemos. Everything he did was in direct opposition to what we've been taught and have lived out our whole lives. He certainly wasn't the Son of God. He was a fraud trying to lead the people astray," he remarks, distaste encompassing each and every word.

"Right," I nod along, and he raises his eyebrows. "What?"

"Please don't tell me there's a part of you that wants to believe him," he says. What Carian said makes sense. That man clearly isn't the Son of God, but the prospect of Him being here was kind of exciting. How cool would it be to walk among Him? It'd be like the beginning of time; except I wouldn't screw it up like the first humans did. I would bask in His presence, soaking up everything He had to offer. It would be paradise before Heaven. "Niemos?" Carian questions, bringing me back to the here and now.

"No, I don't believe him. He definitely was a fraud," I finally answer, and he nods his head.

"A dangerous fraud, too. He had those people convinced he was their savior. That's why we need to make the Sanhedrin aware of him so we can find a way to move forward before he draws in any more of the simple-minded," he tells me, determination encompassing him. His eyes have begun to survey the area before us where the people had been. He must already be planning what he's going to say to the Sanhedrin. My mind has never worked like his, but each time I'm around him is a chance to try and emulate the way he thinks.

"You're right," I agree. That man is a danger to our way of life. We need to find a way to convince the people of that.

10 AURAN

"Dominus, I'm glad I caught you," Deslan lets out, running over to me from the direction of the temple. I was just on my way home for the day, but I don't mind staying a bit longer. Home is full of things I don't want to think about. Whatever problem Deslan is bringing to me right now can't be worse than all of that.

"Is everything alright?" I check when he reaches me. Nothing about him seems abnormal at the moment, and strangely, that disappoints me. *Am I really that desperate to avoid home?*

"Yes, I just wanted to apologize for not being around to give you the nightly report this morning. I was with a merchant who was attacked by thieves last night," Deslan explains. I will admit that Deslan not being there this morning threw me off, but as soon as Ren told me where he was, I completely understood. While we're primarily here for the interests of our own people, we're also here for the Jewish. That man needed him and he showed up. I'd never condemn him for that.

"You don't need to apologize, Deslan. You did the right thing taking care of that man," I tell him, and he smiles.

"Thank you, Dominus," he responds, and I nod.

"How is he?" I ask. Attacks like this used to be few and far between, but lately it seems that the thieves are getting bolder. Part of me wonders if I'm to blame for that. I haven't had the wherewithal to deal with everything happening on the streets after seeing my boy bound to his bed every morning. Somehow, those up to no good have sensed this weakness and they've decided to capitalize on it.

"He was in rough shape, but he pulled through. He described the attack to me when he was more coherent. There were at least two attackers who had been hiding in the field next to the road last night. He doesn't know if they had been waiting for him specifically, or if they just got lucky," he details.

"What do you mean got lucky?" I follow up, curiously.

"He sold jewelry. Everything they took from him was worth more than you and I make in a year," he answers. If they had known he was that rich prior to the attack, they probably would've followed him home instead of attacking him on the side of the road. The thieves were waiting for anybody, and they had no issue carrying out their attack once this merchant was unlucky enough to stumble across them.

"We need to do more to stop things like this from happening," I state. Deslan seems confused that I've chosen to have this conversation with him. If I'm honest, it has nothing to do with him, I just need to get these thoughts out now before other things get in the way. I'm powerless in the things happening in my own home, but maybe, just maybe, I can do something about the things happening on the streets.

"What are you thinking?" he poses.

"Stationing more guards out there for starters. Well, now that I say it, I don't know if that would be very helpful. Even with more guards the darkness would still give the thieves an advantage. Maybe we need to impose some sort of curfew for the merchants to make sure they make it home before nightfall? They may complain about that, but I don't know how else to keep them safe," I think out loud.

"We could make an example of the next thief we catch. Make sure the rest of them think twice about stealing after that," he suggests. That would be an easier sell to my higher-ups should they catch wind of this. It also puts the punishment on the right group of people, rather than the people who are being targeted.

"I like it," I tell him.

"Thank you, Dominus," he responds. He starts to walk away and I can feel the pit in my stomach begin to form at the idea of going home. I know it has to happen eventually, but I want to put it off longer. I'm not ready for the silence. For Domitia's harsh glances. I need to find something else to talk about so I can be here longer.

"Deslan, why were you coming from the temple?" I pose, and he turns to face me, his eyebrows raised.

"You didn't hear about what just happened over there?" he asks.

"No," I answer. This could be troublesome. Things involving the Pharisees tend to be.

"You know the blind man who sits on the temple steps?" he begins, excitement seeming to pour out of him at the chance to explain whatever happened. *What about the blind man could be making him this excited?*

"I'm familiar," I confirm.

"He's not blind anymore," he lets out enthusiastically.

"What do you mean?" I immediately inquire.

"The man was blind, but now he can see. I didn't see the miracle itself take place, but I saw him after the commotion, so I know that much," he declares, a smile on his face as he relives the memory.

"What commotion, Deslan?" I ask, leaning toward him, my confusion somehow greater than before. He smiles at first, but then he seems to remember he's speaking to a superior and forces a neutral expression to his face.

"The man that healed the blind man started speaking afterwards and people crowded around him to listen. It might be the biggest crowd I've ever seen by the temple. That must be why the

Pharisees noticed. Two of them came out of the temple and forced their way toward the man. Words were exchanged, then the man disappeared and the crowd dispersed. The Pharisees didn't seem very happy, but I'm not sure there's much we can do about that," he details.

I don't even know where to start trying to comprehend all of this. I've passed by that man on the stairs day after day and so has Deslan. I know he was blind. There's no question about that. I also know that Deslan wouldn't mistake him for someone else. It's just like he said: the man was blind, but now he can see.

Miracles are possible. It's a short statement, but it has the potential to change lives. It can change my life. Medicine has fallen short in treating Maxian, but miracles don't fall short. The simple fact that miracles are possible and that one has occurred on these very streets means that Maxian's fate isn't sealed.

I know I should be more focused on what happened with the Pharisees given that it has the potential to complicate my job, but I can't get my mind off of this mystery man and what he did. Nothing seems to matter right now except for finding out more about him. I don't care what problems the Pharisees found with him. He did something I've never seen them even come close to doing in all their self-righteous glory.

"What can you tell me about the man who performed the miracle?" I pose, surprising Deslan after being quiet for so long.

"Not much. He was pretty average. Dark hair down to his shoulders, tall, but not super tall, probably in his early thirties. He didn't give his name. He didn't seem to want the focus on him, but I have a feeling this isn't the last we'll see of him. I think he's here to start something. I don't quite know what it is, but I know it's going to be big," he shares. Again, I should probably be worried, but all I can think about is finding him. If he's not finished, then maybe he'll consider my family worthy of one of his miracles.

"Thank you, Deslan," I respond, an overwhelming sense of relief taking me over. Even though I didn't see the miracle. Even though I know nothing about the man. Even though my hope had been lost as of late. Hope has a new face now.

"You're welcome, Dominus," he replies, then he heads into the building to find out his assignment for the night. His words replay in my head as I begin to walk home. 'The miracle.' 'The man that healed the blind man.' 'This isn't the last we'll see of him.' The world itself has changed with the arrival of this man. The impossible is possible.

I don't know how it is that I'm believing so strongly in something I haven't seen. It's all so hard to process and even harder to describe. It feels as if all that I am is tied to all that he is. This mystery man. Average yet not average at all. Someone who can draw a crowd but wouldn't stand out in one. Causing problems with the Pharisees, yet also being in and of himself a solution to problems deemed unsolvable. I don't have a very good description of him, but I know I need to find him.

As soon as I walk through the door I head to Maxian's room. He's no different than he was this morning, yet it seems as though everything has changed with the day's events. This bed may not be his prison for much longer. I kneel down next to him and put my hand on his shoulder. He doesn't acknowledge my touch, but this does nothing to discourage me as it has before. Hope is among us now.

"Hold on. Just for a little bit longer," I tell him.

11 MARY

I feel as if I'm about to explode. I have information that I have to share immediately but home seems like it's too far right now. My feet move as fast as I can make them; my surroundings a blur as I go by. I can hear people questioning me and making comments that aren't very nice. I pay them no attention. Nothing can pull me away from what I just witnessed and my need to spread the news to Laz and Martha so that I'm not the only one mind-blown by it all.

I was at the market searching for fruit that Martha told me to pick up, which I'm now realizing I didn't pick up. *That's not important.* I saw everybody leaving the market and heading toward the temple, so naturally, I followed. There was a massive crowd around something, but I had no idea what from my vantage point, so I pushed forward until I could see.

At that point I was pretty confused. Everybody was surrounding a man, but it wasn't just any man: it was Jesus. The same Jesus from my childhood who I played chase with in the clearing behind our houses. Well, He looks a lot older now, as do I, but it was definitely Him. There's no mistaking those kind, amber eyes, and that warm, yet sometimes playful smile. The thing that everybody was crowding around was most definitely Jesus. *But why?*

I turned to someone near me to make my inquiry. Nobody was thrilled to have their focus pulled away from Jesus, but one woman did half turn toward me and answer my question. It took a second for her words to register within me, but once they did, I was stunned. 'He healed a blind man.' *My Jesus healed a blind man.* Just as I was trying to make sense of all of that, two Pharisees reached Him and the one started arguing with Him, though it wasn't really an argument. The Pharisee was shouting, but Jesus was having fun. It was the most like my brother I'd ever seen Him, and it took everything in me not to laugh.

The next part is what really caused this flurry of excitement within me. Jesus claimed that the only One with authority over Him is His Father, and He said the Pharisees should know who He was talking about. That confused me at first. His father is dead, and a couple of random Pharisees wouldn't have known who he was. Then it hit me; He wasn't talking about the father that we knew.

My breathing is heavy at this point, but I don't slow down. The information I'm privy to is too important for my pace to be anything other than what it is. By the time our house is in sight, my lungs are burning. I nearly run into the door as I reach it, but I shake that off as I pull it open and rush into the house.

"Did you get the fruit?" Martha asks. She's so focused on preparing dinner, that she didn't even look up when she asked the question.

"I come bearing something way more important than fruit," I answer, my voice just as manic as my journey here was. This draws her eyes right to mine, and she raises her eyebrows.

"Care to explain," she requests.

"Laz needs to be here for this," I state, and she rolls her eyes.

"He's in his workshop. Don't scare him when you go in. We don't want to risk him hurting himself again," she comments. There was only one time that he hurt himself because I barged in and scared him. We've both been better about things since then.

I rush out of the house, but slow to a walk once I reach Laz's workshop. I can hear him sawing away at something, so I wait a second for those noises to cease before I open the door and head in. He's blowing sawdust off of his table when he spots me.

"Mary," he greets me, a smile on his face.

"Laz," I return, giving him a smile of my own.

"I'm just finishing up in here for the day. Do you need something?" he poses, noticing my antsiness.

"I need you to be done now and come into the house with me so I can update you and Martha on the *wonderous* thing I saw today," I let out. He tilts his head at this, his interest clearly piqued.

"Can I clean up first?" he asks.

"Why would you waste time asking a silly question like that?" I implore. He laughs and shakes his head as he walks over to me.

"You really are something, Mary," he tells me, patting my shoulder. He'd be reacting the exact same way if he was the one with news as big as this. We head to the house and as soon as Martha's eyes meet mine, I just let it out.

"Jesus is the Son of God," I declare. Martha blinks a few times as she tries to take this in. Laz on the other hand, immediately starts asking questions.

"Jesus, like the kid we grew up with, Jesus?" he begins.

"Yes," I confirm, the excitement spilling out of me.

"And you know this how?" he poses skeptically, scratching his forehead. Martha also seems pretty hesitant, her gaze gentle, but containing an air of concern. *Come on. This is not just a random thought that popped into my head. I have proof.*

"Because He healed a blind man, then He told a Pharisee that His Father is the only one with authority over Him, and the only being with authority over a miracle worker would be God," I spill as if it's obvious even though it took me a while to get it myself. Now Laz goes quiet as he stares off at the wall contemplating this. alright, *I wanted them to be mind-blown, but I can't handle this silence.* "Somebody say something," I prompt them.

"This actually kind of makes sense," Martha finally speaks up, her gaze shifting around as she continues to think this over.

"What about any of this makes sense? We've known Jesus forever. He was just a kid like the rest of us," Laz counters. This feels like it has more to do with disagreeing with Martha than it has to do with what I've said. I'd say something to him, but I want to hear Martha's response. I want to hear how this has been right here in front of us the whole time so I know I'm not crazy jumping to this conclusion now.

"He was not just like the rest of you. He only ever got in trouble when you got Him in trouble, He was extremely empathetic and helped me out without me even having to say anything, and He always seemed to know things that a boy His age wouldn't. All of those things on their own wouldn't be enough to convince me, but now He's healed someone, Laz. There's no doubt in my mind that Mary's right about this," Martha states, the words still washing over her even after they've left her mouth. *I get that. This is a lot.*

"So, you're telling me that all those times I went to temple as a kid and learned about the Lord, His Son was sitting right next to me?" Laz questions.

"Yes," Martha and I answer at the same time. Laz's glance falls on the wall again as he tries to think this over. I don't know what the hold-up is for him. You can't argue with the fact that Jesus just performed a miracle. I don't know why He never said anything to us when we were younger, and it's not really my place to know that. What matters is that I know now, and that, that changes everything.

"I need some time," Laz declares, then he walks out before either of us can say anything.

"Why can't he see it?" I ask, and Martha shakes her head.

"I don't know," she responds, though based on her expression, I can tell she definitely has some theories. I'm about to ask her about them, but she speaks up again. "How do you feel about all of this?"

I hadn't stopped for long enough to fully consider that. I believe it-wholeheartedly-I just… I don't know, it's all very weird to me now that I put more thought into it. It wouldn't be weird if it was anybody else, but this is Jesus. I've been to the house of the Son of God. I've had meals with the Son of God. I've had conversations with the Son of God while we were hiding during hide and seek.

"He was one of my best friends growing up. Not even just that; there was a time I had a crush on Him. I had a crush on the Son of God," I let out, and goosebumps pepper my skin at the thought. Martha starts laughing and I shoot her a look. "It's not funny!"

"Right, sorry," she apologizes, throwing her hands up in surrender. "I don't blame you though. He was the only one of those boys you grew up with who was kind and polite."

"I guess that was just the Lord in Him," I comment, embarrassed.

"It wasn't. He got those things from His mom. He may be God's Son, but that doesn't change the fact that He's Mary's Son, or James' Brother, or Laz's Friend. Jesus is still Jesus, there's just more to Him than we've ever known," she says. That feels like the biggest understatement imaginable.

12 AURAN

As soon as Deslan was done giving me last night's report, I began scanning all the written issues, searching for any mention of the man that healed the blind man. It'd be a lot easier to find him if I had more to go off of than a description that dozens of men in this city fit. Unfortunately, I don't find any issues mentioning him. Not even one from the Pharisees.

They don't tend to come to us with their issues unless their issues are with us. It's not hard to see that they resent our oversight. I understand that it must be hard for them having another people rule over them, but we've been more than tolerant. The fact that they still have their temples and their positions shows that. That doesn't seem to matter to them; we're the enemy and we always will be.

I don't think the Pharisees would have had much more information than Deslan anyway. I'm not exactly sure who would. There has to be people that know this man somewhere, but I wouldn't even know where to start my search. I could try to find the former blind man and see if he has any information, though I'm sure he was a lot more focused on the world around him than the man in that moment. It's the only lead I have right now, so I might as well chase it.

I leave the written issues scattered all over my table and exit the building. Soldiers eye me curiously as I head toward the temple, but they don't say anything. Some of them seem happy to see me out and about. I guess it has been a while since I've really taken to the streets like I used to. That's going to change. No matter what winds up happening with Maxian, I need to go back to being the man that he and all those under my command have looked up to.

The former blind man isn't on the temple stairs, which makes sense since he isn't actually blind anymore. *Where would he go?* I always assumed he had no family and that's why he stayed on those steps day in and day out. I wrack my brain trying to come up with each and every detail I have about him.

I remember seeing people with him at times. Not family, but other people with physical afflictions would keep him company sometimes. *Maybe he's gone to find them and give them company now?* This could be a long shot, but I know there's a pool a few streets over that some believe has healing powers; he could be searching for people he knows over there.

I start heading in that direction, hope beginning to bubble up in me as I go. It feels odd after being estranged from it for so long. Almost as if I'm floating, possibility just within my grasp. It's vulnerable. At any moment, reality could grab my ankle and yank me down, anchoring me in the hell that's overtaken my days since Maxian first fell ill. Part of me screams to just let it. It'll hurt less if I give up on possibility now, but I refuse. A man was blind and now he can see. Possibility has been expanded far beyond my comprehension.

Once I reach the pool, I begin searching for the former blind man. Would I even recognize him? I've only ever seen him on those steps in ratty clothes. He's probably acquired different clothing by now. I also haven't been by the temple recently, which doesn't help.

I continue scanning the people before me and my eyes widen as they fall on a man who matches the description that Deslan gave me. He's standing in front of a lame man, a smile on his face that I can only assume has formed because of what's to come. It seems I'm about to witness a miracle.

"That mat looks a little worse for wear," the miracle worker observes. The lame man faces him, confused.

"I've been this way for thirty-eight years and this mat has been with me the whole time," the lame man states. The miracle worker nods and goosebumps pepper my skin as I wait for the moment I'm sure is coming. The lame man has no idea how much his life is about to change.

"It seems it's time for you to leave it," the miracle worker declares.

"I don't understand what you mean. I have no means of acquiring another mat, and I can never make it to the pool in time to find healing," the lame man brings up. He doesn't know what this man is capable of. He doesn't know that the very order of things has changed.

"You don't need the pool. The work has already been done. Pick up your mat and walk, Benjamin," the miracle worker tells him, using his name even though to my knowledge it was never given to him. Benjamin gapes at him, but his expression doesn't waver. *Has the miracle really taken place already without Benjamin knowing it?* "You could stay here, but that seems a little silly now that you can walk," the miracle worker goes on.

Benjamin stares down at his legs, then starts wiggling his toes. His eyes nearly pop out of his head at the sight. He faces the miracle worker as if to ask if this is real; the miracle worker nods. Benjamin braces himself using his hands, then begins to push himself up. His knees bend, then his legs take over the motion and he's on his feet. He stares at the miracle worker, dumbfounded, and the miracle worker smiles at him.

"I told you," the miracle worker says. Benjamin throws his arms around the miracle worker, and the miracle worker pats his back.

"I want to thank you, but I know that's not enough," Benjamin lets out as he releases the miracle worker.

"It's not, but it doesn't need to be. I didn't come for personal gain, but for the gain of all who choose to believe in me," the miracle worker responds. His statement started with a smile, but it's dampened by the end of it. Those words seem to carry a heavy toll for him. *Do they have to do with what he's here for?* I'm still none the wiser as to what his grand plan is.

A crowd begins to form around Benjamin as he bends down and picks up his mat. The miracle worker walks into the mass of people and I try to follow him, but he seems to disappear. My eyes dart everywhere looking for him, but he's nowhere to be seen. Benjamin cranes his neck, searching for him as well until a Pharisee obstructs his sight.

"What are you doing? You know you cannot carry your mat on the day of rest," the Pharisee scolds Benjamin, but instead of obedience, he's met with laughter. His face reddens and he stands up straighter to try and assert his authority, but Benjamin clearly isn't impressed.

"Do you not realize what me carrying my mat means? I've been healed! The man who healed me told me to pick up my mat and walk. The idea was unfathomable, yet here I am doing it!" Benjamin lets out, the joy that comes with such a miracle radiating off of him. I add that joy to the things waiting for me along with possibility.

"Who healed you?" the Pharisee questions him.

"That's what you're choosing to focus on?" Benjamin poses, his eyebrows raised. The Pharisee's eyes remain locked on him, waiting for an answer. "He didn't identify himself, and he's not here anymore," Benjamin tells him, clearly disappointed about the Pharisee's focus. The Pharisee scoffs, then he walks away.

Benjamin rolls his eyes, then heads off in the other direction, his mat in his hands. I decide to follow him. I could sense that there was something he wasn't saying to the Pharisee that he may be more willing to tell someone who doesn't start the conversation by accusing him of something.

After following him down a couple of streets it occurs to me that I have no idea where he's going. *Should I just give it a rest? Am I wasting my time? No, right? He knows something more about the miracle worker. I can feel it.* I continue to follow him, and I'm soon rewarded; the miracle worker steps out from a side street and greets him.

"I see you're well," the miracle worker states, and Benjamin laughs.

"It seems you knew I would be the whole time," Benjamin says, and the miracle worker nods. "You know much more than the average man, don't you?" he goes on.

"I do," the miracle worker confirms. Two words. That's all he uttered, yet the atmosphere seems to have shifted with them. "I was going to tell you this earlier, but I knew the Pharisee was coming…" he begins.

"Did You sense him?" Benjamin questions, wonder in his expression.

"I saw him over your shoulder," the miracle worker laughs, and Benjamin nods, semi-embarrassed. "I was going to say go and sin no more. That would please my Father," he finishes his original thought. *His father?* I have no idea what he's talking about, but Benjamin's entire posture changes in response to that statement.

"Of course," Benjamin immediately agrees. The miracle worker puts his hand on Benjamin's shoulder, a smile on his face. "Can I ask You a question?" Benjamin inquires.

"You just did," the miracle worker jokes.

"Right. Can I ask You another?" Benjamin responds, and the miracle worker raises his eyebrows. "Right, I just did again… I'll just ask the actual question now. Did You choose to heal me on the Sabbath on purpose?" Benjamin finally poses, and the miracle worker chuckles. I forgot that it's the Jewish day of rest. If the miracle worker is Jewish, then he just broke one of their rules by 'working' on the day of rest. Now I get why he left before the Pharisee could bother him about that.

"Would you rather I had waited?" the miracle worker

checks, a smirk on his face.

"No," Benjamin responds with a knowing smile.

"There you have it. I have to go now. There's somebody I need to talk to," the miracle worker says.

"Ok. Thank You again," Benjamin reiterates, and the miracle worker nods. Benjamin continues to head in the direction he was going and I expect the miracle worker to walk away as well, but to my surprise he looks directly at me.

13 AURAN

"You've been searching for me," the miracle worker speaks up, his gaze still on mine. I don't know what to say. I don't know what to do. I don't even know if I'm worthy of standing in his presence, yet here I am, his sole focus. I try to find words or move closer to him, but I seem to be frozen at this moment. Despite my apparent lack of effort in this interaction, he smiles and makes his way over to me. "I'm Jesus," he introduces himself, holding his hand out to me.

"Auran," I return as I shake his hand, my brain finally operating again.

"It's nice to meet you, Auran," he tells me, his smile still shining bright.

"You too," the words immediately tumble out of my mouth, though those words obviously don't convey how honored I am to be standing across from him right now. Silence fills the air between us, but he makes no sign of leaving. I get the feeling that he knows exactly what I'm going to ask him and he's just waiting for me to do it.

I want to ask, but I'm struggling for words again. He really does seem normal up close, but I know that he's anything but that. This man granted sight to the blind. He struck movement into dead legs. Those are just the things I know about. I know without a doubt that he can heal Maxian too, but will he bestow his kindness upon me? I'm not even of the same people as him. Yet here he is, smiling at me, just waiting for me to say the words.

"My boy is sick. I know you can heal him," I state. It's a crazy statement, yet I've never been surer of anything.

"I can," he confirms, nodding. Those words nearly stop my breathing as his majesty clouds my head. This is all actually going to happen. Maxian is going to be up and moving again, and it's going to be all because of this man before me. I can't even express the amount of joy rushing through me right now.

"I uh-I'm not worthy to have you come to my home, or take up much more of your time, but I know if you say he is well, it will be so. I mean, with my limited authority, I'm able to make soldiers come and go using just my words, and your authority far surpasses my own. Yeah, you just need to say the words," I let out, looking over at him, anticipation gripping every inch of me. He faces me with admiration in his expression.

"I haven't even seen this level of faith in my own followers or anyone else in this region. Your boy will be better just as you've said," he tells me, putting his hand on my shoulder. All the anguish that had been built up in me since Maxian first fell ill begins spilling out at once. My chest heaves and tears leak from my eyes as I try to process it all.

He pulls me closer to him and I start to sob into his chest, unable to contain all the swirling emotions within me. He pats my back wordlessly, impatience absent from his demeanor. I'd be embarrassed if I wasn't overtaken by so many other emotions. He holds me until my breathing evens out, then he releases me, that kind smile on his face as he meets my eyes again.

"Thank you," I say, knowing just as Benjamin did that it's not enough. No words could ever be enough for a gift of this magnitude.

"You're welcome," he responds anyway. There's so much else that I want to say to him, but I don't know where to start. It's not every day you come across someone like him. I'm not sure that there really is anyone else like him. "You should go see your boy," he tells me.

I want to see Maxian more than I can express, but I also don't want to walk away from him just yet. He has this invigorating presence about him that seems to fill me with purpose and potential just by standing near him. Deslan was right; whatever he's here to do is going to be big. I don't know if I have any business knowing this, but I have to ask.

"What are you here for?" I pose.

"One day you'll know," he answers, his smile wavers as his gaze leaves mine. It's the same reaction he had earlier when he told Benjamin that he was here for the gain of those who choose to believe in him. What does that mean? "Give Maxian my best," he speaks up, the smile back, then he walks away.

I never told him Maxian's name. I'm starting to question if this man is even a man at all. His capabilities seem to go far beyond those of any man I've ever come across. He knows things. Not just Maxian's name. He also knew that I was trying to find him, and exactly what I was going to ask him about. He heals. Nothing seems to have power over him. Whoever he is-whatever he is, he has my utmost respect and loyalty.

I turn around and start heading back toward my house. It's hard not to stop and tell every person I pass about what has just been done in my life. I want to shout it from the rooftops! My boy was plucked from death's doorstep! The only thing stopping me from letting everyone know is my desire to get to Maxian. I'm practically running through the streets to get home, which seems to be scaring a few people, but I'm not worried about that right now. For once, I'm not worried about anything. The joy in me is too radiant to coexist with worry.

As soon as I turn onto our path, I spot Maxian outside with Domitia. She still seems dumbfounded, which is fair. It's a lot for me and I know what caused this miracle, or rather who did. Once

Maxian spots me, a smile overtakes him, and he runs over to me, closing the gap between the two of us. He throws his arms around me and squeezes me tight, something that I never would've dreamed was possible back when he was bedridden.

"I held on, dad," he tells me.

"You heard that?" I say, letting go of him and meeting his eyes. I intended for him to, but I had assumed that he didn't because he didn't respond in any way.

"I heard everything. I wanted to answer you all. To talk to you. To hug you. I never really had the energy… I'm sorry," he apologizes, his face downcast. There's no cause for downcast faces on a day like this. He was going to die, yet here he is, alive and well in my arms as if the illness had never existed! There's only cause for celebration!

"Maxian, do not apologize. You've been healed! A man cured you without even being in the same room as you! That's all that matters right now!" I let out. He smiles and I ruffle his hair. His smile grows, and somehow the joy inside of me does too. I put my hand on his shoulder and we start heading back toward the house.

"I heard him, you know," Maxian says.

"Who?" I pose.

"The man who healed me. I heard his voice. He said, 'Get up, child,' and suddenly I had the energy to do just that. It gave Domitia quite the scare," he tells me. It baffles me that Jesus could have spoken to him while being with me, but I guess nothing about him should really surprise me at this point.

As we reach the house, the second part of what he says starts to hit me. Domitia still has no idea what happened. She had already accepted the fact that Maxian would be dead, yet here he is, up and active just like before. I should probably talk to her.

"Why don't you go find your mom, and spend some time with her for a bit," I say.

"Ok," Maxian agrees, heading in the direction of the stream where his mom is probably washing clothes. I walk up to Domitia.

She has a faraway look in her eyes.

"I know this is a lot…" I start, and she snaps her head toward me with an eyebrow cocked.

"A lot? He was practically dead, and now it's as if nothing has happened! How are you even thinking straight right now?" she questions, more flustered than I've ever seen her. Domitia is a woman who finds comfort in facts. She can count on them. They're regular. There's nothing regular about what happened in our home today.

"Because I believed in this miracle wholeheartedly. In fact, I asked for it. A man did this for us, Domitia. A man who transcends everything I've ever known," I report. She gapes at me. That's understandable. Just a few days ago I would've had a similar reaction if she was the one telling me this. At once, she starts laughing, surprising me.

"I hope you thanked him," she says, her chuckle continuing through her words.

"Of course I did," I assure her. She takes a step closer to me and sets her head on my chest. I put my hand on her back, holding her close.

"He's alright," she lets out, a deep breath following the proclamation.

"He's alright," I confirm. Miracles are possible. There's absolutely no denying it.

14 TIRNAN

A year ago, I went through every merchant's worst nightmare. It nearly ended my life. The first few days, I was still convinced that it would. Deslan was able to patch me up, but pain continued to torment me. He came to check on me every day for a week, but there was nothing he could do about the pain. It's all kind of ironic; I complained of being lonely, and now here I am with this unwavering ache as my constant company.

Edrik has visited me every day without ceasing. He had been worried about me when I didn't show up at the market the day after the attack, so he came here and had quite the shock when he saw me. He blamed himself at first. Said it was his fault because he wasn't with me for longer that night, but that wouldn't have made a difference. I still would've walked home alone because he doesn't live near me. There's also that fact that we live very different lives outside the market. He has people expecting him to be home. I don't.

Edrik went and got my parents after he found me. They used all of their connections and a considerable amount of their money trying to fix me. Doctors from the highest places were brought in to get me back on my feet. The pain isn't everywhere anymore, but it won't leave my right leg. Every step is excruciating. Nothing has been able to change that. I am the way that I am now. Unfixable.

So, as someone who has a particularly hard time walking, the life of a merchant isn't really for me anymore. I sat here in this giant, empty house for a long time, slowly losing my mind, then I got to thinking. Before the attack I had bright spots in my life, but I was unhappy. Was part of that because I was too caught up in my feelings to recognize what I had? Yes, but there was more to it too. I've been coasting through life on decisions made for me. That much I already knew, but before I wasn't willing to do anything to change that. Things are different now.

My parents would have me continue making jewelry and partner with someone like Edrik to have him sell it every day. Edrik himself would probably also encourage something like that, but I don't want that. I don't want to sit in this house surrounded by all of these things. I don't want to live a life that was handed to me. I want to forge my own path. I have no idea what that really looks like for a former merchant with a limp, but I'm committed to figuring it out.

Part of building a new life is breaking down the old one. I don't want something to fall back on. I'll never truly be able to go off on my own with a safety blanket within my grasp. This house. This stuff. This fortune. I need to shed all of it. I'll take some money with me, but only a reasonable amount, not enough to go out and start another business somewhere else.

My parents aren't going to be happy with this decision, which is exactly why I'm not going to tell them. I'm going to make Edrik do that part. Is that the move of a coward? Maybe, but it's the least Edrik can do for me; I'm leaving him everything. He's always said that his house is too cramped. He doesn't have enough money to do this or that. He won't have to worry about that anymore. I've reflected. I know I took his companionship for granted all these years. It's about time I repay him for being the one part of my life that I actually enjoyed.

"Tirnan, have you eaten yet today? I can make you something if you haven't," Edrik offers as he comes into the house. He's learned not to knock because it takes me forever to get to the door and he knows I'm home anyway.

"I'm fine Edrik," I tell him. He doesn't seem convinced by this answer. "Come sit," I say, gesturing to the seat across from me.

"Is everything alright?" he asks, hurrying over to the chair, his full attention on me. *Are my nerves that obvious?* I'm not nervous about going off on my own; I'm nervous about how he's going to take it. I don't want him to think that this is about leaving him because it isn't at all. I just need to leave here. Leave the shell of my old life that I could never return to even if I did want to. I hope he'll get that. "Tirnan, you're worrying me," he speaks up.

"I need to tell you something," I start, still searching for the right way to put this. You'd think I'd have it after all this time alone, but I never landed on one.

"I assumed that's why you told me to sit," he responds.

"Yes, it is," I confirm. He stares at me, waiting for more. *Where do I start with all of this?*

"Tirnan," he prompts me, concern shrouding his features.

"I'm leaving," I let out.

"You're leaving?" he poses, confused.

"Yes," I state.

"Where are you going? And are you sure this is the best time? Maybe you should wait until you're feeling better," he suggests, taking the tone I've heard him use with his children. *Does he really think I'm acting like them right now?*

"Edrik, I'm not going to feel better! It's been a year!" I shout. He jumps, shocked by my raise in volume. "I'm sorry. It's just-I can't sit here and pretend that things will go back to the way that they were because I know they won't, and I don't want them to. I never wanted to be a merchant. I just did it. I'm glad I did because it's how I met you, but there's something about getting the rug pulled out from under you that really makes you think. I don't want to spend the rest of my life fitting into other peoples' plans for me. I'm done with that," I messily explain. His eyes drift over to the wall as he thinks about what I've said. His silence is comforting; I know he's actually taking me seriously now.

"Where will you go?" he asks. It's a similar question to before, but his tone has completely changed. He trusts my judgment. That brings me more reassurance than I thought it would.

"I don't completely know yet. I want to leave the city. Find somewhere that I can start a new life for myself. I don't have many ideas as to what that might look like, and to be honest that intrigues me. It's about time I face some uncertainty," I voice.

"You've faced a lot of uncertainty quite recently," he comments.

"Good uncertainty that doesn't surround the question, 'Will I make it to tomorrow?'" I clarify. He nods, his eyes on the wall again. "You have doubts about this," I observe.

"I do," he confirms. He pauses a beat to collect his thoughts, then he returns his gaze to me. "A year ago, I came here and found you nearly dead. I can't help but worry about you after that. I don't want to see you hurt, Tirnan. Not just because of all you've done for me, but because you're one of the best friends I've ever had," he sighs, then continues. "But you seem really sure of this. Surer than I've ever seen you about anything. If this is something that you want to do, then I think you should do it no matter what doubts I might have."

I am sure about this. I've needed to make a change for years, and it's kind of sad that it took getting jumped for me to realize that. I'm not going to waste any more of my life pushing this off. It's time for me to take a leap.

"I appreciate your support," I tell him.

"Of course, Tirnan. You'll always have my support," he declares.

"I know. That's why I'm leaving you everything," I reveal.

"You're what?" he questions, eyes wide as he tries to figure out if he's understood me correctly.

"You need the extra space that this house has. The money will help you get more creative with your business. You can sell the stuff or keep it, I don't care. I just want you to have all of this for everything you've done for me-everything you've been for me," I explain. He gapes at me as he tries to process this gesture. I know it's a lot. Anything less wouldn't really be adequate considering the type of friend he's been for me.

"Shouldn't it all go to your parents," he finally says.

"They have more than I do. They don't need more," I respond.

"Then you should keep it. Maybe you'll want to come back to it all," he points out.

"I won't, Edrik. I want to move on from all of it," I reply.

"It's too much, Tirnan," he finally lets out what he was truly thinking. I had a feeling he'd do this. He has an easy time bestowing kindness on those around him, but a hard time accepting it himself.

"You said you'd support me," I bring up.

"I support what you want to do for yourself," he counters.

"I want to give you this. I want you to have plenty because over the years I've known you, you've given me something I never had before; you gave me companionship. I can't even imagine what my life would've been like without you in it. In my opinion, everything I have isn't enough to thank you for all of that," I proclaim. His defenses begin to fall as he takes in the sincerity of my expression.

"Are you sure?" he checks.

"I'm sure," I promise him.

"Thank you!" he exclaims, heading over to me, and wrapping me in a gentle hug. I laugh as I feel his breathing pick up from the excitement of all the doors I've just opened for him. Nothing could make me happier than knowing that I caused this joy for him.

"You're very welcome," I respond. "How are you going to tell Aila?" I pose.

"Hopefully better than how you told me," he responds, and

I laugh. *That's fair.* "You're going to do great out there, Tirnan. And if you ever need anything, do not hesitate to ask me," he adds, remembering how all of this started.

"Thanks," I reply. I don't know what my future will be like, and to be honest I don't really care. It's not guaranteed anyway.

15 TIRNAN

The unknown is the most enticing thing I've ever experienced. I could go anywhere. I could do anything. Well, not anything now that I have a busted leg, but there's still more possibilities than before when I was just following the path my parents set out. For the first time in a long time I actually feel like my life is going somewhere. I may not know where it's going, but it's somewhere new. Somewhere exciting. Anywhere I want.

Traveling isn't exactly easy in my current state. It's not deterring me at all, but it's definitely worth noting. Edrik made me wait to leave until morning because he didn't want me all by myself on a random road at night. I didn't give him much pushback on that given past events.

I've been using a walking stick that Lazarus made for me, and I've just barely reached the next city over by the time the sun starts going down. It's weird being in another city that seems so similar to my own. I can almost picture myself wheeling my cart along these streets toward the market. *Am I really already thinking about the habits of my old life? How am I supposed to move forward like this?* I need to be thinking of things I haven't done and run toward those things. Well, not actually run, but I need to excitedly pursue them however that looks for me now.

I continue heading through the city. There are not many

people around. It sends shivers down my spine as I think about the last time I thought I was alone on a road. I didn't even think about how it would feel to be outside my house again; I was too focused on actually getting out of the house.

It's fine. I still know I'm doing the right thing. My life wasn't just going to magically get better from inside the house. Leaving was necessary, no matter how fast my heart is beating right now. *Hold on, I don't think it's ever beat this fast before. Am I dying? Did I survive an attack by thieves just to keel over on some random street a city over?*

"The sunset is breathtaking tonight," a woman says somewhere near me. I clutch my chest, shaken by the sudden break in the silence. Once I recover from the shock, I process what was actually said. *Was this woman talking to me?* I don't even know where she is. I crane my neck, searching for her, but I don't see her.

"Tell me about it," a man responds. Alright, so she apparently wasn't talking to me. I'm about to continue on my way, but then she speaks up again, and I can't help but listen.

"The sun looks like it's dropping into the water, bringing a shroud of deep orange with it that's reflecting over the water," the woman starts. Water. I turn in the direction of the river behind me, and I find two people sitting at its edge: a woman with no arms and a man with cloudy eyes. His hand is on her shoulder as she gazes out ahead of her. "The sight of it evokes the feeling of taking a deep breath after you've just accomplished something small, but meaningful. There's also a rich blue that somehow blends into the orange despite the fact that they're contrasting colors," she continues.

"It sounds like you and I," he interrupts.

"Only if you're the blue," she responds.

"I can't tell if that's an insult or not," he says.

"The orange is fiery. It commands your attention, but hurts your eyes at the same time. It's what makes the whole thing unique, but it wouldn't be the same without the blue. The blue is what makes the experience serene. It's what brings calm to the whole ordeal of a giant ball of flames making its last blaze of glory for the night. The orange can't function without the blue and the blue is made more magnificent by the orange," she explains, and he smiles.

"I guess it's not an insult," he states.

"You guess?" she questions.

"I know," he laughs, kicking a little bit of water in her direction. She laughs as she kicks some back at him. "You make me magnificent," he adds, turning his head toward her. His eyes are pointed too high, but she doesn't seem to mind.

"And you keep me sane," she tells him.

"Ah yes, the hardest task I've ever had to tackle," he teases, and she kicks water at him again as she tries not to smile. Her gaze shifts past him-directly toward me.

"Hello," she calls to me.

"Hi," the man responds, confused.

"Not you. There's a man just beyond us with a fairly large bag and a walking stick," she explains to him. I didn't know it would feel so weird to hear myself described by someone. She boiled me down to the most basic observations. It's kind of freeing. She didn't tell him that I'm a merchant. She didn't tell him that I come from money. She doesn't know those things. I'm just a man on the street to them.

"Hello," the man greets me, waving in the completely wrong direction.

"You'll have to excuse him. As you can tell, neither of us are exactly whole," she apologizes on his behalf.

"Not on our own," he corrects, and she smiles.

"Yes, not on our own. Together we basically make a complete person. I'm his eyes and he's my arms," she tells me. He smiles at this. Neither of them seems to feel slighted by what they're missing. He doesn't need to see the sunset when she's there to paint a picture of it with her words, and I haven't seen it yet, but it sounds like he does similar things for her when she falls short. They're each broken, but together they're whole.

"I'm Jahre by the way, and this here is Ruriel," the man introduces them, putting his hand back on her shoulder.

"I'm Tirnan," I return.

"I've never seen you before. What brings you around, Tirnan?" Ruriel asks. *How honest do I want to be here?* I was enjoying the fact that they knew nothing about me, but I really have no reason not to tell them the truth.

"I was a merchant a city over, but I got jumped. I left in search of a fresh start," I summarize everything.

"Do you know what that fresh start will be?" Ruriel poses.

"No clue. I'm figuring things out as I go," I answer. She studies me. It's kind of unnerving.

"Jahre, let's have a word," she declares suddenly, speaking to the air behind her. Jahre takes that as a sign to turn in that direction. They exchange hurried whispers for a while before Jahre nods and they both turn back toward me. "If you would like, you can join us. We have a place not far from here. It's not much, but it's shelter for the night, or for however long you need," she offers.

She's offering me a place to stay? The offer is surprising, but what's more surprising is how much I want to say yes. I was just going to stay in an inn tonight and decide my next move tomorrow. Standing here across from them I feel like I know my next move. There's just one thing I need to know first.

"Why are you offering me this when you barely know me?" I pose.

"Because I do know you, Tirnan. I am you. Jahre is too. We know what it's like to be different out there all on your own. People see what's wrong with you before they see anything else, if they ever do see anything else. We aren't like that. To us you'll be a piece of our whole. Any weakness you have will be filled in by us, and all we'll ask for is the same in return," she answers.

This is it. I know it's barely even begun, but I can already tell that this is what I've been searching for this whole time.

Companionship that looks beyond what I bring to the table. A family.

“I’d love to join you,” I declare.

16 NIEMOS

For over two years the Pharisees have been trying to figure out what to do about the false Son of God. His words are blasphemous, that much is obvious, but he's always been careful about how he says them. He leaves room for deniability. Not just that, we need to be able to identify him and his crimes if we're to level any sort of punishment at him. The testimonies of myself and Carian aren't enough for that. We need three witnesses. Because the people are so enthralled by this hack, they'd never be a part of anything that could get him in trouble. It's going to have to be three Pharisees.

We've all been trying to find him and watch him perform another false sign, but we're always too late. We arrive as people speak of a man that healed them, but they never say who he was, and he's nowhere to be found.

It absolutely infuriates Carian, and I happen to find it fairly frustrating too. Nobody's really been able to focus on their temple duties with this guy out there, and even if they could, the people ask for our guidance much less now. Carian was spot on with his assessment that this man, this fraud, is dangerous.

The people have never been very committed to the rules, and now they use this man's words as an excuse to leave them behind. It's an insult to our ancestors who have been dedicated to these practices for generations. And for what? Because this man has supposedly healed people?

Even if it's true what they say of him, his lawlessness overshadows these signs. I mean, he's done them on the day of rest. How can the people not see that that's a slap in the face of centuries of tradition that started with the Lord Himself? My heart is burdened by how easily these people have swayed.

I've given more thought to the Son of God since all of this started. I'm still not quite sure what I expect him to be. We don't often talk about the texts that refer to Him. Our religious leaders have always been more concerned with studying the rules than the distant prophecies foretelling a Savior. They've always said that it's more important to pay attention to our actions and make sure we're following the law properly than it is to spend our time obsessing over something that likely won't happen in our lifetime. That used to make sense to me, but now I'm starting to wonder if I should spend more time with the prophecies.

"Are you ready, Niemos?" Izal poses, walking up to me with Amon by his side.

"Yes," I answer, and we begin walking through the city. One of the latest strategies we've employed along with stationing Pharisees at random points throughout the city, is that Carian and I have been taking two other Pharisees around the city trying to find the man we saw. We're hoping that if we can find him, we'll be able to get him to perform one of his false signs for us. It's a long shot, but it has a better chance of success than just waiting and hoping we stumble across him performing a sign.

Izal stares disapprovingly at every man we pass as if they're all the fraud. While they're not, any one of them could be wholeheartedly believing all his lies, and there's not much we can do to remedy that. Not when this fraud is still out there drawing crowds with nearly every appearance. It confounds me how he always manages to slip away before we can see him. I think back to the first time I saw him outside the temple. He walked into the crowd, then he was nowhere to be seen. *Who does that?*

"You're paying attention, right Niemos?" Izal checks, facing me with stern eyes.

"Yes," I confirm, forcing my mind back to the task at hand. We continue through more of the heavily populated areas of the city to no avail. That doesn't really surprise me. The fraud makes an effort to avoid us after each sighting. Of course he's not hanging out where we'd easily stumble across him.

Izal gets visibly impatient as we get closer to the edge of the city. Part of me wants to apologize until I remember that it's not my fault we haven't come across him. He's hiding because he knows exactly what he's doing and what he should be facing for it. We reach the edge of the land that borders the sea, and suddenly, I stop.

"That's him," I declare, pointing to a man sitting on a rock with about twelve others around him. They all appear to be busy with various tasks, including the fraud; he's carving something onto a plank of wood. "How are we going…" I start to ask, but Izal is already closing in on the fraud before I finish my question.

"What do you think you're doing?" one of the twelve questions, cutting off Izal before he can reach the fraud. His fists are balled at his side, and he has a menacing look on his face.

"Peter, back down," the fraud speaks up, setting his plank and knife down and getting to his feet calmly.

"Are you sure?" Peter checks, sizing us all up. As my eyes drift to the rest of the men, I realize that he's not the only one assessing us as if we're a threat. About half of them have stood up and moved closer to us. Two of them have even begun cracking their knuckles. I never even imagined that approaching the fraud could be dangerous…

"I'm sure. I've been expecting them," the fraud states, putting his hand on Peter's shoulder. *Is he saying that he knew we were coming today, or he knew he'd see us eventually?* Peter gives us one last death stare, then steps to the side so we can talk to the fraud. "It's a beautiful day today. The heat finally seems to be giving us a break," the fraud says, a friendly smile on his face. *Is he really trying to have small talk with us right now?*

"We're not here to speak of the weather," Izal remarks, glaring at the fraud.

"No, you're not," the fraud states as if he knows exactly what we're actually here for. The certainty of his tone sends shivers down my spine.

"My associate here saw you heal a blind man and there's been word that you've performed several other signs since then," Izal begins. Peter shifts uncomfortably, but the fraud seems unfazed just as he was with Carian.

"I've heard that chatter as well," the fraud responds. Again, his words leave room for deniability. Izal doesn't seem too pleased with that.

"Forgive me if I don't believe the chatter without having seen it myself," Izal goes on, still managing to be somewhat cordial despite his annoyance.

"You're forgiven," the fraud replies, that aggravating smile on his face. He's doing exactly what he did to Carian. Only giving the bare minimum of what's required in his response. He knows there's going to be follow-up, but he does it anyway, all with that smile on his face. *What exactly is it that he's trying to accomplish?*

"I'm looking for a little bit more than forgiveness," Izal comments, his patience thin.

"Ask away," the fraud replies. He knows exactly what will be asked of him. That much is obvious. Whether he's going to do it or not, I'm still unsure of.

"I would like to see one of your miraculous signs. To truly understand what all the chatter is about of course," Izal requests, barely keeping his composure.

"This generation," the fraud remarks with a sigh, then he turns to Peter. "Peter, what is faith?" he poses.

"Believing in something without seeing it," Peter answers, still glaring at us.

"Exactly. Belief is all I ask for, but this generation is almost incapable of that without seeing a sign first. I did not come to impress the masses with neat tricks. Truly, I tell you, no sign will be given to those without faith," the fraud declares. He shakes his head at us, then turns around. "Let's go," he says to the twelve. They all begin gathering up the things they were doing and bringing them to a boat nearby. The fraud is almost to the boat when I realize something.

"Wait!" I call. He turns around and faces me, his interest piqued. "Why did you come?" I ask. He said it wasn't to impress the masses with neat tricks, but he never said the real reason for why he's here. Having this piece of information could help us learn more about who he is and how much he plans to shake things up.

"That will all be revealed to you eventually," the fraud answers. I expect to see his little smile, but humor is absent from his face. He turns back toward the boat and gets on it along with the rest of the twelve. They depart, leaving Izal, Amon, and I behind with what feels like even less than we came here with.

"That man is definitely dangerous just as you and Carian reported. We need to change the way we're approaching all of this," Izal states, his eyes on the boat as it gets further and further away. He turns around to leave, but Amon speaks up, stopping him.

"He left whatever he was working on," Amon observes, pointing to the rock where his plank still sits. We head over to the rock to inspect it further. At the top of the plank the word 'MIRACULOUS' had been carved in large letters, then below it in smaller letters, 'is this what you were looking for?'

"A miraculous sign," I let out as I process it. Izal snatches the sign up and breaks it over his knee in a fit of rage.

17 CATO

Everybody in my family has gotten food every day for years now. It's a statement I take great pride in. I went out there and I made things better. So much better in fact, that we're better off than we've ever been.

I stopped stealing food about a week after I started. I had gotten good at it, but I also realized a couple of things. First off, stealing food from people during a grain shortage will hurt what little profit those merchants were bringing in at the time. My goal has never been to pull my family out of poverty at the expense of someone else's family. Secondly, while stealing food went toward ensuring my family ate, it was also kind of low risk, low reward. I don't just want my children to not starve; I want them to have everything they want.

These realizations led me to change my strategy. I switched to stealing money from wealthier merchants. It's not even enough that they'd notice, but it's enough to make a huge difference for my family. My kids have toys now that aren't worn from years of use. We actually have variety in our meals now because I can buy all different kinds of food. And today, on Kassia's birthday, I'm going to bring her home a gift for the first time in years.

Life is looking up. All I had to do was bend the rules a bit. In the grand scheme of things, it doesn't really matter. The people I steal from now have clothes more expensive than my property. They can spare a generous handful of coins to brighten the lives of me and my family. Who knows? Maybe they would even be happy about the fact that they're putting a smile on my kids' faces. Of course, they'll never actually know, but it's worth noting.

Today my target will be a booth that sells jewelry. I've been watching it for a while, as soon as I got it in my head that I would get something for Kassia for her birthday. The booth had exploded in popularity over the last couple years because another booth that sold jewelry isn't here anymore, or so I've heard. The reason doesn't really matter to me; all that matters is that busy booths make great targets, especially busy booths with merchants that aren't that used to being busy.

I've watched this merchant walk away from the pouch where he keeps his coins for long stretches of time while he talks with his customers. I would've already stolen from him if I hadn't decided his booth is where I'm going to be getting something for Kassia.

I head through the market, stopping at a few booths, pretending to look at things. It's best to do that first so it actually seems like I'm here to buy things. I found that the only times I've ever noticed eyes on me are when I've quickly made my way to the booth I'm targeting for the day. I had to linger, picking things up as if they interested me, then setting them down until people weren't watching again. Stalling for that long caused anxiety to bubble in me in a way it hadn't in a long time. I do not wish to do it again.

I scope the jewelry booth out for a while before I actually head over to it. I had to decide what I was going to take for Kassia before getting there so I can make a quick exit once it's time for that. There's a necklace near the pouch made with gold and orange beads that Kassia would love. She'd probably love anything I could grab since the only piece of jewelry she currently has is the ring I got her when I married her, but I really do think she'll be pleased with this specific piece; orange is her favorite color.

"You seem a bit lost," the merchant says to a man at the far end of the booth.

"Is it that obvious?" the man asks sheepishly, and the merchant laughs.

"Don't worry, I've been at this for years, I can help you. Who are you buying for?" the merchant poses. This is my window. I quietly slip my hand into the pouch, pull out a handful of coins, slide my hand out, grab the necklace with my other hand, then I'm off. As usual, nobody sees anything.

I've found that people tend to be too caught up in their own lives to pay much attention to the actions of others. I'm not saying that as if I'm better than everybody else. I'm sure people could've been doing exactly what I'm doing now back before I was and I wouldn't have noticed. Life throws us enough of our own troubles that we subconsciously block out others'. Before I was so worried about feeding my family that I could care less if a merchant was being robbed. Even if I had seen it, I probably wouldn't have said anything.

I sound bleak. I know that. A lifetime of struggle will do that to a person. I'm actually surprised it took me this long to be honest with myself about the world. Even after everything I went through for the majority of my life, I still tried to have hope that things would get better. I clung to that hope. I was stupid. Things didn't get better until I let go of that foolish little emotion and made things work myself. The world has always been a cruel place that preys on those who try to navigate it with care.

My life would be a lot different if I had learned that lesson earlier. That doesn't matter now. I have a beautiful family that I love and I now have the gall to go out there and provide for them without relying on anybody else. It's a pretty good place to be in.

We already have enough food at home for tonight, but I stop at a booth with all different kinds of fruit and buy a pomegranate anyway. They're Kassia's favorite, and I really want to make today special for her after years of it just being a normal day in the past. She deserves even more than the treasures I'm bringing home today, but I can't steal the whole world, so what I have in my arms right now will have to do.

I leave the market with no issues as always. The walk home is peaceful despite all the craziness around me. I breathe it in, thinking back to all those days I felt like I was on the outside of all of this. I've come a long way since then. I'm a part of things now. A part that refuses to be swallowed up by misfortune again. I reach my house and head in.

"Daddy!" Viridi lets out, running up to me.

"Hey sweetheart," I greet her, patting her head. She smiles, then she notices the necklace in my hand and her eyes widen.

"What's that?" she asks.

"It's a birthday gift for your mom. Do you want to give it to her?" I inquire. A big smile spreads across her face, and she nods her head repeatedly, her enthusiasm shining through. I laugh as I stretch the necklace out to her. She takes it, then carefully carries it to the kitchen where Hale appears to be 'helping' Kassia with dinner.

"Happy birthday, mommy!" Viridi exclaims when she reaches Kassia, holding the necklace out. Kassia smiles as she tilts her head down toward Viridi, then shock enters her eyes as she spots the necklace. Her eyes find mine, seemingly searching for something. "Are you going to put it on?" Viridi questions, and Kassia returns her attention to her.

"Of course," Kassia tells her, accepting the necklace with that warm smile back on her face. Viridi beams as Kassia unclasps it, then clasps it around her neck.

"It's so pretty!" Viridi declares excitedly, staring at her mom in awe. It's certainly pretty, but Kassia's beauty was awe-inspiring even before the necklace adorned her neck.

"Not as pretty as your mom," I state. Viridi giggles, and I wait for some sort of reaction from Kassia, but nothing comes. She simply looks over at me, searching for something. What exactly it is she's trying to find, I have no idea. Eventually, she gives up and allows a slight smile.

"It's beautiful," Kassia agrees. She bends down and gives Viridi a hug, then she begins collecting some of the things on the counter. "Why don't you and your brother start bringing the food to the table," she requests, passing things to the kids. They scamper away, doing as they were told. I head over to Kassia, extending the pomegranate.

"Happy birthday, my love," I say. She takes the pomegranate, a hesitant grin finding its way onto her features. *She's probably just a little overwhelmed by the gift.* I pull her close to me and give her a kiss. "Thank you for the grace you've shown me these past few years and all the years before those. This family wouldn't be what it is without your kindness and your love," I tell her, giving her hand a squeeze. She's silent, her eyes surveying the room as she tries to find the words to form her response, but her thoughts are interrupted.

"Done," Viridi lets out.

"Let's go eat," Kassia states, letting go of my hand and heading to the table. *Alright, that was definitely weird. Did I do something?*

18 CATO

Kassia was weird all throughout dinner. She basically only talked to the kids. I mean, she would answer me if I asked her a question, but other than that, she made no effort to have a conversation with me. The entire time I cleaned up the table, I wracked my brain trying to come up with what it is that I did wrong.

I feel like I did everything right. I got her jewelry. I got her favorite fruit. I was home on time despite lingering at the market for longer than usual. I got the kids excited about the fact that it's her birthday. I offered to clean the table and I'm now following up on that offer. This is all commendable husband behavior. I don't get it.

After I finish up in the kitchen, I head to the kids' room to help Kassia finish tucking them in. Hale's already conked out as usual, but Viridi is doing everything she can to fight going to sleep.

"How old are you today, mommy?" Viridi poses, a yawn following the question.

"Viridi, you never ask a lady how old she is," I tell her. I turn toward Kassia, expecting a chuckle, but her expression remains neutral. *Seriously, what did I do?*

"Fine. What were you like at my age, mommy?" Viridi asks, trying a new line of questioning so she can extend her bedtime.

"I spent a lot of time in my imagination. I used to run around the field behind my friend's house with her and we would pretend we were somewhere else," Kassia details.

"Where's your friend now?" Viridi follows up, her eyes nearly closing. Kassia drops her gaze; a small sigh escapes. I know what friend she's talking about. She cut contact with Kassia because of Viridi, just like her parents did. She had claimed that her parents were making her do it because they didn't want Kassia's bad choices rubbing off on her. She looked right at me when she said that. She wanted me to know that I was the bad choice she was referring to. That was after I faced the wrath of Kassia's dad; I was already aware that people saw me as a bad choice.

"She's probably off somewhere with her own family now," Kassia comes up with. A neutral response for a situation anything but neutral.

"What about you, daddy? What were you like at my age?" Viridi asks, blinking a few times then turning to face me. What was I like? She's not old enough to learn about the events of my childhood. I'm not sure I'll ever tell the kids how I grew up. That's all behind me now and I want to leave it there. As far as I'm concerned, my only family are the people in this room.

"I was certainly better about going to bed than you," I tease her, ruffling her hair, and she giggles. "One more question, then we're going to head out and go to bed because we're tired too," I tell her.

"Alright, alright," Viridi responds. She stares at the wall, thinking hard about her last question, then a smile comes to her face and she turns toward us. "What did you think about mommy the first time you saw her?" she poses. *Well, that's an easy one.*

"I thought that I was lucky a woman that beautiful was even looking in my direction. Then I learned I was beyond lucky when she decided I was worth more than just a glance," I answer. Viridi smiles as she glances back and forth between the two of us. Kassia smiles too, but it seems like it's more for Viridi's sake than for mine. I definitely need to talk to her. "Bedtime," I tell Viridi.

"Fine," Viridi agrees. I kiss her forehead and Kassia does the same. We turn away and start walking to our room. Kassia's pace is slow, and her shoulders are tight with tension. Her hand furls and unfurls on the necklace. My chest begins to feel heavy as I try and prepare for whatever this conversation is going to bring. I wait for her to say something once we're in our room, but she remains silent.

"Is everything alright?" I ask. She won't meet my gaze. Instead, she stares at the necklace which she's taken off and set on the dresser in front of her. "I'm sorry if it's too much, but you really deserve much more than that. I meant it when I said that I'm lucky to have you," I tell her, coming up behind her and putting my hands on her shoulders. She pulls away from my grasp and turns to face me, a serious expression clouding her features.

"Where did it come from, Cato?" she questions. That's what this is about?

"I got it for you," I answer vaguely. I haven't told Kassia what I've been doing, and I don't want to do it right now. I don't want her to worry about me. I've got everything handled.

"How? We've never been able to afford something like this," she brings up.

"Things change," I respond, trying to get her to drop this.

"What changed, Cato? We've been in a grain shortage for years, yet you've been bringing home more food and money than ever. I know your daily wage didn't increase, so where is this extra money coming from?" she interrogates. I knew she would notice that we've been better off lately, but I was hoping she wasn't going to question it.

"I told you I would handle things," I remind her.

"Why won't you tell me where the money is coming from, Cato?" she asks, fear creeping into her eyes. This is exactly why I don't want to tell her. I don't want her to freak out like this. *Why can't she just let it be? Trust that I've got this?*

"You don't need to know where it's coming from. All you need to know is that we won't be starving again," I declare. Her breathing picks up and she puts her head in her hands. "Kass," I try, reaching for her, but she shakes me off.

"You're stealing it, aren't you?" she poses, her big brown eyes boring into mine. I sigh and drop my gaze as I search for a gentle way to respond to her. If I'm honest, I'm really trying to find a good way to deflect the question. "It's a yes or a no, Cato," she lets out, her voice nearly breaking.

"Yes," I say, meeting her eyes again. My admission causes tears to well up in them. I go to put my hand on her shoulder again, but she slaps it away. "I'm only taking from people who don't need it, Kass. I doubt they even notice," I tell her, and she gapes at me. "What?" I ask.

"Do you even hear yourself?" she questions. I'm starting to grow frustrated with this conversation. We were in a bad spot and I got us out of it the best way I could. Why can't she see that?

"Kassia, our family is finally going to bed full. This is a good thing," I point out.

"Stealing is a serious crime both to our people and the Romans, Cato," she brings up, tears continuing to drop from her eyes.

"You think I don't know that? I'm being careful, Kassia. I'm not an idiot," I remark.

"Well, you could've fooled me," she comments, her tears beginning to slow down as her fear starts to make way for anger. Why is she angry? I'm going out of my way to provide for my family and she's refusing to acknowledge that! I should be the one who's angry right now!

"I'm doing this for you! For the kids!" I cry.

"Don't you put that on us! What do you think happens if you get caught, Cato?" she questions.

"I won't get caught!" I insist.

"You can't be sure of that! This is your problem, Cato. You get tunnel vision and you don't think about the consequences of your actions. If something happened to you, the kids and I would have nobody! We'd waste away and it would be all your fault," she declares, her chest heaving as her mind gets stuck in the grim possibilities she's suggesting.

Her words hit me like a ton of bricks. I thought I was making my family proud, but according to her I'm just as much of a failure as ever. If I keep stealing, the consequences of my actions could bring my family down with me, but if I stop, then we'll all probably starve anyway. There are no good options for people like us. At least the way I've chosen to do things I'm not leaving our fate up to the whims of the harvest.

"What would you have me do, Kassia?" I question.

"Stop," she answers, her eyes pleading with me to heed this advice.

"That's not an option," I respond.

"It is," she tells me.

"It's not," I counter. I won't roll over and let my family starve. That's not who I am.

"It is, Cato; you're just too prideful to take it," she insists. *Does she really think pride is the main thing driving me right now?* Sure, I might find a little bit of pride in what I'm doing, but it's only because I'm finally able to provide for my family. That's what's driving my actions. I've never been provided for. I hated that. I vowed that I wouldn't continue that cycle with my own family. That they would always be the first thing on my mind when I made any decisions.

I get that what I'm doing right now is dangerous. I really do get that. I get that I'm a letdown. I'm sure I'm not the type of man that Kassia dreamt of marrying as a little girl. It would honestly be embarrassing for her if I was. I just don't know what else I can really do here. I am who I am. I'm not a man with a handful of paths set out for him. If another option presents itself, I'll take it in a heartbeat, but I just don't see that happening. I have to do this. I have to do this, and she's just going to have to find a way to make peace with that fact.

"Kass, I can't stop," I say with finality, and she sighs.

"Is that what I'm supposed to tell the kids when you're dead or in jail? Sorry, Daddy couldn't stop. He had to keep going. He knew things would end like this, but he just couldn't stop," she goes on. I close my eyes as I try to keep my composure. This conversation is going nowhere. It's best if we just stop here.

"I'm going to go to bed before either of us says anything else we don't mean," I state.

"I meant it, Cato," she declares, then she slides past me and gets into bed.

19 LAZARUS

Though I've had time to mull over the fact that Jesus is the Son of God, I still haven't quite gotten used to it. How is one supposed to get used to something like that? I had other friends growing up, but Jesus was the best friend I ever had. No matter how troublesome I could be, no matter how annoying I could be, no matter how overcome by emotions I could be, there was Jesus, right by my side as always.

Maybe Martha was right and we should've known He had the Lord in Him based on how He always knew what to do. When my parents died, Jesus was the one who got me through that. I was horrible to be around, but He never left. Leaving someone in crisis has never been in His nature.

I remember being so lost the night we lost them. None of us knew what to do, Martha included. She brought us next door, but didn't know what to do next. I wandered into Jesus' room because that's what I always did when we went over there. It was clear by His messy hair and tousled clothes that He had been sleeping, but He didn't turn me away.

"They're gone," I had said, surprised that my voice even worked. I hadn't uttered a word until that moment. He took a step toward me and pulled me into a hug. He didn't ask who 'they' were. Looking back on it knowing what I know, He probably already knew.

We stood there in the middle of His room with me silently sobbing and Him just holding me. He didn't say anything. I think if He had, I wouldn't have been able to take it in. He knew that. He knew that I just needed to be held.

He's always known exactly what I've needed. When I got frustrated with my slow progress with carpentry, He would patiently walk me through the parts I was struggling with. When I was causing a lot of trouble, He would talk to me to find the root of why I was doing it. When my house felt too empty without my parents, He would come over unprompted, reminding me that He was there.

So, yeah, maybe we should've seen this coming. It's still weird to think about though. When we went to temple as kids, He sat there and let the teachers read scrolls about Him and give their take on it all without a peep. I would've never been able to stay silent in those moments if I was Him. Well, maybe if I had the Lord in me things would be different, but as I am right now, I would've taught them a lesson instead of the other way around.

"Guess who I saw?" Mary lets out as she runs into the house. She said she would be out for the majority of the day gathering flowers, but I'm definitely glad she's back early because I feel like Martha's been waiting to scold me about something for a while. She's said practically nothing to me all day, but she keeps glancing in my direction.

"Who?" I ask.

"Jesus! He's going to come over with all of His followers!" Mary answers excitedly. Perfect. Martha won't scold me with people here. It will be a little odd seeing Jesus though. We've heard nothing from Him since Mary told us He was the Son of God, though we've heard many stories of His miracles.

"How many followers does He have and when will He be here?" Martha questions, already starting to tidy things up around her.

"He didn't introduce me to them, but there were somewhere

around ten. Maybe twelve? Also, He said He's stopping to see His mom first, then He'll come here," Mary details.

"Come here when? Soon after seeing His mom, or later?" Martha interrogates, her cleaning frenzy already in full swing as the words leave her mouth.

"I don't know. Trust His timing," Mary responds with a wink. Martha stops her hurried movements and gapes at Mary. I feel I should step in now.

"Mary, let's go to the market and get some fruit for everyone," I say.

"Alright," Mary agrees. We head out of the house and through the streets to the market. Mary seems to be in her own world as she thinks about the coming visit. There's a twinkle in her eye and a bounce in her step propelling her forward. My strides are normally longer than hers, but right now I have to actively try to keep up with her.

People wave to me from various booths as we walk through the market. Though I don't sit in the market every day, many of my clients do. As we walk through the various pathways formed by booths, I notice things I've made. A cart for a merchant selling clothes. A display table for a merchant selling soap. Bowls for a merchant selling food. I wave back at them as we pass. Usually, I would go over and talk to them, but I'm trying to keep an eye on Mary right now. I'm sure they understand that.

"Twenty servings of berries please," I request as we reach one of the booths. The merchant cocks her eyebrow, but she doesn't say anything. She begins gathering the berries together, eyeing Mary who's practically bouncing with excitement.

"We should get Him figs! He loves figs!" Mary suggests, turning to me with bright eyes.

"And one serving of figs," I add. Those can be just for Him. He is the Son of God after all; He does deserve special treatment. The merchant hands me a container with all of the requested fruit in it, and I dump a handful of coins on her table. She quickly counts them, then smiles at me and Mary as we head off.

As soon as we get back home, Mary takes a seat near the window so she can see Jesus as soon as He gets close. I put the fruit on the counter where Martha's already begun making something, then I back out of the kitchen to make sure I don't get in her way. I take a seat near Mary, but I don't attempt conversation because I know she's too overcome by anticipation.

"He's here!" Mary lets out after a while, jumping up and running out the door. I follow her out, but Martha stays where she is, furiously trying to finish preparing food for everybody before they come inside. I'd tell her to come out with us to greet Jesus, but I don't want to get killed.

Jesus smiles as soon as He sees us. He holds His arms out and Mary runs right into them, squeezing Him tight. He holds her until she lets go, then He heads over to me and I give Him a hug. It's no different than when we were kids and hadn't seen each other in a while.

"Boys, this is Mary and Laz, and Martha should be around here somewhere," Jesus introduces us to His followers. He cranes His neck to try and spot Martha in the house.

"She's preparing food for everybody," I fill Him in.

"Ah, finally, something to make these boys stop complaining," Jesus jokes. Some of them laugh, but others definitely just want to get inside and find out what Martha's making. "Martha, come out here for a second," Jesus calls. There are a few scattered noises inside, then Martha appears, slightly disheveled.

"It's very good to see you, Jesus," Martha says as she straightens her clothes.

"You as well," Jesus returns, giving her a warm smile. He gestures to His followers beside Him. "There's a lot of names to say, so I didn't want to do introductions twice. From left to right, we have Peter, Andrew, John, Big James, Philip, Nathanael, Thaddaeus, Matthew, Little James, Thomas, Simon, and Judas," He stops and takes a breath. "I know that's a lot to remember. Luckily, they all respond to 'hey you' if need be," He assures us.

"Nice to know," I respond, knowing most of those names have already slipped my mind.

"Someone mentioned food," Big James brings up, staring at Martha. I'd say something to him about staring at my sister if I thought it had anything to do with her, but it's clear he's just interested in a meal after what's probably been a long time without one. It can't be easy feeding all of those mouths, and none of them look rich.

"Go inside and make yourselves comfortable. We'll bring the food to you when it's ready," Martha responds, then she rushes back in first so she can finish everything up. Everybody files in and finds somewhere to sit. Jesus takes the seat next to me, then turns to face me with a kind smile.

"How's carpentry going?" Jesus poses. I hadn't expected to be talking about myself when I heard the Son of God was coming.

"It's going well. I'm using every little trick Your dad taught me," I answer, thinking back to the days when my current workshop was his and the three of us were in there for hours on end. "I actually always imagined that's what You'd be doing right now too. You were good. Better than me. If You were still in the game I'd have no business," I admit, and He laughs.

"That's why I had to stop. You need all the help you can get," Jesus teases me.

"What have You been up to? You know, besides healing people and amassing a following," I say. He smiles, but it doesn't linger as long as His smiles normally do.

"My current pastimes seem to involve a lot of making powerful people angry," Jesus responds. That seems like the sort of thing that I was destined for, not Him. Martha begins bringing out little trays of food for each sub-group of people in the room, starting with Big James and the two others sitting with him.

"Tell them about the miraculous sign," John lets out through a mouthful of food.

"I've heard of the miraculous signs," I state.

"Not this one," Peter comments, a smirk on his face. I turn to Jesus curiously.

"As I've alluded to, the Pharisees aren't very happy with me. I knew they were going to come ask me for a miraculous sign, so I carved the word miraculous on a plank of wood," Jesus shares, matter-of-factly. Again, that screams me.

"That's not all it said," Philip speaks up, a big grin on his face.

"What else did it say?" I venture, my eyes on Jesus. *I didn't realize He had that in Him, and now they're telling me there's more? I need to hear this.*

"'Is this what you were looking for?'" Jesus quotes. *No. Way.*

"I guess I really rubbed off on you, huh?" I say, and He sighs.

"Just a little bit," Jesus responds, a small chuckle escaping Him as His cheeks flush. Again, it feels just like when we were kids and His mother was scolding us for something I dragged Him into. He was always quiet and took it, knowing I was the one at fault. Come to think of it, He really never did anything wrong when we were kids. He just stood by me after I didn't listen to Him when He tried to talk me out of something. I guess if the scrolls are correct, He's incapable of wrong. He has to be to save our people.

"Why now?" I can't help but ask. He's been around for years, but He hasn't made Himself known until now, and I know there has to be a reason for that. Jesus sighs and drops His gaze. I don't know if He's searching for something to tell me, or just straight up ignoring me. Martha places a tray in front of us, and that's when I realize that Mary's been sitting on my other side this whole time. She reaches for something on the tray and Martha scoffs.

"Seriously, Mary? You left me alone to cook and clean all day, then you left me alone to serve next. Now you want to just sit there and eat? You should be helping me, right Jesus?" Martha questions pointedly, turning to face Him. He meets her gaze, compassion in His eyes.

"Martha, you worry about so many things, all of which could've waited. I don't need to walk into a spotless house. My followers don't need to be immediately fed," Jesus begins. A few of His followers seem like they're about to say something, but He shoots them a look and they all stay quiet. "Mary has picked up on what's important. I'm not going to scold her for that," He finishes. Martha looks hurt, but she does her best to reign her reaction in.

"What is it that You need?" Martha asks.

"You," Jesus responds. A tear falls from her eye, and He gets up and pulls her into His arms. "All I really want from any of you is your heart," He declares, His eyes surveying those gathered around Him from over Martha's shoulder. I know there's a lot I still haven't processed about all of this, but I can be sure of one thing.

"You have it, Lord," I promise, and He smiles at me, His eyes bright and glistening with happy tears.

20 NIEMOS

After the whole miraculous sign-fiasco, Izal immediately insisted we update the Sanhedrin and come up with a new plan. I'd never seen him so worked up before. Supposedly he was picked for his position because of his ability to separate himself from the aggravations we face daily, but he certainly didn't do that by the sea.

Of course I was angry too, but the miraculous sign remained on my mind for other reasons. The fraud had carved it before we had even gotten there. He also said he had been expecting us. That tells me that he chose to make the sign because he knew he'd see us eventually and he got lucky with the timing, or he knew exactly when we'd show up and exactly what we'd ask for.

There are little things that make me think it's the latter. He knew we would specifically use the word miraculous. We could've just asked for a sign, then it wouldn't have worked. He also had an air to him that made it seem like he was in control of the conversation the whole time. He wasn't thrown off at all. The sign was already finished by the time we got there. The boat was right there giving him a quick escape.

I'm honestly ashamed to have found this much sense in the matter. I want to be able to explain these things away to myself like everybody else does. This man is not the Son of God. I know that. I just don't know how he keeps pulling things like this off. I like when things have explanations, and there aren't really any here that don't make him seem legitimate. I'm just naive. That's what Carian would say. I like the idea of the Son of God, so part of me just wants to abandon what I know and believe it's Him. But it's not. I'm sure of that.

Right now, I need to leave these thoughts behind and head into the meeting Izal called with the Sanhedrin. I walk in and take a seat next to Carian. He's quiet. I told him about what happened with the miraculous sign and he got even more worked up than he did when he was face to face with the fraud himself. Now he's eagerly awaiting what Izal has to say about all of this despite their differences.

"Thank you everybody for being here. We have matters of great importance to discuss," Izal announces once the last of us have come in and found seats. All eyes fall on him, and he continues. "As you all know, there's a fraud among our people claiming to be the Son of God," he begins.

"This again? Don't tell me you want to pour more of our resources into the hunt for this man," Joseph interrupts, and murmurs spread throughout the room. I turn to Carian and find him shaking his head disapprovingly. He may not be the biggest fan of Izal, but even he can see that Izal is right in going after this fraud.

"This *fraud* is turning our people away from centuries of tradition. He makes blasphemous claims and shows no respect for our authority. We don't even know the extent of the damage he's causing because he always manages to slip away before we show up," Izal lets out, the uncontrolled side of him I saw yesterday peeking through. It causes more murmurs to sound around us, and earns a laugh from Joseph.

"Can't you see that you're contributing to the damage he's causing? You've let him get under your skin and turn all of your attention away from your duties and toward him. As I've repeatedly said, the best way to handle this situation is to ignore this man instead of giving him more attention," Joseph states.

"Get out!" Izal exclaims. His outburst shocks everyone. For once, it's dead silent.

"Excuse me?" Joseph questions.

"If you refuse to take this threat seriously, then you're no longer welcome at this meeting," Izal declares, glaring at him. Joseph turns to Caiaphas for help since he's the ultimate leader here, but he says nothing. Joseph shakes his head, then peers around the room, eyeing each and every one of us. It's almost as if he's asking 'This is the man you're choosing to listen to?' I stop breathing when his eyes fall on me.

There are parts of what he's said that I agree with. We have neglected our duties in an attempt to handle this situation. I wish that wasn't the case, but I do agree with Izal that we have to do something about this. I've seen this fraud twice now and left both interactions confused. If I'm faltering after being around him, then the people who have far less discipline stand no chance at turning away from his foolish teachings.

Joseph finishes surveying the room, then he shakes his head again. He seems like he's about to say something, but then he decides against it. He walks out of the room just as he's been told to do, and now the murmurs start up again.

"He didn't belong here anyway," Carian remarks.

"Right," I agree, keeping my response short so he doesn't pick up on the fact that I don't completely disagree with Joseph. *I don't know what I would do if he told me I don't belong either.*

"Is there anybody else who's ok with the fraud continuing as he is?" Izal poses, bringing everybody's attention back to himself. Nobody says anything. "Good. As I was saying, this fraud needs to be stopped. His teachings may be foolish, but he is not. Our current strategies are falling short. We need a new one. One involving not just catching him, but exposing him for the fraud he is to the people. We need to trip him up in his own words," he states.

"How do we do that? You just said that he's smart," Amon points out. I was thinking the same thing, but I never would have asked the question myself in front of this many people.

"His teachings go against our scrolls. That much we know because we have spent a considerable amount of our lives in the scrolls, but the people have not. We need to question him until he starts going against things that even they know to be true," Izal explains.

"We would still have to run into him," Carian brings up. I hadn't expected him to speak today. He usually only pokes holes in Izal's policies in private. He knows the position should've been his, but he still has respect for Izal since he's the one who got it.

"We'll make it impossible not to. Stopping this fraud is our number one priority right now. Because of that, I'm proposing a strategy that involves everybody in his region spending time in the streets waiting for him to show himself. There will be no more taking shifts and leaving gaps; all of us will be out there all day, including myself," Izal details. *It's a good thing Joseph isn't here to hear that.*

This is a really extreme strategy. He's suggesting that we neglect reading the scrolls. Neglect being in the temple to guide those who come to us. Neglect everything we're expected to do in order to catch this one man.

I wait for someone to say that this is too far, or to even call it crazy, but nobody does. There doesn't even seem to be hesitancy in the faces of those around me. Everybody wants this man gone. Everybody is willing to do anything it takes to make that happen. I guess I just have to get on board with that. This man is not the Son of God. The people need to know that.

"We will proceed as you have suggested," Caiaphas declares after thinking it over, and Izal nods his head.

"We'll start with this strategy tomorrow, meeting at the temple to decide who will stand where. Each morning we'll meet up to give updates on the prior day, then we'll go back out to our spots. We won't stop until the people see him for what he is, or until we have grounds for a stoning," Izal declares.

A stoning? This man is a nuisance, yes, but again this seems far. Yet nobody's questioning his words. People nod, some jeer even, fully on board with the highest punishment we can get away with for this man. My muscles tighten as people begin to disperse. It's been decided: this man will die if we don't manage to discredit him.

21 CATO

After years of being a nobody, I finally thought that I was worth something. Sure, I'd never have been able to tell people what I was doing, but that wouldn't matter; they'd look at my family and the things we had and think, 'Wow, he must be a good father.' That's all I've ever wanted as soon as I found out about Viridi.

I was young at the time. Kassia and I first met when I got a job working in the stables across from her house. She kept coming up with excuses to come over and it took me a few weeks to realize she was actually coming over to see me. The idiot that I was, I just thought she was really into horses.

Once I did realize that she liked me, I invited her over to my house after work, which was actually just a tiny shack near the stables that the owners had given to me because they felt bad for me. We hit it off and she kept coming back every day for months, always making sure that she returned home before her father.

About half a year in, she decided she wanted to introduce me to her parents. While she had always respected me for the manual labor I did, her father didn't. He had people for that sort of thing. People who's names he didn't even bother to learn.

He wanted his daughter to be with someone more like him. Someone rich. She was used to being able to have whatever she wanted whenever she wanted it. Things like pomegranates weren't a special occasion. Someone with power and status. He didn't speak with anyone who didn't own a considerable amount of land, and he was disgusted to find that his daughter had been. He had high expectations for the man who would marry his daughter. I didn't meet a single one.

That night was the real turning point in our relationship. Things had been pretty innocent before that, but after we found out that her father would never let someone like me marry her, we decided to skip a few steps. One thing led to another, then about a year into our relationship, Kassia found out she was pregnant.

I never had my sights set on being a dad. I didn't think I'd be any good at it. Not only did I not have a good example of a father, I also didn't have a good example of any parental figure. I wouldn't say that I was actively avoiding becoming a dad. Obviously I wasn't, but I never really thought about it being a thing in my future.

Kassia had been afraid to tell me at first. She was really just afraid in general. One night she broke down crying and let it out. When I heard those words leave her mouth, my entire view on the subject changed. I wanted kids. I wanted kids with her. I wanted to do everything that had never been done for me and show her that being with me wasn't a mistake. I would be the best father, and she would love me for it.

I decided that I'd be the one to tell Kassia's father about everything. She was sick with worry over what he'd say to her, and this option made her feel better. That didn't go very well. I was beaten, we were shunned, and I lost my job and my home because of the influence Kassia's father had with the owners of the stables.

The following months weren't easy, but I made them work. By the time Viridi was born, I had a job again and we had a home. From the very first moment I held her tiny form in my arms, I vowed that I would never let things get bad again. She was never to know the struggle that Kassia and I went through before she was around. When Hale was born, I doubled down on that vow.

I wasn't naive enough to believe that I could control

everything around me, but I believed that I could navigate life no matter what it brought. And for a long time, I was successful with that. We didn't have much, but we had enough to get by, and we had each other, which is more than I had when I was growing up. It wasn't glamorous, but it was enough.

Until recently. Things spiraled out of control and I did my best to navigate it, but Kassia's right; I'm still a letdown. Our family might have a few nice things and full bellies now, but at what cost? If I'm caught, they'll be in a worse position than Kassia and I had been in all those years ago. I've been careful this whole time, but there's only so long I can go undetected.

Kassia may be right, but I was too. Although what I'm doing is bad and, in all likelihood, probably won't end well, I have no other option. Even with the extra money I've gathered during this time, we'll still starve probably within a month of me making my normal wages. The odds aren't great for me when it comes to the whole stealing thing, but they're even worse if I abandon it.

So, not only am I still a failure, I'm also a common criminal now, and I can't change either of those things. This is the dung pile that life has dropped me into, and I just need to learn to live in it now.

I am going to be changing the way I do things a bit. I'll always know I'm a failure, but Kassia doesn't have to know that. I'll still be stealing coins and using them to buy food, but I'll buy less than before. Just enough for all of us to eat and no more. I'll hide the rest of the money I take so that Kassia has some money to keep the family afloat if I ever were to get caught. For now, the hope is that she'll think that I stopped and then I can at least pretend that I'm not going out there letting them down every day.

Today, I linger in the market for a while, making sure to avoid the eyes of a couple of Pharisees who seem to be searching for something or someone. When no one is watching, I grab a handful of coins from the pouch of a merchant selling extravagant fabrics. Quick and easy. I buy a bit of food, pocket the rest of the coins, then head home.

I feel as if I'm being mocked by the strange amount of Pharisees I pass on the way home. They don't know what I've done. If they did, they wouldn't just be standing there leaving me alone, but passing them reminds me of every wrong I'm committing. From the act of stealing itself, to the lies I'm about to tell my wife, it seems I'm the poster child for sin.

I know what the Pharisees would say about it all, but I wonder what God would say to me right now. He's never really shown up for me in the past, and that was before I was a criminal. I'm sure He hates me. How could He not? I've explicitly ignored major commands that He's set out for our people. There's no way I'm ever going to see Heaven; He won't want to spend eternity with me. I'm surprised He hasn't smote me already for my crimes like He's done to people who have disobeyed Him in our people's past.

I'd deserve it if He did that. I'm not the type of creation to be proud of. I never really have been. My father tried to convince me of that early on, but I managed to convince myself he was wrong. I thought I'd escape from him, then I'd amount to something, but all I did was find Kassia and manage to drag her down with me.

My hands shake when I reach the house. I can't let Kassia see me like this. She won't believe my lies if she does. I take a few seconds to gather myself, then head in, my shaking diminished. I'm immediately greeted by both Viridi and Hale, and I hug them close to me, trying not to think about what they'll do if I ever don't come to the door one day. *Will they wait up for me? Will Kassia let them?* I know she'll know what happened. She'll probably tell them that I'll be back in the morning just to get them to go to bed, then she'd break the news to them the next day. 'Sorry, Daddy couldn't stop. He had to keep going. He knew things would end like this, but he just couldn't stop.'

"This is less," Kassia whispers, coming over to me and taking the food I've brought home out of my hands. She hands it to the kids, then they run toward the table with it.

"It is," I confirm.

"So, you're not doing it anymore?" she checks, knowing fully well that we both know what 'it' is. There's desperation in her eyes and she nervously taps her side as she awaits my answer. I still have a chance to tell the truth right now. She'll know I'm a failure, but at least I'd be an honest failure like she's always appreciated.

"No, I'm not," I tell her, giving into my need for her to see me as more than what I am. More than what I've ever been.

"Thank you," she lets out, throwing her arms around me. I return the hug, patting her back as she takes deep breaths of relief. In her mind I'm safe now. As if safe is something I've ever been.

22 MARTHA

I was an idiot earlier obsessing over all the details of this visit. From the moment Mary told me about it, all I could think about was getting the house ready and being the perfect host. I hadn't seen Jesus in years, yet I didn't go out to greet Him until He called me out. I felt really bad about it all after He spoke to me in front of everyone, but He didn't seem to be holding it against me. That's the thing about Jesus; nothing you do could ever push Him away.

His followers made sure to thank me over and over again after my little outburst. I think some of them did it because they knew that's what Jesus would want, but there were some that seemed like they actually meant it. I didn't really care either way; I didn't do it for them, though I'm glad I was able to give them a meal. Apparently, Jesus has them on the move a lot, so meals aren't really a constant for them. Part of me feels bad, but the other part of me remembers that they get to learn from the Son of God every day. There are so many figures in our people's history who would've loved to be walking in their shoes.

Overall, they're an odd group of people, but I don't think I could see Jesus walking around with anyone else. He's always been welcoming to everyone He's come across, so it's no surprise that they all come from different backgrounds. The only thing that they all have in common is their desire to follow Him. It's actually kind of beautiful.

There were a couple times throughout the day where a few of them tried to talk to me or Mary one on one, but Laz was quick to shut that down. The furthest I got in an individual conversation was finding out that John was a fisherman before he joined Jesus. He asked how I spend my days, and that's when Laz interrupted. He was clever about it too. He told John that Peter was talking about him, and that made John immediately walk away. Laz was so proud of himself. Honestly, I found it more funny than annoying. I was only humoring John and Laz gracefully ended that conversation for me so I wouldn't have to.

The day was filled with fun and laughter. It was good to see that revealing himself as the Son of God didn't really change Jesus. Slowly, people began peeling off to go to bed. Mary went in the first wave, then Laz in the second, until it was just Jesus, Peter, and me. Peter has been yawning incessantly for the last ten minutes while Jesus has been telling me about the years between the last time I saw Him and His first miracle.

"Peter, go to bed," Jesus finally says.

"I'll just go when You go," Peter responds, barely getting his statement out without another yawn.

"Peter, go," Jesus repeats.

"Alright," Peter reluctantly agrees, then he heads off. Now that Jesus and I are finally alone I can apologize to Him for my behavior before.

"I'm sorry about earlier. I just wanted everything to be perfect," I tell Him, and He sighs.

"Because I'm the Son of God?" He poses.

"Actually, no, not because of that," I answer, and He raises His eyebrows. I'm almost embarrassed to admit the real reason to Him. I should've just gone with the whole Son of God thing.

"There's not much you could say that could surprise me," He raises. I guess that's fair. For all I know He already knows.

"When we were younger, I was a mess. I had no idea what I

was doing at all, but You were always there in the midst of things. I was out of my mind, but when You were around, I knew I was going to make it. Today, I just wanted to begin repaying the debt I owe You," I detail, and He laughs.

"Martha, you don't need to repay me for any of that. That's not why I did it. You needed me, so I was there," He says simply. None of it was that simple for me. I feel like I was always on the verge of losing it, but He never judged me for it. He was younger than me, yet so much more put together. I could never state how much all of it meant to me.

"Jesus, it wasn't that simple and You know it. Laz, Mary, and I would've all drowned in the chaos had it not been for You," I declare, and He smiles.

"I know it seemed like chaos to you, but for me it was a time to put down the burden that surrounds being 'the Chosen One' and experience some normalcy," He tells me. I hadn't even thought of it like that. He knew from the time He was a kid the path that was set out for Him.

I didn't go to temple like the boys did, but I've still heard a lot about the Son of God. It's said that He'll save humanity. He'll reunite the Lord with His creation. I know a popular theory is that He'll save us from our earthly rulers, but I never believed that one. That wouldn't bring us back to the Lord. From what I understand, we can only be among God if we're somehow made right. Jesus is going to have to make us right, and I don't imagine that'll be easy. The fact that He's made Himself known now means that the hard part is probably coming.

"You won't be able to put that burden down again anytime soon, will You?" I guess, hoping I'm wrong. I know I'm right when His smile disappears and He begins tracing His fingers across the seams of His clothes like He used to do when He was a teenager.

"The things that our people have been prophesying about for centuries in regards to me will soon come to fruition. It will bring pain, both for me and for those around me, but in the end, it will be worth it. There will be a bridge between the Lord and His people once more," He proclaims. Goosebumps pepper my skin as His words wash over me.

He's going to suffer. I'm going to have to watch Him suffer. All for my sake and the sake of those around me. *How has He known this His whole life and just existed with that information?* I think I'm starting to see how He was able to appreciate the chaos of my household growing up.

"Thank you," I let out, wrapping my arms around Him. I thought the debt I owed Him from childhood was big, but with what He's eventually going to do for me-for us all-I'm truly never going to repay it. He knows that, yet He smiles at me. He knows that, yet He hugs me. He knows that, yet He's still here. He's never left and He never will.

"You don't need to thank me. I know you can't find words to describe how much I mean to you. It's the same for me. At least, I can't put it into words you'll understand," He teases, and I laugh. "You're all imperfect, but you're still mine. There's no pain I wouldn't endure to be with you in Heaven," He proclaims. I let go of Him and look Him in the eye.

"How bad will it get?" I ask softly, afraid of the answer. He faces the wall as He considers what He'll say to me. "I can handle it," I assure Him. In all reality, I don't know if I can, but I don't want Him to have to carry this alone anymore. He's already been doing that all His life.

"Sometimes it's better not to know," He says. I've never seen Him look so burdened before. Somehow, it's even more jarring than it was when I found out He's the Son of God. I don't want to see Him like this; His eyes downcast, His shoulders slumped, His hands resting heavily on His knees as if He can't support the weight of everything He's carrying. I don't want to, but this is only the beginning and there's nothing I can do about it. I guess I can do one thing.

"You can always come to me if You need a hug, or anything

else really. You don't have to tell me things to let me be there for You," I point out. He lets out a deep breath and a small smile comes to His face.

"I really appreciate you," He lets out, the words in and of themselves a sigh of relief. I never would've guessed that I'd hear the Son of God say that to me, but here we are. "I should probably go get some rest. I've got a big day tomorrow," He tells me.

"Am I allowed to know what it entails?" I tentatively ask, and He chuckles.

"The Pharisees have it in their head that they're going to trap me in my own words," He shares. I think back to the bits and pieces I heard about the whole miraculous sign story earlier.

"You're going to make them look silly, aren't You?" I guess.

"You've always caught on quickly," He responds, and I laugh.

"You'll have to tell me all about it the next time I see You," I tell Him. I expect Him to let out some cheeky comment in return, but instead His smile falters. *What's that about?* "Am I not going to see You for a while?" I ask, and He sighs.

"Goodnight, Martha," He says instead of answering my question. He gets up and puts His hand on my shoulder. I can almost feel the weight of the world trickling down until He removes His hand and walks away. I'm starting to get the feeling that whatever's in His future is far worse than I could ever imagine.

23 TIRNAN

I've been staying with Jahre and Ruriel for over a year now, and I absolutely love it. They really do know how to fill in all of each other's gaps. Describing things out loud is practically second nature for Ruriel, and Jahre always seems to know when Ruriel will need help, even when she doesn't ask for it.

At first, I was worried that I wouldn't really fit into everything they have going, but I was quickly proven wrong. They've both begun to pick up on my weaknesses and find ways in which they can help me.

Today my leg ached from the moment I woke up. It only seems to be getting worse as I get ready for the day. On the days where this happened at home, I would just abandon all efforts to try and make myself seem like a civilized person and wait for Edrik to get there to eat. It wasn't a great situation.

"Bad day?" Ruriel presumes, nodding to my leg as I take a seat at the table after struggling to move from one side of the small house to the other.

"Yeah," I confirm. I find the admission leaves my mouth much easier than it had whenever Edrik asked. "What's the plan for today?" I continue, attempting to avoid that particular topic.

"We're going to go gather berries, then drop some off at the market in exchange for other food," Jahre fills me in. That sounds like a lot of walking. There's no way I'm going to be able to handle that when my leg is like this.

"Don't worry about it. We'll fill in the gaps," Ruriel assures me, noticing my hesitancy. I don't know what exactly she has in mind, but I'm not going to question it.

"Thank you," I respond, relieved. I've never been particularly good at asking for help, but I don't have to with them. They know what I need and show no hesitancy in bringing it about.

"Tirnan, we've been over this; there's no need for thanks. Being there for each other is what we do," Ruriel reminds me. I almost say thank you again, but I manage to stop myself. Instead, I offer a smile. *Wait, Jahre can't see that I'm smiling. Do I narrate my smile, or am I supposed to find something to say?* I've never had to be this intentional with my words before. Edrik could usually tell what I was thinking without me even saying anything.

"I appreciate that you've extended that promise to me, and I promise to extend it to you both as well," I describe the reason behind my smile, and Ruriel nods with a smile on her own face. I guess I did a good job.

"To your left," Ruriel states. *What's she talking about?* I turn to my left, but realize she wasn't talking to me when Jahre's hand brushes my arm, then finds my shoulder and gives it a squeeze. I totally forgot that he uses physical touch to interact with the world.

At first, I thought that he often put his hand on her because there was something romantic going on between the two of them, but Ruriel made sure to tell me that they're just friends when she noticed I was a tad bit uncomfortable my first night here. I was worried I was a third wheel. It became clear that she was telling the truth when Jahre started dropping his hand on my shoulder as well. I've never been a touchy person, but I understand why he does it, so I don't mind.

We finish eating breakfast, then I help Jahre clean up the table. All I had to do was hand him things and tell him what they were. At that point, he knew exactly where to put everything.

Muscle memory is a more powerful tool than I ever gave it credit for.

"Ready?" Ruriel asks, getting to her feet and standing near the door.

"I guess," I answer. I'm still not quite sure what she's planning in terms of helping me get around today.

"Hop on," Jahre speaks up, turning his back to me and patting it.

"What?" I pose, my brow furrowing. I don't know what I had in mind, but it certainly wasn't this.

"I'm going to carry you," he states obviously. I'm not so sure about this. Not that I don't think he can carry me; he's remarkably strong from what I've seen. I just-I don't know. I'm not very eager to be a grown man letting another grown man carry me.

It's demeaning, isn't it? That's what my parents would say. Someone from my family has no business accepting that kind of help, especially when other people are going to see. *But I'm not like my parents anymore, am I? If I ever even was in the first place. 'Hopping on' isn't the equivalent of swallowing my pride like they'd frame it to be.*

The assistance that I've watched Jahre and Ruriel provide for each other has nothing to do with pride. It's about companionship. That's what this is too. They don't want to leave me behind, so they're making a way for me to come along despite my inadequacies. Hopping on is how I show them that I want to be around them too.

"Alright," I finally agree. I do as I was told. Once I'm on his back, Jahre puts his arms under my legs, securing me, and then we're off. Ruriel leads the way as we head towards the wilderness at the edge of the city. She doesn't do it by giving directions. Instead, she just makes sure to keep a steady conversation going so he can follow her voice.

"There's flowers on the side of the road," she tells him.

"What kind?" he raises.

"All different kinds. Light blue ones in clumps that are like a baby's laugh. Bright yellow ones that pop up in random places like little globs of joy. Spindly white ones that give off the feeling of a freshly made bed," she describes.

The way she's able to so quickly equate everything to a feeling or a sound mesmerizes me. It's beautiful how her world has expanded to that level of detail just so she can pull him into everything she's experiencing. I wonder if the world will expand the same way for me as I spend more time with them. It already feels so much brighter and more inviting than it ever was.

"The clouds are pretty today too," she says.

"Are they puffy?" he asks.

"Some of them. There are a few different types up there right now. Some of them are like sheets, spreading out across the sky with little ripples in them that let some of the blue shine through. Then there's the puffy ones that look like sheep. I like to imagine them as God's own flock, prancing around up there," she answers. Jahre's body shakes a little as he chuckles.

Ruriel continues to describe all of the sights around us as we go. The fields are like the overlapping voices in the market. The birds like the tartness of a pomegranate. The wilderness ahead is like a cool breeze in the summertime. I find that I'm so caught up in her words, I barely process the fact that we've made it to where the berries are.

"And we're here. Tirnan, Jahre can lean down so you can reach the berries, or he can put you down if you're feeling up to it," Ruriel says. I think back to how difficult moving around was this morning. I don't think I'm up to trying again, and I actually feel safe enough with them to admit that.

"The first option works best for me," I tell her.

"That's perfectly fine. Just tell Jahre what he needs to do," she responds.

"Alright," I agree, and then it begins. The process is a little rocky at first since I'm still pretty new at giving directions like this, but eventually I get the hang of it, and we start going quickly. It doesn't take long to fill the containers we brought.

Once that happens, we turn back and start making our way to the market. I thought Ruriel would've run out of things to talk about since we're passing all the same scenery, but somehow, she manages to pick out new things and describe them to Jahre. I truly am amazed by the way she notices everything.

When we reach the market, my mind begins to drift to how I used to be just a couple years ago. Back then, I would've only entered the market with fine clothes and my cart. Now I'm in normal clothes and I'm being carried by a blind man. I think back to the lonely state of mind that overtook me when I was a merchant. How I'd watch people like the fishermen laughing together and wish I was that happy. Now I am like those fishermen; nothing else around me seems to matter. *My heart is full. I'm truly happy for the first time in my life.*

24 NIEMOS

I've been stationed a few streets away from the market to try and spot the fraud. There's a few Pharisees in the market, but other than that, there aren't very many others anywhere near it. Izal thought that the market was the least likely place we'd see the fraud based on what we know about him. I can't say I disagree. From what we saw by the sea, it seems that he and his followers do as much as they can themselves.

All this to say that there's not really anyone close to me right now. Most people have been stationed further out in the city near places where reported healings have taken place. I'm not thrilled to be standing out here by myself all day instead of sitting at my spot in the temple reading the scrolls, but I guess I can see why this strategy has been deemed important, so I won't complain.

I've been giving thought to how I would trip the fraud up in his words if he were to walk into my zone. I haven't really heard him speak much, so I don't know the best way to go about this. I know that he doesn't seem to take the commands set out for us very seriously. That's evident by what he said the first time I saw him with Carian, and also by the way he's reportedly healed people on the day of rest.

Bringing up his healings probably isn't a good idea given how easily charmed the people are by that. *I'll just have to find a way to draw attention to other ways in which he shows little respect for the commands. That is, if I ever see him. Wait, there's no way. Is that? Yup. There he is. He only has four men with him instead of twelve like last time, but I'm sure it's him.*

After the way all my encounters with him have ended, I could never forget his face. I've spent a lot of time thinking about how those interactions could've gone differently if I'd been more confrontational. *Could I have crushed his popularity before it even had the chance to grow to this level?*

The fraud's eyes meet mine and he smiles. At this point, that smile is a regular in my nightmares. He says a few things to the followers he's brought, then he sits on a nearby wall, and begins to speak.

"The Kingdom of Heaven is like a man who planted good seeds in his field," the fraud starts, and people nearby stop what they're doing to listen. "However, as the plants began to grow, the man found that weeds placed among his field by an enemy had also grown. When his workers asked if they should pull the weeds, the man told them no. He didn't want the surrounding good plants to be ruined while the weeds were being pulled. Instead, he told them to let both the good plants and the weeds continue to grow. At harvest time, the weeds will be collected first and thrown into the fire, then the good plants will be collected and brought into his barn," he finishes.

The people stare at him in awe as they meditate over what was just said. I glare up at him and find that his gaze has met mine with that stupid smile. *Can't the people see that he's one of the weeds in the story he just told? He's trying to corrupt all those who follow the commands of the Lord! Could that be any more obvious? It's time I try to make it more obvious for them.* Luckily, he's given me a fairly good transition to do that.

"Given the way you speak of Heaven, you must be familiar with the law," I speak up, and the crowd's eyes flick to me, many of them annoyed. They'd be a lot less annoyed if they knew that I'm just trying to help them not lose their place in Heaven.

"Yes, I'd say I'm familiar," the fraud confirms.

"Then tell me, what is the greatest command in the law?" I pose. In the past he's spoken of the commands as if they serve no purpose. Whatever he has to say in response to this question will surely go against what even the common people know of the commands set out for us.

"The first and greatest command is that you should love the Lord with all your heart, soul, and mind. The second isn't much different; you should love all people as yourself. Every law found in the scrolls stems from these two commands," the fraud answers. This response does nothing to dissuade the people from him. If anything, they seem to be marveling at him even more now. *How do they not see that what he just said goes against everything we believe?*

"The commands of the scrolls were not meant to be rolled up into two overarching concepts. Each is to be memorized and followed with the utmost reverence. Simplifying them in a way such as you just did leaves room for people to disregard the things seen as little," I let out, doing my best to keep frustration out of my voice. I quickly scan the crowd around me, and it doesn't take long to find exactly what I'm looking for. "Like the command to put on our prayer tassels each morning. That man isn't wearing his. What do you have to say about that?" I ask. There's no way the people will continue to marvel at him if he straight up approves of a command being disregarded.

He studies me, his eyes prying into my soul. Shivers go down my spine. It feels as if he's somehow seeing me for everything that I am, and everything that I believe all without me saying another word. I half expect his little smile to make an appearance, but just like when I asked him what he's here to do when we were by the sea, the smile is absent. Finally, he speaks.

"You spend your life chained to traditions, entirely missing the point of why they exist. Do you think that wearing prayer tassels makes you more holy? That lording your dedication over others is pleasing to God? Truly I tell you, He doesn't care what adorns your body. His only focus is your heart. Tell me, Niemos, is yours as pretty as the outside?" the fraud poses, his gaze locked on mine.

I didn't tell him my name. I've never seen him in the temple. The only times I've seen him he never heard my name. Yet he just said it. Not just that, he used it in an accusatory question in front of all of these people. I'm torn between shock and anger. As I consider my next move, I know I can't give the fraud the satisfaction of shocking me.

"Your words are a disgrace to everything we've been brought up to believe! One of these days the people will realize that you're a blasphemer, and you'll be punished accordingly," I spit out. His followers begin to edge closer to me, some balling their fists at their sides just like they did at the sea, but the fraud just shakes his head.

"It saddens me that you view the Lord as a prison guard intent on punishment. That's not who He is. He cares very deeply for His children," the fraud states. His eyes finally leave mine. He scans the crowd until he seems to find what he's searching for. "You. You've been sick lately, haven't you?" he inquires, though it doesn't come out like a question. The crowd parts revealing a woman with sunken eyes and pale skin.

"Yes," she rasps. Those closest to her move further away.

"Come to me," the fraud tells her, sliding down off of the wall. The woman stares at him, confused. He smiles at her, and nods, assuring her that he means it. She slowly moves toward him until she's standing right in front of him.

"What now?" she asks.

"Now you're not sick," the fraud answers, putting his hand on her shoulder. At once, color floods into her face and her eyes are no longer sunken. She breathes deeply as she takes in the change that just occurred within her.

"Thank You!" she lets out, throwing him into a hug. He pats

her back, then he lets go and looks me directly in the eye.

"This is who the Lord is," the fraud declares. *Did he purposefully heal someone and then lump himself in with the Lord right now because I'm the only Pharisee here to see it? He will not get away with that!*

"Come with me to the temple at once!" I exclaim.

"It's not my time," the fraud responds, then he begins to walk away, his followers right behind him. I storm after him, but the crowd closes in, forcing me to push through them. By the time I reach the other side, both he and his followers are gone. He's done it again. I'm starting to question if we'll ever be able to stop this man, or if he's about to ruin our whole way of life.

25 LAZARUS

Something is wrong with me. I don't know what, I just know that I started to feel so exhausted earlier that I had to stop working. I stayed in the workshop though because I didn't want to go inside and worry the girls. *They don't need to know about whatever this is. I'm sure it'll pass. Tomorrow I'll wake up and I'll feel much better.*

When I do come in from the workshop, Martha's busy in the kitchen, and Mary's putting new flowers in the jar. There are blue ones in the bunch. Those don't grow close to us, so she must have gone far to get them. I'd say something, but I'm not feeling very talkative right now. My head feels heavy. If nobody interrupted me, I think I could sleep for a week. I head into the living room and take a seat.

After a while, Martha starts bringing food to the table and Mary rushes to help her. Once they put the last few things down, I get up, which takes a lot more effort than I'd like to admit. I head to my spot at the end of the table in the dining area. *I was supposed to finish making a table for a client today. I hope that doesn't become an issue.* I glance up from my plate and find that the girls are eating, so I move food around on my plate to make it appear like I am, too. Finally, Mary can't take it anymore.

"It was good to see Jesus after so long," Mary says, a smile on her face.

"It was," I agree.

"His followers were all so nice," Mary goes on. She's clearly been reflecting on all of the details of yesterday all day. I think Martha has been too, but she hasn't said much about it. She's actually been a lot more quiet than usual. I'd point it out, but if I did that, then she would start paying more attention to me right now, and I don't want that. I really am going to shake whatever this is, so I don't need her fussing over me.

"Not all of them. There seemed to be something not quite right about Judas," Martha brings up.

"Which one was he again?" Mary asks through a mouthful of food.

"The one who was sitting quietly in the corner watching the rest of them," Martha answers.

"Maybe he's just shy," Mary offers.

"I don't know about that," Martha responds, unconvinced.

"What do you think, Laz?" Mary asks, and both of them turn their attention to me. Martha's gaze falls to my untouched plate, then meets mine, a skeptical expression forming on her face.

"Mary's probably right. In a group of twelve men there's bound to be one shy one," I weigh in, then I immediately shove food in my mouth so Martha will see me eating. I'm not hungry at all, nor do I feel like maneuvering all of this food into my body, but I'm going to have to do it if I want to keep Martha off my back.

"You wouldn't be saying that if he was one of the ones who tried to talk to Mary and me," Martha points out. I was hoping she wasn't going to notice me conveniently breaking up every one-on-one conversation she and Mary had with the guys.

I wasn't trying to be controlling or anything like that. And I'm sure Jesus' followers are great people and all. I simply didn't like them presuming to make advances on my sisters in my own home. Anyone who would seek out their host in that manner while there's a handful of other people around is too desperate and therefore not worthy of my sisters' attention.

"You two can do better than all of them," I say, and Martha laughs.

"I don't know, I think I liked a few of them," Martha prods, a sly smile on her face.

"Oh yeah? Which ones?" I challenge.

"Simon was pretty cool," Martha answers.

"Wasn't he the one with those weird baggy pants?" I question. I could be wrong. There were so many of them to keep track of. I think I accidentally kept mixing up Nathanael and Thaddaeus, but neither of them corrected me. The only reason I'm convinced I got it wrong is that I kept getting looks from the other guys.

"Apparently he's very active," Martha tells me.

"Did he tell you that?" I remark.

"Peter did. Apparently, he and Simon are Jesus' main 'guards.' They're also both technically Simon. I was told Jesus changed his name to Peter somewhat recently," Martha shares.

"Simon recently called Peter and Simon still called Simon. That's not confusing," I comment.

"Keeping them all straight is probably the biggest miracle Jesus has pulled off," Mary says, and Martha chuckles. "I mean, I certainly wouldn't be able to do it. Peter, Andrew, James, and John all dress the same. The only one that I could firmly identify was Andrew, and that's only because he was so much quieter than the other three," she goes on.

"Can we all agree that John was the most annoying?" Martha poses, shaking her head just thinking about him.

"Did he talk to you too?" Mary asks.

"Yeah, I think I actually owe Laz for leading him away from me," Martha answers. I really wish I was at full strength right now so I could capitalize on that statement.

"Did he tell you that he's Jesus' favorite?" Mary checks.

"No. He said that to you?" Martha questions, and Mary nods. "That's so arrogant," she comments.

"That's exactly what I was thinking," Mary laughs.

"I'm pretty sure Jesus isn't even allowed to have favorites anyway," Martha brings up.

"If He did, it certainly wouldn't be John. I bet it would be Matthew. He and Jesus seemed to have some unspoken connection," Mary explains.

"Yeah, I know what you mean," Martha agrees.

"What do you think, Laz?" Mary asks. I need to quickly say something that sounds like me before Martha realizes that I didn't get far with my attempts at eating.

"I think we all know that I'm His favorite," I come up with. Mary laughs and Martha rolls her eyes. It seems I've escaped their notice.

"I wonder when we're going to see Him again?" Mary says. Martha's face falls and she immediately gets up.

"I think I'm going to go to bed. I didn't get much sleep last night, and today has been another long day," Martha states, then she heads back toward her room. She definitely knows something, but I'm so exhausted I can barely move, and my head feels so cloudy that I don't think I'd be able to find the words for a conversation with her.

"I'm headed to bed too," I tell Mary. My body aches as I get up, protesting any sort of movement. I take a few deep breaths, then start heading back toward my room one increasingly difficult step at a time. I have to stop again once I reach the edge of the living room. I peer around the room, pretending that I forgot something, but I don't think Mary's finding my act believable.

"Laz, are you alright?" she inquires, worried eyes studying me. Her body is completely still, something abnormal for her. Luckily, she's not as observant as Martha. All I have to do is divert her focus and I should be able to dodge this.

"Yeah, I'm just thinking about the way Martha left. Do you think Jesus said something to her after the rest of us went to bed?" I throw out there.

“Were they the last ones awake?” she asks, her gaze finding the wall as she ponders this.

“It was just the two of them and Peter after the rest of us called it a night,” I inform her. I’d follow this train of thought further myself, but all I want to do right now is lay down. “Maybe it’s nothing,” I say with a shrug that she’s too lost in thought to notice.

“Yeah, maybe,” she agrees, her tone unsure. Good; she won’t notice the rest of my struggle to get to my room.

“Goodnight, Mary,” I tell her.

“Goodnight, Laz,” she returns, eyes still locked on the wall. I start slowly making my way forward, forcing myself to keep moving until I’ve made it past my doorframe. At that point, I practically collapse onto my bed from exhaustion, nearly missing it. I’m starting to get the feeling that this isn’t that type of thing that’s going to go away by tomorrow.

26 TIRNAN

Everything I had in my old life pales in comparison to what I have here with Jahre and Ruriel. The only thing that I miss is my time with Edrik. I'm sure I'll visit him at some point down the road. Maybe I'll even bring Jahre and Ruriel. I feel like Edrik would really appreciate Jahre's heightened sense of smell.

I know a meet up like that is far off, but I can already feel myself growing excited by the possibility. All of them feel like such a big part of my life, and I just want them to meet. It's good to actually be looking forward to things. I might be thinking too far ahead. A trip like that isn't possible for me unless Jahre's carrying me the majority of the time, and although I'm not ashamed to let him carry me, I wouldn't want to make him do it for that long.

I want to start getting better at moving through the pain. It doesn't feel the greatest today, but it isn't debilitating enough that I can't walk with my walking stick. I think I'll take a walk to the river while everybody's finishing getting ready for the day. It's not too far from here, so I should be able to manage going there and back.

"I'm going to take a walk to the river," I tell Ruriel as I get up and grab my walking stick from where it's leaning against the wall.

"Good for you. We're not doing much today, so don't feel like you need to rush," she responds.

"I appreciate that," I reply. She smiles, then I head out. The first few steps almost make me turn back, but I force myself to keep going. It'll get better the more I do it just like the quality of my jewelry did. At least I hope it will.

I take in the sights as I slowly make my way down the path. The scraggly little yellow flowers that spring up on the side of the path, pushing their way into a world that doesn't seem to invite their existence. The uninterrupted sky that allows the sun to freely blaze, blinding you in a way that you're almost grateful for. The soft footprints in the dirt that show a piece of the journey undertaken by the travelers before you. All things that make the world seem more alive. All things I never would've noticed before spending time with Jahre and Ruriel.

I find that I'm paying a lot more attention to the things around me now. I've even attempted to describe things to Jahre a few times. I don't think I did a very good job, but he didn't complain. I guess he wouldn't know if my descriptions are off. He truly has to trust every word that comes out of my mouth. Before the attack I was a man who did not bond easily with others, but I've found that Jahre's unwavering trust in me has made it easy to trust in him. He believes that I will guide him forward, and I subsequently believe that he won't drop me.

As I near the river, overlapping voices begin to crowd my senses. It's pretty early for there to be a rush of people moving toward the market. *Maybe the market here just has different patterns than the one where I worked?* Soon, the people come into my line of sight and I realize that they're not moving toward the market; they're moving out of the city. There's also a lot more of them than I thought there was.

"What's going on?" I ask somebody close to me. She turns toward me and I realize that she has a bandage over her arm. I assume the bandage was once white, but it's now more of a yellow tint and has been soaked through in multiple places, causing an odor. I can't remember any of the wrappings over my wounds ever being that bad, though I had money when I was recovering. This woman's clothes are in just as much of a state of disarray as her bandages, telling me that she does not appear to be financially blessed.

"There's a man who said to bring all the sick and injured to him. He's healing them! He's going to heal me!" the woman exclaims, then she hurries forward with the rest of the group.

There's a man healing people? I need to go tell Jahre and Ruriel! All of our lives will change if we get there before this man is done! Jahre would finally be able to see all of the things that Ruriel's been describing to him. Ruriel will finally be able to squeeze Jahre's shoulder back. I'll be able to walk again without any pain.

I move as fast as I can back toward the house. While today hasn't been the best day pain-wise, knowing that there's an end in sight propels me forward. Once I reach the house, I burst through the door, scaring Ruriel.

"Was the river that exciting?" Ruriel finally manages, her breathing returning to normal.

"This has nothing to do with the river!" I let out, unable to contain the elation flowing through me. They have no idea how big what I'm about to say is!

"So… what does it have to do with?" Jahre asks.

"There was a large group of at least thirty people traveling along the road. I asked one of them why and she told me that they're all on their way to see a healer!" I drop, expecting my elation to spread to them, but neither of them appears to be particularly excited. "The healer said to bring all the sick and injured to him. Don't you see what this means? We fall under that description. He wants to heal us!" I elaborate. Ruriel's shakes her head, her eyes finding the wall, and Jahre's fingers drum rhythmically on his leg, but he doesn't say anything. *Really?* "This is big," I state, confused.

"How do you even know what they were saying is true?" Jahre questions. *Seriously? That's his hold up?*

"I guess I don't, but with the amount of people heading that way, I feel like there's definitely a good chance it is. I'm willing to chase a good chance," I declare. Neither of their expressions change. *Come on! How can they not be jumping at this like I am?* "We have a chance to be whole!" I exclaim, overcome by all this could mean for me. For us.

"We are whole!" Ruriel proclaims, outraged that I'd even suggest otherwise. She rises to her feet and storms out. *Sure, they make things work well with each other's help, but does she really think that's what life is supposed to be like? There's so much more out there for both of them.*

"Tell me you're not actually going to pass this up," I say, facing Jahre.

"She wasn't wrong. We are whole. I thought you understood that," Jahre responds.

"I get that you don't feel like you're missing anything from life because of what she does for you, but come on Jahre, don't you want to see through your own eyes?" I pose.

"She is my eyes. That's enough for me," he answers without hesitation.

"Wanting to be healed wouldn't mean you love her any less. You guys can still be friends without needing to rely on each other to get around," I tell him, trying my best to pull him away from this foolish notion. I know I haven't been with them long, but I really care about both of them and I want them to get everything they can out of life. Passing this opportunity up won't help them with that.

"Tirnan, stop. You're not going to change my mind. Frankly, I think it's stupid for you to even be considering this. You know what long journeys do to you. What if you get there and you find out it's all a lie? You'll be in too much pain to make your way back. Depending on how far it is, it could be a journey you may never recover from," he points out.

He's right. I know he is, but that doesn't change anything for me. I came here because I was done letting outside factors control my life. I still am. I'm not going to let pain keep me away from a miracle. I don't know where this healer came from, or why he's doing what he's doing, but I know in my heart that this is real. *He's real.* I want nothing more than to come face to face with him and let him take my pain away.

"I understand that, but I'm not going to let it stop me. I didn't survive my attack just to be saddled with pain for the rest of my life. I need to go find this man," I declare, and he sighs.

"We were wrong to think that you belonged here," he says, and I feel as if I've been stabbed in the heart.

This was the first place I ever felt like I really did belong. I was finally getting to live in the happiness I'd watched others experience my whole life. I was the fishermen for goodness' sake! Is that really all over because I want to be healed? Does going after what's best for me really mean that I have to give all of this up?

"Are you still here?" Jahre speaks up. *Is he going to take it back?*

"Yes," I reply, my voice barely above a whisper.

"Just go if you're going to go," he says harshly, and my heart sinks.

"I really do love it here," I try.

"Clearly not," he states, his tone guarded. He crosses his arms in front of his chest. I've never seen him do that. Given the way that he experiences the world through physical touch, this feels very pointed. Like he's pushing me out of his world.

"Jahre, I feel closer to you two than my own family. I need you to know that. I need you to know that I'm not trying to separate myself from you guys," I insist. I don't care how hurtful what he's saying to me is; I can't just walk away with him under the belief that this time was a sham for me. That I only enjoyed their company because I couldn't go anywhere else, and now I'm jumping ship the second I get the chance to. That's not at all what this was for me. Not in the least bit. I need that to come across.

"You should go if you want to make it to this guy in time," he tells me. The hostility has left his tone, but I can tell I'm also not going to be able to convince him to come with me. I hate it, but there's nothing I can do about it.

"I'll come back after," I promise him.

"Alright," he responds, waving me away. That's not how this goodbye is going to be. I head over to him and hug him. The sudden contact shocks him at first. He takes a deep breath, then pats my back. I give him a squeeze, then I let go, grab my walking stick and my bag, and head out the door.

27 TIRNAN

I really overestimated my stamina when I first set out on this journey. Not that I want to turn back. I won't. I can't. I believe in whoever it is that's at the end of wherever this path leads. *I sound like an idiot. No wonder I couldn't convince Jahre to come with me...*

No. This isn't stupid. I don't know how I know that, but I know it's not. I'm going to follow these people to the end, and I'm going to be healed. I don't care how long it takes. I'll walk for as long as I possibly can, and if it gets to a point where I can't anymore-well, I don't know what I'll do, but I'll find some sort of way to keep going. This pain isn't meant to be my future. I know it.

Eventually the flow of people slows. We must be close. I peek out behind the person in front of me to see if I can get a better glimpse of what's going on, but there's too many people for me to see much. My leg is throbbing and I want nothing more than to just collapse on the ground right now to try and alleviate as much of the pain as I can. I know I was so convinced before that there's some sort of happy ending at the end of this line, but is it possible that Jahre was right and there's nothing at the end? Is that why we're practically stopped? People aren't ready to move on after the disappointment?

"He's real! The healer is real!" somebody shouts as they run back in the direction we all came from. *I knew it!* The pain is just getting to my head right now, but soon it won't even be a factor in my life. All I have to do is make it to the end.

"Please don't bring this to the attention of any Pharisees!" a man calls, running after the enthused woman. Eventually he catches up to her and they exchange a few words, then the man starts heading back this way.

"What does this have to do with the Pharisees?" I inquire, reaching my hand out toward him. He stops in his tracks and studies me for a second, debating whether he should divulge any information to me.

"The Pharisees would like to see Him in chains. They know now that His time is here, theirs has passed," he answers, his voice quiet so only I can hear.

"Who is he?" I ask. Indecision fills his face again, and I get the feeling he's not going to give me the information I seek this time.

"You'll know when you meet Him," he tells me, a smile on his face, then he walks back to the front. *What does that mean? Is he going to tell me, or is it going to somehow be obvious?* I'm a little unnerved by how much of this seems up in the air but also far too determined to turn back.

As the line starts to move, more and more people start walking past us in the opposite direction with joy exuberating from them. On more than one occasion either the same man I saw before, or a different man has had to run after them and remind them to make sure news of what's happening here doesn't spread to the Pharisees.

I can feel the anticipation continuing to build within me with each passing smile. It's almost stronger than the pain at this point. Almost. The pain is still entirely too present, a sharp ache causing stars in my vision with each and every step. I'm trying not to think about it because I know it'll be gone soon, but it's really hard to avoid at the moment. Every time we move forward, I wind up doing this weird hopping maneuver to try and avoid putting pressure on that leg. I must look like a fool, but I don't think any of the people around me are paying too much attention.

As more time passes, the pain begins to encompass all that I am. I think it's the worst it's been since the attack. Hopping forward is doing nothing to help anymore. I'm starting to question if I'll even be able to reach the front of the line at this point; I feel like I might actually collapse right now.

"Woah there," a man says, coming to my side and holding me upright. It's the same man I saw chasing after that woman earlier. *Am I at the front of the line?* I take a deep breath, then focus on what's ahead of me. There's a group of about seven men including the one currently holding on to me. While all of them seem fairly average, my eyes are drawn to the one in the middle.

"Are you him?" I utter, my voice weak, and he smiles.

"I Am," He answers, and chills go through my body. I know who He is now. The healing. The way I feel with Him across from me right now. The way He said 'I Am.' He's quoting the scrolls referring to the divinity of God. *He's the Son of God. I'm standing across from the Son of God!*

"You're Him," I proclaim, the pain in my voice only a footnote now compared to the awe shrouding each word.

"Yes, I believe we've established that," He laughs. It's a kind laugh. Everything about Him is kind. The fact that He's been standing out here all day for the good of others shows that. "Tirnan," He grabs my attention.

"Of course you know my name," I say.

"You actually sold me a bracelet for my mother when we were both much younger men, but yes, I do know things about you that I haven't been told as well," He affirms. *The Son of God was my customer? How many times have I passed Him on the street and not known it was Him?* "We don't have much time now, but I want you to know that I know what you sacrificed to be here. You will be rewarded for that, but more than that, you should know that you have always belonged. My Father has called you His own from long before you took your first breath. If you find me tomorrow, you'll hear more about that, but for now, I think I should get to your reward," He says.

There's so much I want to say to Him. Words catapult around inside my head and I try to make sense of them so I can find something to give to Him right now. He smiles at me and I know that He isn't really expecting anything from me. All day He's stood here taking away pain without question. He's here because He loves and cares about each and every one of us even if we didn't know who He was until today.

"Consider me Your servant, Lord. Whatever You need, I'll be there. You have the rest of my days," I declare, painstakingly making my way to the ground to bow before Him. He kneels down in the dirt across from me and puts His hand on my shoulder.

"Your faith has healed you," He proclaims, and suddenly I feel just as I did before the attack happened. *The pain is gone. It's really gone.* He gets to His feet and I do the same, still awestruck by the lack of something I've been so familiar with these past couple years. "For now, make sure you don't spread what happened here to the Pharisees. There will come a time where I'll take you up on your offer and have you spread news of me to the people. It won't be easy, but that doesn't seem like it will stop you," He guesses.

"It won't," I confirm, and He smiles.

"Have a nice walk, Tirnan," He tells me, and I can't help but laugh.

"I will," I respond, then I turn around and start heading back the way I came. As I walk past all the people that I was just among, I think back to how I felt standing in that line, especially when I was further back.

The pain was so overbearing. I was close to losing hope that there was even anybody at the end of this line. I can't just leave other people to think that. I head a bit further back in the line until I've reached a point where the beginning won't be visible for a while, then I stop and face the people beside me.

"There is healing at the end of this line. I can promise you all that. I know the wait is long and many of you are in pain. I'm here to help. If there's anything I can do for you while you wait, let me know," I announce. Some people let out a sigh of relief, others appear to be confused, and a few seem like they want to take me up on my offer. I hope they do. I want nothing more than to reflect the kindness of the Son of God until they reach Him.

28 TIRNAN

Yesterday was the best experience of my entire life. The fact that I'm not only referring to getting miraculously healed and meeting the Son of God just shows what level of amazing the day was. One of my favorite parts was getting to stand by all the sick and injured in line. I got them food and water, I physically supported those who were having a hard time standing, and I listened to all their stories.

It was so interesting to hear where all these people came from. Some people were like me and had had some sort of accident or attack that did this to them, while others were born this way and had never known anything different. The only thing we all had in common was this pull of sorts leading us to believe that there was healing at the end of this line.

Getting to see all of those afflictions fall away throughout the day was so beautiful. People who were at the end of their rope suddenly had a new life in front of them after one quick interaction with Him. And though He was growing tired as the day went on, His smile never wavered. The men around Him took breaks, sitting over at a nearby campsite, eating and drinking, but He stood there the entire time. Leaving these people even for a second wasn't something He would consider doing.

As it got dark, less people were flowing in. He didn't stop

until the very last person was whole. At that point, the exhaustion was evident in His features. His movements slowed and yawns escaped Him. Even so, He still met my eyes and gave me a smile before He went into a tent set up at the campsite, and that was the last that I saw of Him for the night.

There were a handful of people who had come from far away when they had heard of the mysterious healing, and they were too tired to travel back home. I gathered them together, then went to the nearest city and got rooms for all of them and myself. Some of them offered to pay me back, but I insisted they keep their money. The Son of God didn't charge for kindness, so I won't either. Plain and simple.

Come morning, many of the people were ready to get back on the road, but a few of them decided to follow me back to the place where we were healed. He told me that He would be speaking today, and I intend to listen attentively to every word. By the time we reach Him, there's already a small crowd around Him, including a Pharisee. I wonder if this means that He's going to watch His words.

"One who does not enter the sheep pen through the door, but rather finds another way to infiltrate it is a thief and a robber. On the contrary, the shepherd of the sheep enters through the door. The gatekeeper knows Him, and lets Him in. He calls His sheep by name, and they know His voice. When He has called them out, He goes before them, and they follow. They will not follow a stranger, fleeing instead, because they do not recognize the voice of a stranger," He begins.

"Why do you speak of sheep? I was told your words hold deep meaning," someone from the crowd says, and He sighs.

"Truly I tell you, I am the door of the sheep pen. Those who come before me are thieves and robbers, but the sheep pay them no regard. I am the door. Those who enter by me will be saved. They will go out and find pasture. The thief only does bad things. Robbery. Murder. Destruction. I am not like that. I have come to bring about life, and I will bring it without end. I am the Good

Shepherd. For it is the Good Shepherd that will lay down His life for His sheep. A hired hand would not do that; the sheep are not his. He would flee and let danger close in on the sheep, scattering them. He does not care for them," He pauses, and I watch His eyes drift to the Pharisee.

I take this moment to try and take in everything He's said before He continues. *We're the sheep. He's the shepherd. He calls us by name. He did that with me yesterday. Before He even spoke, I knew it was Him. The one here to save us all.* I'm starting to get the feeling that that doesn't mean what I always imagined it meant. He just said that He will bring about life, but He also said that He would lay down His own. *He's not going to save us through some military conquest like they always made it seem when we were growing up, is He?*

"I am the Good Shepherd. I know my sheep, and they know me, just as the Lord knows me and I know the Lord; and for my sheep, I lay down my life. This is why the Lord loves me. Because I lay down my life that I may take it up again. No one can take it from me, but I lay it down by choice. I have the authority to lay it down, and just the same I have the authority to take it up again. This authority I have received from my Father," He goes on.

He can take up His life again? I've seen Him do miraculous things one after another, but defying death is a whole other level. Is He really saying that He can do that? Is He going to have to? He's spoken a lot of laying His life down. The scrolls speak of Him saving our people. I know that all of these things are connected, but I can't quite process how.

"Your mother and Your brothers are here to speak to You," one of the men from yesterday tells Him.

"Who is my mother, and who are my brothers?" He poses, and the man stares at Him, confused. He gestures out to the crowd, then He speaks up again. "These people are my mother and my brothers. Whoever does the will of my Father is my brother and sister and mother."

“And who is your Father?” the Pharisee questions, his eyes almost ravenous.

“I believe we’ve had this conversation before, Niemos,” He answers, His expression calm.

“Yes, but you weren’t clear in your answer last time. Why don’t you tell these people who it is that you are?” the Pharisee suggests, gesturing out to us all. This is a trap for Him. The Pharisee wants Him to make a claim that can be used to put Him in chains. He’s kept quiet this whole time just waiting for the perfect opportunity.

“I think these people would be interested to hear who it is you think I am,” He responds, a smirk on His face. *He has a plan for this. Of course He has a plan for this. He’s the Son of God. He probably has a plan for everything.*

“I *know* you’re a fraud,” the Pharisee declares, his face red with embarrassment or anger, I can’t tell. Perhaps it’s both.

“You seem confident,” He replies, His tone unchanged.

“I am,” the Pharisee insists, not a hint of humor in his expression.

“Who is it that you think I’m pretending to be then?” He raises, angling His head while keeping His gaze locked. The Pharisee stares at Him, confused, trying to figure out if he’s now being set up instead of the other way around. I have to admit, I have no idea what His plan is. I don’t think the men around Him do either. They keep shifting uncomfortably trying to anticipate what will be needed of them.

“The Son of God,” the Pharisee finally says, and whispers start spreading throughout the crowd.

“And how did you come to that conclusion?” He asks, a smile on His face. Pure rage floods the Pharisee’s features now that he knows he fell into a trap. I don’t think it matters if he tries to backtrack here; he’s already associated the title ‘Son of God’ with a man who was healing hordes of people just yesterday. There’s no getting that out of people’s heads.

"I will not play your games!" the Pharisee remarks at last, most likely coming to the same conclusion that I have.

"It's time," He states.

"Big James, find a path," one of the men next to Him orders, getting to His side along with another one of the men.

"Over here," a man announces, beginning to part some of the more willing people in the crowd.

"That's not what I meant," He speaks up, and all of the men gape at Him, confused. The Pharisee stares at Him, anxiously awaiting His next move. At this point, I think everybody here is anxiously awaiting what will happen next. The crowd is silent, and I can feel the people behind me leaning closer. His eyes leave the Pharisee's and survey the masses before Him. He nods His head, then releases a breath I hadn't realized He was holding. "You want to know who I am? Any of the hundreds of people I healed could tell you, but I'll save you the trouble of tracking them down and getting it out of them: I am the Son of God," He declares.

29 NIEMOS

This fraud may have made me look stupid multiple times, but it's all worth it now. He just gave me exactly what I needed. It doesn't matter how many times he's twisted my words. It doesn't matter how many times he's flashed that stupid smile. It doesn't matter that he sent his followers to distract all of us Pharisees yesterday while he performed multiple signs. He just messed up big time.

Falsely identifying as the Son of God is a serious charge. He may have been able to keep word of his miracles down, but there's no way he's going to be able to keep people from spreading this. Not everybody will believe him, and we'll have our witnesses. We'll be able to get rid of this problem once and for all.

"You've made a grave mistake," I tell the fraud.

"If you think that was a mistake, then you weren't paying attention to a word I said," the fraud remarks. I don't think I've ever seen him this close to anger. Even when I confronted him about his disrespect of the commands, he still had a remarkable air of calm to him. Now he's staring at me with fiery eyes. It chills me to the bone, but I force myself to get over it so I can capitalize on this moment.

"Oh, I heard what you said. You're just not fooling me. You're not the shepherd; you're the thief. You've come here to destroy our way of life and turn our people away from generations of tradition," I retort.

"You think tradition is what's going to get you into the Kingdom of Heaven?" the fraud questions.

"Following the commands earns one a spot in Heaven. You would know that if you actually read the scrolls you're trying to claim are all about you," I comment, and he scoffs. One of his followers starts to head toward me, fists balled at his sides, but the fraud sticks his arm out, holding his follower back.

"The Kingdom of Heaven is perfect. No matter how closely you follow the commands, you are not. Imperfection cannot be allowed anywhere near perfection. Are you hearing me clearly or do I have to state it more obviously?" the fraud poses harshly. I will not let him paint me like an idiot again, especially after making a claim like he just did.

"Your words come from your own mind, not the scrolls. You're spinning a narrative that fits the false ideals that you want these people to believe. It's all blasphemy," I declare.

"You say this based on your interpretation of the scrolls. Truly I tell you, I've been around for longer than the scrolls. I watched them all get written. The only one who knows them better than me is my Father. I assure you, if you read the scrolls considering what I've said here, then you'll see that everything lines up. Every day you do wrong. Whether it's less than the person next to you or not, it doesn't matter. You need to be made right in order to enter the Kingdom of Heaven, and you cannot do that on your own," the fraud proclaims.

How dare he!? Of course it matters if I've done less wrong than the person next to me. That's the whole point, isn't it? Heaven only accepts those that are as close to blameless as a human can get. I've dedicated my life to not only fitting that definition, but to guiding others towards it. *I don't need anyone to make me right; I already am.*

And does he really think that people are going to believe he's been around for longer than the scrolls? That claim marches past blasphemy into the realm of ridiculous. He's a man intent on destruction just as I said before. I'm going to make these people see that.

"I suppose you want people to believe that you're the one who's going to make them right?" I pose.

"I am the door to the Kingdom of Heaven. No man can enter without going through me. The scrolls are clear about this. Humanity ruined their chance to dwell with God in the beginning. The Son of God is needed to justify them so that they may be in God's presence once again. This is what I want people to believe because both the Father and I want nothing more than to spend eternity with Our people. I'm desperate for each and every one of you to grasp this, but I can't make you do it," the fraud says, his voice wavering toward the end. Tears start to well up in his eyes, and my breath catches. In this moment I can see why people believe the things he says. I take a deep breath, forcing that realization away. This crowd cannot see me captivated by this man.

"Your words do nothing but convince me that you're a fraud," I spit. His eyes drill into mine, prying out each and every thing I've hidden under the surface. I feel as though he's uncovered that my attachment to the rules comes from the lack of structure from my parents. I feel as though he's uncovered my insecurities about being less than Carian. I feel as though he's uncovered that there's a part of me that wants to believe him.

"Not everyone who minds the rules will enter the Kingdom of Heaven, but only the one who does the will of my Father. On the last day many will say to me, 'Lord, did I not wear my prayer tassels? Did I not say my prayers? Did I not follow each and every little command to the best of my ability every day and make atonement when I fell short?' And then I will tell them, 'Depart from me; I never knew you, you creature of lawlessness,'" the fraud declares.

Lawlessness? There's no way he can equate someone who spent their entire life following the rules to lawless, right? I don't know what to say to him right now and I'm afraid that if I do say something he's going to respond directly to me, calling me out for everything he extracted with that one glance.

I turn around and push my way through the crowd, then head back toward the city, thoughts swirling my mind. *He's a fraud. He has to be. If he's not, that means that I've been going about my whole life wrong. Practically swearing off joy. Scolding others for not doing the same. That can't be the truth. This man is a fraud. He says things that sound important, but that's it; they're not actually important.*

Heaven is for people like me who have lived by each and every command set out for us, no matter how small. On the last day the Lord will see our sins, but He'll also see everything we did to atone for them. That's the way that things work. There's no middle man there keeping us out. *That's not how things work!*

I break into a run, the importance of stopping this fraud suddenly hitting me. His words are dangerous. He cannot be allowed to speak to the people for much longer. If he does, there may be irreparable damage done to our way of life.

I got him to say that he's the Son of God among many other blasphemous claims. I just need to tell Izal and he'll be able to proceed with that information. What exactly proceeding with this information looks like, I don't fully know, but I'm pretty sure it ends with the fraud dead.

There was a time when that bothered me. There was a time when I wanted to be more peaceful in the way we dealt with him. That time has passed. I can accept now that he's too dangerous to be kept anywhere people can still hear his ravings. If we put him in prison, his followers will just continue to spread his blasphemy, but if we make sure he ends up dead, they'll be too afraid to even utter his name. The fraud will die. This is the way things have to be.

I run into the temple, startling those around me, but I don't care. What I have to say needs to be spread, and they would understand that if they knew the information I'm privy to. I continue on, all the way to Izal's quarters. His gaze finds mine when I enter, his face scrunched in annoyance at my sudden intrusion.

"What has gotten into you, Niemos?" he questions. His eyes flash to his right where Caiaphas is seated next to him. *I didn't know he'd be here... You know what? It's best he is. This information should be spread to the leaders with the most power immediately.*

"I just witnessed the fraud tell a big group of people that he's the Son of God," I drop, and Izal's eyes widen.

"That's blasphemy," Izal remarks.

"I know. We have grounds to stone him now," I state. Izal seems excited about this, but Caiaphas' expression hasn't changed.

"How did the people react?" Caiaphas finally speaks up. That's not what I expected.

"I wasn't really focused on that, but from what I can gather, many of them seem to believe his lofty claims," I report. Caiaphas nods his head as he takes in this new piece of information. *What is there to think about here? This man is dangerous.* "We need to get rid of him before they believe any more," I say. Izal's eyes widen at me, disturbed with the way I'm speaking to the High Priest, though I doubt he disagrees with me.

"A stoning would not be the right move if the people are this attached to him. It could cause riots, and the Romans would not be too pleased with that," Caiaphas states.

"Then what are we supposed to do?" I immediately ask.

"It would be best for the people if the Romans themselves killed him," Caiaphas declares.

30 MARTHA

"Where's Laz?" I ask Mary. I haven't seen him all day. I assumed that he had gotten up before me and went to his workshop, but he would've come back for food by now if he'd been out there this whole time.

"I don't know," Mary responds, continuing to messily cut the cloth she's using to make clothes. She got it in her head about a month ago that this was something she wanted to try. I've encouraged it because it's occupied her time. Unfortunately, her endeavors haven't exactly proved to be fruitful as of yet. There's a pile of mishappen garments in her room that she likes to look at 'for motivation.' I don't understand my sister sometimes, but I try to support her anyway.

"He's been quieter lately, hasn't he?" I think aloud as I take a seat next to her. I haven't had to use his full name at all these past few days, which never happens.

"Maybe? He seemed a little tired the night after Jesus visited," she tells me distractedly, her eyes locked on what she is doing. I think back to that night. He didn't eat very much. Now that I think about it, he hasn't eaten much at all since then.

"Mary, what do you mean by tired?" I question.

"He was slow walking to his room, and he stopped a few times on the way to it," she answers. He what!? That's not tired, that's something much worse!

"Why didn't you say anything to me?" I let out, and she finally averts her gaze from her work.

"I don't know, it didn't seem like that big of a deal. You were tired too, but I didn't say anything about that either," she defends. I wasn't tired, I just didn't want to tell them about my conversation with Jesus! I let all of that distract me and I missed whatever it is that's going on with Laz right now… I need to go check on him.

I practically run through the house toward his room. His door is shut. I usually respect that, but I can't do that right now. I swing open the door and my eyes are immediately drawn to Laz's bed where he's still laying despite the fact that half the day has already passed. Laz never sleeps in this late. His work ethic is one of the only redeeming things about him. He knows that his income is our only source of money and he takes that seriously.

"Lazarus!" I exclaim, crouching down beside his bed. I want to yell at him for not saying anything. I want to ask him what hurts and fix it like I did when he was younger. I want to go back and notice this all sooner so I could do something about it before it got this bad.

"Martha," he says weakly, his eyes barely open. I think he's trying to sit up, but he barely moves. I've never seen my brother like this before. It takes my brain in a slew of different directions, none of which are helpful right now.

"Is he alright?" Mary inquires, walking into the room. As soon as her gaze reaches Laz, she stops moving and her eyes widen in panic.

"I'm fine," Laz tries, but nobody's convinced.

"Martha, what do we do?" Mary questions, her voice close to breaking.

"I don't know," I answer, trying to force all the unproductive thoughts out so I can come up with a way to make this better.

"We have to do something," she insists as if I'm not taking this seriously. She starts subconsciously biting her nails as fear continues to flow through her.

“I’m fine,” Laz repeats. He begins to push himself up with his hands, but the effort exhausts him, stopping the process before he even makes it a few inches. Sweat gathers at his brow and the sight of it at such little exertion makes my heart drop.

“You’re not fine! You look an inch away from death!” Mary exclaims, tears in her eyes.

“I just need… a day. I’ll be… better then,” Laz gets out. If he actually believes that then he’s stupider than I always thought he was.

“Martha, he’s going to die!” Mary cries, falling to her knees.

“He’s not going to die!” I assert. Mary’s body shakes as she tries to cut off her cries to hear what I have to say. To be honest, I don’t know what to say. I just can’t let the idea of Laz dying hang out in the air like that.

I’m not ready to lose another family member. I know it’s been years, but most days I still feel just as fragile as I was back then. The only thing that kept me going was taking care of Mary and Laz, and now I’ve failed at that. Laz is sick. Sicker than I’ve ever seen anybody before. I can’t fix this-but there is somebody who can.

“I’ll get word of this to Jesus. He can fix this,” I declare. *I know that He has a lot on His plate right now, but He’ll come. He’s always been there in the past whenever I’ve needed Him, no matter how small the situation I was in. This isn’t small. He has to come. There’s no way I can get through it without Him.*

“Do you know where He is?” Mary asks, her voice small.

“No, but His mom might. I’ll go talk to her,” I decide, standing up. I haven’t seen Mary in years. She has no reason to help me with this, but I know she will. She’s a lot like her Son; she shows up for you whether you do the same for her or not. Maybe that’s one of the reasons she was chosen to be His mother.

“What do I do while you’re gone?” Mary utters, a shimmer of hope on the verge of shining through her tears.

“Keep him company,” I answer, then I turn to Laz. I can tell how much he hates this. As much as I've always taken care of him, I can see now that he's taken care of me too. "Please hang on," I beg him. He gives me a weak nod.

I head out of his room. Pass the back door that leads to his workshop where he should be right now. Pass the spot in the sitting room where he hit his head on the ground as a child, nearly giving mom a heart attack. Pass the kitchen where he's annoyed me throughout the years while I've prepared countless meals. My brother is in every nook and cranny in this house. *If this plan doesn't work, that may be all I have left of him.*

As soon as I'm outside I begin a mad dash toward Mary's house. I find that I'm running fairly recklessly, nearly tripping a few times, but I don't stop. I don't know how much time Laz has left. I need to get word to Jesus as quickly as possible. I wouldn't even know what to do with myself if this all went wrong because I didn't act fast enough.

I'm a mess by the time I arrive, but I don't care. Her image of me is not what's important here. My fist raises and I knock on her door so hard that it hurts. I wait a couple seconds and nobody comes, so I continue knocking, each frantic move taking a piece of my sanity with it.

"Woah there," James says, catching my fist with his hand. He must've opened the door. I hadn't even processed that. My mind is consumed by what I'm here to do. "Are you alright?" he asks me, lowering my fist, his eyebrow raised as he meets my gaze.

"I need to talk to your mom," I insist, annoyed that he doesn't seem to be picking up on the fact that this is important. I thought he was smarter than this. He always seemed very bright when he was younger, but it has been a while since I've seen him.

"What about?" he ventures, still not getting it.

"Just get her, James," I tell him. Confusion fills his face, but he walks away from the door to go get his mom as he was told. It takes a minute, but eventually he comes back with Mary. He stares at me one last time, trying to find out what's going on, then he gives up and walks away.

"Martha, come in dear," Mary says, gesturing inside. I don't really want to go in because I want this to be quick, but I'm not about to argue with the mother of the Son of God. I follow her inside and take a seat in a worn chair. I know this chair. I remember sitting in it the night my parents died, trying to figure out how to move forward. She was so patient with me that night, and I can see the same patience in her eyes now.

"Do you know where Jesus is?" I ask her, getting right into things. She may be patient, but I don't have the time I did that night. This all needs a happy conclusion within the next few hours, or my brother may never leave his bed again. She studies me, concern in her eyes. *I don't have time for concern.* "Laz is sick. Without Jesus he'll…" I trail off. I don't want to say the words, and I know she can fill them in herself.

"I saw Him yesterday, but He's moved around since then because He enraged a Pharisee. He doesn't tell me where He goes, but James and John's mom always seems to keep tabs on where they are. I'll go to her and make sure she gets word of this to Him," she promises me, her eyes blazing with empathy.

It tugs at my heart. Her heart aches for me because she knows what it's like to lose someone. I wasn't there for her when she lost her husband even though I knew all too well what the death of a close family member was like. Empathy wasn't enough to bring me to her door. Yet here she is, ready to hold me together all over again while I try to process this situation I've fallen into.

"I'm sorry," I spill, my voice small.

"What do you have to be sorry for?" she prompts.

"I've ignored you for years because I was afraid to talk to you about Joseph even after all you've done for me. I should've returned the favor, but instead I was a coward," I say, and tears begin to spill from my eyes. For how I treated her. For Laz, laying still in bed. For my parents. It seems as if all the tears I've held inside my whole life are pouring out right now. All in front of poor Mary.

"I never held that against you, Martha," she tells me, coming over to me and wrapping me in her arms. I fall into her, the tears still streaming. I didn't realize how much that would mean to me until she said it. I want to respond, but words feel far from me right now. I just want to stay curled up in her arms forever. But I can't. Laz needs Jesus and she needs to go work on getting Him.

"Laz," is all I manage to get out as I start to sit back up.

"I'll go talk to Salome," she states, getting to her feet. I follow her to the door, trying to get myself together as I go. She stops just before we walk out. "I'm here for you Martha. Please don't hesitate to come to me as this progresses," she says.

"I won't," I agree, and I mean it. I don't want to continue to lock emotions inside like I have in the past.

31 TIRNAN

It's been a day, but I'm still mulling over everything the Son of God said. I have a feeling those words will stick with me for the rest of my life. I'm still trying to piece together what exactly it all means.

There are things I definitely understood. For starters, He's the way to Heaven. I don't know how it'll work, but I know that much. I also picked up that He views us all as family. That must be what He wanted me to hear when He told me I'd hear more about how I belong. It's really comforting to know that He and the Lord both view me like that. There were definitely stretches of time where I felt like I was alone because the Lord thought I deserved to be. I'm overjoyed to find out that was never true.

Then there's the things He said that I can't quite figure out. He's going to lay down His life. He's going to take it back up again. He said it as if it was simple, but I can't seem to wrap my head around it. I'm sure I'll understand how it all works one day, but for now, I'm at a loss.

I'm on my way back to see Ruriel and Jahre. I don't quite know what I'm going to say to them, just that I need them to know everything that happened to me. Maybe they'll change their mind about everything and I can take them to the Son of God to have their lives changed. Or maybe I can get them to grasp all that He is without standing across from Him, and their lives will change due to that. That's the hope at least.

The trip goes much faster now that I can walk without pain. I left first thing in the morning, and the sun has barely reached its peak in the sky as I make my way down the road where just days ago I heard about a healer and decided to take a leap of faith. I walk toward the house, reflecting on just how fortunate I was to hear what I did when I did. *My life has been forever altered. If I hadn't been in this city, everything would be different. If I hadn't gone for a walk that morning, everything would be different. If I hadn't asked that woman what was going on, everything would be different.*

I find my pace quickens the more I think about it. Everything happened the way that it did to lead me to the Son of God. It goes all the way back to the attack, something that I couldn't understand when it happened, but that I couldn't be more grateful for now. *I know the Son of God now! I get to introduce Him to two people that I care about through what He's done for me!* I've always struggled with purpose, but now I know I have one.

Once I reach the house, I swing the door open and burst in, my excitement over sharing all that He is taking me over. Ruriel jumps a little from shock. When she realizes it's me, her eyes drop to my leg, then immediately widen.

"I'm back," I announce for Jahre's sake.

"Tirnan?" he questions.

"Yup. Minus the limp now. The healer is real. I watched Him heal affliction after affliction after affliction. There seems to be nothing He can't do," I tell them. Ruriel still appears to be resistant to everything I'm saying despite the fact that I'm living proof that this is all real. Jahre seems to be deep in thought. I want to give him a second to process all of this before I tell them the even crazier part.

"How did he do it?" Jahre finally asks, and Ruriel turns to him. She seems to be upset that he's even entertaining any of this. Not that he knows that.

“He told me that my faith healed me, and then the pain was just gone,” I answer.

“How did that work? Who is this guy?” Jahre wonders, unable to hide his curiosity. I was waiting for this question.

“He’s the Son of God,” I announce, and Ruriel scoffs.

“Alright, so you’re actually insane,” she comments.

“How do you know that?” Jahre poses, taking a calmer approach, though I can still sense disbelief in his tone.

“At first, I sensed it. I don’t know how to describe how that worked. You’d have to feel it yourself to understand. I just knew it was Him. The next day, I went to hear Him speak. A Pharisee questioned Him about who He was, and after toying with him a bit, He told the Pharisee that He’s the Son of God,” I report. I get goosebumps just thinking back to that moment. The Pharisee thought that he had Him, but He quickly turned that idea on its head. He did what He did for a reason. I don’t quite know what the reason was, but I trust He knows what He’s doing.

“You really just believed him?” Ruriel asks, trying to keep her reaction to a minimum. She doesn’t want to admit how intrigued she is. It hurts to see her reject Him like this. I know He is who He says He is, and I want both of them to know that too. He’s the door. I can’t let them miss that.

“He healed multitudes with no issue, including me. Who else would be capable of that?” I bring up.

“I don’t know, but it can’t be the Son of God,” Ruriel responds.

“Why not?” I prompt, my eyes begging her to stop resisting. This is real. The Son of God is here and healing is the least of what He can do for us. He’s here to save us, to make us right. There is nothing more life-changing than this!

“Because it can’t be, Tirnan. He’d be making Himself more known if He was actually here. This is just some guy that you want to believe is Him because you need to believe in something to make yourself feel better after everything that’s happened to you,” she retorts, harshness lacing each and every word.

"Ruriel, that's too far," Jahre speaks up, facing her general direction with disappointment on his face. She gapes at him, unable to process why he's not taking her side here. They've been one for so long that it seems unfathomable to her that he could have his own opinions. Maybe he's finally ready to listen to what I have to say.

"We're His sheep. He calls to us, offering kindness, and relief from the pains of this world, and a way to enter the Kingdom of Heaven to join Him and His Father for eternity. Please don't turn your back to Him. He doesn't want that, and neither do I. I want you to live in the fullness He provides here on Earth and in Heaven," I tell them. I can tell my words are deeply affecting Jahre. He slowly releases a breath, his chin tilting down in thought. He's picking up on just how big all of this is. Ruriel, however, seems more resistant than before.

"My life is plenty full the way it is! I don't need any of your soothing quotes about some magical man!" she exclaims, and her sudden increase in volume shocks Jahre. His face drops down to the table below him as thoughts fly around his head. I don't know if I'll ever be able to convince Ruriel that this is real, but I know I'm close to convincing him. Pushing this could lead to Ruriel refusing to allow me to stay, which would break my heart, but it would also break my heart to know that I didn't do everything I could to try to bring them to Him.

"You're clinging to your pain as if it has the ability to save you. It can't. I don't know how to make that any clearer. You may think that you're living a life with everything you want, but you're not. You need to let go of your pride, or whatever it is that's holding you back right now and turn to the only thing that actually can save you; you need to turn to Him," I declare. Again, Jahre deeply considers my words, but again, I've only angered her.

"Get out! You're no longer welcome here!" she proclaims. I knew that was coming. I don't want to leave. These people really do mean more to me than I can express to them. They took me in and showed me that being broken wasn't the end of things. They gave me a place to belong. But I was wrong when I thought that this is the only place I've ever belonged. The Son of God told me that much. If I have to leave here because I did everything I could to spread His words, then so be it, but before I leave I need to appeal to Jahre one last time.

"Jahre, please. I know you know this isn't a fluke," I plead, my voice raw with emotion.

"Do I need to make myself clearer?" Ruriel questions. I fully believe that she will follow through on whatever it is that she has in mind, but I can't leave without a response from Jahre. His eternity is on the line.

"Say something, Jahre," I beg. He turns toward me and Ruriel glares at him, a warning in her eyes that he can't see.

"I'm sorry, Tirnan. I have what I want from life. He can't give me more than this," Jahre states. He seems to believe that the Son of God is here, he just refuses to act on it. It makes my heart ache, but I know there's nothing I can say to him right now to change it. Maybe I'll come back someday after he's had more time to think about all this and things will be different, but for now I need to respect Ruriel's commands and leave.

"Give it some thought," I tell him. I think about going over to him and giving him a hug before I go, but Ruriel's harsh expression tells me that that's not an option. "I'll miss you both," I say, then I head out.

32 CATO

Today I'm stealing from a soap merchant. He doesn't exactly seem to be the richest of the bunch, but I've already stolen from all of them, and I'm worried about drawing attention to myself by going to the same place too many times. I wait until he's talking to a customer away from the pouch as usual, then I reach my hand in and grab a small handful. I feel bad. There definitely wasn't as much in there as the pouches I usually take from.

"Everybody gather stones!" somebody calls, and my heart starts to race. *They caught me. They're not going to arrest me; they're going to straight up kill me in one of the worst possible ways... Can I run? Is that even a good idea? If I go home, I'd be putting my family in physical danger, so that's not an option, but I don't want to stay here and get pelted with rocks. Is there a way to get out of this? Pretend it was an accident? I don't think I can really do that when the coins I took are sitting in my pouch. What do I do?*

"This woman is an adulterer! She is to be punished according to the laws of our ancestors!" the same person announces. *This woman? That's not me. I haven't been caught. I haven't been caught!*

I turn around and see a circle of people all holding stones gathered around a woman delicately wrapped in a blanket. She trembles as her accuser begins to back away from her, leaving her vulnerable. People around me begin searching for stones, then join the circle. I have to follow their lead, or else I'll stand out, and that's the last thing I want to do right now. I pick up a stone, then fall in among the rest of the people.

"Wait," a man calls, holding his hand up and entering the circle just as people begin to wind up. Two other men start to follow him in, but he waves them away.

"Are you the teacher?" someone from the circle inquires, lowering his stone.

"I Am," the man in the middle confirms. *The teacher? Should I know what they're talking about?* I lower my stone and wait intently to see how this plays out.

“Teacher, the law commands us to stone a woman who has committed a crime such as this. Why do you stop us?” someone questions, confused. The teacher bends down and begins writing something in the dirt. I crane my neck to try and get a good look, but I can’t tell what it says. “Teacher?” the man prompts him. The teacher stands up and turns toward the man.

“She has done wrong, but she is not the only one here who has. Let any of you who are blameless in the eyes of the law throw the first stone at her,” the teacher announces, then he bends down and begins writing in the dirt again. Whispers fly throughout the circle. My breath catches as I carefully watch to see what everybody else is doing. Suddenly, a Pharisee drops his stone to the ground, his eyes on the teacher’s. The teacher nods at him, something unspoken between them, then the Pharisee walks away. One by one people begin following his lead.

I stare down at the stone in my hand. *Was I really going to throw this at another human being?* Shame overtakes me as I think about just how far from blameless I am. How evil am I that I was perfectly willing to hurt someone else when worse sins sit in my own heart? The stone feels like it’s burning in my hand, so I quickly drop it and retreat to the edge of the market, away from the woman.

I know I should keep walking and go home, but I can’t. My shame keeps me planted in this place, my eyes locked on the scene still unfurling before me. I watch as the rest of the people in the circle drop their stones and disperse, the youngest of the crowd leaving last. The only one left with the woman is the teacher. He stands up, meeting her gaze and she trembles before him.

“Where’d everybody go? Have they not condemned you?” the teacher poses, and the woman stares at him.

“No, Teacher,” she finally answers.

“Interesting. I don’t condemn you either. Go, and sin no more,” the teacher responds. The woman’s trembling ceases as she takes a massive sigh of relief. She almost goes to hug him, then she seems to remember that the only thing covering her is a blanket, and her face reddens. "Let's go get you some clothes," the teacher says, kindness in his eyes despite her current state.

"I don't deserve to have You come with me," the woman utters, making herself small so the blanket covers as much of her as possible.

"You have been made right today, and a day is coming where all of your sins will wash away forever, past, present, and future," the teacher tells her. *What does that mean? He's not seriously saying that that amount of wrong can go away, is he?*

He puts his hand on the woman's shoulder and leads her over to a booth with clothes. Now that the commotion has ended, normal activity is beginning to resume in the market. I think back to everything I just witnessed; the teacher wrote something in the dirt. An overwhelming urge to know what it was overtakes me. I run to the where he knelt down to see what it says before it gets trodden over by the market-goers.

'I am greater than the law. I know what you've done. I am also greater than all of that,' it reads. A shiver ripples down my spine, and I scooch back. These words hold a power I can't grasp. This man is claiming to be greater than something passed down for generations, and I believe him. He just stopped a stoning by using his words. That's not a small feat.

The part that I'm struggling with is what comes after that first statement. *How can he be greater than what we've done?* The extent of my transgressions keeps me up at night. Surely, he's not greater than that. This message must be meant for those who live better lives than I do. I'm too far gone for a statement like this. I close my eyes and breathe deeply as I try to contend with what I've done-with who I am. *I was about to throw a stone at a woman no worse than me for goodness' sake! There's nothing and nobody who can redeem that.*

I rise to my feet and head over to a booth with food. Just as I've been doing for the last week, I get just enough bread and fruit to feed my family, then I drop the proper amount of coins on the table. Just like the stone, the coins seem to burn in my pouch, reminding me of all I've done. I try to dampen my shame as I begin to walk out of the market. If I don't, Kassia will sense it on me, then she'll see who I really am.

"Cato," a voice says behind me, and I stop dead in my tracks. Despite how long I've lived here, nobody really knows me by name. Kassia and I have always stayed to ourselves because of how our experiences with people have played out in the past.

I turn around and see the teacher before me. The men who tried to follow him into the circle aren't too far behind him, with the woman, now clothed, between them. Despite the situation she had just found herself in, she's now smiling. *How is that possible? How has she found peace that quickly?*

"How do you know my name?" I question, returning my gaze to the teacher.

"I know you, Cato," the teacher states simply. *That's impossible. I've never met this man.* "I know that you feel that you're not enough for your family, and I know what that's driven you to do," he goes on. While that was vague, it was also extremely spot on. He truly knows the things I've done. I don't know how, but he does. It terrifies me.

"I have no other options," I say, feeling the need to defend myself. If he really knows all this, then he must understand that.

"Follow me. The rest will take care of itself," he tells me, his eyes carrying no judgment despite the things he's somehow privy to. No. That's not how things work. Things don't just work out. In my experience, every possible thing goes wrong. He must've missed that part when he somehow gathered all this information about my life.

"I need to get home," I decide, snapping out of all the confusion he's stirred up in me. I start to walk away, but I stop when I hear his voice again.

"We will meet again, Cato. The circumstances are up to you," he states. I don't know what that means, but I don't want to stand here and try to decipher it. No matter how much he thinks he knows me and my life, he doesn't. I continue forward without so much as turning around to acknowledge him.

33 MARY

Over the past two days I've watched my brother lose more and more of himself. After the first day he stopped talking. Opening his mouth and letting words out was somehow too much for him. My whole life my brother has never let a moment sit without some sly comment, but now there's only silence.

It hurt, but I could deal with it because he would still smile at me every once in a while when he saw I was by his side. He was still in there. Buried under that stupid illness, but still there. Then as this second day has gone by, the smiles have stopped. He just lays there, motionless on the bed.

Hurt is not enough to describe the way sitting next to him now makes me feel, but I can't leave him. What if there is a small part of him still in there, and sitting here is the only thing that's keeping him from slipping away? Getting up would be letting him go, and I can't do that. *I can't lose him too.*

"When was the last time you ate, Mary?" Martha asks as she walks into the room. She's been taking the opposite approach as me to all of this. Busying herself so that she doesn't have to see him. I guess it shouldn't surprise me; she had a similar tactic when our parents died. She threw everything she was into taking care of Laz and me. She's never stopped even after all these years. I know they would be proud of her, but I also know that they would've wanted her to start living her own life at some point. Isn't that what Laz is always on her about? She could have her own family by now, but instead she's devoted herself to being there for us. Why have I never seen that until now?

"Eat this," she says, putting a plate of food down next to me.

"I'm not hungry," I tell her.

"Mary, this isn't healthy," she states. *I'm sorry, she thinks that the way I'm handling things isn't healthy? Has she looked in a mirror recently?*

"Martha, you won't even let yourself sit down for two seconds because if you do you might have a thought about all of this, and that's too much for you," I spit, and I hear her scoff behind me. I turn to her just in time to catch the end of her eye roll. "What?" I demand.

"Nothing," she remarks. I might not be the most attentive person, but even I can see that there's something she wants to say right now.

"Just say it, Martha. We're both grown women now, you don't need to watch your words around me anymore," I snap.

"Alright. I was going to say at least I'm not watching him slowly inch closer to death with each passing moment. Do you realize how sad that is, Mary?" she asks, and my heart sinks. I know it's sad. I'm well aware of that, but I have to stay here. There's still a chance that Jesus will come, and I can't have Laz thinking that we forgot about him and letting go before He gets here.

"I won't leave my brother alone. He needs to know that I'm here. He needs to know that I love him," I tell her.

"Do you think that that's going to make him better somehow?" she ventures, judgment in her tone.

"No, but Jesus will," I declare, and she sighs.

"Mary, if Jesus was going to come, He would've already," she says, sitting down beside me. She goes to put her hand on my shoulder, but I jerk away from her.

"He's going to come. Laz is His best friend, He won't let

Him go like this," I state. We've known Jesus all our lives. He's not the type to leave a friend in need. I don't know why He's taking so long to get here, but I know He's coming. I'll stay by Laz's side until the very moment He gets here, no matter how stupid Martha thinks I am for it.

"Mary…" she starts, but she cuts off. I turn to her and find her face pale. I follow her line of sight to Laz and try to see what she's seeing.

"Martha, what's wrong?" I question. She stares at Laz's chest, and that's when I realize it; his chest has been weakly rising and falling all day, but now it's still. "No," I let out, refusing to believe what my eyes are telling me. Martha leans forward and feels for his pulse. I wait for her to say that she's found it, but she doesn't say anything.

This isn't real. He's not gone. I was here. I was right here! He was supposed to hold on! Jesus was supposed to come! It can't just end like this! My brother is too much of a loudmouth to go out that quietly. He's just playing some horrible prank on us. Maybe the prank is just on me and Martha's helping him with it. That's why she's so quiet right now. They're trying to really sell it. Before I know it, Laz is going to shoot up and say something like 'You should've seen your face.' That's what has to be happening here.

"We need to go get Mary. She said that she would have the boys take care of things for us," Martha finally speaks up, letting go of Laz and getting back to her feet. There's no humor in her tone, but this has to be a joke. Because if it's not…

"Alright," I agree. I bet we're leaving so that Laz can set up some big scare for me. That has to be what's happening right now. It's twisted, but Laz has been known for letting his pranks get out of hand. Granted, this is more messed up than anything he's ever done in the past, but it has to be because Jesus wasn't here to keep him in check like He did when we were younger. That has to be it.

I get up and follow Martha out of the house. She's quiet the entire walk to Mary's. She must not want to give up the joke. There are tears in her eyes, but I'm sure she can fake cry. This is all a part of it. When we get there, she knocks on the door and it's quickly answered by Mary. One glance at Martha, and her face falls. She must be in on it, too.

"James, go get your brothers and meet me at Martha's house," Mary instructs, then she joins us and we begin heading back home. This is all really elaborate for a prank. I'm going to have a lot of notes for Laz once the ruse is up.

The walk back is just as quiet as the walk there. When we get home, I find everything the way it was when we left. *That doesn't make sense. Didn't we leave so Laz could set something up?* We head over to the sitting room and Martha immediately starts crying. Like, really crying. I've never seen her like this before. Mary cradles her close, and when I see the look in her eye, it hits me; this is real.

"Why didn't Jesus come? He could've stopped this!" I let out, finally beginning to process everything that's happened. Martha sits up and faces me with watery eyes. Despite the argument we got into before, she wants to comfort me now, but I don't think she has the words. Mary rubs her back, and turns to me.

"I don't know why my Son does things the way He does, but I do know who's plan He's privy to," Mary responds. *Is that supposed to make me feel better? My brother is dead!*

"Why would God have Laz dying in His plan?" I question, angry tears starting to slide down my cheeks. Laz has done nothing to deserve something like this!

"I've wrestled with that question myself," Mary replies honestly. If the mother of the Son of God has wrestled with this question, then what am I supposed to do with it?

"Did you ever get an answer?" Martha wonders quietly. It's almost as if she's afraid of the answer. Mary sighs, and now I find myself fearing her next words.

"No," Mary admits. *No? What am I supposed to do with that?* "I actually still wrestle with it sometimes, but it's hard to stay mad at God when you live with His Son. I've never understood His plan, I won't pretend that I did, but during every low point our family has ever faced Jesus has been there to comfort us all. He was grieving, yet He did everything around the house so I could process things. He showed up for all His brothers' messy emotions. He was there to hold His sisters for as long as they needed. Losing Joseph was hard, and I don't know why it happened, but I've never felt the love of God more than I did during that time. I know that's not what you want to hear, but it's all I've got," she finishes.

She's right; that's not what I want to hear. I want my brother to be alive. I want her Son to have come in time. I want to feel that same joy that He used to spur up during our childhood with all the little things He did for us. But my brother is dead. Jesus didn't show up. He didn't do what we needed Him to do. And I don't know what to do with that.

34 MARTHA

My brother is dead. The words still bring tears to my eyes when they come to my mind even after four days. This shouldn't have happened. He was in perfect health before this illness struck, yet it took him so quickly. I needed more time to prepare myself for the sudden quiet that now fills every inch of the house. The empty chair at mealtime. The customers of his who come by asking how they can help, but only ever wind up reminding me that my brother is gone and we now have no source of income.

Jesus' mom has been staying with us to keep us afloat while we process this. I'm really grateful for her, but at the same time her being here reminds me that Jesus never came. He didn't even come when we buried Laz even though we got word to Him about when that would be happening.

I don't understand it. I don't understand why He would do this to us. How could He refuse to come when He knew Laz was dying? The last time I saw Him He told me that He can't even put into words how much He loves and cares for us, but if that's true then where is He? I want to be able to understand why He's done what He's done, but for the life of me I can't make sense of it. He should've been here. There's no excuse.

"He's coming," James whispers to his mom as he walks into the kitchen with food from the market. There's only one Man he could be referring to right now. I immediately jump up and start heading for the door. I need to hear what He has to say for Himself. "Martha, wait…" James tries, but his mom puts her hand up, stopping him.

"He can handle this," she states. At first, I get annoyed with her phrasing, but then I realize that she's slightly annoyed. She wants to know just as much as I do why her Son let this happen.

I run out the door and start heading in the direction of the market. I don't know where exactly He is, but I know that this is where James came from and he must've seen Him on the way to our house. I spot Him in a side street about halfway to the market. It's not very hard considering He has all twelve of His followers with Him right now.

"Where were you?" I question Him. His followers all duck their heads awkwardly so that they don't have to face me, but He meets my eyes.

"I couldn't come yet," He answers as if that clears anything up. I get that He's the Son of God. I get that He's probably pretty busy because of all that. But one thing I will never get is how He's managing to justify all of this to Himself right now.

"You're all-powerful! You could've done away with his sickness, but instead You stayed away! Do You really expect me not to be mad about that?" I exclaim. His face falls for a beat, and He takes a deep breath, then His eyes return to mine.

"Do you truly believe that I'm all-powerful?" He prompts. *Seriously?*

"That's what I just said, isn't it?" I remark.

"Then what's limiting me now?" He asks. *What's limiting Him? My brother is already dead! He was too late!* Yet He's looking at me right now as if that's not the case. What if it isn't? What if healing the living is only the start of what He can do?

"It's not too late for You to fix this," I realize. Most of His followers gape at me, but He faces me with a small smile beginning to form.

"Go get your sister," He tells me.

"Yes, Lord," I agree, then I take off running back the way I came. I don't know how all of this is going to play out, but I know that He is in control right now and that's the best place for Him to be. Everyone jumps when I come bursting into the house.

"You didn't beat my Brother, did you?" James checks, and even his mom seems to have a little worry in her expression.

"No," I answer obviously, then I turn to the sitting room where Mary's been stuck the majority of these last four days, staring out the window towards Laz's workshop. "Mary, He wants to speak with you," I say.

"What if I don't want to speak with Him," Mary responds, not even turning away from the window.

"Mary, I know you're mad at Him. I was too, but then He said some things-you should really just come and hear for yourself," I tell her. She slowly turns to face me, and her eyes search mine. They're red and puffy and skeptical. It hurts seeing her this way, but I know it'll all be over soon. Jesus is all-powerful.

"Fine," Mary agrees, getting up and following me out the door. James and his mom trail along behind us as we make our way through the city. Jesus is in the exact spot I left Him, and He smiles when He sees me.

Mary heads right up to Him and stares daggers at Him. I think she wants to yell at Him, but instead, she drops to her knees and begins to sob. Jesus' smile falters as He looks at Mary weeping at His feet.

"Where is he?" Jesus inquires, His voice shaky.

"I'll take you to him," I answer. He nods, but He doesn't move. His gaze shifts from me to Mary, then sorrow that I now realize has been within Him this whole time fully overtakes Him, and He falls to his knees next to Mary, joining her in her weeping. Because though He is in control, He still just lost His best friend.

"Did he not know this was going to happen?" Judas whispers to Thaddaeus.

“Shut up,” Thaddaeus responds, trying to focus on Jesus and gauge how he can help Him.

“We received multiple messages,” Judas reminds him.

“Not the time,” Thaddaeus seethes.

“Let’s go to the tomb,” I speak up, annoyed with the whispers. I kneel down and help Jesus up. Once He’s on His feet, He takes a deep breath, then extends His hand to Mary. She accepts it, then we head to the tomb in one muddled lump of grief, comfort, and hope.

As we move through the city, people eye our group, and some even join in. I don’t know if they recognize Jesus or just want to see what’s going on. Jesus doesn’t acknowledge any of them; He just stays close to Mary and me, all of us sniffling as we go. By the time we reach the tomb, our group now numbers around forty.

“Move the stone,” Jesus instructs, wiping his eyes, then gesturing to the large stone we used to seal the tomb. My breath catches as my mind brings me back to the day we put him in there. I find reality clashing with everything I believe to be possible in my head.

“It’s going to smell. He’s been in there for four days,” I point out, the hope built up inside me beginning to flicker. I still believe that He is all-powerful, but I can’t get the image of my brother wrapped in burial cloth out of my head. He wasn’t here for that. He doesn’t know the pain that will come with seeing it again.

“Do you still believe, Martha?” He raises, turning to me. My eyes are drawn to the tear stains on His face. He understands perfectly the state He will find Laz in, yet He wants to continue. He is still in control.

I nod my head and He motions to His followers. They hesitate, but eventually Peter, Simon, and Big James come forward and begin to roll away the stone. As soon as a crack has been revealed, the smell wafts out, but they continue until the stone has been fully removed. They step back, uncertainty in their eyes, and Jesus steps forward. My hope, which wavered only a minute ago, now burns bright. Jesus raises his eyes, then starts to speak.

"Father, thank You for listening to me. I know that You always listen, but those around me tend to doubt. Show them who You are in this moment so that they will be just as confident in You as me," Jesus proclaims, and chills run through me despite the warmth of the day. God has never felt more real than in this moment. Jesus turns back toward the tomb and raises his fist. "Lazarus, come out!" He cries out, all He is, Lord and Man, seemingly poured into those three words.

Noises stir within the tomb in front of us, and people gasp around me. I do not. I do not breathe at all as the footsteps start. I do not breathe as a form, my brother, comes into view at the mouth of the tomb where the stone separating him from the living once stood.

"What are you waiting for? Unbind him," Jesus directs. Air fills my lungs again and I rush over to my brother, once dead, now alive. I tear the linen strips away from his hands and his feet and pull the cloth away from his face. His eyes meet those of his Savior, and he falls down at His feet, weeping.

"Lord!" Laz chokes out, his voice hoarse.

"That was quite the nap you had," Jesus jokes, kneeling down next to him. Laz falls into His lap, and He pats his back.

"Was he actually dead?" someone in the crowd whispers.

"Yes. He died four days ago. I was there when they buried him," someone else responds, awestruck.

"We've just witnessed the greatest miracle there will ever be!" someone lets out. I couldn't agree more! I turn to Jesus and find that His smile has faltered. I think back to our last conversation before Laz was even sick. He told me that things were coming that would bring pain for Him and those around Him. I can see now that this is one of the things He was talking about, but something tells me that this isn't the end of it. Something greater is coming, and it's going to rip Him apart.

35 LAZARUS

I was dead. That is a statement that's not meant to be said seriously by any man, but here we are. I was dead. Now I'm not. I have to think about it simply because if I try to actually make sense of it all, my head spins. Dead people generally don't live to see another day. That's kind of how it works.

Things are different for me. Not because of who I am, but because of the kid who grew up next door to me. I've known Him all my life, seen Him countless times, but I've never seen Him how I saw Him today. When the cloth was removed from my face and my eyes met His, I was overwhelmed by all that He is. It's one thing to hear your best friend is the Son of God; it's another thing entirely to be snatched from death by Him.

I've been asked a few times what death was like. It's hard to put into words, but I've been trying my best. People who saw the miracle think they know all it entailed, but they don't. They don't know how dark it was. Darker than closing your eyes. And it wasn't just dark, it was silent. There was nothing. From my experience, death seems to be the absence of everything. Emptiness in its purest form.

Jesus pulled me away from that. I heard Him call my name, then the only darkness around me was that caused by being in a tomb with a cloth over my head. Everything rushed back all at once because of Him, and I've never appreciated it all more. Somehow that includes Martha incessantly tending to me.

It's not even just her either; Mary's been all over me too. Both of them partly blamed themselves for not noticing that there was something going on with me sooner and doing something about it. I've been slowly getting them to believe that that's not true. My best tactic has been to reiterate that I'm an idiot and should've said something to them. It's been pretty humbling.

Jesus and His followers have been here all day, and I've been waiting for the chance to talk to Him alone. Peter and Simon seem to be wary about leaving His side, and Martha and Mary still don't want to leave mine. I would tell them to go away, but I feel like that might be unreasonable considering I was dead just this morning.

After a while, Jesus' followers finally start peeling off to go to sleep, until Peter and Simon are the only ones left. I'm tired too, but I'm not going to bed until I've talked to Him. He brought me from death to life. That's not a little thing.

"Laz, are you good if I go to bed?" Mary asks after what I think was a string of ten yawns in one minute.

"Of course. You should probably go to bed too, Martha. You've had a taxing few days," I suggest.

"How would you know?" Martha challenges me, and Jesus smiles.

"Any day you have to get through without me is taxing," I respond, and she rolls her eyes so aggressively that her head moves.

"On that note, I think I will go to bed," Martha states, getting to her feet.

"Why don't you show Peter and Simon to their rooms," Jesus suggests.

"We know where our rooms are," Peter says, confused.

"That was a hint, my friend," Simon tells him, patting his shoulder. "We'll leave you to it," he adds, getting up. Peter takes one last look at Jesus, then gets up and walks out with Simon and the girls. I almost ask why Peter behaves the way that he does, but I decide against it. There are much more important discussions to be had right now.

"I don't want to sound like I'm complaining, but why did You wait until after I had died to come? We both know You could've healed me before anything happened and saved my family the pain they went through," I raise. I hate that I just said that to Him, but I know the question would plague me forever if I didn't. He nods His head as if He was expecting this. Of course He was. Even a normal person would've expected that question after how everything played out.

"It wasn't just your family that went through pain," He starts, His face falling as He thinks back to the state of things before He showed up. I hadn't even thought about how it had all affected Him. I figured since He knew He could bring me back, He wouldn't have grieved me, but His expression tells a different story. "The last thing I wanted was for this to happen to you, Laz, but it had to. I can't really explain it to you in a way that you'll understand. I guess to put it in its most simple form, it had to happen so that people would know that I have dominion over death," He tries.

"Woah," I let out.

"Woah indeed," He agrees, a smile on His face that doesn't quite reach His eyes.

"Did You always know that we'd wind up here?" I ask, the question suddenly hitting me.

"Yes," He confirms. I wait to see if He's going to elaborate, but He doesn't. I guess I should leave it there.

"So, what have You been up to? I mean, besides raising people from the dead," I clarify, and He chuckles.

"I've only raised you for now, my friend," He jokes. *For now? Should I ask about that? I feel like we've moved away from the serious part of the conversation, so I won't, but I'll definitely keep it in mind.*

"I knew I was Your favorite," I respond instead.

"I don't have favorites," He denies.

"You have to say that, don't You?" I inquire, tilting my head.

"Do you even want to know what I've been doing?" He asks, raising His eyebrows.

"Of course," I reply, and He smiles.

"I healed the masses, then the day after that I identified myself as the Son of God to a Pharisee, then not too long after that I stopped a stoning," He details.

"What?" I immediately question, sitting up straighter in my seat as the shock of his statement washes through me.

"A woman was to be stoned, but I got everybody to drop the stones by pointing out their own sins," He answers. *Really? He's not going to be able to redirect me that easily like He did when we were kids.*

"You know that's not what I was reacting to," I comment, and He nods His head.

"Ah yes, the whole Son of God thing. The Pharisee tried to bait me and I turned it around on him. It was actually quite funny. You would've loved it," He tells me. He's still trying to redirect me from the serious nature of this situation through jokes. This must be worse than I'm imagining.

"No Jesus, I wouldn't have loved it. You're taking things too far," I say.

"And you're going to explain to me why with your extensive knowledge of the world?" He inquires. I know He's making fun of me, but this is serious. The whole miraculous sign debacle was one thing, but this? This gives them grounds to try and kill Him. As someone who just experienced death, I don't want that for Him.

"The Pharisees are valuable because they read and interpret the scrolls. You're valuable because You fulfill them. One of those things is clearly better than the other. They'll stop at nothing to stay in control," I spell out for Him, and He sighs.

"You're not telling me anything I don't already know," He replies, humor now absent from His tone. If He knows all this, then why is He pushing them? I need Him to see that this is a bad idea.

"They're going to kill You, Jesus," I proclaim, and He shakes His head.

"Lazarus, do you believe that I'm the Chosen One?" He asks. *Did He really just use my full name? Is He mad at me?*

"Of course I believe that," I assure Him.

"What is it that you believe I've been chosen for?" He follows up. This seems irrelevant right now, but I guess I'll engage.

"Conquest. You're here to free us from our captors," I answer obviously, and He shakes His head again.

"I think you need to read the scrolls more closely," He tells me, then He gets up and starts to walk out of the room, but He stops just short of the hallway. "It will get harder, Laz. You're going to have to be sure about the things you believe," He adds, then He walks away.

What is that supposed to mean? It's going to get worse than my own death?

36 MARTHA

Jesus and His followers left fairly early in the morning. He wanted to get to where they were going before there were any Pharisees out to spot them. Apparently, they've reached their limit with Him. He doesn't seem scared about it, but I can tell it comes with some kind of burden for Him.

Before Jesus left, He warned us to keep a low profile. Word about Him raising Laz has apparently spread remarkably fast, and many people are starting to believe in Him. Unfortunately, that's making the Pharisees even angrier. Jesus doesn't want any of their anger pointed at us.

He told Laz that he can continue to work, but that all orders will have to be taken and delivered by James. I was anticipating pushback from James on that considering that he has his own life and all, but he agreed as soon as Jesus asked. I think he's still taken aback by everything that happened, which is fair. If I saw my brother raise someone from the dead, I would be too.

I'm still pretty taken aback by it all, but for different reasons. I was mourning Laz, then four days later he was back. It's kind of a hard thing to just move past. At least I'm not the only one going through it. Mary also winds up randomly staring at Laz throughout the day to make sure he's still there.

Laz has asked us for a little space, so right now Mary's working on making clothes in her room, and I'm cleaning up everything from last night in the kitchen. I wasn't going to make the mistake of cleaning while Jesus was in my home again.

I haven't said anything to Laz, but I do keep glancing over to where he's sitting. He hasn't noticed; he's too caught up in whatever he's reading. I'm actually kind of curious. I quickly prepare a snack for him, then I head over.

"You seem like you're going mad," I say, setting the plate down next to him.

"Jesus said I was interpreting the scrolls about Him wrong, but I can't seem to come to any other conclusion," he responds, scratching his head as his eyes continue to race across the words in front of him. I love my brother, but it's not uncommon for him to interpret situations wrong, so his inability to interpret these scrolls doesn't shock me.

"And what conclusions have you come to?" I pose.

"He's going to raise an army and free us from the chains of the Romans," he states matter-of-factly. *Of course that's how he's reading things.* Life under the Romans hasn't always been the best, but there are things far worse than them. Things an army can't touch. There's also a very big flaw in his theory now that we know that Jesus is the Son of God.

"Has Jesus ever seemed like a fighter to you?" I raise. I have vivid memories of Him going to great lengths to avoid killing bugs. I don't think that behavior goes with being a military commander. I mean, of course He could do it if that was the plan, but I'm pretty confident that's not even close to what the plan is.

"No, but it says here that He has come to break every chain. What else could that mean?" he asks, pointing to the line he's referring to. I don't even have to look at it to answer his question.

"We're enchained by more than just the Romans, Laz," I say, and he gapes at me, confused. *I swear, he's so dense sometimes.*

"Laz, you should know more than most the things He's capable of freeing us from," I try to make it more obvious for him. He stares at me for a second, then seems to realize something and quickly begins scanning the scroll in front of him. His eyes go wide, then His gaze finds mine.

"He's going to die," the words tumble out of his mouth. I hadn't fully grasped that, but the idea had definitely been swirling around my head. There are lines in the scrolls where He's referred to as the Lamb. In our people's history, lambs have been sacrificed to atone for wrongs. If He is to bridge the gap between us and God-make us right-He's going to have to sacrifice Himself.

It makes sense why He didn't want to outright tell me about that when I asked. It's hard to think about. I'm sure even though He is who He is, it's hard for Him to think about too. It's a lot. But it's also necessary. And that's probably what hurts the most about it all for Him. His people cannot be right on their own. We're not worthy of entering the Kingdom of Heaven and spending our eternity with Him and His Father. It's a fact. But Jesus. He was sent to rewrite the way things work. To make us right by being the perfect sacrifice.

"He's known this His whole life. How does one live knowing they'll die?" Laz murmurs, his eyes downcast. *Is he really asking that?*

"We all die, Laz," I remind him, and he shakes his head.

"But He knows exactly when and how He'll die…" he trails off as something crosses his mind. "Surely He can stop it. We've seen Him do crazier things," he presents, gesturing to himself. *He really doesn't get this, does he?* I don't like it either, but it's clear that it's supposed to happen. Jesus wants it to happen.

"Stopping it would mean leaving the world in chains. He could never do that," I declare.

"But He has dominion over death, doesn't that mean that it shouldn't lie in His future?" he raises. *Wait a minute.*

"The phrasing you just used. Where did that come from?" I question.

"Last night Jesus told me that he couldn't just heal me because people had to see that He has dominion over death," he answers. Jesus is going to die, but that's not going to be the end of things.

"Give me those," I say, snatching the scrolls from Laz.

"What are you on about?" he asks, and I shush him. He puts his hands up in surrender, then peers over my shoulder as I scan each and every word before me. Goosebumps pepper my skin as I read about the Son of God being despised and rejected. It brings me back to my conversation with Jesus during His last visit. He told me He's going to suffer many things. The scrolls confirm it.

He didn't say anything to me about coming back though. The closest He got to that was saying that it would all be worth it in the end, but that could mean so many things. I keep taking in all the lines of the scrolls, hoping for something that points to my theory. He wouldn't have used those words with Laz by accident. He has dominion over death. That includes His own. My eyes jump from word to word until I find it.

"Here," I state, pointing to the lines, and Laz leans closer.

"For You will not leave my soul in the realm of the dead nor let Your Righteous One see decay. Martha, this is a psalm of King David. What does it have to do with Jesus?" he inquires.

"Keep reading," I prompt him. He shakes his head, then returns his eyes to the scroll.

"You will forge the path of life and make it known to me; You will…" he continues.

"Stop there," I interrupt him, and he cocks his head. "Do you not see it?" I question.

"See what, Martha? This is a fairly standard psalm of David. We read them all the time at temple," he states, clearly trying to portray the idea that he knows more than me because he went to temple. Their teachers didn't even realize they had the Son of God as a student, so I'm not shocked they also missed things in the scrolls.

"Except it's not a standard psalm of David, Laz. Who do you think 'Your Righteous One' is referring to? And what do you think it means when it says He won't see decay? And how about when it says that He'll forge the path to life? Tell me you're getting this Laz," I practically beg, excitement pouring out of me, but he just stares at me blankly. "Seriously? Nothing?"

"Martha, it's just a psalm of David," he reiterates. I can't believe him right now.

"Laz, Jesus is the Righteous One. He's going to die, but He won't see decay because He has dominion over death, just like He told you. His death and resurrection are what's going to forge the path to life that we're all going to get to take when we die if we believe in it," I explain to him in a way that could not be any clearer, yet he still hasn't seemed to have grasped this.

"Resurrection? Are you hearing yourself, Martha?" he says as if I'm the stupid one.

"What would you call what just happened to you?" I ask, glaring at him.

"I guess resurrection is a pretty good way to put it…" he starts.

"Exactly," I cut in.

"But that doesn't mean that you're interpreting this right, Martha. It could just be a psalm of David, and you want to see it as something else because you don't want to think about losing Jesus," he finishes, his infuriating 'I know best' look on display. *Is he really going to shut himself off to this revelation because he didn't come up with it?*

"You're right that I don't want to think about losing Jesus; I'm still trying to get over losing you and you're here next to me right now, but that has nothing to do with this. This is about what I know Jesus is capable of. It's about how the idea of bridging the gap between us and the Lord is actually going to work. It's about not only Jesus' future, but the future of all of creation. I don't know why you can't see that," I voice, frustrated.

"Because it's crazy, Martha," he responds.

"So is the fact that you're breathing right now, Lazarus. Is that really where you're going to draw the line?" I question. He's quiet for a while as he ponders this. I know it's crazy, but nothing has really been normal since Jesus' first miracle. The blind see. The lame walk. The deaf hear. The dead breathe. I wholeheartedly believe that there's nothing He can't do.

"I don't know, Martha. This is all a lot," he finally responds, then he grabs the scrolls from in front of me and heads to his room. That's an understatement, but it doesn't make what I'm saying not true. If things are really as close to happening as Jesus has made it seem, then Laz will see that I'm right soon enough.

37 AURAN

Things have been great at home since Maxian was healed. Laughter and smiles fill my house again, leaving no room for any sort of anguish like what we were steeped in before. I began training Maxian shortly after he was healed, and he's picked up on things very quickly. He'll make a great Praetor one day.

I've been doing better at work now that I'm not shrouded in doom and gloom. Being back out on the streets among the people has been so refreshing compared to holing up in the building all day going through written requests. The sun shines down on me as I head in for the day, ready to meet Deslan. When I find him, he has panic in his eyes, and he's tapping his side repeatedly.

"What's wrong, Deslan?" I prompt. I don't think I've ever seen him this worked up before.

"Pilate is here by request of the Pharisees. He got in last night," Deslan reports. Pilate is the ruler of this entire region. He's my direct higher up, yet I've only spoken to him maybe five times in my whole career. The fact that he's here right now makes the blood drain from my face. The fact that he's here because the Pharisees summoned him makes me fear for my life. If they say anything that makes it seem like I haven't done my job properly there's no telling what he'll do to me.

"Do you know where he is now?" I ask, my voice small.

"He just left for the temple shortly before you arrived," Deslan tells me.

"Thank you," I respond, then I begin running toward the temple before he's even had the chance to say anything else. The Pharisees have left me no written issues. If they're going over my head like this, this must be serious. Pilate isn't the biggest fan of people barging in on meetings, but I need to know what's going on.

Pharisees eye me as I run through the temple courts, but none dare to stop me. Once I'm inside the temple, I slow my pace. I can't let Pilate see me acting deranged and I have no idea which part of the temple he's in.

I've never actually been inside the temple. There's been no reason for me to go further than the courts in the past. I'm not sure if I'm even allowed in here. The looks I'm getting from Pharisees right now make it seem like I'm not, but again, they don't say anything to me. At first, I thought it was because they're intimidated by my armor and rank, but now I'm realizing it has nothing to do with me. They're up to something. I can see it in their eyes.

I forge ahead, gauging the panic in their eyes to tell if I'm going in the right direction or not. It's like that game I used to play with Maxian when he was younger; calm expressions mean I'm getting colder, and wide eyes mean I'm getting warmer. I know I'm nearly there when the panic starts to spread further than their faces.

"You can't be here," one of them finally finds his voice as I near a door. The meeting has to be happening behind it.

"Need I remind you who's in charge here?" I raise, pointing to the Roman emblem on my armor. He staggers back and I open the door, revealing Pilate at a table with four Pharisees. I recognize the two in the middle as the High Priest, Caiaphas, and a leader within the temple, Izal. They don't seem thrilled to see me, particularly Izal.

"Auran, I didn't send for you," Pilate states when he sees me, his soft features projecting a stern expression that looks unbecoming on him. It's not quite threatening, but it's enough to unnerve me, especially when my eyes find his crown, reminding me of his authority.

"I know that, Dominus. I wouldn't have come if I had not thought that my presence at this meeting was important. I oversee the day to day in this city, and I haven't heard anything from the Pharisees, so I would like to know what was so important that they dared to disturb you," I say, trying to draw attention to the fact that I was not consulted prior to him. I need him to know that I'm not neglecting my duties; I just wasn't made aware of whatever this is. The Pharisees avoid meeting my eyes, embarrassed that I've just called them out.

"Very well. Caiaphas, would you mind filling my Praetor in on what's occurring," Pilate requests, twirling one of his many bracelets impatiently as he faces the High Priest. Based on the way he just used my title, I'd say he wasn't aware that the Pharisees didn't come to me first and he's annoyed about that. I almost let out a sigh of relief, but I hold it back, deciding that that's not a good look. As soon as I find a seat, Caiaphas begins to speak.

"There is a man among the people who defies our ways and pulls the simple-minded to his side using false signs," Caiaphas starts, and I immediately know that he's talking about Jesus. Jesus, the same man who healed my boy. I know I should be quiet considering the fact that Pilate is right next to me, but I can't let this go on any longer.

"A man is not following *your* ways. How does this concern Rome?" I question, trying to make it all sound preposterous. I need Pilate to avoid getting involved in this.

"He has called himself the Son of God. Do you know what that means?" Izal prompts in a tone meant to make me sound stupid. I've heard the title a few times while trying to learn about their culture, but I have no idea what it means.

"Not entirely, no," I respond. Izal turns a scroll around and pushes it closer to our side of the table, pointing to the middle of the page.

"It's said that the Son of God will break every chain. What do you think that's referring to?" Izal asks as I quickly scan the scroll in front of me. The words in it carry power. The Pharisees know that. Their leadership is the only thing they've ever cared about. That's why they're so resistant to us. They won't let a challenge to that leadership succeed.

"Are you insinuating that this man will incite some sort of revolution?" Pilate questions, his eyes glued to the page in front of him, dissecting each and every word.

"That's what we're afraid of," Caiaphas responds. *Wait a second.*

"These are *your* scrolls. This man is from *your* people saying that he's a figure that *your* ancestors have waited generations for. Why would you bring this to our attention?" I ask. If I can prove that they have some sort of ulterior motive, then maybe I can pull Pilate's focus away from what was just said.

"Because this man is not who he says he is. He's using a title meaningful to our people to create an army and we won't take that lightly," Izal replies, ready for the question.

"What if you're interpreting the scroll wrong?" I pose.

"I've dedicated my life to these scrolls, so that's unlikely, and even if I am interpreting them wrong, it wouldn't matter. He's out there convincing people to join him, telling people that he'll set them free. This man is a threat whether you believe our scrolls or not," Izal declares. He's got Jesus all wrong. I don't know what he's here for, but I know it's not conquest. The only people he's a threat to is them.

I don't know how I'm supposed to convince Pilate of this though. If I tell him that I've seen Jesus perform miracles and that I believe he's not here for harm, then he'll think that I'm a part of this supposed revolution and I could lose not only my job, but my life. I need to find some other way to stop this, but I can't think of any.

"What would you have us do about this?" Pilate finally asks, his tone neutral.

"What your people do so well to revolutionaries like him," Caiaphas answers.

"You want us to crucify him?" I question, unable to contain my shock. Pilate turns to me, his eyebrows raised. "I mean, doesn't your own law require three witnesses before inflicting any sort of punishment that drastic? We can't just sentence a man to death without being sure that he's guilty," I bring up. Pilate turns his attention to the Pharisees, his eyebrows still raised.

"My fellow Pharisee, Niemos, was there when he claimed to be the Son of God, as well as when he performed false signs," Izal starts, gesturing to the Pharisee on his left. "And my fellow Pharisee, Carian, has also seen him perform false signs and allude to being the Son of God before he officially announced it," he goes on gesturing to the Pharisee on the other side of Caiaphas.

"And the third witness?" I question, desperate for him to say that they haven't found one yet and for this all to just be over.

"One of his own followers who has been with him for all of his false signs and proclamations has come to us. He has identified the man as Jesus, son of Joseph, and has agreed to lead a group of soldiers to him for his arrest," Izal states. *No. This can't be real. One of his own followers wouldn't actually give him up like that, would they?*

"This man will be arrested and tried, and if he is found guilty then Rome will sentence him to the appropriate form of punishment," Pilate declares. The decision has been made. And there's nothing I can do to stop it.

38 AURAN

As soon as I left the temple, I went to the place where the population records are stored. I need to find Jesus' last known residence so I can find him and warn him. I begin searching for a record with his name and his father's name together to ensure I've found the right Jesus. It's actually a fairly common name. I have to go back ten years before I find a record that has both names. I recognize the other names from another record I'd found with Jesus' name earlier in my search. Joseph must've died in the years after this was recorded.

I backtrack until I find the most recent record with Jesus' name next to these others. There's some variation that's probably due to people moving out, and new families beginning, but there are at least three common names, which convinces me that I have the right record. I commit the location listed to memory, then I tuck the record back where it belongs and head out.

I try to think about what I'm going to say as I go. 'Remember me? You healed my boy. Well, bad news; your own people are trying to have you killed and one of your followers is aiding them in their efforts. Oh yeah, and they don't just want you killed, they want you to be crucified!' It's not exactly the type of news you want to give to someone who changed your life.

What if I go to him with a solution? I couldn't stop Pilate

from agreeing to this scheme, but maybe there's another way out of this. Jesus' arrest has been ordered, there's no way around that, but maybe there's still a way to ensure he's never arrested. As time goes by, Pilate will see that he's not a revolutionary, and this will eventually become low priority. Jesus would have to leave here and move around to avoid Roman detection for a while, but it would keep him from crucifixion. I don't know if I'd call it a solid plan, but it's the best option he's going to have.

I quickly finish the walk to his last known residence, then I knock on the door. Nobody answers. I knock again, and this time I hear footsteps on the other side of the door as someone gets closer. The door opens and a woman faces me. Based on her age, I'd say she's his mother.

"Hello, I'm here to speak to Jesus. Is he around?" I inquire. She surveys me, her eyes pausing on the Roman symbol on my armor. I totally forgot about the fact that I'm in full armor right now. "I know how this appears," I start.

"Do you?" she questions.

"Yes, I do. Your son has a knack for making enemies in high places, and now a Praetor has just shown up at your door searching for him, but I promise he's not my enemy," I assure her. She raises her eyebrows at me, asking for more. That's fair. "My boy was sick a couple years back. He was going to die, but then I heard about your son. I found him and he healed my boy from across the city with just his words. I'm in awe of your son not just for what he did, but for the fact that he did it at all. He didn't have to help me, but he did. I would never do anything to cause him harm," I go on. Her suspicion falls, and she smiles. It looks a lot like Jesus', meeting her amber eyes and radiating warmth.

"He's not here and I don't know where He is, but I can take you to someone who does," she tells me, stepping outside and closing the door.

"He doesn't tell you where he goes?" I ask as we begin walking away from the house.

"He says it keeps me safe," she answers.

"I'm sorry. That must be hard for you," I respond. I can't imagine not knowing where Maxian is, especially if I knew there were powerful people against him.

"You don't even know the half of it," she jokes, though there's no humor in her eyes.

"I'm going to keep him safe," I promise her, and she actually laughs.

"Good luck with that," she tells me. *What's that supposed to mean?* I'm about to ask her, but then she comes to a stop in front of a house. "Wait here," she instructs me, then she goes inside. She's gone for a few minutes before she returns, a large loaf of bread in her hands. "He's camped out in a field just outside the city with all of His followers. Give this to them and tell them it's from Salome. Also, tell Him that I love Him for me, will you?" she requests, handing me the loaf of bread.

"Of course," I agree, and she smiles. "Can I ask you something?" I prompt.

"You just did," she responds, a smirk on her face. That's exactly what Jesus said to the former lame man. *Like mother like son, I guess.*

"What did you mean when you told me good luck keeping him safe?" I ask, and her smirk wipes away.

"I've tried to do what I thought was best for my Son His whole life, but He's always seemed to know better. It's hard to see how these situations He's getting himself into are going to end well, but I know He knows what He's doing, and so does He. He won't do what you want Him to do if it's not a part of His plan," she explains.

"What do I do if he doesn't listen?" I raise, thinking about everything that's at stake here.

"Trust Him," she answers simply. I wish things were that simple.

"Thank you," I tell her, and she nods, then we go our separate ways. The whole walk out of the city, I try to think of a nice way to word my idea. I need him to say yes. I need to make sure he doesn't decide to be stubborn and reject it for whatever reason he comes up with. There's no logical reason to stay here and let himself be arrested, tried, and crucified. He's going to see that. Any man would.

Once I'm about a mile outside the city, I see the camp Jesus' mother was talking about. There are twelve men doing various things, though I don't see Jesus at the moment. I shiver remembering that one of these men has already begun to betray Jesus. *Would I know which one it is if I saw him? Will Jesus know which one it is when I tell him?*

"What do you want?" a man questions me as he jogs up to me with another man right behind him. He has a small fruit knife in his hand, but he holds it as if it's as big as my sword.

"I'm here to speak with Jesus," I respond.

"You're not going anywhere near Him," the man spits.

"Peter," the other man says, poking him, then pointing to the bread in my hand.

"Where did you get that?" Peter interrogates, gesturing to it with the knife.

"It's from Salome. She sent it for all of you," I report. Peter stares at me, confused, but apparently that was enough for the other man.

"Peter will bring this to the campsite, and I'll take you to Jesus," the man tells me.

"Thank you," I reply, handing the bread to a still confused Peter, then following the man as he heads away from the camp toward a more secluded area. After we pass a few trees, I see Jesus in the distance, down on his knees. He must be praying.

"Sorry to disturb You, Lord, but You have a visitor," the man who brought me speaks up. Jesus stands up, then turns to us with a smile on his face.

"Auran," Jesus greets me. Now that it's clear I know him, the man leaves my side.

"Your mom says she loves you," I spill, all other words failing me.

"I'm sure you didn't come all the way here just to say that," he suggests.

"No, I didn't," I confirm. I was supposed to have a good way to get into this all, but I've got nothing. At this point I just need to say something. "I just came from a meeting where the Pharisees initiated a plot to use my people to kill you. One of your followers is going to give up your location to them, but I don't know which one. I've done everything I possibly can to try and stop this, but the Pharisees were ready for everything I had to say. My direct higher up ordered your arrest, and if the claims the Pharisees are making can be proved in a trial, your crucifixion," I tell him. I didn't really expect panic from him, but I was expecting more than just the slightly saddened expression that's in his eyes right now.

"I didn't ask you to do anything," he responds. *Is he serious? He healed my boy. There is nothing I wouldn't do for him. Not to mention his life is on the line right now.*

"You didn't have to, Jesus; I would go to any length for you, including smuggling you out of the city, which is exactly what I'm going to do. You'll still have a target on your back, but if you continue to move around, you'll be safe," I say. It's not perfect, but it's the best I can offer him. The Pharisees were prepared at the meeting, and something tells me that they'll be even more prepared at the trial. If Jesus stays, he's going to die in one of the most excruciating ways humanity has thought up.

"I won't be doing that," he states. *What?*

"Jesus, I don't think you understand how painful this is going to be. My people have mastered torture. What you will endure during your last day on Earth will be worse than you could ever imagine," I proclaim. The crucifixions are so brutal that I usually try to avoid going to them if I can. I've been in wars. I've watched men cut down by other men. But the slow, agonizing death that a crucifixion brings; that's human suffering at a concentrated level that's hard to stomach.

"My imagination extends far beyond your comprehension," he informs me.

"You know what I mean, Jesus. If there's any way for you to avoid this, you need to pursue it," I insist. He sighs, his eyes on the ground, then he returns his gaze to me. I've never seen a man before appear so burdened. There's a gloomy look on his face, and his shoulders slump. It's a stark contrast from the smile that usually adorns his features.

"There is a way, but it would lead to separation from my children," he tells me. I've searched through his records and I haven't seen any mention of children or even a wife.

"You don't have children," I point out.

"My children are those that do the will of my Father," he elaborates. His Father. He's not talking about Joseph. I didn't understand what the Son of God meant until right now. His Father made this world and everything and everybody in it. According to what I saw in the scrolls during the meeting with the Pharisees today, He was there for all of that. He has divinity in His own right.

Breaking every chain and freeing the people has nothing to do with us Romans. We're not on His level. The scrolls are referring to other chains; chains only He can break. The chains of sickness. The chains of affliction. The chains of death.

"What is your will for me, Lord?" I inquire, dropping down to my knees to acknowledge His glory. A smile that doesn't quite meet His eyes comes to His face.

"Let me be God, and you just focus on being man," He says.

"Yes, Lord," I respond, bowing my head.

39 CATO

After lingering in the market for a while, I decide that the spice booth will be my next target. I've never actually bought spices, but I've heard they can be expensive, so there should be a decent amount of money in the pouch.

I wait for the merchant to move away, then I head up to the booth. I reach my hand into the unguarded pouch and grab a handful of coins. The process, once automatic, now takes every ounce of me to complete as I drop the coins in my pouch. They burn just like they have every time I've repeated this action since seeing the woman caught in adultery.

I feel like an even worse person admitting this, but it irks me that she gets to walk away from all of that shame and live in peace while I can't even look at a coin the same way now. I don't want to feel this way. I hate it. It's every horrible thing I've ever thought and been told about myself all rolled into one big ball of shame, and there's no escape from it.

My whole life I've tried to be good. Good enough that my father would leave me alone. Good enough that nobody would leave me like my mother did. Good enough for Kassia. Good enough for her father. Good enough for my kids. Good enough for that stupid voice in my head that screams the exact opposite at me.

The voice is right. It always has been. A good man doesn't

do the things that I do. All I've managed to do with this life of mine is prove everybody who ever said anything bad about me right.

"Can I help you?" the man behind the booth asks. I'm still in front of the booth where I stole. *This isn't good. I've never had to interact with someone I've stolen from. What do I do?* "Hello?" the man inquires, facing me with concern in his eyes. He's concerned for me. I just stole from him, but he's concerned for me. *I can't do this.*

I turn around and start running away. I don't know where I'm going, I just know I need to get out of here. The exit is in my sight and although I didn't buy any food for my family tonight, I make a beeline for it. Just when my escape seems sealed, something shiny gets in the way and I screech to a halt.

"What do you think you're doing?" a voice questions. That voice is attached to the shiny thing. It's Roman armor. I've just been stopped by a Roman soldier. This is the worst of all the worst-case scenarios that have flown through my head since Kassia found out I was stealing! *I need to say something, but what do I say?* The coins burn in my pouch and all sensible words have slipped my mind. *I'm done, aren't I?*

"You," another voice says from the other side of me. It's the merchant I stole from. I don't even dare to turn around.

"You know this man?" the soldier asks. My eyes drop to the ground. I can't be a part of this interaction even though I'm at the center of it.

"He was standing awkwardly in front of my booth, then he took off. I checked my coin pouch, and it's lighter than it was before I saw him," the merchant reports. I should try to deny this, but I can't speak right now. It's almost as if this is happening to someone else.

In my head I call myself an idiot as if I'm some separate entity. I tell myself that I should be doing something. I should've played it cool with the soldier. I should've talked my way out of this. And now that I've let things get this bad, I definitely should've run by now. Yet I just stand there, letting my life happen to me like it always has. Only this time I've given up the illusion that I have any control over it.

"He stole from you?" the soldier questions.

"I can't be sure that it was him, but given that he ran away, I think there's a strong likelihood it was," the merchant responds.

"Empty your pouch and show me your hands," the soldier orders, but I just stand there. He stares at me, waiting for me to move, but I don't. I can't. Everything in me has simultaneously shut off. I'm just existing here right now with no choice in the matter.

The soldier sighs and takes a step closer to me. He reaches his hands into my pouch and forces my closed fist open. In my fist he finds the few measly coins that I earned for a full day's work. In my pouch he finds the handful that I took just minutes ago. I couldn't bear to put them all in the same place. The honest keep and the loot. If they were separate, then I could keep those parts of me separate too. The honest laborer and the thief. Two different men.

"Did you steal these?" the soldier questions me, though he doesn't seem hopeful that he'll get an answer. He sighs, then looks past me at the merchant. "Does this seem like the right amount?" he prompts.

"The pile on the left does," the merchant confirms, gesturing to the coins gathered from my pouch. The soldier drops those coins in the merchant's hand, then returns the sad, miniscule, little amount of coins that started all of this into my pouch.

"Go back to your booth," the soldier tells the merchant, and he obliges, then the soldier turns his attention back to me. "You're coming with me," he declares, pulling shackles from his belt and securing my wrists with them.

He begins leading me out of the market and I shuffle along wordlessly, still processing that this is all happening to me right now. The shackles that bind me are cold, a stark contrast to how the coins felt in my hand. I wasn't meant to have those, but these chains; they belong to me. There's no injustice with what's happening right now.

We head into a building that has more soldiers within. They all eye me, most likely wondering what I did. *Could the thoughts in their mind be worse than my actual transgressions? Would that make me feel better or worse? Is there even a way to feel better while in chains?*

"Dominus," the soldier with me greets the Praetor sitting before us.

"Yes?" the Praetor asks, seemingly preoccupied.

"I caught this man stealing in the market. How do you want me to proceed given the new focus on theft?" the soldier raises. *New focus on theft? Of course I chose the worst time to turn to thievery.*

"Take him to the prison and find out the extent of his crimes. Report back to me before you leave today and I'll decide what to do with him," the Praetor answers. Prison. I guess I knew this would end there, but actually hearing the word makes my heart drop.

"Yes, Dominus," the soldier responds. He leads me out of there, and into another nearby building. We walk past people chained to the surrounding walls. Some of them avoid eye contact while others laugh as we go by them. The sight of it all makes my heartbeat slow, as if my own organs want to give up on me like those in my life always have.

I expect the soldier to attach me to the empty shackles at the end, but he leads me past them. Instead, he brings me into a room with a table and a few chairs at one side and what I can only describe as a torture chamber on the other side. My legs begin to tremble as my eyes are drawn to spots of dried blood on the ground.

"You have a choice here. Admit to me how long you've been at this," he begins, gesturing to the side with the table. "Or I'll find out one way or another," he goes on, gesturing to the torture chamber. "And trust that if you lie, I'll know," he adds. I'm not a bad liar. I've been lying to Kassia for a while now, but I still believe that he'd see right through me.

"I'll tell you everything," I say, my voice shaky.

"So, you do speak," he comments as he leads me over to the

table. He secures the shackles on my wrists to something on the table, then sits across from me. “Get going,” he tells me, eyeing me impatiently.

“It started a couple years ago. I didn’t have enough to feed my family, so I found another option,” I begin, and the words all flow out of me after that. Every nasty detail coming to light.

40 CATO

I am to be crucified. I stole too many times for them to let a lower punishment slide. It's hard to explain what it's like finding out that you're going to be brutally killed. There's still a small part of my brain that hasn't seemed to accept it yet. I've done bad things. I failed my family. But crucifixion? That's for murderers and other people on that level. I didn't kill anybody. People barely even noticed that I stole from them! Yet crucifixion is now in my future. I don't really know what to do with that. I guess I don't have to think about it too hard given the fact that I'll be dead soon.

It was clear the soldier who brought me in felt bad for me when he came and gave me the news. He knows why I did what I did. He probably knows that he wouldn't have behaved much differently if he were in a similar predicament. Because he felt bad, he offered to let me see my family one last time.

I went back and forth on whether I'd accept his offer. I wanted to see my family again, I did, but I didn't want to see their reaction to all of this. I could not possibly have let them down more. But they deserve some kind of closure. It'd be selfish for me to deny them that, so I accepted the offer.

There's only one private room in the prison, and it's the one with all the torture devices in it. The soldier put a curtain up to hide all of that from view, secured me to the table, then left to get my family. My leg shakes under the table and my shoulders slump as I wait for them. I know this was the right move, but I have no idea what I'm supposed to say.

Is there even anything I can come up with to make this better for them? An apology would probably help. I also need to tell Kassia where I hid the money I've been saving. Other than that, I really have nothing. I wish I did. I wish there were words out there that could counteract all the pain I'm about to put them through, but there just aren't. I'm leaving them in one of the worst ways possible.

All of a sudden, the door opens and I sit up straighter, forcing a collected look to my face. Kassia comes in and stops as her eyes drift to the shackles on my wrists. Her eyes are red and puffy, but she's not crying right now. Instead, her expression is practically unreadable as she takes all of this in. She draws in a breath, then continues on and takes a seat in the chair across from me. She stares at me, and I wait for her to say something, but she doesn't.

"Where are the kids?" I ask.

"I wasn't bringing my kids into a prison," she answers harshly. *Her kids? So that's how this is going to play out. I'm already dead to her.*

"Do they know what's happening to me?" I raise, and she rolls her eyes.

"Did you really think I was going to tell them that you're being crucified?" she questions, leaning forward with her fists clenched, angry with me for even suggesting that.

"I could've told them if you had brought them," I say, and she shakes her head.

"You really don't get it, do you Cato?" she retorts.

"Get what?" I ask, too disheartened to play her guessing game. I'd rather she just let it all out. It's what's best for both of us. She shakes her head, and my shoulders tense up as I prepare myself for the onslaught of words she's about to release.

"You've been sentenced to one of the worst deaths out there! The kids should never know about this!" she exclaims, and it hits me like a punch in the face. I recoil as I take it in. I know that I should be more focused on the fact that I'm going to be brutally killed, but what hurts the most is that I'm never going to see my kids again. I wasn't even sure if I wanted to just yesterday, but now that I know I never will, it brings tears to my eyes. "It's a little late for tears, Cato," she scoffs.

"I'm sorry. About all of it. Please Kassia, you have to know that," I tell her, trying and failing to get myself together.

"What do you expect me to do with that, Cato? You said you were done! You told me you had stopped! You lied to me, and now look where you are!" she exclaims, gesturing to the shackles binding me. I know this is bad and I know I don't deserve more than what she's giving me right now, but that doesn't make it hurt any less.

"I'm sorry," I repeat.

"Stop saying that!" she shouts, putting her head in her hands. When she returns her gaze to me, I can tell she's done with this conversation. *I'm not ready for her to leave!* This is the last interaction that I'm ever going to have with a member of my family. After she leaves, I'll be all on my own. *Completely alone.*

"I hid some of the money," I say, moving my hands up to try and wipe my eyes, but the shackles keep them from reaching.

"Great," she comments, shaking her head.

"It's in a pouch underneath Hale's pillow," I go on.

"You had him sleeping on top of your spoils?" she phrases, disgusted. I knew it was safe there because he doesn't move around a lot in his sleep unlike the rest of us. I'd say that to her, but she clearly doesn't want to hear it. She doesn't want to hear anything from me right now. I'm not done with this though.

"What will you tell the kids about me?" I ask.

"Does it really matter, Cato?" she poses.

"Yes, Kass. I want to know how they're going to remember me," I state. My mom left with no warning, and that's always haunted me. I need to know that that's not the lie she's going to feed them. If they have to live their lives thinking that I did that to them, well… I was going to say I wouldn't be able to live with that. I'll be dead anyway so I guess that's not really the right phrasing here. I would really hate it. I'd die being what I always vowed I wouldn't be to them. A cruel parent who put themselves first. I can't think of anything worse.

"I'll tell them you died in an accident at work. That's where they think you are right now," she finally relents. It's not great, but it'll probably be easier for them to live with than the truth.

"Thank you," I say, and she nods. Her eyes fall to my shackles again. She sighs, then she starts to get up. *No. Not yet.* "Kass, wait."

"What?" she questions, now at her feet. Her tone is so cold. So unlike the woman I married. I guess I don't exactly appear like the man she married right now. I look like someone who deserved her father's disrespect. That's probably what she's thinking right now. I don't blame her for wanting to leave, but I'm not ready.

"Please don't go," I beg her, leaning toward her. I can feel tears welling up in my eyes, but I refuse to let them fall. She'll find them pathetic.

"What am I supposed to do, Cato? Sit here and stare at you in this sorry state? Console you for all the bad decisions you made? Waste my time with a corpse?" she retorts. My heart drops and even though she's made it perfectly clear she'll provide me no comfort, I'm utterly terrified of her leaving. *I don't want to be alone. Not here. Not again.*

"Just don't go," I urge, my voice small. Her eyes find mine and I see the exact moment she decides she's completely done with me.

"I need to go," she puts forward, turning toward the door.

"I love you, Kass. I need you to know that," I declare. She stops for a second, then she continues forward and leaves me here. Alone. *That was really the last interaction I'm ever going to have with my wife.* Tears sting my eyes and this time I let them fall. My life is over now. There's no point in trying to stop them.

I'm full-on sobbing by the time the soldier comes in to get me. He releases me from the table, but he doesn't make any further movements. Does he not want to bring me back to my spot among the other prisoners looking like a pathetic mess? Will my red eyes and loud cries disturb the peace out there? I try to even out my breathing, but that ultimately makes it worse.

"I'm sorry," he finally speaks up, and I can tell that he really means it. If only that meant anything to me.

"I don't deserve your pity," I respond, and he sighs.

"I shouldn't have brought her here. I'm sorry for that," he rephrases. He couldn't have known that she was going to react like that. Based on the way that I described her to him, I made it sound like she loved me. It turns out I was a little off in my assessment. At least, she doesn't love me anymore.

"Just bring me back among the other criminals," I say. He seems like he wants to say something else, but he decides against it. He leads me back to my spot on the wall, attaching my shackles to the waiting chain, then leaves. The irony that the soldier that arrested me cared more for me than my wife leading up to my last day is enough to keep my tears falling.

41 AURAN

I awaken suddenly in a cold sweat. My sleep has been continually interrupted with images of what will happen to Jesus all night. He doesn't deserve any of this. I don't understand why He's just letting it happen. I don't understand it, but I need to go with it. He's God. I'm man. I need to trust Him.

That doesn't make it easy. My people are the ones who are going to be doing these vicious things to Him. They'll be following orders. My orders. They may originate from higher than me, but I'm going to have to be the one to tell them to hurt Him. With words, He snatched my boy from death, and with words I'll be driving Him toward His own. It's all deeply troubling me.

"Are you alright?" Domitia ventures, sitting up next to me.

"No," I admit, knowing I can't lie to her right now. It's all too much. I don't want to do this. I don't want to be a part of it all. The very thought of it makes my soul ache, but Jesus said this needs to happen. I need to obey.

"What's going on?" she asks, putting her hands on my shoulders and gently massaging them. This is what she used to do back when I returned from war and nightmares of the things I saw would plague me. Her actions do nothing to ease my mind now. The distress has to do with my future, not my past.

"Today I have to arrest the man who healed our boy," I tell

her. She stops what she's doing and faces me.

"Why would you do that?" she raises, upset with my statement. *That makes two of us.*

"Because somebody has to and I told Him I'd do it," I answer. The only thing anybody else knows about Him is that He's a potential revolutionary. If they were to arrest Him, they'd treat Him as such. I won't. I know who He is. I want to keep Him from pain for as long as I can, and the only way I can do that is to arrest Him myself. He didn't seem to care if it was me or not, but I do. I care too much about Him to let it happen any other way.

"Why is he being arrested?" she asks, tilting her head as her frustration falls away and her inquisitive nature takes over.

"Because He made the wrong people angry. He's the one they've been reading about for generations, but they're too caught up in their own thirst for power to accept that," I detail, and she gapes at me. "He's the Savior prophesied about in their scrolls. The only one who can make everybody right," I elaborate. Her eyes dart around as she thinks this over. I get it; it's a lot to take in. We knew He was capable of physical healing because of what He did for Maxian, but we didn't know how far it extended beyond that.

"Has He done that yet?" she finally inquires.

"What?" I prompt.

"Has He made everybody right?" she rephrases. *Has He? Not to my knowledge. I would know if He had. Yeah, I would know.*

"No, He hasn't," I reply.

"Then this won't be the end for Him," she proclaims. No, no it won't. I was so focused on what He was asking me to do that I didn't realize that. He's not finished. I don't know how everything will fall into place, but He still has more to do.

"Thank you, Domitia," I say, leaning over and giving her a hug. She pats my back, then releases me.

"From the moment He healed Maxian, He chose you to be a part of this. Try to focus on that today," she suggests, building me up just as she's done throughout my whole career. This is bigger though. My career means nothing in comparison to aiding Him. She knows that. I can see it in her eyes. She believes in Him too.

"I will," I affirm, and she nods. I take a deep breath, then I get out of bed and start getting ready for the day. Each and every movement feels forced. Putting my armor on. Stepping out of the house. Walking to work. All of it takes a conscious effort as I think about what I'm heading toward.

I have to keep reminding myself that He knows this is coming. This isn't a shock to Him. It wasn't even a shock when I told Him. He's in control now even though it seems like He isn't. I'm doing exactly what He wants me to do. Exactly what He chose me to do.

Once I reach my place of work, I find a man sitting at one of the chairs by my table. I recognize him as one of Jesus' followers. His leg bounces up and down, and he toys with a pouch sitting on his lap. He's about to completely betray the Man he dedicated his life to. It makes me shudder as I head over to my side of the desk. He hides the pouch and rises to his feet when he notices me.

"Praetor, I'm Judas Iscariot. I'm here to lead you to Jesus, son of Joseph," he asserts, his voice wavering. His eyes won't meet mine. I almost ask him why he's doing this. Tell him that it's not too late to go back. But it is too late to go back; the money is already in his possession. He has already betrayed his Savior. The bead of sweat on his forehead despite the breeze outside tells me that he knows that. He won't meet my gaze because he's too ashamed to be seen.

"Let me gather my men, then you'll do as you've told me," I respond, and he furiously nods his head. I go into the other room where a group of soldiers are waiting, including men from the temple guard. They were already informed yesterday of what they'd be doing. "It's time," I tell them, then I turn to Judas. He takes a deep breath, trying and failing to steady himself. He shakes his head, then begins leading us out of the building.

We head down the same path I took yesterday when I went

to see Jesus. After a few miles, the campsite comes into view. Judas bypasses it before we can be spotted, instead opting to go into the wilderness. We follow a trail that leads us to the exact clearing where I spoke to Jesus.

"He's the one in the middle," the follower tells us, pointing to where Jesus is kneeling down. He's praying just as He was yesterday, except this time His body trembles and blood seems to be mixing with sweat, dripping down His face. He knew this was coming, yet He's deeply unsettled. It sends chills throughout me.

"What are you doing back here with them?" Peter demands, quickly approaching me with fury in his eyes. The man who was with him yesterday is nowhere to be seen. Instead, two other followers flank him, both equally as upset about my presence.

"I tried to warn Him," I whisper, so my men don't hear, and Peter scoffs.

"What are you here to do?" one of the other followers asks. My men start to surround the followers to make sure that they know there's no way out of this.

"Leave them alone. You're here for me," Jesus declares, laboriously rising to His feet and turning toward us. He seems as if He's been tortured already even though none of that has begun yet. I want to walk away. I want to make things better for Him. His mother's words come back to me. 'Trust Him.' I do. He has some sort of plan.

"Back off. We're only to arrest that Man," I order, pointing to Jesus. My men back away from the followers, but they stay close behind me as I take steps toward Jesus. Just like this morning, I have to force my feet to move. This is easily the hardest thing I've ever done. I reach for the shackles strapped to my belt, and Jesus nods at me, reassuring me that this is what He wants. I take a deep breath as I step closer to Him.

"You won't take Him!" Peter cries, suddenly advancing toward me. I see the flash of the sun reflecting off of his outstretched knife and duck out of the way. He misses me, but comes into contact with the High Priest's servant who was lingering behind me. He falls to the ground, clutching the side of my head. Blood seeps through his hand, and I spot his ear on the ground next to his leg. My men start to advance on Peter, but the last thing this situation needs is more weapons drawn.

"Don't!" I order, blocking anybody from reaching Peter. My men stare at me unsure of this decision, especially since Peter still has a weapon pointed at me, but they don't move any further. Peter stares at all of them like a wild animal who's been cornered. He steps in front of Jesus and waves his knife around, warning them all away.

"Peter, put the knife down. This is the cup the Father has given me. No force from here or above will keep me from drinking it," Jesus declares, stepping out from behind Peter. Peter stares at Him, slowly bringing his knife down, but not fully convinced by what He's said.

Jesus moves past him and kneels down in front of the High Priest's servant. He picks his ear up off the ground, gently moves his hand away from his head, then presses his ear back where it belongs. The High Priest's servant takes in a huge breath, pain now absent from his features. Jesus removes His hand and the High Priest's servant's ear stays where it is, good as new.

"Who are you?" one of my men lets out, his voice trembling.

"I am the Son of God. I was sent to lay down my life for the good of those who follow me," Jesus states, rising to His feet and holding His arms out to be bound. I take a step closer to Him, the shackles in my hand, then I secure them to Jesus' wrists. He looks me in the eye, then speaks again. "Though I lay my life down, I will take it back up again. This is the plan."

"What plan?" one of my men questions, but Jesus doesn't answer. He's freely heading to His death, but that won't be the end. Just as Domitia said, He has more to do. I don't know how it will all happen, but I wholeheartedly believe it will. He is in control.

"Go," Jesus says, facing Peter. "Tell the others that the time has come."

42 NIEMOS

Today the fraud, Jesus, son of Jospeh, will have to answer for his crimes, and when he can't he'll be sentenced to death. The Sanhedrin, along with a few other Pharisees such as Carian and myself, are gathered within Caiaphas' courtyard where Jesus will attempt to defend himself in front of the High Priest himself. After we undoubtedly find him guilty of falsely claiming to be the Messiah among other blasphemous claims, he'll be sent to Pilate for further judgement and punishment.

Caiaphas is positioned above us all along with his father-in-law, Annas, facing a table where Jesus will sit. Carian is next me, and although people talk all around us, neither of us say a word. We've known about this fraud from his very first false sign. This is different for us.

The buzz of conservation cuts off immediately as Jesus is led in by the Praetor. His expression is unreadable as he takes a seat at the table in front of him. It's gratifying to see him in a compromising position without that stupid smile on his face. We finally got him, and he knows it.

"Izal, you have accused this man of serious crimes against our people's ways. You may now question him in accordance to the law," Caiaphas begins things. Izal nods, then moves to the front of the courtyard, face to face with Jesus. I take a deep breath as I prepare myself for all that's about to come.

"What is it that you're teaching the people?" Izal starts.

"I haven't spoken in secret. Many times, one of your own was present during my teachings as well as many other Jews. You don't need to ask me about my words. Ask those who have heard them; their testimony should be enough for you," Jesus answers. There is not one bit of respect within this man.

A Pharisee close to him jumps up and slaps him before the soldiers nearby have time to react. He continues delivering strike after strike until he's pulled off of him by the Praetor.

"Your claims have caused waves of harm to wash through our people! You will take this seriously!" the Pharisee cries as he's dragged away.

"Leave his punishment to Rome!" Caiaphas proclaims as soon as he's gone. Silence overtakes the room, and all eyes fall on Jesus as everybody apprehensively awaits his response. He touches his hand to his mouth, then pulls it away, examining the blood that transferred onto it. *Surely this will make him take things seriously.*

"If any of the things I have said have been wrong, then state exactly what they were, but if the things that I have said are right, then why do you attack me? Why do you seek to cause me harm? Who am I, and what chord have I struck that you felt the need to go to the Romans to do away with me?" Jesus questions. Of course he would ramp up after that. It's infuriating how little he lets things get to him.

"You know exactly the things you have said, and as to who you are, why don't you tell us?" Izal prompts, and Jesus laughs.

"Even now you act as if you are in control. You ask me leading questions as if you're about to trip me up. Truly I tell you, I've known everything you're going to ask me before I stepped foot into this courtyard. I know you want me to say that I am the Son of God. I know you have been convincing the Romans that means I am some sort of revolutionary. I know you want me to use language when I am before them that will make them fear me just as much as you do so that they'll have just as much of a motive to kill me. And you know what? I'm saying these things of my own volition. I know what that means for me. As I've said repeatedly, I will freely lay down my life, and if you think that's crazy, wait until you see what happens next," Jesus declares.

Conversations immediately break out all throughout the room as people react to everything he's just said, but I can't bring myself to speak. He gave us everything we need to kill him. *This man is either insane, or he is who he says he is. It can't be the latter. No, it can't be. He's insane. That's what this is.*

"Quiet!" Caiaphas orders, banging the ledge in front of him. He has to do it three times to get all the voices to cease their hurried whispers. "What happens next?" he interrogates, staring at Jesus before him.

"Death will not last. You will kill me, but I won't stay dead. I have authority over all things, including death itself," Jesus proclaims, and my veins fill with ice. *I hate that he can cause that reaction in me so easily! He's a liar! His words are just that: words. They will not come to pass!*

Conversations break out again, but this time they won't be quieted as easily. This man has just claimed that death means nothing to him. I've heard him speak many times. He usually leaves some room for interpretation, but he was very clear in what he just said. He truly believes what he's saying, and he won't be able to separate himself from it. He said he's going to rise from the dead. If he doesn't, that's it; everything he's said will be invalidated. But if he does…

"Everything you have said is blasphemous! You will be sent to the Romans to face the full extent of their punishment!" Caiaphas shouts to be heard over all of the noise around us.

"It will play out as I have said," Jesus responds, his voice remarkably even.

"Get him out of here!" Caiaphas orders, disgust in his eyes. The Praetor pulls him up from the table and leads him out of the courtyard with a group of soldiers following closely behind him.

Caiaphas stares at the spot where Jesus had been sitting, his countenance undone as he tries to process everything that just occurred now that the moment is over. He'd never heard Jesus speak before. That man is more than anybody could ever put into words in the most terrifying way possible. He wows crowds. He twists words. He's always so calm, giving the illusion of control. He's the perfect disruptor.

"Niemos," Carian says, waving his hand in front of my face to grab my attention.

"What?" I ask.

"What? Did you not see what I just saw? The man that we discovered turned out to be just as dangerous as we said he was. Do you know what that means for us?" Carian raises. *He's focused on what all of this means for us? A very deranged man was just sent toward his death. My own ambitions are the last thing on my mind.*

"Carian, this is bigger than us," I respond.

"That doesn't mean that we can't use it for our gain. I mean, you were the one who got him to say that he was the Son of God. Even Caiaphas has to acknowledge that none of this would've happened without you," he asserts.

I didn't do this for my own gain. I thought that he was in this for the same reasons I was: to protect our people from being swayed by a false teacher. I feel as if I'm seeing him for the first time, and I don't like it.

"I need to go," I say. I don't give him time to respond. I jump out of my seat and make my way out of the room. I don't even realize where my legs are taking me until someone speaks up.

"You've had your turn," the Praetor states, right in front of me with his soldiers surrounding him. I'm not even sure how to respond because I didn't mean to be in this situation in the first place.

"I would like to speak with him," Jesus announces, his eyes locked on mine. The Praetor looks turns him, confused, but his expression doesn't falter.

"Let's go," the Praetor tells his men, still confused even as the words leave his mouth. They stare at him, bewildered, but they do walk away with him, leaving me standing across from Jesus. His gaze is somehow kind as he looks upon me, his hands in shackles that I helped put him in.

I don't know much right now, but I do know that part of what Carian said was right. This man would not be where he is if it wasn't for me. I know he's made me appear stupid in front of the people multiple times, and I know this is what I wanted not too long ago, but things are starting to feel different now. I didn't do this for me like Carian suggested. I did it for the people. I care about the people, and I care about getting things right. Standing here before him, I'm not fully convinced that I am right. He's a part of the people. I owe him a chance to explain things to me more clearly. I need him to tell me who he is and why he's here before he's sent off to his death because of me.

"Niemos," Jesus grabs my attention. The first time he said my name he was questioning if my heart looked as good as what I portray to the world. This moment is different, but it feels like we've been heading here this whole time. I can't explain it, but everything about this seems to be wrong, starting with the chains on his wrists. "This is what you wanted," he says, holding up his bound wrists.

"Who are you?" I ask, not realizing that those words were going to leave my mouth until they did.

"The Son of God," he answers.

"No," I immediately respond. *Why would he lie right now? It's just the two of us; he can tell me the truth now.*

"Why not?" he raises, his kind eyes inviting to believe in him at last. But I can't put my faith in him. He's not the Son of God.

"Because I would know if you were," I reply. I don't know how, but I know I wouldn't have missed it for this long.

"You will," he states, and it comes out like a promise, sending chills throughout me yet again. *This was a mistake. I don't know what I thought I was going to get from this. I need to leave before any more of his insanity rubs off on me.* I start to walk away, but I stop when he speaks up again. “I see you, Niemos. The Lord sees you. You are loved. You never had to earn that.”

His words cause tears to well up in my eyes. I quickly wipe them away, then run as fast as I can in the opposite direction. I don’t know who he is, but he’s not the Son of God. His words don’t actually mean anything.

43 CATO

Today they brought somebody new into the prison, but it wasn't just anybody; it was the teacher that stopped the stoning. They took him straight to the back room and based on the sounds that came from there, they immediately started torturing him. Not too long after, he was brought out by a high ranking Roman, before being brought right back in. The whole charade repeated itself, but the Roman left by himself the second time.

I've been trying to make sense of it all since it happened. It beats thinking about my upcoming death. It also makes me insanely curious. He locked eyes with me as they dragged him past me. Insanity surrounded his journey through the prison, but he still took the time to do that. It wasn't quite an 'I told you so' look, though it may as well have been considering he did tell me so. I believe 'we will meet again, Cato,' were his exact words, followed ominously by 'the circumstances are up to you.'

He knew I was going to get arrested. He knew he was going to get arrested. Whatever's happening to him behind that door right now is brutal. *Why wouldn't he have dodged this fate if he knew about it?* I know I would've stopped if I knew all of this was going to happen to me. Well, I guess that's not completely true. I had a good idea I'd be arrested, and there was even a moment I was afraid I'd be killed, but that didn't even slow me down. But him? He didn't seem as stupid as me.

Wait, what is he even being arrested for? They said he's a teacher. How does a teacher wind up getting arrested and beaten immediately upon his arrival to the prison? They didn't even treat me that poorly and I was stealing for years. *Could this man have done worse things than me? No way.* He stopped a woman from being stoned. He can't be worse than me, someone who was about to participate in said stoning.

The door to the back room is thrown open, and the teacher is thrown out. Blood covers his body from a plethora of wounds, and a crown of thorns has been shoved onto his head. My throat tightens just glancing at him, I can only imagine how he's feeling right now. The Praetor lifts him to his feet gently, then starts carrying him out of the prison with a few soldiers behind him.

"It's time," the soldier who arrested me says, unhooking my shackles from the wall and leading me out. Another prisoner is unhooked from the wall a few people down from me. I've heard whispers that he frequently attacked merchants in the night and stole everything they had. I understand why he's being crucified, and I understand why I'm being crucified, but why is the teacher being crucified?

"Who is the man they just brought out?" I ask the soldier escorting me. He doesn't say anything at first, but one glance at him tells me it's not because he's refusing to talk to me. "What has he been charged with?" I rephrase.

"Claiming to be a King," the soldier answers. *What? That doesn't seem to line up with what I know of him.* Before I can ask any further questions, we reach the outside of the building where there's three crosses waiting. "You have to carry it," the soldier tells me, pointing to the cross on the right. I wonder what would happen if I say no. I'm not particularly inclined to figure that out, so I do as I was told. The teacher grabs the one in the middle, his already labored breathing becoming worse. The other criminal grabs the last one, then we begin heading to the edge of the city.

I struggle to continually move my feet forward with the weight of the cross on my back. I look over and find that I'm not the only one. The other criminal takes shaky steps, and the teacher keeps stumbling. There are a few times where he falls down and we're ordered to wait for him to get back up. He falls again, but this time he struggles getting to his feet. The Praetor bends down to help him up. By the time they're both back on their feet, one of the soldiers has dragged a man over.

"Who is this?" the Praetor asks.

"My name is S-Simon. I was just passing by on my way h-home to Cyrene," the man responds, fear encompassing all that he is. He trembles, and I can tell this bothers the Praetor.

"He will carry the cross the rest of the way," the soldier who grabbed him decides. While it comes out like a statement, he doesn't move as he waits for the Praetor to speak. The Praetor's gaze moves back and forth between the Teacher and Simon of Cyrene, unsure how he wants to proceed. In the time he's taken to make his decision, the teacher has begun to sink to the ground again. The Praetor sighs, helps him up, then turns back to Simon of Cyrene.

"You will carry the cross. This is not a punishment, nor will it be a fruitless act," the Praetor assures him. Simon of Cyrene nods, terror locking his words away. The soldier releases him, and he picks up the cross, officially joining the procession. "Keep moving," the Praetor orders. The teacher stumbles beside him the whole way to the hill where this is to all go down. Simon of Cyrene drops the cross, and we drop ours on either side of it. The Praetor ushers Simon of Cyrene away, then he turns to his men and nods.

"Lie down," my soldier instructs me, pointing to the cross. I find that my body moves in slow motion as I fulfill his request. My arms spread out over the wood and I shiver as I think about what happens next. I don't want to see it coming. I close my eyes.

Pain races through me as my soldier drives a nail through my right wrist, and I let out a yelp. I hear the other criminal and the teacher let out similar noises as they face the same fate as I do. The second nail in my other wrist is just as bad as the first, and comes with the same chorus of yelps. Just when I think it can't get worse, my feet are forced together and the last nail is driven through both of them, causing the loudest cries.

I open my eyes and watch as a few soldiers haul the cross up using ropes. Somehow the movement causes more pain to rush through me. I close my eyes again, until the apparatus holding me up is completely still, then I open them. A crowd of people is gathered in front of us. I search for Kassia. I know she won't be here, but I figure I should still check. A tinge of disappointment hits me when I don't find her. It's quickly overshadowed by the pain that comes with breathing in my current position. It turns out the Romans don't mess around when it comes to their execution methods.

"Blasphemer!" someone from the crowd shouts, throwing a rock at the teacher. It hits him square in the shoulder, and he winces.

"Where's your power now?" more taunt, and a couple more stones fly in his direction.

"Father, forgive them. They don't know… what they're doing," the teacher lets out, his eyes upward. *Father? Who is this guy?*

"Could not the very same man who healed multitudes save himself from this? If he is the Son of God, it should be easy for him," someone in front of us remarks. *The Son of God!?* He knew exactly who I was without ever having met me. He stopped a stoning with His words. He's apparently healed multitudes. He really is the Son of God. There's no way anyone else could do all of those things.

"Yeah! Save yourself! Isn't that what you're here to do? Be a savior?" someone else jeers. The scrolls call Him a Savior yes, but they never say how that will occur. *Is that what's happening right now? Is He saving humanity by taking their penalty? That goes along with what He was saying to the woman and what He wrote in the dirt.*

"If you are the Son of God… get us all down from here!" the criminal to His left orders. You don't order the Son of God around.

"He is far above us… He won't take orders from you. We've all been condemned to the… same sentence, but He doesn't deserve it. He's blameless, but we couldn't be… further from that," I declare, rebuking the other criminal, and he sneers.

"Do you remember what… I wrote?" the teacher asks, struggling to get the words out.

"You're greater than the law?" I recall.

"Yet you still landed here," the other criminal comments.

"What else?" the teacher follows up. I think back to that moment. There was a second statement. One I didn't believe. He knows what I've done and He's greater than that too. I'm hanging on a cross right now for my transgressions, that really can't apply to me too. "It was for everyone," He insists, somehow knowing exactly what's on my mind.

"I'm a bad man," I tell Him. My own wife couldn't tell me that she loved me when she knew it was going to be our last conversation together. If she couldn't give me that, then how in the world could anyone justify forgiveness for me on that level?

"That doesn't deter me… or my Father," He assures me. I painstakingly turn my head toward Him. His chest heaves, and blood drips down his face from the crown of thorns. I can barely handle the pain of this process and He's dealing with more than I am, yet He's insisting on talking to me right now. *He really does care. He really does mean what He's saying.*

"You are greater… than the things I've done. Remember me… when You reach Your kingdom," I say, the words more important than any other words I've ever uttered. His lips start to curl up as He attempts to smile.

"Truly I say… today you'll join me in the… Kingdom of Heaven," He gets out, somehow conveying joy through the massive amounts of pain. And I feel the joy. I believe him! Once this is over, I'll be with Him and the Lord! It doesn't matter what I did. It doesn't matter what everybody always said about me. It doesn't matter what I always believed about myself. He is greater!

"Thank You!" I exclaim.

"You're both crazy," the other criminal remarks. *What's crazy is that I get to go to Heaven despite my sins! What's crazy is that I've been made right! Me! Of all people! This is hope, isn't it?* It's not an emotion at all and it's not for the weak. Hope is a reaction you can't help but have when you know He's taking care of you. It might not even play out how you imagine it will. He's not going to bring us down from these crosses, but that doesn't matter. He's invited us into His embrace. That's enough. That's far more than enough. I'm a dirty, rotten man, but in His arms, I'm clean. That transcends words.

44 AURAN

My memory of all of the events of today is cloudy. Some moments are vivid, and I know I will never forget them, while others blend together and I don't know if I will ever truly process them.

First, there was the arrest. Peter attacked the High Priest's servant, then Jesus made it as if it had never happened. Though my family has experienced His healing before, it still felt otherworldly to watch Him perform another miracle. A miracle is hard to process even when you already know they're possible. For some of my soldiers, it brought awe, but for others, it brought fear.

Next came the trial. Jesus was, well, Jesus, and that did not make the Pharisees happy in the slightest. I didn't know that they were capable of vicious attacks until I had to drag one of them off of Him. Jesus tends to cause strong reactions within people. Whether those reactions are good or bad seems to depend on the heart of the person.

For Pilate, His words caused alarm. I don't know exactly what he believes Jesus is, but I know he wanted to wash his hands of all of this. He tried to hand Jesus over multiple times, finding no fault in Him after various conversations, but the Pharisees wouldn't allow it. They practically threatened Pilate, telling him that if he didn't sentence Jesus to death for claiming to be a King, then he was no friend of Caesar. While Pilate seemed to respond to Jesus in a way the Pharisees had not, he wasn't willing to risk his career to stop their plot. So, Jesus was sentenced to death. Death by crucifixion. I knew it was coming, but it still made my heart drop.

I just kept telling myself 'trust Him' over and over again. It became the mantra of the day for me. As I watched my soldiers beat Him. *Trust Him.* When He wanted to talk to one of the very Pharisees who got Him into this situation. *Trust Him.* He is God. I am man. *Trust. Him.*

Before it was time to crucify Him, He asked to talk to me. This is one of the events of today that will stick with me forever. I told my soldiers to clear out, and He took a second to catch His breath, then He looked up at me from where He was sitting in little puddles of His own blood on the ground.

"I have to go away for a bit," He started, and I just stared at Him. He was heading toward crucifixion, of course He was going to go away. "I'll be back. On the third day," He continued. He coughed up blood after that statement. Despite that, I still found myself wholeheartedly believing Him. He had said that death has no authority over Him. I guess this is what He meant. *He's going to rise again after three days.*

"I'll be waiting," I had responded. I didn't know what else to say at the time. He tried to laugh, but just wound up coughing up more blood. "I'm sorry," I spilled, and I hid my face from Him. I did this to Him. Not physically, but it was under my orders. I could've tried to make things easier for Him, but instead I let my soldiers torture Him.

"Don't apologize," He immediately told me.

"But I…" I had started.

"Auran, I need you to listen," He interrupted me.

"Yes, Lord," I agreed. He took a few deep breaths, His battered form heaving. His pain was clear, yet He was insistent on speaking to me. I knelt down in front of Him, and He put His shackled hand on my shoulder.

"Take care of my sheep. I know you've grasped that I'll…

be back, but a lot of them haven't. They'll need somebody there for them. I trust you," He professed, His eyes on mine. All day I had been telling myself to trust Him, and there He was saying He trusted me. My answer came immediately.

"Of course, Lord," I assured Him. He let out a sigh of relief. His people mean the world to Him. *That's why He came, isn't it?* He wants to be with His people forever. He spent more time than I can process separated from them, and that tortured Him. Worse than any torture that we inflicted on Him throughout the day. That's why He didn't resist any of this. This was always the plan. He came because of His abundance of love for us, and seeing His blood-covered form in that moment, I saw it clearly.

Eventually the time to crucify Him came. He tried to carry His cross like the others, but His body couldn't handle it, His earthly form already starting to slip away. One of my men found a passerby and he took the cross from Him.

The next parts are where things get fuzzy for me. I know the cross was set down. I know I nailed Jesus to it. I know I was one of the ones to get the cross situated. I was there the entire time. It lasted hours, but I have no recollection of any of it until the last moment. He was weak. Weaker than I'd seen Him all day. He tilted His head up, a strenuous movement for Him.

"It is… finished," He got out, then His head dropped. Right after, the ground began to shake below us. The people in the crowd all started turning to each other, terror in their eyes. They called for His crucifixion. They stood there and mocked Him. They realized He was who He said He was.

A Pharisee stood close to the front, staring at the crown on His head. I didn't recognize him. I don't think he came to the trial earlier that day. I moved closer to him and found tears spilling from his eyes.

"I should've stopped this," he cried, dropping to his knees and bowing his head.

"You couldn't have," I spoke up, startling him. His gaze fell on the Roman symbol on my armor, and he quickly rose to his feet. "I tried to stop it," I revealed, separating myself from my people in his mind. He gaped at me. "He healed my boy. I wanted to repay the favor, but then I realized who He is. He didn't need my unprompted advice, or help. He is God. I am man. This was His plan. I was not going to stop it," I told him. He stared at me a little longer, then he took a deep breath.

"I always believed Him," he admitted, and tears began to spill from his eyes. He put his head in his heads as his cries started to rise in volume.

"He knew," I promised him, and it was as if a load had been lifted off of him. He threw his arms around me, and we stayed like that for a while, both of us reflecting on the weight of the moment.

"Where will His body go?" he finally said, letting go of me and wiping his eyes.

"There's a pit nearby where we dump them," I answered, hating the words as they left my mouth. He doesn't belong in there.

"I have a tomb near here. Let me give Him a proper burial," he requested. My answer was an immediate yes. I even told him I'd help him. I wasn't sure how Pilate would react to it all, but if I'm honest, that wasn't even a factor in my decision.

The Pharisee stayed by my side after that. He waited patiently as we broke the legs of the criminals on either side of Jesus to speed up their deaths and ensure we were able to get Jesus down before the day of rest. I could tell it was a lot for him, but he didn't go anywhere. Jesus is just as important to him as He is to me.

"They're all dead," Deslan reports, coming to my side. He eyes the Pharisee next me. The crowd is long gone by now, so his presence here is odd.

"Bring the two on the ends to the pit. I have other plans for Jesus," I declare.

"There's something different about him, isn't there?" Deslan asks, a seriousness in his gaze that I don't see often.

"Yes," I confirm, not having the capacity to add much to the answer, though it doesn't seem like he needs more. He gazes up at the dead body of humanity's Savior, awe in his eyes. Then he heads over to where the other soldiers are standing and repeats my instructions to them. They split up and get to work getting the two criminals on the ends down. I head to the middle cross where the Man who changed the entire trajectory of not only my life, but of the whole world hangs, lifeless.

I freeze. *He's dead.* I know He's been dead for hours now, but standing under Him right now it suddenly hits me. The Son of God is dead. He said this would happen. I've had so much preparation. *He's dead.* I'm going to pull Him off of this cross as if He's some criminal. His lifeless form will be in my arms. *He's. Dead.*

I fall to my knees before Him. Last time I did this was when I realized who He was. Who He is. He's still the Son of God. Death has no authority over Him. He told me that He'd be back in three days. I'm going to pull Him off of this cross and I'm going to bring Him to the Pharisee's tomb and in three days He'll… I actually don't know how it's going to work. *Will He just get up, air filling His lungs once more? Will He disappear from the tomb, then reappear somewhere else good as new? Does it really matter? He'll be back.* This is far from over.

"I'm waiting," I proclaim, getting back to my feet and looking to Him.

45 MARY

Jesus is dead. I wasn't ready to hear that. James told us that He had been arrested this morning. I couldn't do anything all day. I just stared out the window, waiting for Him to show up and say that they couldn't hold Him, or some other Jesus comment like that, but He never came. Instead, James came back and told us He had been crucified.

Martha had offered to go back to his house with him to help them all process everything, but he said that it was best if we stayed here. He was worried that there would only be more animosity toward us from the Pharisees now that Jesus had been branded a revolutionary. He left shortly after he came, and we were all alone with this new piece of information that seemed to be sucking the air out of the house. *Jesus is dead.*

None of us have really spoken to each other since we heard about it. The weird part is, we've all been in the same room. Just sitting. Staring. Lost for words. Because what can one really say after hearing something like that? *Jesus is dead.*

There's a knock on the door just after nightfall. If it was James, he would've done the special knock we've been using since Laz's resurrection. My heart skips a beat as I think about people on the other side of the door here to harm us. *Haven't they already taken enough?*

"Stay here," Laz orders, getting to his feet.

"Not a chance," Martha remarks, getting up herself and cutting in front of him to get to the door first.

"At least wait," Laz seethes as he runs after her. Well, I don't want to be the only one sitting. I follow them to the door. Martha swings it open, revealing Andrew, Simon, Thomas, and Matthew standing there, the darkness unable to hide their sunken eyes. We stare at them, and they stare at us, nobody really knowing what to say at first.

"Where is everybody else?" Martha finally asks, ushering them into the house, then closing the door. We reach the sitting room before any of them speak. They seem to be in a collective state of shock. I can't say I blame them.

"John and Big James went with their mother to support His mom," Matthew starts, then he trails off, his eyes stuck on a random point on the wall as thoughts drift around his head.

"I haven't seen Peter since the sentencing," Andrew reveals, slight panic in his tone. Simon squeezes his shoulder trying to give him some sort of assurance that I don't think he believes himself.

"Philip, Nathanael, Thaddaeus, and Little James are all hiding. If the Pharisees recognize us, there's a good chance they'll want to hurt us," Simon continues their explanation. He says it so calmly as if we don't all know what the Pharisees are capable of. As if they didn't take someone that we all loved. Jesus has been a staple in my life from the time I was kid. Even during the years we didn't see much of Him, I still felt His presence. I could go find Him if I really wanted and reminisce on the good old days. I can't do that anymore. He's gone.

"And Judas?" Martha inquires. Thomas' gaze drops to his feet, Andrew and Matthew appear as if they forgot how to speak, and Simon takes a deep breath.

"Judas is… Judas is gone," Simon answers. He doesn't elaborate, and he doesn't need to. We all know exactly what 'gone' means.

"Why aren't you all hiding?" Laz changes the subject. All their eyes fall to Andrew. It takes him a few seconds to notice.

"There was something He was working on before... everything," Andrew starts, reaching into his pouch. "He never told any of us what it was or why He was doing it. That wasn't necessarily uncommon for Him, so we all kind of forgot about it. After the arrest, we all left the campsite in a rush, grabbing things, but mainly focusing on getting out of there. We just started going through things. Nobody was really in the mood to talk to each other. His bag wound up with my stuff, and I found it. Seeing it finished, I knew exactly who it was for," he goes on, pulling something wooden out of his pouch.

He holds it out to me. It's a lily carved within a circle. It's so intricate. It must've taken Jesus days to get just right. I take it from Andrew and trace each and every ridge with my finger. I picture Jesus sitting somewhere in the quiet between His teachings and miracles, gently carving into the wood with me on His mind despite what He knew was coming. Tears sting my eyes.

"It's beautiful," I utter, my voice small.

"He always was better at that than I'll ever be," Laz comments, admiring the lily from his spot next to me. Though it was meant to be a joke, his face falls as his mind goes to Jesus.

"He was the Son of our world's literal *Creator*, so don't feel too bad about it," Simon responds, and a smile edges its way onto Laz's face.

"I guess you're right. When we were kids, He used to put so much detail into things. He nearly made His dad cry with how beautiful His works turned out," Laz says, then a thought seems to hit him. "I was referring to Joseph, though I'm sure the Lord Himself was proud too," he adds, and Simon laughs.

"I never imagined the Son of God as a carpenter, but I have to say, He's made us some pretty cool things," Simon shares.

"Like the little fig tree He carved for Nathanael," Andrew brings up.

"Or the fish that He made for the four of you with all of those funny faces," Simon adds, and Andrew laughs.

"Are we really going to pretend that nothing happened?" Thomas challenges, his voice full of emotion. I think this is the first time he's said something the whole time he's been here.

"We're not pretending it didn't happen. We're choosing to focus on the good moments we had with Him," Simon replies, trying to make his words as gentle as possible, but they do nothing to wipe away the tormented look on Thomas' face.

"You say that as if He died of natural causes. He was crucified! He was brutally tortured before that! And all of this-it all happened because Judas gave Him up! Someone who walked among us. Someone that I considered a friend. He turned on the Man we all pledged our lives to, and now they're both dead. There's been so much death lately," Thomas lets out, his eyes falling on Laz, then he shakes his head and drops his gaze. "I almost wish I never answered His call," he admits, his voice shaky.

"Thomas, don't say that," Matthew scolds him.

"Why not? It's true! If I had known there was going to be this much pain and confusion, I wouldn't have followed Him! It's all too much!" Thomas cries, tears streaming down his face. I want to condemn him like Matthew did, but I don't think I can. This *is* all too much. I just got Laz back, and now I've lost Jesus in one of the most brutal ways that exists. If I had known that all of this was going to happen, I can't say that I would've welcomed Jesus back into my life.

"It's a lot, but there's a reason behind it all. You just need to trust Him," Matthew tells him.

"Trust Him? He's gone! What reason could there be for that?" Thomas exclaims.

"He did it for us," Martha speaks up.

"What?" Thomas questions, turning toward her, his expression a mix of anger and confusion. I'm not quite sure I know where she's going with this either.

"He died for all of us. To make us right. That's the whole reason He was here in the first place. He and the Lord both have an inexplicable amount of love for us. They didn't want to spend eternity without us, so Jesus came here to be our sacrificial lamb. It hurts now. I know that. I know that you're trying and failing to make sense of all of it. I just went through that when Laz died, but look: Laz is back. There was a plan for all of that. There's a plan for what's happening now too, and I'm not just saying that to say it. Think about your time with Jesus. He didn't make a single move without a purpose. He knows what He's doing right now. I can promise you that," Martha proclaims.

My eyes drop to the lily in my hand. I think back to when we were kids and Jesus would accompany me to the flower fields because Martha didn't want me going by myself and Laz considered himself too cool to care about pretty things. One day Jesus and I came across a patch of lilies.

"It's beautiful isn't it," He had said, picking one and handing it to me.

"Is it," I responded, taking in all the little details. The way it was shaped. The way the colors blended into each other. The way it smelled. It all seemed perfect.

"Yet it does nothing to look like this. It just exists; the Lord takes care of the rest," He pointed out. I had never thought of that. Thinking back to that moment knowing He was talking about His Father sends chills throughout me, especially considering what He said next. "The Lord loves us all infinitely more than the lilies. How much more will He take care of us?"

The lilies are made perfect without any effort on their own part. The Lord makes them perfect. The things that Martha said are starting to make sense to me. How much more will the Lord take care of us? He wants to make us perfect too so that we can be in Heaven with Him. For the lilies He uses rain and sunlight. For us He's using Jesus. His perfect Son.

"I don't understand it," Thomas mutters, snapping me out of

my thoughts. His head is in his hands and he squeezes his eyes closed as if he's trying to force an explanation to appear in his mind.

"He loves us," I share the part that's most concrete in my mind. I don't understand everything that Martha said, but that part is all I need right now. *He loves me. He gave everything for me, submitting to death even though He's greater than it. That's what matters.* I don't need to understand His full plan as long as I understand that.

"He's gone," Thomas reiterates. He quickly gets to his feet, then leaves before any of us can say anything to him. Matthew gets up to follow him, but Simon holds up his hand.

"Let him go," Simon says, his expression solemn. He knows he can't fix this. I think the only person who could is Jesus, and that's not exactly going to happen right now. "We should all get some rest. It's been a taxing day," Simon suggests.

"You're all welcome to take whatever rooms you want," Martha states, as she stands up.

"Thank you," Simon replies, and she nods. Everybody gets up and starts heading toward the hallway.

"Andrew," I utter, and he stops in his tracks. He turns around to face me, quickly trying to wipe the exhaustion from his face.

"Yes?" he inquires, his eyes on mine. Though he's tired, there's something else in his gaze. The care that Jesus always showed me seems to be reflected on his features. Jesus may not be here physically, but He's still present.

"Thank you for bringing this to me. I know leaving was risky for you guys," I say.

"Jesus' bag wasn't near mine the night before the arrest, yet somehow, I wound up with it. I don't think that was an accident. I think He wanted us to be here," he tells me, a small smile on his face. *Jesus didn't want us to have to deal with this alone. He really did think of everything.*

46 TIRNAN

This last week has been so fulfilling. I've been traveling around nearby cities, telling them all about the Man who made me whole. The reactions have been mixed. Some of the places that I've been aren't Jewish, so they don't have the background that the scrolls provide for the Son of God. Even so, there's still a considerable number of them that wound up believing in what I had to say. It's hard to deny the healing that took place in my life.

Of course there are those that don't believe I was ever injured. That's the hard part about going to those who I don't know. I need to find a convincing way to describe the way my life has changed so that they won't be able to deny. Sometimes my words change depending on the crowd before me, but my message is always the same: our Savior is here, and He's willing and able to change all of our lives if we put our trust in Him.

I look out at the group of people in the market before me. A few people have prayer tassels hanging from their clothes, which tells me that there are at least a few Jews here. Hopefully they're the ones that don't require extra convincing.

"A couple years ago I was jumped," I begin, and people turn towards me. I usually open with that because it's a good way to get people's attention, especially in a market. "I nearly died that night. While I was able to pull through, I was left with lasting damage: a pain in my leg so intense that I could barely walk most days," I continue. Eyes drop to my legs and confusion fills their faces.

"You seem fine," someone close to the front states the obvious.

"I am now. The pain is completely gone, and it wasn't medicine that made this happen; it was a Man. He healed multitudes, not just me. All He had to do was tell me I was better, then I was," I go on.

"Who is this man?" someone interjects. This is my favorite part.

"The Son of God," I reveal, and whispers start to circulate throughout the crowd. I give it a minute before I continue. "He and His Father both care for us all deeply. They want to spend eternity with us. All They ask for from us is our heart. He's capable of life change. I've seen it. I've experienced it. All you have to do is believe," I finish. I get all sorts of looks from the people before me.

"Believe in what?" someone finally speaks up.

"That He is who He says He is and that He has the power to save," I answer. I'm sure there will eventually be more, but for now those are the big things. He is the door. That can't be missed. Some people walk away, annoyed they took the time to listen to me, while others seem to actually be considering what I said. I hope it's more than just a few of them. I scan the faces of the people before me, and someone familiar catches my eye. "Dad?" I utter, heading over to him. I didn't see him before, but now that the crowd has started to disperse, it's clear it's him.

"Son," he returns, taking me in. His eyes stop once they reach my leg and widen. I've found that seeing proof of a miracle tends to have that effect on people. He blinks a few times, then he meets my gaze again. "You look different," he says. This is the first time he's seen me in normal clothes rather than the fancy stuff mom picked out for me.

"I picked these out myself," I tell him, gesturing to my clothes, and he chuckles. I wait for him to say something, but he doesn't. I guess it's up to me to address the big thing being left unsaid between us. "What are you doing here dad? How did you even find me?" I ask. Even Edrik doesn't know where I am right now, and I actually spoke to him before I left.

"Your mom and I were worried when your friend told us that you left. I've been reaching out to old associates in nearby cities asking if they've seen you. I just wanted to know that you were alright. When I heard that your leg was fine, I knew I had to come see it for myself," he reveals.

He's been searching for me? I knew they would worry about me, but I thought it would be more of a performative worry for the sake of showing that they didn't know what I was doing. Their friends aren't the type of people who would support someone leaving a successful business behind. My parents like to keep up appearances. I figured that's all they would be worried about, not my actual safety. I didn't know they cared for me on that level. I didn't know they were capable of care on that level.

"Thank you," I proclaim, my voice full of emotion.

"For what?" he inquires, confused.

"For searching for me. For caring enough to actually come," I respond. He eyes me, surprised that I seem thrown off by this.

"Of course. Your mom and I have always cared for you. I'm sorry if we haven't done the best job showing it," he apologizes. Those words mean more to me than he could ever know. My whole life I thought that the only time they ever cared was when I was doing what they expected of me, but here he is, telling me he cares when I'm in another city dressed as a common man.

I throw my arms around him, surprising him, but he quickly recovers and hugs me back. I can't remember the last time I hugged him. Our whole family isn't really big on physical touch, but it seems this moment would settle for nothing less. He pats my back, then he lets go of me and looks me in the eye.

"Son, you should know something," he states, his tone laced with gloom.

"What is it?" I ask, suddenly worried about my mom.

"The Man you speak of. He was crucified by the Romans yesterday," he tells me. *Crucified? That's one of the most intense forms of death. How did this happen? What wrong could the Romans have found in Him to justify something as extreme as that?*

"What was the charge?" I raise, trying to hold back my reaction until I have all the information.

"They say He claimed to be a King. From what I've heard, the Pharisees brought His claims to their attention and convinced them He was a threat to Caesar," he reports. He studies me, trying to gauge how I'm taking all of this. This is hard to hear, but it's not a complete shock. In fact, I expected this.

"He said He was going to lay down His life. He said that right before He identified Himself as the Son of God. That's what happened here. This doesn't disprove who He is, it only goes to show that He is who He says He is. He has divine knowledge of the future; He is the Son of God," I ramble, trying to make myself sound convincing. He needs to see that this was intentional. He needs to see that the Man I met was the real deal.

"Son, I believe you," he responds, not a hint of doubt in his voice.

"What?" I venture, surprised.

"The last time I saw you, you barely left your couch. Even before the attack, you were never really passionate about anything. It's clear that this Man has made more than just an outward change in you," he asserts.

He's right. I've been a new man since I met the Son of God. My own desires and inclinations have started to decrease, with His taking their place. And I couldn't be more thrilled about that. I want nothing more than to spread the good news about Him and all He's done for me and all He will do for us all.

"You're really alright with what I'm doing?" I ask. This doesn't exactly line up with the family image.

"Am I thrilled that my son is going around announcing the

majesty of a Man who was just crucified for being a threat to Caesar? No, it obviously scares me, but I can see this is what you need to be doing, so I'm not going to stop you," he answers. *Is he being sincere right now or is this some sort of trick?*

"You're not upset about me leaving the business?" I check.

"I wish I had had the courage to leave the business at your age," he drops.

"Really?" I react, and he laughs.

"I wanted to own a field. Contribute resources that the people really needed. Instead, I followed in my father's footsteps and got comfortable with the wealth, so I pushed the same path on you. I couldn't be prouder of you for being the one to break the cycle," he tells me, giving my shoulder a squeeze.

"Does mom feel the same?" I ask. She's always seemed to equate wealth with worth.

"She's a little confused. You did go without saying anything," he reminds me. I did do that… I don't regret that choice because I know I probably would've backed out of everything if I had gone to them first, but I should probably try to make things up to her.

"Maybe I should come visit for a few days. Explain everything to her myself," I offer.

"She would love that," he responds, warmth in his expression. It seems she's not the only one.

47 AURAN

I found most of Jesus' followers soon after I left His tomb. They were wary of me at first, which I guess is fair, but eventually they warmed up to me. I brought them more supplies so they won't have to leave before Jesus comes back, and I stayed with them a little while to help them process things. There was maybe one or two of them who seemed to know that He was even coming back. I would've stayed with them longer to try and explain things further to them, but one of them was worried because his brother was missing, so I set off to go search for him.

The missing follower isn't just one of the twelve: it's Peter. Given what I know about him, finding him is of the utmost importance. The look in his eye when he attacked the High Priest's servant flashes in my mind and chills go through me. If that rage is still within him, he could be out there getting himself into serious trouble.

I walk through the whole city as the day goes on to no avail. Either he's on the move, holed away somewhere, or outside of the city. I don't know which option scares me the most. I just need to find him. I promised Jesus I'd take care of His sheep, and I can't let Him down.

Suddenly, jeers start to sound from a tavern near me. *Oh no.*

I would rather him be out of the city than down there in the midst of whatever's going on, but something tells me that's not the case. He left without so much as a goodbye for his brother. I know a thing or two about staying quiet. It's what you do when the thoughts in your head can't be formed into anything productive no matter how hard you try.

I run down the stairs right behind Ren, who also happened to be nearby, and my heart sinks as I take in the scene before me. Peter is on the ground trading punches with a guy twice his size. He appears remarkably unharmed considering the size mismatch, but he does have a large gash near his eyebrow that's causing blood to drip over his eye. Unsurprisingly, he keeps getting hit on that side because of the hindrance to his vision.

"Break it up!" I order, but neither of them ceases what they're doing. "Ren, get the big guy," I tell him.

"Yes, Dominus," Ren responds. I insert myself into the situation, grabbing Peter and pulling him away while Ren does the same with the other guy.

"You got lucky!" Peter shouts as I drag him up the stairs and out of the building. He doesn't turn to face me until we've reached the top. "You. You arrested Him," he places me. He twists around in my arms, increasing his efforts to escape my grip to no avail.

"I was going to sneak Him out of the city, but He said it had to happen this way," I tell him, and he stops struggling as he thinks this over. I bring him down a nearby side street that appears to be empty. After deciding that he seems too caught up in what I've said to try and run away, I let him go.

"Why? I don't understand it all," he says, putting his head in his hands and leaning against the wall behind him. Jesus said that a lot of them never grasped it. *Do I tell him what He told me? Would he even listen to me right now?*

"I know it's all very hard to understand, but He does have a plan with all of this. He made it sound like He told you all about it," I prompt, trying to jog his memory, though I'm not sure how helpful that's going to be. I'm pretty sure he's drunk right now.

"You want to know what He told me? He said that I would deny Him. Three times. I told Him that that was preposterous. I love Him. I would never do that," he trails off, sliding down the wall behind him until he's on the ground. "When it came down to it, I guess He knew me better than I know myself. Three times I was asked if I was one of His followers, and all three times I said no. I let my own self-preservation stop me from declaring that He's Lord," he goes on, tears starting to well up in his eyes. I lower myself to the ground next to him and put my hand on his shoulder as he cries.

"You messed up, Peter, but that doesn't mean He or the Lord love you any less. He knew exactly what you were going to do, yet He didn't shun you, and He never will no matter what you do," I console him. He wipes his eyes and turns to me.

"I don't deserve His love. I don't even know why He called me in the first place. I was a mess then, and I'm no less of a mess now. You of all people should know that given what you've seen me do," he reminds me. Ah yes, his attack at the arrest. I can't deny that made things messier, but it's not like it ended poorly.

"Everyone walked away unharmed," I point out, and he gapes at me.

"Are you really downplaying my actions? I physically attacked someone during a time I should've been listening to His words. Not to mention that you were in the middle of making an arrest. I should've walked away in shackles with Him," he points out. He definitely should've, but given that there was technically no damage, I didn't see any reason to do that.

"You did attack someone, and it was fairly disruptive, but it gave Him a chance to show His majesty in front of my soldiers. I'm pretty sure some of them believe in Him now because of that," I reveal, and he cocks his head.

"Really?" he murmurs.

"Yeah," I confirm. I didn't get the chance to talk to them

about it, and I'm not sure they would admit it given the danger that comes with associating with Him at the moment, but there were definitely a few of them that were being respectful to Him throughout the day despite what He was being charged with. Thinking back on it all from this lens, I actually think it was a good thing it happened. They wouldn't know Him if it hadn't. "I think I know why He chose you," I say.

"Why?" he questions, facing me with desperation in his eyes.

"You are a mess, but that gives Him a chance to shine through you. If you were perfect, then His impact wouldn't really stand out as much, would it? You screw up or fall short and He makes things work despite that, and in doing so people get the chance to see His glory," I explain, figuring it all out as the words leave my mouth.

Peter may get himself into bad situations, but He can turn any bad situation into something beautiful. He did it when He healed Maxian. Our family has never been happier than we are now and it's all because of what He brought us out of. He's doing it again now with His death. The Pharisees want to show that they still have power and the people still need them, but that's all going to be thrown out the window when He comes back. He's making the people right and simultaneously showing them His power.

"I know this is all painful, Peter, but He's going to use it for good. That's who He is," I assert. He sniffles a few times, staring out at the wall ahead of us. His brows knit as he thinks through everything I've said.

"Who He is," he says, processing the words as they come out. "Who He is," he repeats, this time with more confidence. That's not what I thought he was thinking about, but I guess I'll go with it. "He's alive. He never died!" he exclaims.

"Not quite. He is dead, but He won't be for long. Death cannot hold Him," I declare, and he gapes at me. He may be too drunk for this right now. It's hard enough to grasp sober. "Is there somewhere I can bring you?" I ask him. I don't want to bring him to the others in this state. They've been through enough.

"Yeah," he answers, getting to his feet with his mind elsewhere. He starts walking away, so I jump up and follow him. He walks through the city somewhat aimlessly. *Should I really be trusting his sense of direction right now? Maybe I should just bring him home with me. Domitia can probably clean up his cut.*

He stops at a door, then proceeds to knock on it, getting blood on it. Whether it belongs to him or the guy he was fighting, I have no idea. The door opens, revealing a woman somewhere around Peter's age. She takes in the two of us, confusion on her face.

"Andrew, can you come here?" she requests. *Andrew? Isn't that...*

"Peter!" Andrew exclaims, running toward us as soon as he spots his brother. He throws him into a fierce hug, and Peter winces. Andrew quickly releases him and takes his current state in, worry in his eyes. "What happened to you?" he questions, and tears well up in Peter's eyes again.

"I denied Him just like He said I would," Peter details, shame in his tone. Andrew sighs and puts his arm around him, leading him inside.

"You're only human, Peter," Andrew tells him as they walk away. The woman who answered the door stares at me. I should probably introduce myself.

"I'm Auran. Jesus healed my boy. He uh-He told me to look after everybody while He's away," I try to explain how I wound up with Peter in a succinct way. She raises an eyebrow at the last part, but unlike Peter it seems like she actually knows what I'm talking about.

"Thank you for following through on that," she says. She seems to be deciding whether to let me in or not. As much as I would love to meet more people that He cares for, I should probably get home. Domitia's worried about me because of how involved I've been in everything that's going on.

"Of course. Will you be able to patch him up?" I venture.

"My sister has experience in that area given the fact that our brother is both a carpenter and a blunderer," she assures me.

"Alright. I have to head home. If you need anything, please don't hesitate to send for me. I may wear this symbol on my chest, but my loyalty is with Him and those He cares for," I tell her, and she smiles.

"He'll be grateful for all you're doing," she affirms.

48 NIEMOS

Jesus has been dead for three days. For whatever reason, he was put in Joseph of Arimathea's tomb near the site of the crucifixion. Nobody has seen Joseph since we found out, but there's been lots of whispers going around about him. Some people are suggesting that he's been an inside man for Jesus this whole time, warning him every time we developed a plan against him. I have a hard time believing that. Jesus seemed to pick and choose when and where he showed himself. It didn't seem to have anything to do with what strategy we were pursuing at the moment.

Now that Jesus has an official resting place, the Romans have stuck soldiers near it at the request of Caiaphas. In his request, he cited Jesus' claims that death does not have authority over him. Caiaphas said that Jesus' followers may try to steal his body to make it seem as if the things he said are true. The Romans seemed to agree that wouldn't be a good look, so they fulfilled the request.

I thought the people would start to come back to the temple like they had before now that all of this is behind us, but even after three days we haven't seen many of them. Just a handful, and all of them have wanted to know about the scrolls surrounding the Son of God, not about the scrolls that teach them the proper way to live. It's discouraging seeing how much Jesus was able to change things around here. He destroyed the very system he claimed to have created.

I'm sitting at my table, going over some of the earlier scrolls, when two soldiers come running into the temple. *Why are they here? They have no business inside our sacred places.* All of the agreements that were put in place between us and the Romans seem to have been relaxed now, and I don't like it.

"You're not supposed to be in here!" I proclaim, but the soldiers don't slow down. They run all the way through the temple and into Izal's quarters. This can't be good. I chase after them and enter just in time to hear them start throwing out panicked words.

"There was a man!" the first lets out.

"There was a man where?" Izal questions, annoyed. There's too much fear within the first soldier to even attempt any more words. *What would make a soldier who's been in the midst of battle this terrified?*

"At the tomb! The man was at the tomb!" the second exclaims, his horror matching that of the first.

"Shut the door," Izal orders, his eyes on me, and I do as he says. He stares at the trembling Roman soldiers before him, thinking carefully about his next words. "What did this man look like?" he finally asks.

"Like lightning!" the first declares, putting his head in his hands as the image comes back to him. *What does that even mean? How could a person look like lightning? They had to have been hallucinating.*

"And his clothes were white as snow despite the fact that he was sitting on top of the stone!" the second adds, and shivers go throughout him at the memory. *Could they have both been hallucinating the same man? Is that a thing?*

"What stone?" Izal prompts, trying to make sense of all they're saying. I'm not sure there's much sense to it at all.

"The stone in front of the tomb! He rolled it away as if it weighed nothing, then he sat on it!" the second clarifies, starting to breathe heavily.

"Did he take the body?" Izal questions. *He thinks this is real? A man like lightning who rolled a stone away?*

"We didn't see him do it," the first answers quietly.

"Is the body still there?" Izal interrogates.

"No," the first admits, his head low. The fraud's body is gone? How is that possible? The stone in front of the tomb would've taken at least three men to move, and even then, they wouldn't have been able to do it quickly. There's no way the Roman soldiers could've missed something like that.

"Did the man you saw come close to you in any way?" Izal inquires. *Where is he going with this?*

"No. He just-he appeared out of nowhere. He was definitely not a normal man. I-I need you to explain this to me," the first gets out.

"Why would he be able to explain this to you? He wasn't with you when it happened," I argue. The soldier turns to me, his chest rapidly rising and falling. The terror in his eyes is the purest I've ever seen. Whatever this soldier saw, he truly believes it was real. *Can hallucinations cause a reaction this strong?*

"Because this man was otherworldly. He has to be in the pages of your scrolls," the first declares. *In the pages of our scrolls? Is he serious? He thinks he came across something divine? That's not possible. Nothing divine would dare associate with a fraud like Jesus.*

"I need you both to listen to me," Izal starts, and the first turns back toward him. "You're going to tell the people that the followers of Jesus came by and stole his body. You won't tell anybody the things you just told me, especially not your Praetor. Are we clear?" he finishes, pulling out a purse full of coins and tossing it onto the table. *Is he bribing them? Why is that necessary? He doesn't think they're telling the truth, does he? They can't be. The things they spoke of-they don't make sense.*

"I don't want your money. I want-I need to understand what I saw. Normal men are not like the man we saw, nor do they move stones that big on their own," the first insists, shaking his head. *He's denying the money? If my knowledge on Roman wages is correct, Izal is offering them each more than they would make in multiple months. Who turns that down?*

"You're going to take the money and do as I've said, or I'm going to go straight to Pilate himself and tell him that you let the followers of a revolutionary steal his body. If he happens to hear about this on his own, I can speak on your behalf if you make the right choice," Izal threatens them. *Since when do we as Pharisees threaten people? Nothing about any of this seems right.*

The soldiers stare at Izal as they consider his words. *Do they really believe in what they saw enough to test him?* If Pilate is told that they let the followers of a revolutionary steal his body, he'll kill them. There's no question about it. The Romans are a violent people when it comes to punishment. Look at what they did to Jesus.

Finally, the first soldier steps forward and grabs the pouch off of the table. He thumbs the coins within, getting a relative count of them, then he tucks the pouch away within a pouch under his armor. He and the other soldier move toward the door, but he stops short of it. Izal is glaring at him before he even turns to face him.

"The man we saw was not of this world. You won't be able to keep what happened quiet for long," the first soldier warns. Despite the fact that his words come out calmer now, the fear that occupied his eyes from the moment he entered has not dwindled one bit.

"You better hope I can," Izal remarks. His general attitude right now is reminiscent of what it was like when he broke the miraculous sign over his knee. The soldier shakes his head, then leaves the room, but his words stick with me. Not just what he said, but the way he said it. I've seen men claim to have had a divine experience before; none of them were as convinced that it had happened as those soldiers, and the soldiers aren't even Jewish.

"Why did you go to those extremes with them?" I ask, turning to Izal. His eyes drop to the table in front of him. *Why is he avoiding answering this? Does he believe that what they saw was actually divine?* "What do you think happened at the tomb?" I urge.

"I know the followers of Jesus took his body," he quickly answers, his gaze meeting mine. I can't tell if he believes what he just said or not. "The Romans are a people easily swayed. The followers took advantage of this. They pulled some stunt to get the body so they can try and convince the people something divine happened in order to continue spreading his blasphemous teachings," he goes on, trying to sound more convincing.

"You really think they would do that? That they would be able to?" I ask. Sure, there were twelve of them, but that's not the case anymore. The one who gave him up is dead now, and the rest of them haven't been seen since the arrest to my knowledge. Besides that, none of them seemed capable of taking down trained guards. The most they seemed prepared for was crowd control.

"You haven't fallen for their tricks too, have you Niemos?" Izal challenges, his eyebrows raised. *No, that's not what I'm questioning right now. What am I questioning right now? Maybe I'm overthinking all of this. Reading into things that aren't there.* "Niemos?" he prompts, a threatening air in his voice.

"No, of course not," I respond at last.

"Good. I need you to keep quiet about the things you heard here today. You understand why, right?" he asks. His tone makes it clear what my answer should be.

"Yes, I do," I reply right away. I need him to know that I don't actually believe any of this. The small doubts swirling my head are stupid and I will push them out. Jesus was a fraud. His followers must've taken his body just like Izal is saying.

"Great. Now please go back to your duties for the day. We need to get the people back on track after everything that's happened," he asserts.

"Yes, Izal," I say. I am a Pharisee. It's my job to set the people straight. Maybe in the process I'll manage to set myself straight, too.

49 AURAN

It's the third day. I don't know what to expect, but I know the tomb will be empty. Anticipation fills me as I get ready for the day. I wonder when I'll see Him. *Will He come to me, or will I have to find Him? Will I see Him at all? He didn't say that I would. He just said that He'd be back.*

I try to gather my thoughts as I head into work. I still need to show up and act relatively normally. As far as the people around me are concerned, today is just a regular day. Nothing divine is on the schedule. That would be silly.

"The body is gone," Deslan announces as soon as I'm within earshot of him. I pull him to the side so that our conversation can be somewhat private.

"As of when?" I ask.

"This morning. The soldiers who were on duty are saying that His followers took Him, but I saw them run into the temple trembling before they came out and started spreading that story, so I don't think it's true" he answers. The Pharisees know what happened. They're trying to keep it quiet. If I were them and I knew I'd sent the Son of God to His death, I'd be trembling. Not that Jesus would do anything to them, but they don't know that.

"I don't think it's true either," I agree. Even if I didn't know that He was coming back today, I still wouldn't think it's true. His followers are a wreck right now; they wouldn't be able to pull something like that. Most of them are still too terrified to leave the house they're holed up in, and the ones that have left haven't done it often.

"He's alive, isn't He?" he asks, all he is poured into that question. Deslan has never personally interacted with Him, yet he's managed to pick up on this. I'm impressed with him. Jesus' own followers have been struggling with that type of faith these past couple days. I don't know if I'm supposed to spread the news that Jesus came back quite yet, but I know He would approve of me rewarding Deslan's faith right now.

"He is," I confirm, and his eyes widen.

"Do you know where He is?" he urges, childlike wonder radiating off of him.

"No, I haven't seen Him yet," I report, a small chuckle escaping me as the joy of the moment takes me over.

"Well get on that," he immediately follows up, starting to usher me out of the building. "I'll cover for you," he adds, pushing me out the door, then heading back inside, a pep in his step. I guess I'm going to find Jesus now. He probably won't be out in the open right away, but it doesn't hurt to check.

I head to the market and begin scanning the faces before me. *Will he look the same? The body is out of the tomb, so He must have the same one.* That sounded weird, but I don't know how else to phrase it. All of this is dealing with concepts that transcend human understanding. I continue peering around, and I spot a familiar face in line at a booth with various fruits.

"Mary?" I prompt, walking up to her. She turns to me, too much joy on her face for someone who just lost her Son. *He really is back. She's seen Him.* I knew this would all happen, but proof like this causes wonder to shoot out in my mind like streamers. *He actually did it. He actually rose from the dead.* "Can I see Him?" I ask.

"I'm sure He'd like that," she responds, a smile on her face.

It doesn't matter to her the role that I just played in everything. Jesus cares for me. That makes me a part of the family. "I have a few more things left to buy, then I'll bring you to Him," she says.

"Thank you," I reply, and she nods. She grabs some figs, then starts to reach into her pouch for coins. "Are those for Him?" I ask.

"Yes, they're His favorite," she answers.

"Let me," I tell her, pulling out coins of my own and dropping them on the table. The merchant seems confused to see me do this, but he doesn't say anything.

"I didn't know what to think about you at first," Mary raises as we move on to another booth. That's fair. I'm a soldier who's not even of her people.

"And now?" I venture.

"Now I'm glad that my Son chose you, and not just because of the figs," she presents, sending me a small smile. Her approval means more to me than I could've imagined it would. This woman raised the Son of God, and she thinks that I'm a good person to have around. Honestly, that's a higher compliment coming from her than it would be if it had come from Caesar.

"Thank you," I respond.

"Thank you for doing what you could to take care of Him. I know you did things that put you in danger all for His sake. That is not lost on me, nor is it lost on Him," she promises me. *That's how she sees things?* I've been trying to get images of the things that were done to Him under my authority out of my head this whole time, yet none of that seems to matter to her. All she sees is what I did for Him.

And that's all He sees. Not the man who ordered His torture, but the man who looked after His followers. It seems that I haven't just been made right by Him, but that I've also been made better. In serving Him, my actions are becoming those of a righteous man. I won't be perfect like Him, but I'll be a better reflection of Him. Here in this moment, I know that that's better than anything I've ever strived for.

Mary picks out a few more things that I wind up paying for, then we start walking to her house, everything that she bought in my arms. I'm not going to watch the mother of my Savior carry things when I'm right there, willing and able. When we reach the house, she opens the door, and we're immediately met with some sort of conversation between Jesus and His brother.

"I don't think it's ridiculous to ask for You to warn us next time a death won't be permanent," His brother asserts, holding his hands out as if he's just proved a point. Jesus stares at him, an eyebrow raised.

"I warned you several times over the span of all of my teachings," Jesus points out, and His brother shakes his head.

"Only You could manage to annoy me hours after rising from the dead," His brother comments, and Mary sighs.

"Boys, we have company," Mary announces, gesturing to me. I put everything in my arms down on a nearby counter, then I face them.

"Auran," Jesus greets me, the same warmth in His eyes that was there when I met with Him in the clearing despite all that's happened between now and then. I'm sure I don't even know the half of it.

What has He been going through this whole time? Scars cover His body from where we tortured Him. How are the wounds scarred already? They were inflicted days ago. Has more time somehow passed for Him? How would that even work? And where was He? I know His body was in the tomb because I put it there, but where was He actually?

"Do you two mind leaving us?" Jesus requests, facing His mother and His brother. Mary nods, and pulls His brother away with her. Jesus waits until the door closes, then He turns to me. "You have questions," He says. As always, there's no impatience in His tone. He's ready to meet me exactly where I'm at.

I don't even fully know how I'm feeling at the moment. I'm

confused, that's for sure, but do any of the questions that have been bouncing around my brain really matter? I don't need to know how it all worked. My Savior is right here before me, just having come back from making me right. Trying to understand it all can wait.

"Thank You!" I exclaim, hugging Him. He quickly reciprocates, patting my armor-clad back. It's so surreal to be hugging Him right now. The last time I saw Him was when I was laying His battered body in a tomb, and now here He is, breathing.

"You did well, Auran," He tells me.

"How do You know?" I ask, letting go of Him. He raises His eyebrows at me. Fair. I don't know why I even bothered questioning it. "I feel like I could've done better with Peter," I say, thinking back to the situation I found him in the other night.

"Peter is a tough one to watch over," He admits, his eyes veering to the side as He thinks about him. "He cares so deeply. He's always the first person to ask for clarification because he wants to understand the things I say. He likes to know where I am at all times so that he can be there if I need something. He has the most blind faith out of any of them. He just needs to work a bit more on getting out of his own way," He explains. I can see that. He doesn't always seem to fully think through his actions. I've seen proof of that.

"Why did You tell him that he was going to deny You?" I ask Him. That's what made him so upset with himself.

"I wanted him to know that I knew what he was going to do, but it wasn't going to make me love him any less," He explains.

"He didn't really get that," I point out, and He laughs.

"He got more of it than it seems," He replies. I didn't really see that, but I guess He would know better. "Auran, are you ready to hear something difficult?" He raises. *What? Does it get more difficult than what we just experienced?* "We don't have to get into it now if you're not ready. We can sit here as long as you want," He adds.

Am I ready? I have no idea what He's about to say right now. He's giving me a warning. He's never really done that before. I mean, He did tell me about the whole three days thing, but that wasn't like this. *Can I handle what He has for me right now?* I turn toward Him. His eyes meet mine with unwavering support. I don't know if I can handle whatever He has to say on my own, but I'm not on my own; whatever it is I can handle it with Him.

"What is it?" I prompt, and He smiles before He speaks up.

"I'll be going away again," He begins.

"They're not going to kill You again, are they?" I immediately venture, my heartbeat rapidly picking up.

"No, I'm done with death," He laughs, and I let out a deep breath. "I'm going back up to Heaven to be with the Father again now that I've accomplished what I was sent here to do," He reveals, a melancholy expression overtaking his features. *What about that makes Him sad?* "This world was never my home, but it was nice to be among my people, interacting with you every day. I'm going to miss being able to hug Andrew when he's feeling down and the deep conversations I would have with Matthew late at night and my mother's cooking-oh I'm really going to miss that," He says, and I laugh. "Anyway, I was going to tell you something, wasn't I?" he remembers.

"Yes, something difficult if I remember correctly," I respond, and He nods.

"Well, we actually already got to the difficult part. The other part has to do with you. I have a very important role for you," He introduces.

"Whatever You need, consider it done," I respond, and He smiles.

"I need you to keep looking after my sheep. They're all going to face many trials as they spread the good news about me, and I need you to do everything you can to keep them safe. It's not going to be easy as you already know, but your heart for people makes you perfect for it," He details. It still baffles me that He trusts me this much.

"It would be my honor, Lord," I instantly agree. Confidence

fills me not because I think I can do all He's asking of me, but because He does, and His judgment far surpasses my own.

50 NIEMOS

"What can I help you with?" I inquire as a man takes a seat at the table across from me. I'm grateful for his presence. I need to get back into doing something familiar.

"What do the scrolls say about the Son of God?" the man before me asks. I can't deal with this right now. The report of the soldiers caused questions to swirl in me that I shouldn't be having as a Pharisee. I need to re-root myself in the facts of the scrolls. All of the rules and procedures that have kept me going all these years. Those are what I need right now.

"We're not here to go down that rabbit hole. Do you have any questions about the everyday requirements of our people?" I pose, and he shakes his head, frustrated.

"I know everything the scrolls have to say about the shall and shall nots. You Pharisees love to talk about that constantly. I want to know more about the man that was just put to death," he spells out.

"That man was not the Son of God," I immediately deny.

"How am I supposed to know that if I don't know what the scrolls have to say about Him?" he questions. He does somewhat have a point there. Maybe reading those scrolls will help me convince myself that I'm being ridiculous and there's nothing weird going on here because the arrival of the Son of God is still a long way off.

"Fine, let's go through the scrolls about Him together," I agree, sifting through the many scrolls on the table until I find the one that I'm searching for. "The Son of God has come to break every chain…" I begin.

"I've already heard that part. It's all anybody seems to know about Him. I want you to tell me what the scrolls say about the circumstances of His arrival, or the circumstances of His departure," the man clarifies. *The circumstances of His departure? He just wants to try to link this to Jesus in any way he can.* I should not have entertained this.

"I'm sorry but…" I start, but I'm cut off.

"He's alive! The Son of God is alive!" a man yells as he runs through the temple. *No. This man doesn't know what he's talking about. The Son of God is dead. No. The Son of God isn't here yet. The fraud we crucified is dead. Jesus is not the Son of God.* I'll make sure this man gets that so he doesn't keep spreading these dangerous rumors. I get up, leaving the man in front of me and head over to the man who's hollering.

"The Son of God hasn't come," I tell him, but that seems to have no effect on him.

"I don't know what the holdup is for you Pharisees! A Man shows up performing miracles and you put Him to death for it, only to kick off the greatest miracle He's ever performed. The tomb is empty!" the man declares.

"The tomb is empty because his followers stole his body," I reason, and the man shakes his head, a smile on his face.

"Then how was he spotted on the streets by multiple people?" the man challenges. *He was what? No. There has to be some sort of mistake here. He wasn't spotted. He couldn't have been spotted. He's dead.*

"It was just somebody who looks like him," I come up with. Perhaps it was his brother. From what I've heard, Joseph had multiple sons. That has to be what's going on here.

"It was Him. They saw the scars on His wrists from where He was nailed to the cross, and the scars on His head from the crown of thorns. He is the Son of God. No amount of denying that fact will make it untrue," the man states. *That's impossible. These people must be mistaken. I need to talk to them.*

"The people who say they saw him; where are they?" I press.

"Out spreading the good news," the man answers as if it was obvious. He wholeheartedly believes that what they told him truly is good news, not blasphemy. I need to get to the bottom of this before more damage is done.

I run out of the temple. I'm not sure where I'm going, just that I need to find these people. There are lots of people around me smiling and whispering. While they're probably talking about what the man came into the temple shouting, they're not the ones who spotted Jesus. I push past them and move along, forcing myself to focus on my goal even though I want to stop and correct them.

"The Son of God is alive!" I hear a woman shout from not too far in the distance. That really didn't take long. *How many people are out there?* I run toward where the shout came from. "The Son of God is alive!" the woman repeats. I can see her now. I recognize her, but I don't know why.

"Have you seen Jesus, son of Joseph?" I call out, running up to her. She turns to me and points at me, recognition in her eyes.

"You. Don't tell me you still see Him as a problem?" she prompts, thoroughly confused by my insistence on seeing him as anything other what she thinks he is.

"Who are you?" I interrogate, still unable to put my finger on where I know her from.

"You won't know me by who I am, but rather by what He did for me. I was sick, and He brought life back to me. Now He's brought Himself back from even further!" she shouts, excitement flowing out of her. She was the one that he healed when I tried to trip him up. No wonder she believes in this delusion. People nearby are paying close attention to her each and every word, and I know I need to shut this down.

"Have you seen Jesus since he was killed, or not?" I bring her back to my original question.

"I did not see Him myself, but I heard He was spotted and I have no reason to doubt that that's true. When He healed me, I could feel all that He was radiating through His touch. Death is no match for that," she declares. People start coming closer to her to ask for more details. *No! That's not how this was supposed to go! I need to find whoever it is that actually claimed to have spotted Jesus quickly.*

I leave her and run further away, trying to get her words out of my head as I go. Whatever she felt must've been some side effect of whatever he was using to perform his false signs. He does not actually have power over death. No man does. I just need to find whoever started this rumor, then I can prove that. I can prove he isn't the Son of God.

"The Son of God is alive!" another shout reaches my ears. I find its source just in time to hear the next declaration. "I've seen Him with my own eyes! They nailed Him to a cross, but that did nothing! He is victorious!"

"How do you know it was the man who was crucified?" I challenge, shoving through the people gathered around the man.

"Well, first off, I would recognize the Man who granted me sight anywhere," the man begins. So, he's another person caught up in false signs. Before I can point that out, he continues. "Secondly, I saw the holes in His wrists where the nails were driven through. Scars like that don't come from anything else. Whether you want to believe that He's the Son of God or not, you can't deny that He was crucified."

No. This can't be right. He has to be mistaken. I mean, he said he was blind, right? Maybe there's still something wrong with his vision? Maybe there was something else on this person's wrists and he just thought they were scars. That has to be it. Crucifixion is not something that people come back from.

"Maybe not, but I can deny that you saw what you think you saw. You were blind after all," I raise, and he gapes at me.

"I *was* blind. He has made me new. He was dead. Now He's not. I believe you Pharisees are the ones who had Him killed. Is that why you're so desperate to deny this? Are you afraid of what He'll do to you for your role in it now that He's back?" the man prompts.

His words hit me like a ton of bricks. Not because I'm afraid, but because if he's right and Jesus is back, then I know exactly what he'll do to me: nothing. He told me that I'm loved and that I don't have to earn it. If this is all real, then I just took part in killing the most innocent man in existence.

51 TIRNAN

"So, He just told you that you were healed, and then you were?" Edrik restates after I finish telling him the story of my first interaction with the Son of God. I decided to come visit him while I was here because I wanted to tell him everything about how my life changed. He's a lot more accepting than Jahre, Ruriel, and all the people I've come across while spreading the good news. I honestly think seeing me was all he needed to believe that the Son of God was upon us.

"Yeah," I confirm, flexing my leg as proof that the pain is gone. His jaw drops as he watches the movement. He took care of me for a long time. He knows just how bad things were. *Then came Jesus.* His eyes find mine again.

"He's dead now, but you don't seem to think that's the end," he observes. There are definitely big thoughts swirling around in his head. I hope they're the ones I think they are. I hope he can see Jesus' majesty as clearly as I can.

"He said He would lay down His life and that He would take it back up again. He's already done the first part, the second is coming," I lay out. I've never been more sure of anything in my life. His death was some sort of stepping stone. The logistics of it all aren't something I have right now, but I know they're coming. I know His biggest miracle is on the horizon.

"They say He brought Lazarus back from the dead shortly before His own death," he tells me, looking off to the side.

"Lazarus died?" I follow up, my eyes widening in shock.

"A sudden illness took him out. The whole community mourned him, but then four days later he was back. I haven't seen him, but I've heard people are still ordering things from him, so I don't doubt that he's back," he explains. So, Jesus really can raise the dead. Of course He can. He's practically the living embodiment of life.

"Death will not hold Him," I declare.

"I believe it," he agrees. The weight of that statement sits over us until the silence is interrupted.

"Honey, we're almost out of berries and the kids are about to fight each other over the last ones," Aila says, as she approaches Edrik and me. She has an apologetic look on her face, feeling bad about interrupting.

"I'll go get more," I offer.

"You don't have to do that," she immediately responds, holding her hand out. She hasn't let me do a thing since I walked through the door. Not that she hasn't been a generous host in the past, but she used to let me help out when I offered. I think she knew that it made me feel like a part of the family. Now that I've given her my house, she doesn't know how to treat me.

"No, I don't, but I want to. I haven't been to the market yet since I've been back, and it would be nice to see everyone again. Plus, this guy is taking a day off, so it wouldn't be fair to make him go," I joke, pointing to Edrik. Aila gives a polite laugh, then turns to her husband for guidance. Edrik nods his head and her gaze returns to me.

"Alright," she agrees, then she hurriedly starts heading toward the counter. "Let me get you some coins," she calls as she goes. I could point out that the coins she's getting likely came from me, but that would be counterproductive. "Here you go," she asserts, as she rushes back over and drops some change in my hand.

"Thank you," I reply.

"No, thank you. You've seen how the kids can get when they're fighting," she comments. I certainly have. I love Edrik's kids, but there have definitely been moments where they've made me glad that I was an only child. I once watched his son put his daughter in a headlock and she subsequently bit his arm. I may have been lonely as a kid, but I never worried for my safety.

"I called it!" a shout comes from the other room, and Aila sighs.

"I better head out," I state, and Aila nods, her eyes past tired.

"You're a lifesaver," Edrik pronounces, putting his hand on my shoulder, his features spelling exhaustion. I laugh, then I head out. I start down the same path I used to take every day to get to the market, noticing so much more than I ever did. The flowers on the side of the path are like little drops of the sun, their beauty illuminating the way. The fields I go by look like the way Jahre's laugh sounds, the uneven elevation reminding me of the way his body would shake while he was carrying me.

Eventually other people wind up on the path around me. I never really thought too much about the people around me until recently. Each and every one of them has their own life. All different. All known by Him. It's hard to process that He can keep track of that much. Not just all the events, but everything in each of our hearts. It's almost harder to imagine than Him coming back from the dead.

"The Son of God is alive!" I hear a woman shout. *Already?* I search for the source of the voice. "The Son of God is alive!" she repeats as she rushes down the road. I hurry over to her, reaching my hand out to stop her. Her joy seems to latch onto me even before I've heard any more than just those six words.

"He's back?" I venture, and the biggest smile comes across her face.

"He was spotted earlier this morning! The tomb could not

keep Him!" she declares.

"The Son of God is alive!" I echo her statement, and she nods, her smile seemingly never ending. I continue on toward the market so I can share this news with as many people as possible. *He's alive!*

I reach the market and find it fairly busy. Perfect! All these times I've been spreading news about Him to people, all I've had to tell was my story, but now I have something even better: His story. He's back, and that's the only thing that matters to me now. This is the big thing to believe in! Not just that He can take pain away as if it's nothing, but that He can trample over death as if it's nothing. And not just that He can trample over death, but that He chose to go through everything He did for us, His sheep. He is the Good Shepherd!

"The Son of God is alive!" I shout, and eyes start to land on me, including the eyes of a handful of Pharisees I hadn't noticed were in the crowd. I know what they think of the words I have to say. I don't care. I'll declare them until my dying breath if that's what it comes to. "The Son of God is alive!" I repeat, and fury fills the faces of the Pharisees. They march on over to me, their fingers outstretched accusingly.

"You are spouting nothing but blasphemy!" one of them yells. If they're offended by that, just wait.

"The Son of God is alive because He has the authority to take up His life. He said that much the day after He healed me and countless others, and now He's proven it. This is big, but I urge you not to gloss over the fact that He was dead. That day He also said that he has the authority to lay down His life. He said that He would do it for His sheep. We are His sheep. All of us who believe these things. He laid down His life and took it back up again to bridge the gap between us and the Lord. That is why He came! To make us right! To save us! And that's exactly what He did. We don't have to spend eternity away from Him and the Lord if we believe this. He is the door. He's opened the gates of Heaven for all who choose to go through Him," I declare.

The reactions of those around me are mixed as always. I can tell that my words have struck some people to their core. Others think I'm a rambling lunatic. Then there's the Pharisees. They seem very unhappy with me right now. They're looking at me the way I've seen them look at Him. That only invigorates me more!

"This is real. He's been spotted for crying out loud! These men thought they were stopping Him, but they really just helped Him fulfill His purpose. Our sins do not define us anymore: He does! We don't need to be perfect; we just need Him," I go on, and the Pharisees have managed to get angrier now that I've called them out. I'm starting to get the feeling that this won't end well for me, but I don't care. I know where my future lies.

52 NIEMOS

"Everything you're saying is blasphemy! There is a punishment in the law for such speech!" Izal declares, but the man before us seems unaffected by his words. *He wants to stone this man? Does he really think that killing another person is going to fix this? It certainly didn't fix our last issue.*

"Do what you must. I won't revoke my words," the man states, holding his ground. I want to scream at him to stop, but I can't do that. I'm not completely sure that he's wrong. It hurts to admit that after so long denying any proof that the Son of God was here, but I don't know what I believe anymore. From the miracles, to the knowledge of the future, to the report of the soldiers this morning, then the reported sightings, my entire world has been rocked. *What if this is real? What if Jesus is the Son of God?*

"Then by the law of our ancestors, we have the right-no, the duty to stone you!" Izal exclaims, that ferocious side of him on full display. It almost makes me ashamed to be associated with him. He's out here killing people he doesn't agree with, while all Jesus ever did was ease peoples' pain. Which one of them do I really want to associate myself with when I face the Lord on my last day?

"Niemos, get yourself together," Carian tells me, handing me a stone. He has one for himself as well, and so do the rest of the Pharisees around me. I don't feel right about this at all. Before I even have my thoughts straight, stones begin flying at the man in the middle. The man brave enough to preach of a Savior knowing what would happen to him for it.

He falls to the ground as the stones continue to fly at him, tearing apart his skin. He grunts and cries out in pain as blood begins to spill out of him, but he doesn't take back his words. That's the only thing that can save him right now, but he won't do it. He can't.

"I'm coming home… Father," the man barely gets out, turning his head toward the sky as the stones continue to pelt him. Father. I think back to what Jesus said the day he identified himself as the Son of God. He said anyone who does the will of his father is his family. This man knows that he's a part of the family of God because he's doing His will; spreading the word about His Son.

I'm not sure of much right now, but I know that we were wrong. Men don't heal people. Men don't know the future. Men don't rise from the dead. Men don't love the way that He does. It's an eternal love that existed long before I was born and will continue long after I die. He has it because He's been around that long. Jesus is the Son of God. *This changes everything.*

"Stop!" I shout, holding my hand out and entering the circle. A couple of stones hit my chest before they stop flying. That was only two stones and it was probably the worst pain I've felt in my life. *How is the man in the middle not screaming in pain right now?*

"Niemos, what's the meaning of this?" Izal ventures ferociously.

"I don't think his words are blasphemy," I say. It comes out quietly and laced with fear. I don't know what will happen to me for taking a stand here. The look in Izal's eyes when the stoning started made it seem like he was beyond reason. Even so, I can't let this go on. I need to join this man in declaring the majesty of Jesus. That's the will of the Father, and that's what matters to me now. Not the rules and traditions I was using as a safety blanket. I need to actually let Him in.

"Don't tell me you're buying into all of this, Niemos?"

Carian raises, betrayal in his eyes. This isn't a betrayal, this is me wanting him to see the truth too.

"When was the last time a man performed signs like we've seen Jesus perform? And weren't the last people to do it messengers of the Lord?" I bring up, referring to the men of faith in our history. Miraculous signs aren't new, but it has been hundreds of years since the last ones, and they weren't on the scale we've seen from Jesus. There doesn't seem to be anything that He can't do. That's more than what can be said about our ancestors.

"Those were all false signs!" Izal cries, furious that I'm even entertaining any of this.

"Then let's talk about the miraculous sign He left for us. He knew that we were coming and what we would ask for. That's not even the only time I've witnessed Him possessing knowledge that He shouldn't have. He knew my name without ever being told it, and not to mention He did predict His death," I reiterate what the man on the ground next to me has already said. His body is still. I think he's dead. It's disheartening and reminds me exactly what I'm risking by speaking to Izal this way, but I can't stop. I'm done denying that the Son of God is upon us.

"Saying you're going to die, then doing something to get yourself killed is not proof that you know the future! All it proves is that you're insane!" Izal shouts. He's about an inch away from completely losing control. I don't know if it's because I'm making him doubt himself or if it's because I'm a Pharisee proclaiming the exact opposite of everything we've always taught in public. I'd like to think it's the former, but more likely than not, it's the latter.

All Izal seems to care about is power. It's why he supported having Jesus killed in the first place. Our power was dwindling as His increased. It's also why he wanted the soldiers to spread lies about what happened at the tomb this morning. He doesn't want any sort of validity about Jesus' claims to spread. That's the exact reason I'm going to tell the truth now.

"Except He didn't just predict His death, He also predicted

His resurrection," I spell out, and Izal's face burns red as fury overtakes him. He squeezes the stones in his hands tightly, his knuckles turning white.

"Choose your next words carefully," Izal warns. They've already been chosen.

"This morning a man like lightning, a man who sounds a lot like an angel of God, rolled the stone away from Jesus' grave. I know this much because I heard it straight from the soldiers who were guarding the tomb. Once the soldiers recovered from seeing this man's majesty, they checked the tomb and it was empty. Since then, Jesus has been spotted by multiple witnesses. I didn't want to believe it at first, but I spoke to one of them, and there's no denying what he saw. The Son of God is alive," I proclaim.

The people around me all start whispering. Some of the Pharisees scoff, while others turn to Izal, knowing the soldiers ran into his quarters this morning. Izal's expression tells me he's trying to quickly come up with a way to do damage control here. My eyes drift to Carian, and his eyes meet mine. They seem desperate. Desperate for what, I'm not sure yet, but I hope he's at least starting to undo all of the lies that are in his head.

"Niemos, you've spent your whole life devoted to the rules. Don't turn your back on that now," Carian finally speaks up. That's not what I was hoping to hear. He grips the stone in his hand tightly, and I feel my heart drop, but I don't let it stop me.

"That's the problem. I shouldn't have been devoted to the rules. I should've been devoted to Him. That's what He asks of us and in turn He offers a love that's beyond our comprehension. It isn't earned based on how many rules we follow. It's freely given to all who turn to Him and believe in His Son. I know that much because He told me that when I went to see Him after His trial. I'm one of the main reasons He was on a path that would end in His death, but He didn't care. He still offered me that love because of who He is, despite who I am. It's an offer always on the table for all of us until our very last breath. Do not be blind as I had been and pass it up," I beg the people around me. There's an overwhelming urge in me to lead them to Him. I desperately want them to experience the freedom I now feel despite my current circumstances.

"You brought this on yourself," Carian declares, then he launches the stone in his hand right at my head. It hits my forehead, and the pain brings me to my knees next to the man who started all of this. His eyes covey a peace that seems out of place among all the gashes covering his body.

As more stones fly at me, I know that very soon I'll be like him. My soul will leave my broken body and come face to face with the Lord. Despite the way I've handled Him my whole life, His arms will be open to me, inviting me in because of the decision I made here today to trust in Him. Knowing that that's coming makes all the pain flooding my system worth it. *I'm going home.*

53 AURAN

"You need to go to the market," Jesus suddenly announces, a serious expression overtaking His face.

"What?" I inquire. I was just there with His mom. I don't see a reason to go back.

"Run, Auran," He instructs, urgency in his eyes. *Alright then.* I get up and run out of the house, making my legs go as fast as they can. I have no idea what I'm running to, but He wouldn't have told me to do it if it wasn't important.

I'm out of breath when I make it to the market. I stop and try to even out my breathing when my eyes catch the reason I must be here: there's a handful of Pharisees stoning somebody. My guess is that it's one of His sheep that's been spreading the news about Him. I need to go break this up.

"Stop what you're doing!" I demand as I make my way over to them, trying my best not to sound as out of breath as I am. Some of the Pharisees stop, but a few of them ignore me and continue picking up stones from below them and throwing them at the poor soul in the middle. "That was an order!" I shout, now among them.

"We have an agreement with your people that allows us to freely follow our law, which is what we're doing right now," Izal states, meeting my eyes, then leaning down and grabbing another stone. Stoning is a punishment for various crimes in their law, one of them being blasphemy. I'm now convinced that whoever's in the middle is a follower of Jesus. I have to stop this. It's my purpose.

"Maybe I didn't make myself clear," I remark, pulling my sword out of its sheath. The sound makes all of the Pharisees, excluding Izal, instantly drop their stones and disperse. That's when I see who's in the middle: not one person, but two. One of which is Niemos, the Pharisee who spoke to Jesus after His trial. Based on how he left then, I certainly didn't think he put his faith in Jesus. "He's one of your own," I let out, shocked. I move closer to Izal who glares at me.

"Not anymore," Izal spits. He turns and winds up to throw the stone, but I hit him in the head with the pommel of my sword, causing him to collapse before he has the chance. That's probably going to have repercussions for me later on, but I wasn't going to let him kill Niemos. I don't know why, but Jesus wanted me here to stop this.

"Please tell me you're alive and I didn't just do that for nothing," I say, kneeling down next to Niemos. His eyes slowly flutter open and confusion fills them.

"You're not the… Lord," he gets out. *I guess he's not dead.*

"Nope, but I was sent here by His Son," I tell him, gathering him in my arms. He grunts as I get to my feet with him. I may have gotten here before he was killed, but he took a lot of stones before that. I need to take him to someone who can fix him before he succumbs to his injuries.

"He wanted to… save me?" he utters, his voice weak.

"That's what He does," I remind him. I don't always understand it, but it's a part of who He is. Just like I'm not the man who ordered His torture to Him, Niemos isn't the man who led the charge on His crucifixion.

"I…" he starts, but he quickly trails off, his eyes beginning to flutter closed. I'm losing him. I need to hurry and get him help. My mind takes me back to the events of last night. Peter had me bring him to a house where there was a woman with medical experience. I need to go there.

The way is fuzzy in my mind, especially since Peter and I arrived at night. I wander around, trying to recall every detail I took in. *A lot of the houses around here look alike.* I look down and find Niemos' chest is rising and falling very slowly now. *I need to get it together and find this place!*

Eventually, I spot a door in the distance with blood on it. *That's the house!* I run there as fast as I can and knock on the door with my foot when I reach it. It doesn't take long for it to open, revealing a man who resembles the woman who answered when I was with Peter.

"Now this is a sight one would have to see to believe," the man comments, with shock on his face.

"Laz, who is it?" a voice calls. I think it's the woman from before.

"You'll want to come see," Laz says, still trying to process the scene before him. I'd appreciate a bit more action from him right now.

"Is your sister home?" I question.

"Which one?" Laz wonders, a with a frustrating lack of urgency.

"Lazarus, let them in!" the woman from before orders, suddenly at Laz's side. He moves aside, pulling the door open wider so that I can make it through with Niemos.

"How was I supposed to know that it's safe to let in a Praetor carrying a Pharisee?" Laz asks, as we head into the house.

"Because he's the one who brought Peter to us you fool," the woman retorts as she picks a few things up off the table. "Set him here," she instructs me, and I do as I'm told. "Mary!" she calls into the hall behind us.

"Come on Martha, we eat there," Laz complains, gesturing to the table.

"Lazarus, I'm going to need you to leave the room before I'm tempted to send you to your tomb for the second time," Martha comments, her head in her hands. Laz throws his hands up in surrender, then walks away. Martha smooths her hair out with a deep breath, then heads into the kitchen. "What happened to him?" she asks me as she begins collecting rags.

"He was stoned by his own. I wasn't there for the beginning, but I can only assume they did it because he was proclaiming that Jesus is the Son of God," I fill her in. She comes back over and hands me a few rags.

"Hold these over the bigger wounds to try and stop the bleeding," she tells me, and again, I do what I'm told. If we lived in a different world, she'd make a good Praetor. "Mary!" she yells down the hall again.

"I'm coming!" Mary calls back.

"How did you wind up with him?" Martha asks me as she finds other big wounds and holds pressure with rags of her own.

"Jesus told me to go to the market with no explanation, then I found Niemos here getting stoned," I answer.

"Jesus is back?" Martha immediately questions. She doesn't sound shocked. No, she definitely knew this was coming. It's joy that's rimming the edges of her voice. She didn't know He'd be back this quickly.

"Yes. He was at His mom's house, but He's probably with His followers now. He told me that He was going to visit them after our conversation was over," I detail, and her eyes drift to the door. "I'm sure He'll come here at some point after that," I add.

"Who's coming here?" Mary poses as she walks into the room.

"Jesus," Martha tells her.

"Jesus is alive? Oh my-who's that?" Mary inquires, her eyes widening as she finally noticing the bleeding man on her table.

"This is Niemos. He needs your help," I fill her in. Her eyes fixate on Niemos as she takes in the extent of his injuries.

"I'll be right back," Mary says, then she runs out of the room.

"Is He alright?" Martha asks me, and I raise my eyebrows.

It's pretty clear that he's not alright. "Jesus. Is Jesus alright?" she rephrases. That makes a lot more sense.

"He's covered in scars from everything, but He didn't seem to be in pain. If anything, He seemed lighter than before," I answer. I know that was pretty vague, but I don't know what else to say. The only time He appeared to be sad was when He was telling me that He'll be going away again, and I don't think it's my place to spread that information. Other than that, He was all smiles and jokes. He did what He came here to do. He defeated death.

"I'm glad," Martha responds, a smile on her face.

"Where's the biggest wound?" Mary ventures, returning with supplies.

"Up here," I report, gesturing to his forehead with a nod.

"Move the rag to another spot," Mary tells me, and I do as she says, then she gets to work. This isn't what I pictured when Jesus told me to continue to look after His sheep. It seems to be a job with varying descriptions, many of which could get me in trouble. It doesn't matter; I'll do whatever He requires of me, even if I end up in a similar position as Niemos.

54 MARY

"Where-where am I?" Niemos utters groggily, wincing as he tries to sit up.

"Whoa there," I say, easing him back down gently. "My name is Mary, and you're at my house," I fill him in.

"How did I get here?" he poses, his eyes shifting around as he tries to recall. I probably should've expected that question. In my defense, this is the first time that I've been entrusted with a severely wounded man before. It's not exactly easy. Patching him up was practically endless.

"Auran brought you here," I answer, but that does nothing to alleviate his confusion. "The Praetor. Jesus told him to go get you," I clarify, and his eyes lock on mine.

"Do you know Jesus?" he asks, more alert than ever.

"I grew up with Him. I didn't know who He was back then though. That was a more recent development for me and my siblings," I say, and his eyes widen. The movement causes him to wince because of the wound on his forehead. "How did this all happen?" I ask him. Auran was more worried about aiding in his survival than giving me the full story on what happened to him.

"How far back do you want me to go?" he ventures.

"As far back as you want to," I offer. I figured this would all be a long story the second I saw him. His injuries are consistent with those of a stoning, but he's a Pharisee, so one would expect him to be doing the stoning, not getting stoned himself. When you throw in the fact that Auran brought him here, it just gets more complicated.

"When I was young, my parents didn't provide me with any structure. They went on with their lives as if they had no child," he begins. I hadn't expected him to go that far back, but I won't stop him. It seems like he needs this. "I didn't know what I was supposed to do with myself until I went to temple and was introduced to the law. It gave me the structure I was lacking. It became like a lifeline to me. That's why I became a Pharisee in the first place," he goes on, and his eyes shift to me, his expression apologetic. "You didn't want to know all of that, did you?" he asks.

"I want to know whatever you want to tell me," I say.

"Are you sure?" he checks.

"Yeah. What else are we going to do right now?" I pose.

"You don't have to stay with me if you don't want to. Also, how late is it?" he asks, noticing the darkness outside. I honestly don't know. Auran left once I finished with all the big wounds, and I was still working when Martha and Laz went to bed. Niemos had a lot of gashes. I'm surprised he's able to keep up a conversation right now. I've finished patching him up, but he's lost a lot of blood. "You're tired, aren't you? You should go to bed. I'm sure it's been a long day-night for you," he insists, shyly. I get the feeling that he's terrified of imposing.

"I'm not going anywhere," I assure him. He's had a rough day. I don't want to be the type of person who leaves someone alone after all of that. Am I tired? A bit, but I can always get more sleep later.

"Are you sure?" he prompts.

"You already asked that, and my answer hasn't changed," I promise him, smiling gently.

"Thank you," he responds, still trying to process that I would do this for him. It makes me sad that this is shocking for him. I know that if I were in his position, there would be no shortage of people by my side keeping me company.

He's not going to be alone. I know he has a long recovery ahead of him, but I'm going to be there for him until the very end. Nobody should be alone after getting stoned. *Wait, I still don't know for sure that he got stoned. I should probably bring things back around to his story. If we're going to be spending the rest of his recovery together, I want to get to know him better.*

"Of course. Why don't you continue with your story," I encourage.

"Right," he replies. He looks off to the side as he tries to figure out where he left off. I'd help him, but I'm having a hard time remembering as well. Not that I wasn't listening. I remember him saying something about absentee parents. He needed structure. The law brought him structure. "I was telling you…"

"Why you became a Pharisee," I let out at the same time that he starts back up again. "Sorry," I apologize.

"You don't have anything to apologize to me for. From what I understand, I owe you my life," he says, his eyes containing all of the gratitude his words can't manage to convey. I've never really had this much gratitude thrust upon me. It's always me who's thankful to Martha or on the rare occasion, Laz. I'm not used to this in the slightest, and I don't really know if it's that warranted either.

"I just patched you up. Auran is the one who got you, and Jesus is the one who told him to get you," I reason, and he smiles. "What?"

"You're humble," he says.

"I don't know if that's how I see it," I respond, my cheeks getting hot.

"'I just patched you up,'" he quotes me, shaking his head with that smile still there. *What? That really is all I did.*

"Are you ever going to finish telling me your story or not?" I urge, and he laughs.

"I suppose I should," he agrees. "I became a Pharisee because I needed the structure from the law. If I could follow all of the rules, then I could prove that I was good enough, maybe not to my parents, but to everybody else, including the Lord. When Jesus came on the scene He started speaking of a way around the rules. A way that isn't earned. I couldn't fathom that with how much of a staple the rules had been for me my whole life. I couldn't fathom that He was real," he goes on.

"It was hard for my brother at first even though we grew up witnessing Jesus' kindness," I share. Laz wouldn't like that I'm telling him this, but I think it's something he needs to hear. We all had our own way of coming to Him, none of them perfect.

"Did your brother give the Romans everything they'd need to send Him to His death?" he phrases guiltily, his eyes leaving mine in shame. I guess that is something to be guilty about, but something tells me that Jesus doesn't care.

"When we were all much younger, Jesus' brothers used to try and blame things on Him all the time. Obviously, His parents knew that He wasn't guilty of the things they accused Him of, but when the boys all went to temple, they got away with blaming Him for things," I start.

"Are you trying to make me feel better by pointing out that I'm not the first Pharisee to punish Him for something He didn't do?" he asks. *I hadn't even thought about that angle.* He doesn't seem impressed by it, so I'm glad I have a better one.

"No, I wasn't done," I say, and he goes to put his hands up in surrender, but doesn't get them high before he winces. "Easy," I tell him, putting my hand gently on his shoulder. "What I was going to say is that Jesus never held any of that against His siblings. He took the punishment for them and loved them all the same," I finish.

There's a lot that Jesus put up with in our youth. His brothers blaming things on Him and their scorn whenever the adult in question didn't fall for it. Laz's pranks even though He probably knew the punchline before He was unfortunate enough to discover it. His sisters and I in our teenage years. The point is that Jesus is no stranger to the inadequacies of His people, but that was never enough to change His mind about what He'd eventually do for us. His love went beyond it all.

"I did a little bit more than get Him into trouble," he points out.

"What did you do after?" I pose.

"What?" he asks.

"How did you wind up like this, Niemos?" I rephrase.

"I was stoned after I proclaimed His majesty," he answers.

"If you were out there putting your life on the line for His majesty, do you really think He'd hold everything from before against you. Forget the fact that that's not in His nature, He knows who you really are now," I assure him. He's quiet for a second and I wonder if he hasn't heard me, but then I realize there are tears in his eyes. I wipe them away for him and he sniffles.

"You're really kind," he gets out through his wavering emotion.

"You're easy to be kind to," I reply, and he smiles.

55 MARTHA

When I wake up, I find Mary asleep with her head on the table where Niemos is lying. For a second, I feared he was dead, but then I noticed his chest rising and falling and I let out a sigh of relief. It seems Mary did a good job with him. *I should get her something to celebrate her efforts.* I know we're technically not supposed to go out because of everything that happened with Laz, but something tells me that has left peoples' memories now that Jesus is back, so I think I'm all clear to go to the market.

I quietly grab some coins and tiptoe out of the house, so I don't wake either of them up. To be honest, I don't think that they'd wake up even if I had been loud. Niemos has been through a lot and Mary already seemed exhausted when I went to bed last night. I felt bad for leaving her like that, but there wasn't really anything I could do to help her at that point, and I was pretty tired. We've had no shortage of packed days lately with the undone deaths, grieving guests, and bleeding men being brought into our home.

"Martha," a voice speaks up from the street beside me. It's not just any street, and it's not just any voice.

"Jesus?" I pose, stopping and heading toward His voice. This is the same street where I confronted Him before He brought Laz back. Instead of finding Him among His followers, I find Him alone off toward the side.

"Hi," He greets me once my eyes meet His. They contain the

same kindness as always, but that's not what my eyes are drawn to. He really is covered in scars just like Auran said. I didn't know they did that much to Him. I knew it wasn't great because it was a crucifixion and all, but actually seeing Him right now, I don't think He possibly could've gone through more pain.

Tears start to well up in my eyes. He went through all of that for me. It was so much easier to process when He wasn't right in front of me! He reaches out to put His hand on my shoulder, but all I see is the hole in His wrist from the nail of all of my wrongs, past and future. *He made me right, but at what cost?*

"I'm sorry," I let out, hiding my face in my hands. I don't deserve to be here with Him. I don't deserve any of the things He's done for me. It's all the lies I've told, and all the impure thoughts I've had, and everything else I do wrong that put Him up on that cross. Each and every time I've fallen short, another lash for Him.

"Martha, look at me," He says, His voice no different than it was years ago when He was keeping me sane among all my chaos. I slowly lower my hands and let His tenderness ground me in this moment. "It was all worth it," He assures me.

"How can You say that?" I question.

"Because you and all the rest of my sheep are worth it. Martha, I would endure the pain I went through every day if it was necessary. That's how much you all mean to me and my Father," He declares, intensity in His stare. If I was talking to anybody else, I'd think that was a hyperbole, but I know He's telling the truth. He would face the worst death known to man time and time again just for us. Chills run through me as I try to fathom it. "Lucky for us all, this was all a one and done thing, so I won't have to do it again," He adds to lighten the mood, and I chuckle. He knew I needed a laugh. That this is all too much for me to take in right now. A thought hits my mind, and I know I have to ask Him about it.

"Will I ever be able to grasp all of this?" I pose. His gaze leaves mine as He considers His response. I appreciate that He's actually putting time into answering me. He really doesn't have to be entertaining this conversation at all. He's all-powerful. I'm not. He doesn't have to share any of the things He's privy to with me.

"Not here," He finally answers. *Not here.* But one day I will. One day when we meet again in Heaven.

"What's Heaven like?" I ask. I know a lot of it probably falls into the realm of things I can't process, but there has to be something He can tell me. He smiles and puts His hand on my shoulder.

"It's better than anything you could ever imagine," He tells me. My imagination is fairly sizable, and He knows that. It probably has golden gates and massive houses made of the purest stone. There will be flowers everywhere even grander than the prettiest ones that Mary brings home, and I'm picturing clouds everywhere too. "Are you actually trying to imagine it?" He calls me out.

"Well, You can't just say that and expect me not to," I reply, and He chuckles.

"I bet you're forgetting the best part," He comments, and I narrow my eyes, thinking hard about what it could be.

"No sickness or death?" I guess.

"Well, that part is pretty great, but it's not what I was referring to," He responds. *What could He be referring to?* Surely, it's not any of the frivolous details that I was imagining prior. While He does love details, they're not the most important thing to Him. *What does He value above all else? Wait, I feel stupid.*

"It's the whole spending forever with You thing, isn't it?" I realize, and a small smile spreads across His face.

"I was thinking about the Father specifically, but yeah, I'll be there too," He confirms. I can't believe I left that out. That alone is better than anything I could ever think of. Being around Jesus has always felt like a gift. I can't even begin to imagine what it will feel like being around His Father. *Will I even have words for all of that?*

"Please tell me I'll be well-spoken in Heaven," I say, and He laughs.

"You're not that bad right now," He tells me.

"I feel like a blubbering idiot half the time I'm around You,"

I sigh, my shoulders slumping.

"I spend a lot of my time around a large group of men. Our conversations are a breath of fresh air for me," He presents, and I can't help but laugh, especially since I've had to converse with that large group of men before. I wonder where they are right now. Peter was always so reluctant to leave His side before.

"Why aren't they with You?" I inquire.

"I wanted to visit with you guys without all the… noise," He comes up with.

"And Peter went with that?" I ask.

"Peter has been learning about the bliss of listening before he speaks," He answers. I'm pretty sure He was just trying to find a nice way to say that Peter is learning to follow directions. *You know what, good for him.*

"So, You're coming back with me?" I check, and He nods, that warm smile on His face. "Laz might be a bit overbearing. He didn't believe that You were going to come back until Auran showed up with Niemos and told us that he had been with You," I warn Him.

"I can handle Laz," He responds, as we start heading back toward the house. That makes one of us. Well, I can handle him, but not without wanting to strangle him. "How is Niemos?" He asks.

"Alive," I report. I don't really know much beyond that. "Are You going to heal him?" I pose. He doesn't say anything at first. I didn't realize how much that question sounded like a challenge until it came out. "Sorry," I apologize, raising my hands in embarrassment.

"No, it's a valid question," He replies, then He goes quiet again as He thinks over His words. "The short answer is no. Niemos has a path he needs to follow that doesn't include that. I can't really explain it to you, but know that I'm not holding back to be cruel. I love Niemos just as much as I love the rest of you despite the fact that we met in a very different way," He reveals. That's certainly an interesting way to put that.

"Thank You for being as transparent as my understanding

allows," I relay messily, and He laughs.

"Thank you for keeping an open mind despite my cryptic answers," He tells me. His answers do tend to be pretty cryptic, but I always seem to understand them eventually. There are some that it seems I'll have to wait until Heaven to understand, but I'm alright with that.

We reach the door which I'm just now realizing has blood on it. Whether it came from Peter or Niemos, I have no clue. *Is it weird that I can't identify which bleeding man left a trace on my door?* I don't really want to think about that further. Jesus and I walk in and I quietly head toward Laz's room.

"Laz, come out here," I say, my voice loud enough for him to hear, but quiet enough that I won't wake up Mary and Niemos.

"Coming," Laz responds. There's some shuffling from within his room, then he comes down the hallway. As soon as he sees Jesus, his eyes light up. "Jesus!" he exclaims, running up to Him and throwing Him into a big bear hug. I sigh as Mary and Niemos both start to stir in the room over.

"Careful," Jesus gets out.

"Why? Are You hurt?" Laz questions, immediately letting go of Him.

"No, you were just squeezing really hard," Jesus jokes, and Laz gives Him a play punch, causing Him to laugh. "I missed you too, friend," Jesus says, patting his shoulder. *He says it as if He was just on a trip or something.*

"Was it dark for You too?" Laz asks Him, referring to their shared experience of death. Hearing the question sends shivers down my spine.

"No," Jesus answers. He doesn't say anything else, and it doesn't seem like He's going to. I guess that's just going to have to be added to the list of things I won't know until I get to Heaven.

"Jesus?" Mary murmurs, rubbing her eyes as she squints at Him from the other room.

"Hey, Mary," Jesus responds, His eyes softening as the

corners of His mouth curve up gently. He holds His arms out for her, and she gets to her feet and not-so-gracefully makes her way into them. He pats her back while she silently lays her head against His chest, still in the process of waking up.

"Thank You for the lily," Mary finally voices softly, and He lets go of her so He can see her face.

"You like it?" Jesus asks, a grin naturally making its way onto His face as the words leave His mouth.

"It's my new favorite thing," she tells him, a smile adorning her own features. He beams, then His eyes go to Niemos who is painstakingly starting to sit up, wincing as he goes.

"Can you three give us a minute?" Jesus poses, turning to us.

"You got it," I agree. I've got forever with Jesus. I don't mind giving up a minute.

56 NIEMOS

Seeing Jesus before me right now is surreal. The last time I was face to face with Him was after the trial. His life was already starting to slip from Him despite the fact that He had yet to pick up His cross. I was so angry with Him then for telling me a truth I refused to believe. He had every right to scold me and tell me that I'm ungrateful and closed-minded, but instead He told me I was loved.

I couldn't believe that either. I was used to being ignored, abandoned by the people who were supposed to love me the most. The only time I ever received any sort of positive attention was when I followed the rules. Life became about earning each and every aspect of it, yet there He was telling me that I already had the thing I'd been craving since I was a kid.

Seeing Him now, I couldn't be more certain that He was telling the truth. He bears the scars of a death I sent Him to in more ways than one, yet He has a smile on His face as He faces me. The absurdity of it all makes me laugh.

"I used to hate that smile of Yours," I say, and He laughs too.

"Oh, I'm aware," He responds. He comes closer and helps me off the table. Gently, He leads me to the sitting room, going slow enough for me to shuffle my feet rather than pick them up. I appreciate it. It allows me to avoid as much movement as possible.

He makes sure I'm situated before He takes the seat across from me. His gentleness almost embarrasses me considering how aggressive I was with Him every time we saw each other.

"Did You know what I would do to you back then?" I jump right into things.

"I've always known exactly who you are, Niemos. You always just wanted to understand who I was and what I was doing, but when nobody else reacted that way, you started to hide it. You didn't want to imagine falling out with them, so you tried to convince yourself that they were right. You did some bad things because of that, but I've always seen your heart. You wanted to believe," He lays out, and I get goosebumps. It seems He was more aware of what was within me than I was. *Maybe He can answer something for me then.*

"Why couldn't I?" I pose, and I feel tears starting to sting my eyes. So much would be different if I had just believed early on. He wouldn't be sitting there covered in scars, and things would've played out a lot differently for me.

"You were afraid. You didn't know what following me would give you and you knew exactly what it would take from you," He reasons.

"But why couldn't I just get over that? And shouldn't You be mad at me for getting stuck in that?" I mutter. I'm mad at myself for how I handled everything. I had the Son of God right there in front of me and I couldn't step away from my fear. It made me so blind that I refused to actually listen to anything He was saying. *Why couldn't I just focus on Him?*

"Niemos, I'd never be mad at you for feeling afraid. I've been there too," He reveals. *He's been afraid? I've certainly never seen that, and there were many times that I tried to evoke that exact emotion in Him.*

"How could You be afraid?" I ask, and He laughs.

"You all get so caught up in the fact that I'm the Son of God that you forget I'm also the Son of Mary," He reminds me. *What is*

He talking about? He sighs when He notices my confusion, then He continues. "Yes, I'm Almighty, but I'm also human. I have all the same emotions that you do," He explains.

I hadn't thought about that. While there have been times where I've seen Him display emotions, He's never seemed overcome by them. He's always managed to say what He's needed to say and do what He's needed to do despite everything stirring within Him. *Is that the Lord within Him, or is it possible for me to be like that too?*

"How do you overcome them?" I venture, and He smiles, a proud expression on His face.

"I take them to the Father. He's not afraid of the things that we feel. He wants to take away all of the bad emotions and replace them with peace, but He can't do that if you don't acknowledge them and surrender them to Him in the first place," He tells me. *Is it really that simple?*

"How do I do that?" I ask.

"You just talk to Him," He answers. *Talk to Him?*

"Like my morning prayers?" I pose, and He shakes His hand side to side, letting me know I'm close.

"Prayers yes, but you don't need to use all the fancy, rehearsed language that you've been taught. Think about the way we're talking right now. You're being open and sharing your struggles with me. Talking to the Father isn't any different. Though He already knows what's going on with you, He wants you to come to Him with everything. Peace isn't found in some magic words, but rather in your surrender," He details.

Everything He's saying makes sense, but it opposes so much of what I've been practicing all my life. *How much did we get wrong and then pass down from generation to generation? Is there any of it that's relevant?*

"If the Father is so gracious, does the law even matter?" I ask, and He nods His head like He knew this was coming. I guess asking Him about the law is pretty on brand for me.

"Yes, it matters. There are still things you should and shouldn't do, but doing or not doing those things isn't what justifies you: I am. Just as you and your ancestors slaughtered animals to atone for your wrongs, I was slaughtered to make you right. There's no need for any sacrifices outside of that anymore, but that doesn't mean the law is to be ignored. The Father is pleased by those who follow His commands," He details.

"Then why did You make it seem like the law didn't matter when I confronted you about people violating it?" I question, trying to make sense of it all. I want to make sure I do things right from here on out and I need His guidance in order to do that.

"I have two things to say to that. One, be careful you don't get laws and traditions mixed up. Wearing your prayer tassels every day is a tradition that's been passed down throughout our people, but it was never mandated by the Father. Second, I was warning you not to make the law your master. You should be following the law to please the Father, not because you think it makes you better than your neighbor, or that it can justify you," He explains.

He's right; wearing our prayer tassels is something our people have done all this time, but it was never in the law. I couldn't even tell you the reason why we do it. How many things really fall into that category? I'm going to have to do a lot of digging. Good thing I have no shortage of time now that I can't go back to my old life.

What will I do? Being a Pharisee is all I've ever known. It's too late to learn a skill, and I don't think I have the stamina to work in a field. None of that ever appealed to me anyway. I don't really know what does appeal to me though. I've never taken the time to think about any of that. *Wait, Jesus knows all; he probably knows what I'm supposed to do now that being a Pharisee is out of the picture for me.*

"What am I supposed to do with the rest of my life now?" I ask, and He raises His eyebrows. "What?" I prompt. He saved my life in the market by sending Auran. I know He didn't do that so that

I could wander around aimlessly for the rest of my days. *Can't He just tell me what direction to head in?*

"What are you passionate about?" He asks.

"I don't know," I immediately respond, and He shakes His head.

"That's not true," He denies. *What does He mean that's not true?* I would say I used to be passionate about the law, but we already discussed that. There wasn't really anything else besides that. I mean, I guess there was teaching people about the law, but again, that's out of the picture now. Well, the law part is out of the picture, the people part isn't.

"I'm passionate about guiding people," I assert, and He nods. I wait for more, but He doesn't speak. "What am I supposed to do with that?" I question.

"I can't give you all the answers, Niemos. There are some things you need to figure out on your own," He tells me. *Haven't I already figured enough out on my own? I was stoned for how long it took me to figure things out before.*

"How will I know if I'm doing what's right?" I urge, and He smiles.

"As long as you're glorifying the Father in what you do, then you're doing what's right," He answers. That was vague, and I normally hate vague, but there's something in it that brings me comfort. I can't mess this up as long as I'm putting Him first.

57 LAZARUS

He's back. Jesus is actually back. Even after Auran confirmed Martha's suspicions that death couldn't keep Him, part of me was still skeptical. A man rising from the dead is a hard thing to believe without seeing. Obviously, I was already aware that it was possible, but my brain was so stuck on the fact that Jesus was leading Himself to the slaughter that I completely ignored the fact that He could lead Himself back.

I had Him right here with me for the majority of my life, yet I missed so much. I missed that He was the Son of God, and even when Mary told us I had a hard time believing it. I missed what He was chosen for, and again, I had a hard time finding any sort of sense in it. I missed that the scrolls foretold His return like Martha was trying to tell me, and when He did return, I was slow to believe it.

It seems the root of my problem is belief. The conversation I had with Jesus the night He raised me from the dead comes back to me. He told me that I was going to have to be sure about the things I believe. He was trying to get me to examine everything before all of this went down and I tried, but unbelief took over.

If that happened to me, someone who not only was the recipient of one of Jesus' miracles, but has also had extensive conversations with Jesus Himself, how much more will others be susceptible to it? I don't want that for the people of this world. I'm finally sure of what I believe and I want that to be the case for everyone. The One I believe in has resurrection power within Him, after all. I can't just keep that to myself and let the world forget about who He is and everything He's done for us.

"Something's on your mind," Martha observes, eyeing me.

"Our formally dead Friend who happens to be the Son of God is in the other room talking to a Pharisee who was stoned. What isn't there to think about?" I comment, my head still spinning as I continue to try to get a grasp on everything.

"He has a name," Mary brings up.

"Jesus?" I pose, confused. The point of me not using it was to draw attention to the fact that He's the Son of God.

"Niemos," Mary says, her eyes drifting to the wall between us and the sitting room where Jesus and Niemos are talking. *Should I be worried about that?*

"Laz, what's on your mind?" Martha questions, being more blatant about her inquiry this go around. It's not that I don't want to tell her everything that's bouncing around my head, I just don't know how to word it all. I want the world to know exactly who He is, I know that much, but I don't know what to do about it. "Laz?" she grabs my attention.

"I missed everything," I let out. I expect some sort of 'I told you so' from her, but instead she faces me with a gentle expression.

"This family's been through a lot lately, Laz, nobody is blaming you for not picking up on everything," Martha responds. This isn't the same attitude she had when we were consulting the scrolls. What's happened between now and then? Besides Jesus being crucified and coming back.

"Yeah, I didn't get it all either. All I could really grasp was His love for us," Mary adds.

"That's the thing, it's all hard to take in, even when you're involved in it with Him," I respond, and Mary cocks her head, unsure of what I'm trying to say.

"Laz, where are you going with this?" Martha asks.

"How are the people supposed to grasp it all? This news that we're privy to changes lives! Are we supposed to sit inside this house and just hope they hear it and believe it?" I phrase, and she gapes at me.

"What are you saying?" Martha questions, her confusion overtaking her nurturing instinct from before.

"I'm saying that I want to make Heaven crowded!" I declare.

"Laz, you're making less sense now," Mary tells me, but I can see that Martha's starting to catch on to everything that I'm thinking. Her eyes fixate on the wall in front of her as she sorts through her thoughts methodically. She's always done things that way. Carefully mulling over each and every detail that finds its way into her mind. It's how she was able to figure all of this out before Jesus was even killed.

I don't remember much of our parents, but I have faint memories of our dad being like that. There seemed to be no problem that you could go to him with that he couldn't eventually solve. Granted, my problems were a lot simpler back then than they are now, but it was still impressive. Growing up I wanted nothing more than to be like him. Even more so when he was gone. I wanted to be able to be someone that people could come to, but my brain has never worked the way that his did.

Maybe that doesn't have to disqualify me from helping people. Maybe I am the way that I am because people need to see that if someone like me could grasp this, that could very well mean it's true. People like Martha and our dad can see through all of the metaphors, but people like me need things thoroughly spelled out for them. *Who better to do that than someone who's had it all spelled out in the words and actions of the Son of God Himself?*

"I need to go out and tell people about Him," I assert, more sure than I've ever been about anything.

"Right now?" Mary ventures.

"In general," Martha speaks up before I can. I face her and when her eyes meet mine, I know she's on the same page as me. She has the same overwhelming need to make His majesty known. Normally I would try to discourage her from doing something like this given the fact that the hole-y Pharisee in our sitting room shows exactly what could happen to us, but I can't tell her to walk away from this. Not when I know exactly what she's feeling.

"How far are you willing to take this?" I ask her.

"This is all that matters now," Martha responds, sincerity lacing her words.

"What's going on?" Mary inquires, gazing back and forth between the two of us.

"Martha and I are going to spend our days going out to all different cities telling people about who Jesus is, what He's done for us all, and what that means for them," I reveal, and though the different cities part wasn't spoken aloud until now, Martha has no hesitation in her glance. She knows that this is it; this is the reason we're here. Both of us have a unique perspective into the life of the Man who came down to save us all. People need to hear it.

"So, you're both leaving?" Mary realizes, beginning to process it all. To be honest I'm still processing it too. The logistics are still a bit fuzzy, but I know we'll make it work. We have God on our side.

"He wouldn't survive without me," Martha jokes, to ease Mary's mind.

"And she'd be bored without me," I add, earning an eye roll from Martha.

"What are you thinking, Mary?" Martha asks gently. Mary waits a beat before she speaks up, her eyes finding the wall separating us from Jesus.

"I think it's really great that you two are going to do this. It's hard to imagine you traveling around together without strangling each other, but I'm sure the Lord will be using all of those moments to teach you both lessons," Mary answers. Yeah, Martha and I have always seemed to butt heads a lot. At the root of it all is how much we care about each other, so I'm not too concerned about it.

"Are you going to be alright on your own?" Martha poses, a hint of guilt in her voice, though I don't think Mary picks up on it.

"I won't be alone," Mary declares, smiling at the wall that has her Savior on the other side. "I'm going to have Niemos," she goes on.

"What?" I question, my eyebrows shooting up.

EPILOGUE

Creation was in need of a Savior, and their Creator delivered. He sent His Son to live a life that His people never could and die a death that would wash away all of their sins. Though they hung Him up on that cursed tree, a crown of thorns atop His head and wounds from head to toe, death was not the end for Him.

He rose again. Three simple words that would change the course of history. Death lost its power that morning. He proved Himself greater. A path was forged between creation and their Creator, ready to reunite them once again. In the Kingdom of Heaven, things will be as they were always intended to be: perfect. Nothing will be able to keep the Lord away from His people. Except for His people.

Creation was given free will. Though the Lord longs to have them by His side, He will not force them. He gave His people the ability to choose. Though a path back to Him now exists, He will not make them take it. It is up to each individual to decide whether they will turn to Him, or whether they will repeat the mistake of the first of their kind and take for granted the offer before them.

Some will be caught up in the ways of the world, ignoring the possibility of a Creator at all. Others will find themselves twisted up in traditions, thinking that they can justify themselves. More will hold onto every ounce of control, believing that they can fix their circumstances on their own, or that they simply don't need to be fixed at all. Others will have themselves convinced that they are too far gone to be loved by a just God. And some will simply miss what He's done because it stretches beyond their understanding.

The offer of an eternal paradise extended to all, yet the path is the one less traveled. The Creator at the end of it, arms extended. Waiting. For you. The human He stitched together in your mother's womb. You, dear reader, are eternally known. Eternally seen. Eternally loved. All by a Being that chose you.

Even when you choose the world. Even when you try to be good enough on your own. Even when you refuse to relinquish control. Even when you do things you'd never admit to another human being. Even when you can't comprehend it.

He chose you then. He chooses you now. Turn to Him. Fall into His open arms.

'A'Ω

ABOUT THE AUTHOR

Taylor Funk started writing novels in high school simply because she believed she could, and she never looked back. Now, while pursuing an engineering degree, she captures as many of the stories swirling in her mind as her busy days allow. When she's not writing or in class, she loves taking long drives with great music, finding beautiful places to photograph to share the wonder of God's creation. As someone who's neurodivergent, her interests shift depending on her latest hyper-fixation, whether that's Spiderman, puppies, or something entirely different. She's passionate about exploring the thoughts that fill her head, often through her characters or poetry drawn from her own experiences. She'd love to connect with readers and chat about her stories! You can reach out to her through the contact box on Sheltering Tree Media's website!

DISCUSSION GUIDE FOR SMALL GROUPS, CLASSES, OR INDIVIDUAL INTERESTS

1. Martha stays up late to speak with Jesus after being corrected by Him earlier. What does the way she handles herself during that conversation show us about her, and what can we learn from it?

2. Tirnan's immediate reaction to being healed is to help those around him. How can we embody this in our lives?

3. In chapter 29, Jesus has a fiery discussion with Niemos after identifying Himself as the Son of God. What do Jesus' emotions in this scene tell us about Him, and why is that important?

4. What stops Jahre and Ruriel from seeking both physical and spiritual healing, and how do we see those types of responses in our world today?

5. Jesus calls Cato to turn away from thievery and follow Him after stopping a stoning that Cato had been convinced was for him. How does this relate to the overall message of the gospel, and what does Cato's response represent?

6. Jesus' mother Mary talks about how she's never felt the love of God more than when His Son showed up in her grief. What does that mean for all of us, and how should we respond to the things in our life with this in mind?

7. Jesus tells Auran, “Let me be God, and you just focus on being man.” How can we apply this teaching in our lives?

8. What is the significance of Simon the Cypriot carrying Jesus’ cross, and what does that mean for us as believers?

9. Lazarus and Auran both have tremendous healing occur in their lives, yet when it comes to believing in Jesus’ coming resurrection, they both have different responses. Why do you think this occurs, especially considering that one grew up going to temple and the other did not?

10. Thomas talks about how he wouldn’t have followed Jesus if he knew all the pain that was going to come with that decision. What reaction does this statement evoke in you, and how do you think you would see things if you were in Thomas’ shoes?

11. Though Peter was with Jesus constantly, he still falls short both during Jesus’ arrest, and after His death. What does that show about the Christian walk, and how do you think that impacts the way it’s perceived by others?

12. Jesus and Niemos cover a lot in chapter 56. How did you react to the things said during that discussion, and what lessons can be drawn from it?

13. Throughout the book, Niemos tries to convince himself that the messages and miracles of Jesus can’t be true because they go against what he’s been taught and what those he’s most frequently around believe. What are some ways we can avoid falling into this same trap in our lives?

14. Jesus speaks to the Pharisees very differently than He speaks to the rest of the people He comes across. Why do you think this is, and what does that say about each of them?

15. How did each of the narrators' backgrounds set the tone for the way they interacted both with the world around them and the way they interacted with Jesus?

16. Each character in the book has their own unique way of coming to Jesus. Which one(s) do you feel like you identify with the most, and why?

17. This book focuses a lot on love. How has reading it changed the way that you think about and/or experience the love of God?

18. While you were reading, were there any lines that stuck out to you, and how did these lines impact you?

19. How do you foresee all the characters left by the end of the book impacting the early church?

How to Leave a Review Guide for a ShelteringTree.Earth Book

How to Leave a Review for a ShelteringTree.Earth Book

Thank you for supporting our authors. Reviews help readers discover books that speak to their hearts and spirits. Even a short review makes a meaningful difference.

Here's a simple guide to help you leave a review on Amazon, Goodreads, ShelteringTreeMedia, or any other book review site.

---

1. What to Write in a Review

Your review does *not* need to be long or complicated.

A few sentences is enough.

You can share:

- what you enjoyed
- what you learned
- how the book made you feel
- who you think would benefit from it
- your favorite part or takeaway

You do **not** need to summarize the entire book.

---

2. How to Leave a Review on Amazon

Step 1: Go to the book's Amazon page

Search for the title or use the link provided by the author.

Step 2: Scroll down to "Customer Reviews"

Click **"Write a customer review."**

Step 3: Choose a star rating

5 stars = excellent

1 star = poor

Step 4: Write your review

A few sentences is perfect.

Step 5: Click Submit

That's it — your review is live.

☑ 3. How to Leave a Review on Goodreads

Step 1: Log in to Goodreads

(You can create a free account if you don't have one.)

Step 2: Search for the book

Click on the correct edition.

Step 3: Click the stars to rate the book

This alone counts as a review.

Step 4: Click "Write a Review"

Add your thoughts and click **Save**.

☑ 4. How to Leave a Review on ShelteringTreeMedia.com

Step 1: Go to the ARC tab on ShelteringTreeMedia.com

Step 2: Scroll down to the Review box

Step 3: Fill in the form

Step 4: Click SUBMIT

ARC Team members will be sent a coupon once the review is posted under the book review blog.

☑ 5. Tips for Helpful Reviews

- Be honest
- Be kind
- Be specific
- Keep spoilers minimal
- Share how the book impacted you

☑ 6. Why Reviews Matter

Reviews help:

- authors reach new readers
- bookstores and libraries decide what to carry
- online algorithms recommend the book
- readers discover books that nourish their spirit

Your voice truly makes a difference.

ShelteringTreeMedia.com

www.ingramcontent.com/pod-product-compliance
Lightning Source LLC
LaVergne TN
LVHW020655110826
845149LV00012B/2007